REBUKE

Stern disapproval; to reprove or reprimand…

~A Tranquility Tale~
of love, lust, lies, betrayal and *redemption,*
spanning more than four decades.

April Alisa Marquette

Books by *April Alisa Marquette:*

Fiction

Turnabout

~A Tranquility Tale
Rebuke
Son

~The Cohort Trilogy
Absolution
Progression
Iniquities

~The Sea Isles Series - A Trilogy
Exodus
Affinity
Priestess

~A Sea Isles Series Addendum
Physician

_____ * _____

Non-Fiction

Co-Authored with Jessica Janna

~The Relinquish & Reap Series
Seedling
Sowing
Yielding
 TBA

Ask for them ... at your local bookstore

Books that captivate

For my late father,

The preacher,

Who did what he knew to do,

and carried the saints' secrets to his grave.

...Beware, lest you forget the Lord who brought you out of the land of Egypt, from the house of bondage.

Deuteronomy 6:12

Chapter 1

In the 1990's ~

TOPAZ was an adult. Still, she remembered being a kid and how the choir marched in. They sang *'We've Come This Far by Faith.'* The choir members wore robes. The kind with fluttering sleeves. Angel wings were what Topaz had often thought as the singers passed her, one by one.

As the choir gently swayed to the music, she remembered that an older woman had touched her shoulder. A young one, or two, wearing a fruit-laced scent, had smiled. An older male singer had even given her an officious nod, as en route to the choir loft, all continued to sing.

Topaz Moon could not remember a Sunday morning when she hadn't sat on the second pew from the church front. That was where she and her mother, Naomi, had always sat. In all seasons, the child with the copper-colored skin had been allowed to stand near the aisle. But only during the choir processional. Sometimes Topaz even sang along. However, she usually just allowed the swell of the Hammond organ, the tickling of the piano keys, and the harmonious blend of voices to enfold her. Those times, Topaz felt a type of warmth and anticipation. Both seemed to build at the start of every worship service. Then when the music got so good, Topaz wondered, would it be the same in Heaven? As a kid, she'd hoped so. However, she hadn't seen how a choir of angels could have sounded better than the one at her church. The one made up of humans.

Fallible humans; the adult Topaz mused. Come to think of it, most of her memories of the church had taken place long before the rise of the mega-church. Back then, the only celebrity preacher—if he could have been called that—had been Evangelist Billy Graham. Oh, and Reverend Ike. At the time, a pastor well knew those in his congregation. A church leader knew those in the surrounding neighborhood too, and he was known.

Back in the day, Topaz had wholeheartedly agreed with the bible Psalm that read: *I was glad when they said unto me; let us go into the house of the Lord.* Back then, Topaz had embraced the church with an incomparable love. It wasn't that she didn't love it now. It was just that so many things had happened...things that had caused her to grow up, fast.

No longer a child or childish, Topaz had begun to see people as they were. She saw past their projected images, and Topaz had been disheartened –to say the least.

One of those fallible humans, one who had caused her to feel the most disappointment, had been Naomi, her mother, the church first lady.

In the disillusionment department, Topaz's father, The Right Reverend Elijah Moon, ran a close second... Just maybe, he even held first place. Topaz wasn't sure.

Thinking back, the copper-skinned one only wondered if she would ever forget some of the things that had happened. Then she asked herself one question. Even if she couldn't forget, could she manage to forgive... somehow, some day?

Chapter 2

1966

ELIJAH Moon had become the pastor by default. That was how he sometimes saw it. His father had pastored Greater Bethany Bible Congregation. The handsome older man with the big booming voice and powerful presence had been great at it. When Elijah looked back, it seemed as though Old Preacher had often called down fire from Heaven. Then when the man made altar calls, people surged forward for prayer.

Elijah recalled how he had loved to listen to Old Preacher. Funny thing, Elijah hadn't known why his dad, just fifty-something, had been called that. From stories told, it seemed Elijah's dad had been dubbed 'Old Preacher' when he'd been just a boy. Perhaps because, as a child, Ezekiel Moon had been reserved and observant. Or maybe Ezekiel garnered the moniker because he'd preached since he was thirteen. Elijah really didn't know. All Elijah knew was that he had felt he'd have years to sit and study Old Preacher. Elijah had wanted to learn some of Old Preacher's ways. Then at the right time, Elijah thought, he'd take on more of Old Preacher's duties—thereby lessening his father's burden.

Sure, the younger Elijah had been a junior minister since he, too, had been a teen. He'd progressed through seminary, divinity college. Elijah had then become an elder. Sometimes Elijah wondered if years back, he'd had different dreams. Had he wanted to become something other than a reverend? Elijah no longer knew. All he knew was that his *mother* had wanted the pastorate *for* him, but years down the line.

Yet Old Preacher had told Elijah, "Son, it doesn't matter what your mama wants." Old Preacher looked over his glasses. "You gotta live your life for *you*. Then on that glorious day, you'll stand before the great throne and give an account for yourself. No one else, Son."

Often, Elijah Moon wondered what life would have been like had Old Preacher, yet clad in his clerical robe, not knelt that Sunday morning to pray. It had been his dad's after-sermon ritual. What would things have been like had Old Preacher ever gotten up again? Elijah could still see all so clearly in the eye of his mind... He'd thought it strange that Old Preacher had been on his knees for so long. Usually, the older man said a quick prayer. He thanked God for using him, a willing vessel. Then sometimes, Old Preacher was escorted to his office where he would remove his robe. Wet with perspiration, he might even change his clothing. Other times, Old Preacher had sat on the pulpit until time to offer the benediction. Afterward, he'd greeted the Lord's people. However, on *that* day, before Old Preacher could do any of those things, Elijah knew. *Something was wrong.*

Pulling at the knee of his suit pants, young Elijah knelt. Beside his father, Elijah could smell his dad's familiar, light, non-offensive perspiration. It mingled with his cologne. Down beside his father, Elijah wanted to believe his dad was just a bit winded. It was why Elijah lovingly asked, "How many times I gotta tell you, Dad? Ya gotta quit preaching so hard." Elijah placed an arm around the man that he'd always looked up to, the one who'd recently been diagnosed with a heart condition. Elijah proudly said, "You outdid yourself, ol' dude."

Garnering no response, Elijah was about to ask if Old Preacher was okay. Yet with his very blood going cold, young Elijah *knew.*

His beloved father was gone.

It was not because Old Preacher's eyes were closed, but on his knees, Elijah knew because the big man slumped onto Elijah's chest. Elijah knew because Old Preacher, though still warm, was dead weight.

Placing both arms around the pastor whose shoes he would have to step into sooner than later, tears streamed from Elijah's eyes. Rocking the man who had been his mentor and his friend, softly the younger man asked, "Why couldn't you wait, Old Preacher?" To his own ears, Elijah's voice sounded the way he felt. *Shattered.* "Why'd you have to go—now? I was trying to help you. Why'd you have to leave…me?"

Twenty-four-year-old Elijah Moon had both arms around his father. Holding tightly, with his vision blurred by acrid tears, he became cognizant of something more. Greater Bethany Bible Congregation had grown eerily silent. Within its hallowed halls, the whole assemblage had risen to their feet. It had been as though all present knew they witnessed the significant. In deference, even the frail, old mothers of the church struggled up. Babies were wide-eyed and silent. Children stood at attention, and the organist ceased to play. Everyone remained that way until Elijah no longer knelt on the pulpit beside Old Preacher, the electrifying Reverend Ezekiel Moon, who had quietly gone on…to glory.

Chapter 3

In the 1990's ~

Naomi knew he loved her, even though, down through the years, so much had happened. Still, she was tired. Naomi guessed that might have been how Old Preacher had felt on the day he'd passed. His passing had been so long ago, but never would Naomi forget it. Nor would she forget that Old Preacher's son, tall, handsome Elijah Moon, proposed to her fifteen months after his father's death. That was back in the 1960s.

It had not been romantic, as Naomi had previously believed a proposal should be. Nevertheless, the young woman had guessed. What she got was the best she was going to get, under the circumstances.

One evening at dusk, attractive, young Elijah Moon showed up at the house. He asked Naomi to come out onto her Aunt's porch. "Nae," Elijah began, using Naomi's nickname. "We've been friends for a while, so I know you. I know you wanted this to be different, romantic even. But I don't know how to do this, so I'll straight out ask. Will you marry me?"

In the gathering dark, Naomi extricated her hand. "Why?"

"Why what?" Elijah questioned back. "And why not?"

"You know what," Naomi whispered. "Why *me*? You got all them other girls chasing you. Why not pick one of them? Why ask me?"

"I need *you*, Nae." Forlorn, twenty-something Elijah turned, staring into the dimness. "The others want me because I'm the preacher, now."

Naomi spoke to Elijah's back. "You always were."

Without turning, the young man shook his head. "Not like this, I wasn't. I was junior. Now I'm *it*. To them, I'm some prize, the fatted calf, but you see past that. You see me as I am, as I have always been."

Oh, but she did see him as a prize. Naomi had even loved Elijah from the moment that she'd arrived to live with her Aunt Pet. Petunia. Naomi and Elijah had been in their late teens. To Naomi, Elijah had been a dream. He was sweet, sentimental, and he really hadn't known how irresistible he was to all who met him. Yet, Naomi hadn't been a fool for Elijah. She never would be; it was why she asked, again, "What you want with me, Lijah? You're supposed to marry *up*, I'm down; my daddy's a deacon, not a bishop or clergy. He's several states away, too."

Elijah whirled, his eyes flashing fire, as Old Preacher's had when he'd sent chills down Naomi's spine during his unforgettable orations. "I don't care about any of that! I want *you*, Nae. For me, you are up. You're kind and good; you came here to go to college, then your Aunt got sick. You took care of her." Naomi was shapely and stylish, too, in her laid-back way. She had the most beautiful, thick, glossy brown hair. Elijah didn't say that, but he admitted, "You're pretty; we compliment." He sighed then, wanting to get something right, like he'd practiced. "Nae, your parents live away, but we could drive down south. I could ask your Dad for your hand. If you want that, I'll do it." In the fading light, Elijah tried to see Naomi's face. "Just say yes. Please."

The young, slender, but curvaceous woman with copper-colored skin and beautiful brown hair stared at Elijah's shadowy form. She dared not believe that if she breathed one word, she could wind up Elijah Moon's wife. It was what she had dreamed of, *but* she hadn't wanted it like this. Forced. "Why really Lijah?" Naomi said they had to start in truth.

"I want you," Elijah began and stepped closer. Not touching Naomi, he said, "Because I do. You know me. You don't have a heap of high hopes for me. You see *me*. You won't try to make me over. You're not trying to climb up, on my back." Elijah coughed. "And I love you."

"You love me," Naomi sounded pensive. She knew she and Elijah had chemistry. It had been there from the first. She knew he couldn't stay away from her. He always had to touch her. His eyes tracked her. He'd relentlessly chased her, not caring who knew or saw, so maybe he did love her. He'd never come out and said it though, not before.

Elijah pivoted. "You know I love you, girl, it's always been you."

"Sure it has," Naomi scoffed, "even though you've got women from here to California throwing themselves at you."

"See, that's it." In the dark, Elijah turned, grabbing Naomi's hands. "You never did that. You've never tried to trap me to get the title of 'first lady.' So why not you? Why shouldn't *you* wear my Gran's ring?"

"Why now?" Naomi asked. "You said you'd get married late in life."

Young Elijah's shoulders slumped. "I know, but that was before. Everything's changed. Now. I gotta be what my Dad was, to everybody."

"No. You've only got to be you," Naomi softly reminded her friend.

"See, Nae," twenty-five-year-old Elijah squeezed her hands, "that's why you." She'd sounded just like Old Preacher. "You ground me. You'll be my home, my one true person in the midst of all of this. You love me. You understand that I'm scared. Who else could I say that to – or a hundred other things— without recrimination?"

Naomi swallowed and wanted to cry because, in the space of a few moments, her friend's life had been turned upside down. She'd watched. Afterward, she'd heard the talk. She'd seen the vultures, women who were circling and swarming, seemingly swooping in from everywhere. She'd watched Elijah's mother too, Cozi Moon. Even she, short, corseted, and stylish, had changed since her husband, Old Preacher, died. Naomi wasn't sure those changes were for the better.

Poor Elijah, he really did need someone, Naomi mused, but her? How to be sure this was right? As she stood quietly, assaulted by a maelstrom of thoughts, Elijah pulled Naomi into his arms, right there on her Aunt's darkened porch. "She working tonight? At the college?" Elijah meant the homeowner, Petunia, who wanted to return to teaching in the south.

Naomi couldn't answer because Elijah kissed her then, so tenderly, as though both their hearts were breaking. And in a way, they were, because tonight, a choice would be made, or they would part ways.

Elijah pressed Naomi close. She let her hands slide up her friend's muscular back. Yielding to his kiss, she felt his hands. Up her sides, in the dark, they rose. Naomi gasped as Elijah's big fingers closed around her breasts. Feeling her nipples pebble, Naomi pushed further into Elijah's palms. Beneath his lips, hers parted. She received his tongue, a sweet invasion. Then sure someone, somewhere, watched, she turned.

Taking Elijah's hand, Naomi opened the screen door. With Elijah close, both entered the darkened house. Following Naomi through another doorway, Elijah realized. All before now, he and slender sexy Naomi had only messed around. Many times they'd become heated, but she'd pushed at him. It had been hard, but Elijah had always managed to pull back. He'd been aware that technically, Naomi was still a virgin – but only because he and she had never consummated. Naomi was saving herself. For marriage, she'd said. That Elijah respected. However, on this particular evening, he knew things would be different.

In Naomi's darkened bedroom, Elijah stood. She slowly removed his clothes. Letting Naomi, Elijah nearly wanted to weep as he had not since Old Preacher's passing. Elijah thought, here's someone willing to do something for *me*. In Naomi, he had someone who had never wanted a thing from him, yet she gave. In the dark, Elijah felt fingertips against his lips, quieting him. Oh God, he had been crying. But Naomi didn't judge or think he was a girl. Elijah knew it as he felt slender arms encircle him. Gently, he was walked backward to Naomi's bed. Elijah sat. In silence, he watched as silhouetted, Naomi slowly removed her own clothing. That was another thing Elijah liked about her. Somewhat reserved, Naomi never rushed. Thus, she always appeared sure.

Elijah could not know that Naomi was so scared her hands shook. Tonight, she realized, there would be no protesting, no going back, not if she was accepting Elijah's proposal, such that it was. Naomi exhaled. She told herself she was ready for this, and all that would come after.

Seated, Elijah smelled her, the flower-scented perfume that always rose from her skin. His man-piece stood at attention, and suddenly Elijah ached, mightily, to touch, to taste. He wanted to take, and give, as well.

Naomi stood before Elijah. Lifting his arms, she placed them around herself. On her waist in the back, she flattened his palms. With smaller hands, she cradled Elijah's head. She guided his face to her midsection, where gently she pressed. She was no longer afraid. Desire pushed fear aside. Naomi only wanted to open for Elijah. She wanted to feel him, thick and hard, as he possessed her, fully, body and soul. At last.

Elijah's cheek lay against Naomi's stomach. He heard Naomi's voice that was steady yet soft. "You've done this before, Elijah, I know. I haven't, though, but I've dreamed of doing it—with you, so…" She gave him license to have his way with her, to teach her what he wanted her to know. He could mold her, make her into whatever he desired.

It was such power, Elijah mused; however, other thoughts attempted to intrude. Over those thoughts, he spoke, and Elijah's voice was filled with need. "Naomi, baby, this'll be the first night of many, you know."

"I sure hope so since I'm committed to becoming Mrs. Moon."

Without words, with both his big hands, Elijah squeezed Naomi's rounded buttocks. He kissed her nude body, her stomach, her tiny rib cage, and the curved, soft underside of her fragrant breasts.

Naomi gasped, and Elijah reminded himself as he kissed toward her nipples that he had to take it slow. Drawing a peak into his mouth, he decided. He would not allow Nae to ever regret her decision to marry him. As Elijah sensually slathered and suckled, he knew more. As he slid the fingers of one hand into Naomi's heat, that thought became pronounced. With his other hand, Elijah held Naomi in place, and slowly pleasured her. Then he found her with his tongue. She was slick and ready. After lingering licks, she splintered, and Elijah knew. It was time. Nestling his body between Naomi's thighs, Elijah did not enter her. Instead, he used his rod to again bring her joy. He loved the way she trembled and cried out. She was his. She would be always.

Entertaining thoughts of being inside her, Elijah moved to open-mouth kiss Naomi, *there*, again. When she moaned, raising her legs and making erotic female noises, Elijah could barely wait. Getting them both into place, he ran his large hand over a chubby tit. Allowing that hand to slide down Naomi's body, Elijah grasped his seeking staff. He'd finally get to plug Naomi! What a gift! He nosed into her haven. With his mouth against hers, Elijah admitted, "This'll hurt, somewhat, this first time. But," he said, using a hand to widen Naomi, "I'll take it easy." He nudged onward, saying, "I'll try to be gentle."

Then Naomi felt Elijah spear into her. In the dark, she yelped. Holding her and himself in place, he tenderly shushed her. He kissed tears escaping her closed eyelids. "Wait, baby," he whispered. "One sec, and the pain will subside. Then you'll like it." Elijah sure hoped so.

With his forehead on hers, and both their hearts beating too fast, Naomi nodded. She willed herself to believe. She also marveled at Elijah. He was so big, but now inside her. She tried to relax, recalling that he'd done this before. She told herself to trust him, and she did.

Although he wanted only pleasure for her, Elijah knew that painful first step was necessary. Pecking Naomi on the lips, he asked, "You good?"

Wordless, she nodded. "No more pain," Elijah vowed and began to move, slowly. Now, he thought, he could make Naomi want him for all time. As she too began to move, her body instinctively matching his rhythm, Elijah knew what else was needed. With a finger, he sought Naomi's sentient spot. As he gave her more of his length, he pledged to learn things. They included finding all Naomi's secret sensual appetites. Most she wasn't aware of at present, but Elijah would be diligent. He would bind Naomi to him. Sexy Elijah vowed to create a need so strong within her, for *him*. Why? –Because, for her, he already had the same, an unbreakable bond. She was his whole world. Elijah Martin Moon wanted Naomi Ruth True to be as irrevocably bound to him…as he was *to her*.

Chapter 4

1968

BEFORE the proposal, Naomi had not known Elijah's mother well. Looking down at his paternal grandmother's beautiful ring, Naomi could only think one thing. Now that she was getting to know 'Mother Cozi' – as everyone called Elijah's mom— Naomi was not impressed. For one thing, Cozi was *not* what her name implied. The woman was standoffish like she thought she was better than others, especially Naomi. Short stylish Cozina Anetta Moon had a sharp tongue too, which she often used when things didn't go her way. And pertaining to Naomi and Elijah's wedding, things were definitely not going Cozi's way.

"You're hard-headed," the woman had disparagingly told 'that girl,' the one her son was determined to marry. The one he was a fool for.

Nevertheless, the slender, copper-skinned younger woman thought, the wedding would be hers, so it should be done *her* way. Potluck? Please. For a reception? Naomi didn't think so. Anyway, her parents and her Aunt Pet—Petunia—were willing to help pay for a nice reception. It could be held at a banquet house and not in the church's fellowship hall.

As Naomi pushed Cozi's sniping from mind, she recalled her conversation with Mother See. She was the *official* church mother. The woman had wisdom to go with her years, too, unlike Elijah's mother. Naomi had long known Mother See was wise. Still, during a recent conversation, Naomi had again been reminded of the woman's insight.

Mother See had invited Naomi to her house. There, the lovely rugs and furniture might have been a tad threadbare in a few spots, but they were of good quality. As she'd fixed a pot of tea, the older woman had spoken softly. "You know, a few are upset that you were chosen."

Naomi well knew. Women who would never have had a chance with Elijah now saw her as their mortal enemy.

Mother See opened a biscuit tin. Carefully, with clean hands, she placed fresh homemade butter cookies on a small dessert stand.

Its scalloped edges reminded Naomi of decadent lace.

"You do know those kinds of people—malcontents—will always be around, right? They'll even be present *after* you marry the preacher."

Naomi was aware. She was starting to believe the young preacher's mom was the malcontent crew chief.

Mother See gestured for the younger woman to help herself. "Well, since that's the case, there's no sense in starting off on the wrong foot."

Clearly, Naomi did not understand. "Ma'am?"

"Child, you've got to begin as you intend to continue."

"I don't know what you mean, Mother See."

The woman sighed. "There has been talk of your wedding, your dress, and your reception." The older woman raised a hand. "Let me finish. It's no secret that your ceremony will be held at Greater Bethany," the church. "That is as it should be, with you marrying the new pastor and all. Howsonever, you must not start off beholden to people."

Naomi had a cookie halfway to her mouth. "Ma'am?"

"You must come from a place of strength." Mother See took a seat and explained. "Lil Naomi, I've got some money put by, and I would like to use a bit of it to make sure you get what you need."

"I'm grateful," Naomi said, "but I can't let you do that."

"Gal, you can't stop me." The regal woman who looked like the song stylist Nancy Wilson was tickled. "How about that?" She chuckled. "You trying to tell *me* what to do with *my* money." Mother See no longer laughed. "Listen gal, with *my* money, I'll have *my* say, just like with *your* wedding, you'll have *your* say. Agreed?"

Naomi began to argue. "But my parents and my aunt—"

"I'll help too," the regal, silver-haired woman waved. "This way, you will get what you need. An elegant affair to remember, and *no potluck*."

Naomi munched on a crisp fresh cookie. Swallowing, she said in a barely audible voice, "So you heard about that." It was embarrassing.

"Oh, I see and hear lots of things, most of which I dismiss. Still that, I couldn't let go. It's why I say you can't let naysayers reduce you. They'll try to do so throughout your tenure as the first lady, if you let them. So *go* in this marriage, the way you mean to *be* in, so you can *stay* in."

"I don't actually want to *be* the first lady," Naomi admitted. "Elijah's Mama can keep that title; I just want to be his wife." Naomi wanted to have his babies. She was going to love *getting* big sexy Elijah's babies...

The regal brown woman raised a brow. "Honey, I can see there are a few things you're gonna need to learn."

"Ma'am?" Naomi forgot sexy stunts with Elijah. "Pardon me?"

"First of all," Mother See's voice hardened, "you need to understand. Whether you *want to be* the first lady, that's who you will *become* when you marry the pastor." The older woman's voice gentled. "His mama had her time—Lord knows we thought it would be longer, but with Old Preacher gone, God rest his soul, now Cozi's gotta let go."

Mother See waved. "Say nothing, gal. I know Cozi; I know how she operates and manipulates. You'd do well to learn a thing or two from her because she's not all bad. Circumstances often dictate what a person will and will not do, but all of that you can pick up in time. I suppose.

"Right now, though, lil Naomi, you need to know that ain't no telling what people will do if given half a chance. So get this in your head; you need to feed your own husband. Period.

"Potluck," Mother See harrumphed. "Gal, if you had some ol' tacky reception where people could all bring dishes –why somebody would get the notion to poison you. They'd do it to get you outta the picture. Some woman might even who-do your new husband with a dish that she 'prepared' especially for him." The older woman spoke more to herself than to young Naomi, "Wouldn't be the first time either, or the last."

Mother See shook her head and handed over a fragrant cup of tea. "No, baby girl, we got to keep you safe. The Lord's got work for our young new pastor, but the Lord's indeed also got work for *you*..."

Naomi entered her aunt's home. She nor Petunia would live there for much longer. Realizing it, Naomi knew her life was changing, seemingly every day now.

She thought back a few days. Life had definitely changed quite a bit the day she'd left school to visit Mother See. On that day, the wise older woman had taken Naomi under her wing. That day, the silver-haired regal older woman had become Naomi's mentor, as well as her much-needed confidant.

For reasons unknown to Naomi, Mother See had not only offered cookies and tea, Mother Madonna See had also become Naomi's self-designated, human guardian angel.

Chapter 5

1969

NAOMI was unable to believe it. One week back from her and Elijah's honeymoon, and their new apartment was chock-full of kids!

Ezra, Elijah's stocky brother, had talked gullible Elijah into it.

It seemed Ezra's wife, Tippie, who should have been called Tipsy, was at it again. Drunk, Tippie couldn't manage a lap baby, three-year-old twins, and two older children—a veritable basketball team.

"Why can't they go to their *grandmother*? Where is Cozi Moon?" Naomi hissed. She didn't care that round-bodied Ezra sat out front. Her brother-in-law waited in her and Elijah's sparsely furnished living room.

In the rear with his new wife, Elijah huffed, "Keep your voice down." He eyed her fitted sweater. "You don't want him to hear us—do you?"

"I don't care!" Naomi spat. "Your brother knows we're talking about him 'n his sorry wife. What else would we be doing back here?"

"Forget all that, Nae," big Elijah quietly pled, his voice beguiling. "I told him we'd keep the boys a few days, until their mother gets better."

"Until she gets better?! Y'all acting like Tippie is sick. Topeka drinks!" Naomi was so angry that she trembled. "And Elijah, you told Ez we'd keep those kids—*before* you spoke to *me*! Now you drag me back here, to get me to agree. If I do, that'll mean *I'm* the one stuck, not you. You know I have school. How'm I gonna get my homework done with *five* snot-nosed kids trailing me? Did you forget? I work, too."

Naomi turned away before Elijah could present his argument. "'Lijah, you and your mother made it clear. As the new first lady of Bethany, I need to appear at Ladies Auxiliary Meetings, among other things," *so many other things.* "How'm I gonna do that, with them kids trailing me?"

Elijah forgot the long skirt that clung to Naomi's curves. He held his aching temples and wondered. Had things seemed this chaotic for Old Preacher? It had been over two years since the former pastor had passed, yet Elijah often felt he didn't have a firm grasp on anything. Now, making matters worse, his younger brother, and bro's wife—whom no one was supposed to know was a drunk—were creating problems. For Elijah and his sexy new wife, whom he only wanted to plug.

"Nae," Elijah sighed. He sat on the end of their shared bed. "Take the kids when you go out. *Please.* It's done." Elijah slowly raised Naomi's skirt hem. "I told Ezra we'd help, I can't un-tell him or take it back."

"Don't give me the puppy eye," Naomi ordered. "Another thing, Elijah, this can never happen again. Remove your big hands." They were sliding up beneath her skirt, and felt entirely too good. "Going forward," Naomi managed, as her husband, seated, thumbed the crotch of her panties aside. "You must speak to me, *first*, about anything pertaining to us." She gasped as he slid big fingers into her heat. "*Ohhh...*" She moaned. She nearly forgot what she'd been saying. "Did you hear me?"

"I did." Elijah appeared relieved as Naomi's head lolled back, and she gave herself over to pleasure. Holding her so she wouldn't fall, the large man rose. He kissed the column of his wife's neck, and her cleavage. He had known she would come around. "It won't be bad, Nae," he whispered, his lips nudging their way to a nipple.

He was causing her to feel things that displaced anger, Naomi realized. Forgetting meaningless words, she sought Elijah's staff. Freeing it from confining cotton, she clasped it in two hands. "Give me this, to seal our deal." With her lips on his, she sensually whispered, "And make it *good,* too..." She knew her hips would ache afterward, fooling with his big self, but she didn't care. Getting tangled up with him was worth it.

"But—my brother's out front," Elijah feebly argued, more than ready.

"If I'll keep his kids," Naomi stated, pulling Elijah closer, "Ezra can wait." Lifting her leg, Naomi whispered. "I'm 'bout to baptize you, big preacher, in my special river, even though you don't deserve it..."

Days later, Naomi was sorry she had ever agreed to keep the unruly, whining little monsters. Wondering when she'd get shed of them, Naomi fought feeling sick. However, with each passing day, she found it harder to get out of bed. Therefore, one day she finally broke down and dialed.

Naomi would have called her own mother, but there wasn't much short, plump Mama could do from where she lived, so far away. Naomi could have called Cozi Moon too, but she was ornery, now that Old Preacher was gone. And Elijah's mother truly believed Naomi had usurped her place in the church. Forgetting stylish Cozi, Naomi had also pondered calling Aunt Pet, but Naomi remembered. Days, Petunia taught at the college. At night, the spry little woman packed for her move back to the south. So Aunt Pet couldn't just take off to mind the baby demons.

Therefore, Naomi handled the rotary phone. As she did, her head and even the backs of her eyes ached. Naomi shivered as she said, "Hullo?"

"Gal, that you?" Mother See asked, alarmed. "I can't understand you, not with yo' teeth chattering. Nevamind. Gimme me a few. I'm coming."

Naomi's guardian angel appeared. She morphed into a drill sergeant. With a few words, she whipped the demon-children into shape. Mother See even placed a call to the pastor's aid leader. This middle-aged woman agreed to drive Naomi to an emergency doctor's appointment. While Mother See waved them off, Elijah's nephews stood like statutes.

When Naomi returned, Mother See eyed Ezra and Tippie's kids. The children knew to be quiet as mice. Carrying the lap-baby, Mother See helped Naomi to her room. "Guess no prescription needed, huh gal?"

She'd sounded so sage and knowing until Naomi had to look at the woman she often thought of as her very own fairy Godmother. Noticing the triumph on the nearly unlined face, Naomi whispered. "You...*know*, don't you? You knew when I called. Didn't you, Mother?"

"I know *now*." The regal older woman patted Ezra's baby, resting on her ample bosom. "I wasn't sure when you called, but you have been glowing. I know too," she said, and helped Naomi remove layers of clothing, "you've been happy with your husband." What chemistry those two had! Sometimes it was so intense others couldn't look at them.

As Naomi lay down, wearing a slip and stockings, Mother See pulled the covers up and tucked them around her. "I've also seen that your little figure is rounding out, becoming more womanly, so I supposed."

Naomi closed her aching eyes and allowed her pounding head to sink into the pillow. "*I* thought I had the flu."

"You told me. That was when I guessed. You know, I had men, and a baby, too." The silver-haired woman hung Naomi's wool dress. Then she patted Tippie's youngest. "Now Naomi, we've got to take good care of you, and little Elijah there." The older woman placed a hand on the bedroom doorknob. "I gotta get out here," she said, her voice hardening, "make sure these older hellions ain't 'bout to burn this place down."

Naomi smiled and felt herself drift closer to blissful sleep. However, before Mother See exited, Naomi thought she heard the older woman declare. "I've also got to see about getting these monsters out of here."

WEEKS later, in the snow and the cold, Elijah and Naomi trudged, hand in hand, up their front walk. It sure was nice to be back to normal, just the two of them. They had Naomi's Godmother to thank for that.

True to her word, Mother See had gotten rid of Elijah's nephews.

When asked how she'd done it, the older woman shrugged. "Cozi Moon knows her responsibilities. Ezra is *her* son, not your'n, Naomi." Mother See winked, "When I pointed that out, Cozi quickly saw it. Then she wanted her grandchildren with her, and not with the younger woman who would—if allowed—take everything from her."

"Mother!" Naomi's eyes widened. "You didn't say that –did you?"

Mother See's eyes gleamed. "Who knows? But Cozi got the picture."

"And since she despises me," Naomi surmised, "she took the bait."

"It's what you needed. Is it not?" Dismissively, Mother See waved. "No young marrieds need in-laws, or others, all over them, if it can be helped. Young couples need time to bond and work things out, without interference. I just made that possible."

Naomi hugged her Godmother. "I love you."

"I know, honey."

"You love me too," copper-skinned Naomi grinned, knowing the older woman had a hard time saying some things. Others she had no trouble spitting right out. "I know you love me."

Mother See nodded because the girl-woman in her arms might never know how much. "I sho do, honey. God knows I do."

Starting to show, Naomi, removed textbooks from her kitchen table. Tidying up the small apartment that she and Elijah shared, she mused aloud. "Wonder if Lijah's mama will ever feel differently about me."

Mother See looked away. "She may. Then again, she may not."

Naomi allowed the memory to fade. She saw Elijah glance over his shoulder. He was making sure he'd turned off their car headlights.

Slowly the young couple walked, with big Elijah holding Naomi close. He willed her not to fall on snow undercut with ice. Forgetting mishaps, he said, "I think our session went well tonight. Don't you?"

Naomi let out a breath. She'd been holding it ever since Elijah had said it was her duty to be with him during couples sessions. Naomi had been so nervous, although she and Elijah were married *and* the leaders of their congregation. Naomi felt they were still so new at everything, including marriage. To her, it felt strange, giving marital advice to those who had been married for longer than she had been alive.

In the hallway, she said, "It went okay." Naomi stamped, dislodging snow from her dainty boots. She pulled off her gloves and coat. Classically stylish, both were unlike the outrageous gear worn by Elijah's mother. "I don't know how much longer Sister Eve and Brother Cole will stay together." Naomi's brow creased. "The woman is fed up." *She had eyes for you, too, husband*, Naomi thought but did not say.

"Well, you made some good points," Elijah announced. Free of his outerwear and smelling all too enticing, he took his wife in his arms. "From what shelf of wisdom did you pull those things that you said?"

"Since *we* haven't been married that long," Naomi shrugged, "I thought about my parents. How they'd handle that type of situation."

"Well done, baby." Elijah's voice lowered as slowly he began to undress sexy Naomi. "Now, about another situation..." He had noticed her hips. They were expanding, and he liked. Her cute bottom was becoming more padded, another thing he liked. As Elijah's beautiful hands played over Naomi's copper-colored curves, her breathing quickened. The big man had a way of igniting her, even when it seemed he wasn't trying.

The last of Naomi's garments slipped away. Then amid a fierce desire for the charismatic man with the huge personality and even more significant following, Naomi could not rid herself of one image. As she fondled his heaviness and stroked Elijah's length, Naomi tried to forget. When his hands slid up to caress the undersides of her enlarging breasts, that woman's face came to mind. While big handsome Elijah squeezed, Naomi vaguely saw the woman's husband, too.

As Elijah brought out the devil in her, the one that made Naomi drop to her knees, she realized something. Taking sexy brown Elijah's rod in her mouth, she sucked and kneaded like a hungry newborn. And recognition dawned. Earlier in the evening, during Sister Eve and Brother Cole's marriage session, that woman had not acknowledged her, Naomi. Dark-skinned Eve, a little older, had dismissed the preacher's wife. Attractive, big-boned Eve with the shock of curly hair had only been able to see the preacher. Had Eve's husband noticed? Naomi wondered as her body undulated in readiness for Elijah's staff. She watched as he used his beautiful hands to guide it toward her. Her eyes roamed his muscular, broad chest and the sensual slide of his neck into his strong shoulder. Why did she think such things?

The hands that were so expressive when he preached, Elijah placed on Naomi. Enjoying his succulent kiss, she both moaned and mused. Maybe…she was just possessive; Elijah *was* hers. Or it could have been the baby, causing her to feel more intensely for the man she'd married. Twenty-four-year-old Naomi did not know. She only knew it had become natural to think too many women wanted the preacher. The one whose large hands skillfully parted her curtain, just before he slid his mammoth wand into her. Only her.

Chapter 6

Late 1970 ~

WHEN his baby was born, Elijah forgot to care that she wasn't a boy. It no longer mattered that he hadn't gotten the son he'd wanted. Gazing at his tiny daughter, he told himself he would get his son, in time.

Elijah watched the infant whose skin was a rosy copper color, nearly the same as her mother's. The baby laid on her twenty-five-year-old mother's chest. Baby moved tiny fingers, and Elijah noticed the tawny eyes. It seemed the little thing was absorbing every facet of her mother's face, although Elijah knew his daughter could not yet really see.

He and his wife peered downward, loving all six pounds and five ounces of baby. They spoke in unison. "She has Old Preacher's eyes."

Exhausted from labor, Naomi smiled as Elijah Moon chuckled. Soon afterward, he left the hospital. He had to go back to his job at municipal, the court of limited jurisdiction. There, cases involving traffic and other misdemeanors were handled. Having worked in small claims, the civil division, Elijah now worked in evictions. He hated it. As he walked to his outmoded burgundy Impala, he forgot his job. Instead, he whispered to his father. "Dad, you've got a granddaughter, and she has your eyes."

It made Elijah both happy and sad to say it, and he wondered, as he had many times since that fateful day, why had his Dad had to go, then?

Yet as time passed and his daughter grew, Elijah often thought about his life. It would have been so much simpler had Old Preacher lived.

However, at twenty-eight, Elijah realized he would not have his jewel, Topaz, named for her beautiful eyes. The truth was, he and Topaz Tiara's mother would not have married. Well, not when they had, at any rate. There would have been no need to. Had Elijah's father –who was now legendary– lived, Elijah would not have felt pressured to take a wife. He would not have had to take on the myriad responsibilities and duties that had been flung about his shoulders like a multi-layered and cumbersome cape. Nor would Elijah have felt, every so often, as though he was about to smother. The weight of all that he was trying to tread through, learn and understand often felt overwhelming.

Oh, he should stop being maudlin, Elijah told himself. The church people loved him, just like they'd loved his old man. However, they wanted him to walk in his father's footsteps, and that he could hardly do.

Old Preacher had been content, Elijah now realized, to be just that, an old preacher. However, Elijah Moon had other ideas. Many he wanted to implement. Since the world was changing and television and radio were mediums to be explored, why not? Elijah wanted to get the gospel out that way too. This he'd mentioned in a meeting with the church's board of trustees. He'd been met with unbelievable resistance. Since his pastorate, he had also heard, more times than he cared to count, that his *father* had thought things were just fine, the way they were.

Well, he was not his father! He was Elijah Martin Moon, the new reverend, and his ideas were different from those of his predecessor. Moreover, Elijah's ideas were good. Therefore, at some point, people would have to get on board, or get left behind.

Some ideas Elijah had tried to discuss with Cozina Moon. He didn't altogether know why, but his mother seemed different now. Elijah and his siblings had always believed he was her favorite. Elijah wasn't Cozi's firstborn; he had two older sisters. However, he was the first son. Thus, he had been treated like royalty. Now though, Elijah's mother often acted strange and aloof. She disapproved of Naomi, whom she called gauche.

At first, Elijah had believed that in time, Cozi would come around. Sure, she'd tried to steer him toward the daughters of the church's hierarchy, but Elijah hadn't wanted Bishop Dolman's daughter. Her long face reminded him of a horse. He hadn't wanted Apostle Canady's daughter either. For that secretly whorish woman, Elijah's mother had really pushed, unaware of the young woman's true nature.

Elijah suspected his mother had wanted Ms. Canady for him because the apostle's daughter grabbed attention. "She reminds me of me," his mother said, tacking on that the Canady girl was well-bred. "She doesn't lack the social graces that your girl does, and she has a Master's Degree in education," which, Cozi said, could be such a help to the church.

Elijah mentioned that Naomi was a pretty *woman*, one with laid-back grace. He said she was in college, too, and would help people when she became a social worker. Cozi Moon had rolled her eyes.

"Community college," she'd scoffed, "is not the same as university."

Cozi had then dismissed all talk of 'the girl' who didn't know her place. Cozi had further sang Ms. Canady's praises, as though doing so would change her son's mind. He was married, with a child!

Elijah hated to face it, but his mother was now an angry stranger. Sometimes he felt as though she blamed *him* for his father's untimely demise. Cozi definitely blamed Naomi for stealing her place. She even said, 'That girl will never be me, no matter how hard she tries!'

Elijah defended his wife. He told his mother Naomi wasn't trying to be anyone other than herself. Dismissing him, short stylish Cozi prepared to stalk from his office. Yet she had been the one to show up, unannounced, to deliver word from the church's board of trustees. Before she'd clomped away, Elijah's mother had suggested it was time for him to go into full-time ministry. He knew she spoke on behalf of the board. Slyly, Cozi also asked didn't Elijah think his parishioners had waited long enough for him to get it together. "You know, your *father* was the people's *full-time* pastor, so that's what they're used to..."

As he had in the past, Elijah reiterated that he wasn't leaving his job. It would enable him to purchase his and Naomi's first house. It was, by no means, the home of Naomi's dreams, he didn't add, but it was a start.

"You'd do better to buy that girl some clothes," Cozi caustically screeched. "And you need to forget that stupid house mess 'n do your duty by the church! If you've forgotten, son, *that* is your job, now."

ELIJAH dismissed his mother's increasing antics, which included trying to pit his younger brother, stocky Ezra, against him. Elijah concentrated on his wife, who was also a bit different now. After their copper-skinned baby was born, he and Naomi had moved into their new home. It was in the sleepy town of Tranquility, New York. Invaluable, silver-haired Mother See had helped. Refusing to lift a finger to aid him or Naomi, Cozi Moon had nixed watching her son's baby. Still, Elijah's parishioners had lent hands. Grateful, Elijah knew. There'd be snowballs in hell before he forgave his ornery mother.

Ensconced in his and Naomi's new home, Elijah forgot Cozi Moon. Instead, he recalled that for some reason, he'd believed moving into a house would make his wife happy. Sure, Naomi wasn't sad, but she didn't seem joyful. Naomi even wore shoes—sexy ones, in the house. Her amused husband shook his head. That girl! She did so because she hated the kitchen linoleum. Ever aloof, like his mother, Naomi seemed, like she had tons more to do lately. Elijah knew Naomi worked, and that she'd soon graduate. His wife had the added responsibility of their baby; cute feisty little Topaz was growing like a weed. Naomi had heaps of church duties too, but somehow, Elijah had thought the big house would bring her joy. He had liked the huge, flamboyant old Victorian. But it was drafty, not suitable for a baby—nor for him either because his wife was always cold. Elijah could hardly get at Naomi, bundled beneath layers of clothing. Truthfully, everything about their 'new' house was rickety, but it would be nice when they began to fix it up. They could start with the peeling paint outside. It was an off-putting mustard yellow. There was a lighter shade on the latticework. The trim, shutters, and foundation were brown. Whose foolish idea had it been to paint bricks?

If Elijah forgot all that, he had to admit he really loved the place, the look of it, the lawn, and the home's fanciful details. Those included the rounded porch and the bay windows. The touted spindles, mini-towers, and other flourishes caused the place to look like a rectory. It was the perfect house for a pastor. Elijah also loved that in the tiny town of Tranquility, the house sat close to Greater Bethany Bible Congregation.

When he thought about it, pastoring GBBC really wasn't so bad. The fact was, Elijah Moon was a true son of the church. How many men could say they pastored the very church in which they had come of age? For Elijah, that knowledge often engendered a fierce devotion. In the months following Old Preacher's passing, Elijah had not known he would feel that way. Perhaps the feeling was why, when he wasn't dealing with issues, or refereeing trustee board skirmishes, or poring over parish bills, he could see. He now understood why his old man had never wanted to do anything other than shepherd the flock at GBBC.

Seated in his home office, with its huge bay window, Elijah's mind wandered back to Naomi. She was so busy lately, but she was sexier than ever! Ah, her post-pregnancy body. She even had new clothes. They caused Nae to look more like his mother had when she'd been the first lady. Just thinking about Naomi churned up lust. In heels, she rushed past Elijah's door, trailed by Doggie. Elijah had thought to grab her, but Naomi carried the baby—in a bulky little hat and sweater. Nae had also clutched a textbook, so he guessed that had been no-sex Naomi. Darn it.

Elijah could smell her cooking. From the kitchen—the only warm place in the house—he also heard the baby fuss. The wall phone rang.

Naomi picked it up, and Elijah heard, "Moon residence," just as their big pup began a cacophony of barking. A second later, the doorbell chimed.

Elijah didn't move. Yet he thought, perhaps all those things were why he felt something was lacking in his and Naomi's love life. Elijah felt her *wifely duties* were her lowest priority. But what about *his* needs? Sure, he and Nae had different time constraints now. Still, Elijah wanted to be thanked for the house and for swanky new articles of clothing. A good, long, wet dick suck might pave the way to appeasement. But getting some, too, from the back, on the regular, would be the best.

Elijah's mother crossed his mind. He knew the house and Naomi's new clothes were fuel for the fire of Cozi's simmering rage. However, his mother's attitude was something to which Elijah had resigned himself. He and Naomi had also faced that although Topaz was a beautiful, inquisitive baby, her grandmother might forever ignore her.

Elijah forgot his mother. Maybe he could go lift Naomi's skirt and plug her. If he pressed his hard-on to her pretty, plump backside, and ran it along her cleft, maybe she'd bend and spread wide for him. Behind her, he'd drop to his knees. He'd get her slippery 'n wet, using his thumbs and tongue. *Why* was Doggie barking? Outside Elijah's window, movement and color pulled him from his messy musings. What the...?

Oodles of ladies from the auxiliary club entered his home. No! Through his open door, they called greetings, as most parishioners did when they clomped though the house. Hailing them, Elijah waved all back to the kitchen. He closed his door. Dang! He thought, his equivalent of cussing; so much for his massive hard-on. Now Naomi really would be busy. For hours. No one ate her good cooking and left. They lingered and ate some more. That was what Elijah wanted to do, *after sex*. Plugging Nae made him ravenous. Down boy, he told his male member. No sex right now because such was his life. Still, Elijah wanted a hot, uninterrupted, sweaty, make-a-man's-toes-curl, headboard-banging, good screw session, like he and Nae had before. And he wanted it right then!

SOMETHING was wrong. Naomi knew it as she signed for a package and closed the front door. Naomi felt it in her bones. In the large, old, ugly kitchen she tried to calm hungry, squalling little Topaz. Yet, she couldn't say anything to her husband. He didn't need any more worries. Therefore, she wouldn't burden him with her puny problems. Determined not to be like Elijah's mother, who lamented every little thing, Naomi would keep on keeping on. "Quiet, Doggie," she murmured, just as the doorbell rang. Peering from the window, Naomi saw the ladies' auxiliary club.

Back in the kitchen, under the German Shepherd's watchful eye, the ladies passed baby Topaz around. "How cute!" They spoke of her lavender sweater and matching hat. They all ate while their meeting came to order.

Much later, Naomi dutifully straddled big sexy Elijah Moon. Nude, she was aware that he wanted her to do so more often and with fervor, but she couldn't, and she couldn't tell him why. Riding Elijah, with her breasts jiggling in his face, Naomi couldn't say she wanted a son either, not right then. Desiring Elijah more with each touch, thrust, and sensual slide, she couldn't pretend they were trying to make a baby. Not just yet.

Having another baby would be nice, but first, Naomi had to find out what was going on. If sexy Elijah hadn't noticed, his wife's body had changed since their baby's birth. Sure, when he oiled her up and slid all over her, he saw the outside. But inside, things weren't quite right. Still, Naomi vowed to keep quiet because Elijah, who squeezed her buttocks, wouldn't understand. All he knew was that he wasn't getting as much sex as he would like. Yet 'this' was ridiculous. It was as though Naomi's body wasn't hers anymore. It hurt to think about it, when the truth was: Naomi *wanted* big Elijah. She wanted to lie bare and open beneath his appraising gaze. She wanted laughter and his tickling. She loved cuddling, kissing, and getting re-heated before he would take her soaring again. Knowing he thought she was ambivalent, cut deeply. It hurt more to know she couldn't confide in her sexy virile man, for fear of adding to his burdens. Naomi knew Elijah was pitching radio to the church board. As he speared deeper within her, she knew if he'd get into radio, maybe leaving his job would be worth it. Her stallion was nearly there; Naomi felt it as she rode him. The radio time slot had been garnered, and things elsewhere were falling into place. Therefore, she wouldn't nurse hurt or fear. She'd prayed. Feeling rapturous, she rode big sexy. Naomi moaned and clutched the headboard. She also thought, better be quiet, or they'd wake the baby.

Soon she would go sit with her prayer partner, the only other person who knew. Every single thing to date had happened way too fast. Naomi would take her baby. At the house that was more familiar to her than the giant monstrosity that she and Elijah inhabited, Naomi would voice her concerns. *After* she let big sexy suck her fluffy tits and pull her heavy hair.

And after she'd saturated him with her wet, and performed other skeezy acts for him—*and* her; some of their stunts were for her, too.

Perspiring, Elijah flipped her, saying, "Nae, turn over." With a large paw, he sensually slapped her behind. A truly formidable and generous lover, he did things she really enjoyed. So the truth was: Naomi too often reveled in her and Elijah's messiness. Therefore, on this moonlit night, she would give big sexy what he felt he'd been missing.

Then she would see what was what.

Chapter 7

TOPAZ Tiara Moon was a musical child. Naomi had known it back at mere months old. In church, when the music got going, or the baby daddy sang a hymn, the tiny thing moved. When an upbeat congregational song pulsed, one like *I'm a soldier, in the army of the Lord*, or when many people clapped their hands, so did Naomi's baby.

Why, that child would strain to stand on Naomi's lap. And she, the Mama, would hold Topaz's chubby little arms. Then the baby with old eyes, like they had already seen so much, the beautiful copper-skinned baby with eyes the color of an amber sunset, would dance.

In hard little lace-up shoes, the baby stood on Naomi's lap. The high-top shoes supported her tiny tights-clad ankles. In time with the music, Elijah's baby would bounce. Wearing a cute little dress, often a gift from the saints, who doted on her, the baby would clap her soft pudgy little hands. She would also yip loudly with undisguised glee.

However, what surprised Naomi was that many times when the music ended, the baby would continue to bounce. Perhaps she thought she could start it up again. A few times music hadn't been forthcoming. They'd gotten to a quiet or reverent part of the service. Then tiny Topaz angrily tossed herself backward in Naomi's arms. Thank God Mother See had taught her how to keep a firm hold on the little one, or baby might have gone flying to the floor, a horrible thought.

Naomi clutched her beloved baby close. She also pushed from mind the fact that her mother-in-law, Cozi Moon, eyed her. Naomi forgot that Cozi would have shrugged had Naomi hurt Topaz. Cozi would have then callously reminded Elijah that she had never liked 'that clumsy girl.'

Forgetting her outlandish and surly mother-in-law, Naomi jounced her baby. However, Topaz began to wail because the music had ended. Then the little thing refused to be comforted. Naomi gently shook her head; she knew the white-clad and gloved ushers were ever willing to assist. Yet she rose. She would take her noisy baby from the sanctuary, the baby who had, by then, manufactured tears.

Naomi wore a flattering chiffon sheath. It had delicately fluttering cap-sleeves. As she went, she heard the old mothers murmur, "Bless that baby's heart." "She sho' love the music of the Lord."

While hurrying away on sexy ankle-strap heels, with her glossy curls swinging, Naomi heard her husband too. Behind her, on the pulpit, he stood, wearing his regal robe.

In the hushed and husky voice that called all to attention, Reverend Elijah Moon quoted a scripture. It pertained to God receiving perfect praise, even out of the mouth of babes.

Seeing his demeanor, no parishioner would have guessed. Having glimpsed Naomi rushing away, with her shapely bottom swaying, Elijah Moon had a woody. Beneath his clerical robe, his manhood stood stiff.

Yet at the mention of the scripture, those assembled nodded, even as a few stalwart saints whispered, "Amen, pastor. Amen."

IN 1975, at nearly five years of age, old Topaz could not wait until church was over. Sure, she loved the services. She adored the singing and the music. She even loved the feeling that rose up inside her. She loved when her giant father stood at the podium, and his words rang out over the congregation. She loved the solemnity of 2nd Corinthians 13:14, the benediction. It was said at the close of worship. *"Now may the grace of God, the love of Jesus, and the sweet communion of the Holy Spirit, rest, rule, and abide now, henceforth and forevermore..."*

Topaz loved when her father, Pastor Moon, would deeply intone, "Let all the people of the Lord say..."

"Ahhh-mennn" those assembled would harmoniously sing, but what Topaz loved most was to tear out running afterward toward the piano. Its delicate ivory and onyx keys seemed to call her. Drawn to them, of course, she knew the routine. She had to weave her way through all those with whom she had to speak, all the people to whom she had to be polite. Some of them were older women who smelled powdery. Others were fatter ones; those whose stockings rubbed noisily together between their heavy thighs would give her candy.

While waiting for her to open her small, fake, patent leather purse, the women would ask, "How you doing, lil sister Topaz?" Others would press peppermints to her palm as they inquired, "You been a good girl this week? You getting your schoolwork, darling?"

Topaz would always politely respond. She knew the drill; she went through it weekly. She would thank the women for the sweets and say she was getting her lessons. As she did, her heart would race because within minutes, she would get to sit before her love! She would slip into the space between the tufted leather bench and the shimmering black ballroom piano. Back when her father was a boy, the instrument had been donated to the church.

There, with her heart singing, Topaz would reverently run her small fingers over the manufacturer's name. With fingertips tingling due to anticipation, she would place them on the keys. Then she would attempt to recreate the glorious music recently heard, the music that still rang melodiously in her head.

Topaz hoped that bigger kid, Cedric, would go get on the organ instead of trying to horn in on her piano. She was wary of him. Last year, he'd knocked her down... She and he had gotten into a shoving match because he had wanted to play the piano just to annoy her. He knew *she* always played it after church. Back when she fell, he claimed she'd slipped on the polished wood floor, but that wasn't true. The bigger Cedric kid had even called her a baby. He'd stood over Topaz as she'd cried and touched at the lump that rose fast on her head.

Golden-skinned Cedric had unmercifully taunted Topaz with chants of "Baby. Baybee. You're the pastor's baybee. Baybay..." he ran the two words together. "That's what I'ma call you, Baybay." As on high heels, Topaz's mother rushed up, he'd whispered. "You big baby."

Naomi had said, "Sed-RICK Stable, you apologize." As she brushed off her precious girl, Naomi reminded the boy. He was three years older. "As a seven-year-old," Naomi had advised, "you should know better. You don't hit girls. Nor do you push them to the floor. Be a gentleman." Naomi added, "You wouldn't want me to tell sister Ora, would you?"

His Mom, no. She wouldn't be pleased or proud of his actions.

Forgetting the scared look on the yella boy's face, Topaz approached the piano. She only hoped her tormentor, the bigger boy who often called her cat-eyed, or Baybay, would just leave her alone. All she wanted was to play the piano—her piano—in peace.

There was no one-finger this or two-finger that for her. She'd outgrown that as a toddler who'd sat on her musical daddy's knee. Now Topaz was becoming a big girl, one who could recapture some of what she'd heard. She didn't know how she did it. She only knew that when her fingers touched the keys, it was magic. She had once even said so. Her Mom and regal Mother See had stood staring down at her. They'd asked how she knew to play the hymn *At the Cross* and correctly too.

That had been when Mother See, who was always so good to Topaz, had looked at Naomi. Mother had whispered, "This child's got a gift..."

Not long afterward, Topaz began to take piano lessons. With her parent's blessing, she received the lessons courtesy of Mother See. Mother contacted a man who showed up each week to teach Topaz. Therefore, at the silver-haired woman's cozy little home, Topaz had two invaluable things, her own room and her very own piano!

While other kids despised their lessons, Topaz looked forward to hers. She also loved to place her sheet music on the latticework music rest. To do so made her feel big and important, like a lady.

Sometimes at home, she sang with her father.

Those times Naomi—in heels—asked her family to set the table.

Wearing a button-front shirt and slacks, Elijah dutifully placed plates and glasses there. In tights and a dress, Topaz gathered cutlery, as her dad took her over vocal scales. Other times, with his true tenor blending with her young soprano, the pair, the big father and his tiny daughter, sang hymns.

Topaz only wished she could have a piano at her parent's huge house. Then she could practice whenever she wanted. Why? —Because she knew, even at the tender age of four, as music flowed from her fingertips, that she, Topaz Tiara Moon, possessed something extraordinary.

Indeed, she had a gift.

Chapter 8

EVERY Sunday, Elijah Moon rose in the dark of the morning. He had a routine. After he prayed, then showered, he ate breakfast, prepared by his wife. It never varied. Elijah saw no reason to change. He liked cream of wheat, buttered toast, and coffee. After he brushed his teeth a second time and rinsed his mouth, he patted on aftershave. Then he selected a starched shirt. True, he didn't have as many as he'd have liked, but one day, when the ministry inevitably grew he'd have more. Still, Elijah had to keep up the image cultivated before Old Preacher died.

Donning his wedding band and cufflinks, he checked his creased navy suit pants for lint or loose threads. Naomi would do so again just before he left the house. She would also make sure his suit jacket was hung in the rear of his clean car so it wouldn't become wrinkled before he wore it. Elijah thought he would no longer have to ride in the second-hand, old, long-hooded, burgundy Impala one day. He would have a new car, a shiny, luxurious something. He hadn't yet figured out the make or model, but he knew one thing. It would be fresh off the showroom floor.

Aware that her husband was meticulous, especially about the look of things, Naomi came in from the cold. In heels, she had stepped over shoveled snow to hang her husband's suit jacket in his car. Next time, she vowed, she'd pull on her boots because her shapely legs and feet had gotten cold. While out of doors in the nippy morning air, Naomi had placed Elijah's briefcase on the front seat of his car. She did so after laying fresh handkerchiefs inside. That was *after* she'd made sure his bible was inside. Every time she saw that giant leather bible, Naomi thought of Old Preacher. He had been the previous owner.

If she had a son, Naomi mused, would that bible one day be passed down to him, Elijah Junior? Naomi really didn't know. Soon she'd see her husband off. She would go upstairs to get ready. She'd go back and forth, too, making sure golden-eyed Topaz was dressed. Afterward, the girls would get in the cranky station wagon. It sometimes needed coaxing before it would start. Then Naomi would press the pedal nearly to the floor to get them to service just before the choir processional.

Naomi grasped her pill bottle, needing at least one. She had to quell the ache in the pit of her. It never went away. Therefore, if she was going to get anything else done, she needed pharmaceutical aid.

In the massive old Victorian that the previous owners had painted a hideous mustard yellow, the wooden stairs whined. Naomi looked up. She knew Elijah, who descended, looking so handsome, treated worship and all that led up to it as a ritual. Thus, she dried her hands. She checked Elijah's clothing for lint or loose threads. Naomi thought about what she too would wear.

Unlike her mother-in-law, Naomi didn't own attention-seeking outfits. Hers were simple, well-made pieces that would always be in style. They were things that looked good on her. Thanks to Mother See, Naomi had lovely jewelry too, and a few heirloom pieces.

She helped Elijah into his long wool coat. She handed him his hat and remembered that he liked her stately look. He had even mentioned, a time or two, that she made him proud, in her mysterious way.

Receiving his kiss, Naomi saw Elijah off and was reminded that her husband got to Greater Bethany, the church, early. The ancient boiler might cut up, as it often did in the colder months. However, if caught early, Elijah and a deacon could try to fix it. Closing the door behind Elijah, Naomi realized again. Her husband needed to be on top of things, including her. That she welcomed. Still, she wondered. Was it his way of compensating for another area in which he felt inadequate?

Following his father's death and their marriage, Elijah had admitted it. He had not been prepared for 'all of this.' Sure, in the past, he'd said that given a choice, he'd have preferred being second in command to Old Preacher. However, nowadays, he never spoke of such things. All he talked about was what *his wife* needed to do, to be the proper first lady.

Naomi tried to squash the root of bitterness. She tried to forget that she sometimes felt Elijah was subtly trying to turn her into an overblown slave to fashion. Like his mother, the gaudily attractive but equally as mean-spirited Cozi Moon. Forgetting her mother-in-law, Naomi again realized what she had not known before marrying the big man with the compulsive behavior. He wanted everything just so, and if it wasn't that way, *his* way, big, hard-nosed Elijah Moon wanted to know why.

Chapter 9

In the 1970's

WHEN she was nearly seven, in a ruffled dress, Topaz sat in church. Awaiting the benediction, she fanned herself. She gazed at a photo of people on the cardboard front. A funeral home name was on the back. She remembered the picnic—from the day before. Boy, she'd had fun!

The eve before the outing, filled with anticipation, Topaz hadn't been able to sleep. On Saturday morning, she'd hurried through her wash-up. She'd quickly pulled on the shorts, printed tee, and socks that her mom had laid out. Unlike her friend Caley [KAY-lee], who had spent the night, Topaz hadn't wanted food. She'd gagged on a scrambled egg. Caley Nix had no trouble eating while Topaz's buttered toast stuck in her throat. Abandoning it, she'd looked across the table. Her cousins, Uncle Ezra's boys were always around; Aunt Tippie, their mom drank. With their greedy selves, the cousins heartily ate. Forgetting the five boys of differing ages, Topaz inconspicuously crumbled her toast. From her palm, she let Doggie, the family German Shepherd, gulp it. Then above the voices of the other kids, Topaz said, "Dad, I'm finished."

Seated in the old house, at the kitchen table with summer morning sunlight pouring over him, Elijah Moon read the paper. Aside, high-strung little Caley, whom people said had nappy hair, kept eating. Topaz wanted to scream as she pulled on her father's big arm. It was the hairy arm that church members didn't often see. Usually, he wore starched long-sleeved button-front shirts, suits, or one of a few magnificent robes.

Topaz realized her Dad, who always smelled nice, wore a white tee, something he hardly ever wore in public. His was like hers and Caley's, with the bright blue words 'Greater Bethany Bible Congregation' emblazoned on the front. His shirt-back was different, though. As parishioners, theirs was blank, but her Dad's shirt said 'Pastor, 1977.'

"Daddy, let's go," Topaz whined, and Elijah laughed. "Lil girl, you can tell time; it's not yet ten o'clock. Why you always gotta be so fast?" Elijah glanced over at his wife. "Nae, we rushed too much at the beginning of our marriage. It rubbed off on my baby."

Elijah spoke to Topaz as one of the younger boy cousins climbed up on the big man's knee. "Baby girl, the bus won't leave Bethany until eleven." Elijah hugged the kid striving for his attention. Elijah turned the newspaper page. He did something he always found amusing, too. When she wasn't looking, he lifted the ends of Topaz's long thick hair. When she jerked to face him, Elijah appeared innocent. "Tell you what, Taupe." Big Elijah helped his nephew down. "We'll load up in a few."

A few minutes! Topaz wanted her mom, wearing cute sandals, a sleek denim skirt, and her own tee with 'First Lady, 1977' on the back to forget the dishes. She wanted them in Mama's station wagon—they wouldn't all fit in Dad's Impala—and Topaz wanted them gone! She wanted to *be* at the church. There, the old chuggy bus with the church name on the side would wait. She'd race up to the other kids. They were indeed there by now, screaming their heads off and feeling as excited as she. Topaz wanted the deacons to start the instructions, the headcount, and the loading of food and supplies. Then Topaz wanted hand-holding and prayer beneath the summer sun, before they were off!

Yesterday, Topaz hadn't wanted to wait another minute. The park, sunshine, green grass, and the lake, where they would fish for tadpoles, had been calling. The basketball court, she was sure, had called to the teenaged boys. The softball field should have been calling to her Dad, the deacons, and other men. The strappy chairs and the barbecue grill should have called her mother. Splintery tables covered with plastic tablecloths, on which every kind of food would go, should have called to the other women. Topaz was sure the umbrellas and the trees, under which all the oldies would sit, had called to Mother See. She and others watched the chubby babies as blissfully they slept on pallets made in the shade.

Topaz recalled being in the family kitchen. She'd held back a whine, even though she'd wanted to sob because she'd really wanted to *go*!

Now on Sunday, in church, she slouched. On the hard pew her mom also sat, as did the cousins. Again she could hardly wait, this time for the benediction. Sure, her Dad often said his baby girl moved too fast, but Topaz Tiara Moon couldn't help it. She wanted Morning Service to end. While people shook hands, Topaz didn't want candy, or to say hi to anyone. She didn't want to discuss school. She only wanted to be left alone. Then she could run to her love, the shimmering black ballroom piano. It was the one she never stopped thinking of as her very own.

Chapter 10

TOPAZ asked if she could have a sleepover Saturday night.

Aware that she shouldn't wear shoes in the house, Naomi asked, "Taupe, who would you invite?" Naomi forgot hating the feel of that ugly linoleum under her feet. She watched her child stare at the ceiling.

"Caley—of course, and other girls. Oh, could Lula come too?"

"I don't see why not." Continuing to mop, Naomi wondered why her daughter thought of Tallulah [Ta-LOO-lah]. Lula was a little older. Perhaps Topaz wanted to invite the other girl because Lula really didn't have friends. She had no mother either. Lula simply attended services with her father, an ailing heavy man. Maybe, Naomi mused, Topaz wanted Lula among the number because both she and the older girl had a keen interest in the keyboard; Naomi wasn't sure. All she knew was that her child, who was smaller than others her age, had a good heart. Lil Bit was always trying to make something right for some other kid.

Naomi told Topaz, "I'll think about your sleepover." Minutes later, Naomi said, "Taupe, you know your father works his sermons on Saturday evenings, so it might be too noisy..." Before the whining could start, Naomi raised a hand. Wringing her mop, she said, "But *if* the girls can come Friday night, after church, they could stay over until *Saturday morning*." Naomi winked. "What do you think?"

Topaz quickly hugged her mother. She even offered to make the calls.

FRIDAY evening, while preparing dinner, Naomi partially cooked bacon and put it in a container in the fridge. She was glad that earlier, on her way in from work, she'd stopped and bought milk, fruit, and cereal. She wanted all on hand for breakfast, just in case some of the girls couldn't eat bacon or waffles.

At home, before church that evening, big Elijah mentioned his mother. Buttoning his starched, long-sleeved shirt, he said that later, Cozi Moon wanted to drop Ezra and Tippie's kids off at church. That way, they could spend the weekend with Topaz.

Seated, and brushing her daughter's hair that was so like her own, Naomi stiffened. She was aware of what that meant. *She* would wind up trying to make those hooligans mind. No, thank you. However, before she could say so, Topaz whined.

"Boys, nooo! They'll mess up my sleepover, Daddy—no dirty boys!"

To hide her amusement, Naomi dipped her head. "Well, Elijah," she managed as he chose a tie, "I guess you'll just have to tell Mama Mean we can't do it." Naomi was thrilled. "No boys this weekend."

Normally, when they left for church on Friday evenings, Topaz saw the neighborhood kids out playing dodge ball. Others rode bikes and just plain had fun, while she had to go to church. Usually, she felt sad. Topaz often longed to be a regular kid, like the Puerto Rican kids down the block. They went to church because their father was in the ministry too. Still, they didn't have to go to *Iglesia* every - single - Friday.

Topaz climbed into the back seat of her father's second-hand Impala. They went to Pastoral service; that's what Friday service was called. Thinking about it caused Topaz to feel bad. One reason was on Friday, church members presented her father with what she deemed his pay. But, not many people appeared. But lots of people showed up Sundays, especially the holidays. Some did so just to show off their new outfits.

As young as she was, Topaz felt like her father worked very hard at the church. But he got minimal thanks there, at his *job*. Topaz knew her father loved the church like she did, but from it, he didn't get very much money. She knew that if there were sixty-five people at Friday night service and they gave one dollar each—which some of them did not— that wasn't even a weekly paycheck of sixty-five dollars for her dad.

Topaz waved as she, Caley, and her parents rode past Joaquin and Lisette Eduardo. Topaz stared out of the rear window at Keen and Lissie, her small Latin neighbors. Topaz tried not to think about how somebody would inevitably make their way to her dad after Friday night service. Each week, somebody different begged him for a few of the dollars he'd just received. That person would claim they needed carfare to get to their job the following week. But that person's job paid them a couple of hundred a week! It was all so unfair, Topaz mused, even though her big handsome dad took everything in stride. He felt it was his duty to help the Lord's people, at all times. Things like that were probably why the Moon family lived in the big scary house that always had something breaking down. The golden-eyed child knew her mother added each next item to the broken-stuff list. Topaz also knew what her mother didn't seem to get. Not much would ever be fixed. There just wasn't enough money, not even with her mother's pay from her social work.

Sitting up tall as they neared Greater Bethany, Topaz realized she didn't feel sad on this particular Friday evening. She knew it was because, after church, her friends would pile in the car, and *sleepover*!

That evening during service, Naomi did not fail to notice. With *her* eyes narrowed, Elijah's mother shot daggers. So this was what Mother See had been speaking of, way back. The older woman had said that even after Naomi and Elijah married, there would be malcontents. Well, Elijah's mother was the president of that club.

Seated across the aisle, Cozi Moon wanted her daughter-in-law to know. She was not pleased. Cozi stared at that good for nothing. Why her son had married, against her wishes, Cozi would never understand.

Lazy Naomi could have taken Ezra's kids. For Pete's sake, Ezra was Elijah's younger brother! That she-devil Naomi knew Ezra's wife couldn't handle those boys. And Lord knew Naomi had room, at that enormous mausoleum that she and Elijah lived in, with their one little hoyden. Unlike at *her* home, Cozi cogitated; *she* had precious things, and nice furniture. At Cozi's house, her wild-behind grandsons could do serious damage. However, at Naomi and Elijah's place, the kids could spread out. That raggedy house was full of pieces that belonged to no one. The previous owners had left some of that mess. The rest Naomi had poked about in second-hand stores for. So it wasn't like Ezra's little hoodlums could damage any of that junk that Naomi called furniture.

Cozi cut her eyes, not knowing why Naomi wouldn't take the boys, but she would find out the real reason. Forget that flimsy 'sleepover' excuse Elijah had handed her. Heck, even if there was a sleepover, it wasn't like Naomi had anything more to do; unlike when *she*, the beautiful and fashion-forward Cozina Moon, had been the first lady.

Saturday morning at the mustard-yellow house sorely in need of a paint job, Naomi rose to make batter. She'd allow Topaz and the sleepover girls to make their own waffles, and a mess, but who cared?

The girls straggled in. They were followed by adult Doggie.

After hand washing, Naomi showed the girls how to rinse, slice, and arrange fruit on a platter. She showed them how to set the kitchen table. They had no idea she was teaching them skills they could use throughout their lives. They simply thought it was fancy and fun; "We doing this for breakfast!" one girl yipped. Another stated she'd never had such a nice meal. Naomi smiled as the girls enjoyed cooking, too. Pouring and browning their own waffles, Naomi oversaw all as she finished the bacon. She made Elijah's breakfast because soon, he would make his rounds. He'd see about the sick, the shut-in, and the infirm.

She got big sexy squared away in the dining room. That room she longed to make more elegant. In it, her good-smelling man was pretty much removed from the chaos in the kitchen. Then with heels on, Naomi clomped back to the kitchen to check on the girls who heartily ate.

Leaning to watch her swang that thang, amused, Naomi's husband shook his head. That girl, wearing shoes—and sexy ones too—in the house! He smiled, remembering how she'd awakened him at dawn. Beneath the covers, her tight lips *popped*, as around his plug she'd shushed him. Further, not wanting to wake Topaz's guests, Naomi had climbed the mountain. What a gift!

Grinning, Elijah shook open his morning paper.

Following the man's good-bye kiss—where he got a bit frisky, Naomi returned to the kitchen. There she instructed the girls on clean up.

She remembered her man's big hands on her small waist and shapely bottom. Before he'd left, in the dining room the couple had nearly gotten all tangled up, again. Naomi recalled gently slapping at Elijah's roaming hands. She forgot how curved around her, he'd made her want, again, despite their activities at dawn. Now he was off, to face the day. Back in her large ancient kitchen, Naomi gave each sleepover girl a task. She was surprised that each girl's cheer remained. By noon, Naomi, her young daughter Topaz, and Topaz's taller, thinner best friend Caley Nix, as well as Doggie, waved off the last of the visitors. Standing in the open door, Naomi sighed. Thoughtless, she voiced her heart's desire aloud. "I really would love to have more children." She'd love the making of those babies too, with Elijah Moon.

"But Mama, you've got me, and Caley," Topaz reminded her.

Hugging both girls to her, Naomi smiled. "I guess I do, don't I? And you two," one fast and one wild, "are a handful. Right?"

Chapter 11

ELIJAH ran a hand over Naomi's nude brown breasts. They'd grown so ripe and round until he couldn't resist. Resting on his side, he gazed down at her as she lay beside him. Using his fingertips on the heavy underside, he lifted one. He tasted it. Perfect. Provocative, Naomi raised an eyebrow. She felt Elijah's rod. It was 'bout to be on!

Elijah slid a hand down his wife's body and over the mound. It was his baby, increasing inside her. The thought of a son made him grow harder as he allowed his hand to journey downward. Using thick fingers, Elijah splayed Naomi. Igniting her, he whispered, "Let me in..."

She knew they needed to shower. She had to let Doggie out. Then they'd go; her sexy preacher had to preside over a funeral. Afterward, they'd get Topaz from Mother See's house. However, before all of that, they'd take a few minutes. They'd not be late. They would get to church in time to tend things. It was what they did. That was why Naomi suddenly felt selfish, and like this time was just for her, and her man.

Widening her legs, she felt Elijah use his teeth on her breast.

Not wanting to ruin the moment, she tried not to think. Yet she couldn't forget that she and he had so many responsibilities. Those caused them to have precious little time to spend together as man and wife. Then whenever they happened to be together, something or someone always came up. Instead, she thought, something or someone always tried to come between them. The phone would ring, or a deacon would say, "Excuse me, Pastor..." Or, Eve, whom they had once counseled—along with her husband, long gone—would begin talking to Elijah, or God only knew what else would happen.

Naomi rolled her eyes because Eve was the current church administrator. That gave her first dibs on the pastor, Eve believed.

That was the nature of being in ministry, Naomi reminded herself, she didn't have to like it, but it was how things were. However, she mused, for the next few moments, she and he would *not be* in ministry. Naomi's husband shifted and loomed over her. When he positioned his large warm frame between her thighs, she couldn't wait. For a few precious minutes, they would not be disturbed. For a short time that would be only for them, she and virile Elijah Moon would engage...in hot, sweaty sex.

45

Just thinking about it, Naomi slid elegant hands down Elijah's broad back. She squeezed his firm buttocks and used nasty words to spur him on. Sure, she knew he often wanted to love her with what he called finesse, but since finding out she again carried his seed, she didn't care about subtlety. She only wanted to ride the devil clean out of big sexy.

"*Ohhh,*" Naomi moaned, feeling the familiar knob, then the thrust. Feeling him glide within, she purred. "Oh Lijah," she cried out as he stroked and stirred just right. Arching to meet him, she whispered. "Don't be Pastor right now. Just do me. Harder. Be my man, and—"

"Nae, shut...up," Elijah growled, giving it to her good. Turning her on her side, he raised her leg. Thick and slippery, again he entered her.

"I will not," Naomi grinned, then she groaned in ecstasy when her man hit her sweet spot. He nudged again, and she screamed. His sucking mouth opened on her nape. Despite shudders, she managed to order, "More." Attempting to push back on him, she shifted a bit, squeezing him tightly. "That's it, Big Daddy. Push. Ohhh. Deeper..."

"Nae, shut – it – up," Elijah ground out between clenched teeth. He also chuckled while entrenched and sinking further into her. He knew Naomi knew. Her messy talk did him in. It often caused him to expend himself before he was ready. Right now, he wanted more time within her cushiony body. Yet, coiled around her, he felt sexual healing began to emit. Turning her head, she kissed him, and drove him insane.

"You are one wicked woman," he said, pressing his perspiring face to her neck. "And madam first lady, you're gonna get it when we return." He sounded sexy, fondling her package. "I'ma keep this thang swollen."

Naomi grinned and thought about untangling herself. In Elijah's arms, she wished they had nowhere to go and no one else to tend. "I hope so, big preach," she candidly stated. "I sure do need more of you."

BY the time Advent Season 1979 rolled around, nine-year-old Topaz had heard quite a few people remark on her mother's size. The thing about being a kid was that people forgot she was there.

Topaz had heard her grandmother—who never really had a kind word, and another woman. Cozi and the fat sour sister murmured behind their hands. At Pageant rehearsal, they spoke ill of her mother, Cozi's favorite subject. Cozi whispered about Naomi being 'with child,' whatever that meant. Cozi didn't seem too happy about it.

Unable to stand listening to the women that Uncle Ezra called the cobweb crew, Topaz ran to Sister Myrtle. Seated at a table in the Narthex, the woman handed out paper with bible phrases. Some were short, for the small children. Others were a paragraph, for bigger kids.

Sister Myrtle, handed Topaz one of the paragraphs. The child with the 'cat eyes,' Old Preacher's eyes, wondered why so much to remember?

Topaz could see it; she would stand before the congregation on Christmas Pageant night. Candles would be lit. People who never came on any other occasion would arrive. Their eyes would be on her. Topaz might forget what she needed to remember. Why couldn't she just play or sing? Forcing her to do a recitation could wind up awful.

The child jerked, looking at Sister Myrtle, who smiled. "Yes, it could be awful, Topaz, if you forget your lines. That's why we're rehearsing."

Oh Lord, Topaz cogitated. She had spoken her thoughts aloud! One day she'd keep her mouth shut. Taking a seat with the other kids, she reminded herself. She didn't want to be labeled a troublemaker. Christmas was coming, and the Youth Leaders handed out funny stockings. Troublemakers maybe didn't get the red/white striped 'stockings' They were made of weird plastic-y material. There could be several things in the funny stockings, an apple, an orange, grapes, or a little bag of nuts. Topaz loved those because then her Dad would use his little silver nutcracker at home. Then he'd let her pick out the delicious inside. That was the only time she could ever remember him sitting with her, and the now sixty-something Doggie, for maybe half an hour. Then, having something better to do at the church, her Dad would rush off.

Oh, and she thought about her mother. Mean Cozi said Mama should have known better. Cozi said Naomi had a hard time the first go-round. She was a fool to do it again. Topaz forgot old people talk. She only wanted to think about the Christmas stockings. If she reached far down in her stocking, she might find a game. It could be a small package of jacks or marbles. She might even get a find-the-word book. She loved those. High-strung Caley didn't, but they'd swap because they never got all the same things. Topaz swung her feet. In the stocking, there might even be candy, the striped Christmas kind. In noisy cellophane. If she tried to open it in church an usher would stand over her. They held out white-gloved hands to take candy, until after service.

Topaz loved this time of year, but not standing beside the organ and singing *Gloria in Excelsis Deo* a hundred times. However, she liked the first part of the song. *Angels we have heard on high…* It was so musical and light. She could play it fairly well. She could play while singing other carols, like '*It came upon a Midnight Clear*,' and '*Silent Night*.'

Topaz loved the feeling of togetherness at this time of year. She loved hollering out, "Merry Christmas!" She passed people who also wore mittens and more than one pair of socks. She especially loved the Christmas tree that was put up in the corner of the Fellowship Hall. There, all the church members ate together on different occasions, like after funerals. Topaz loved looking at the decorated and beribboned boxes beneath the tree. *But* the pretty boxes were empty. She knew. The church was always open. Not everybody that entered the doors was a Christian. Topaz's Dad had told her. Some people had evil in them – people like Cozi Moon, her grandmother. Other people might even try to steal the presents. Therefore, the fakes went under the tree. Many people didn't know, but the goody-stuffed stockings were locked away. They were for the church kids and the neighborhood kids. At The Christmas Pageant's end, each child would be called. The stockings would be handed out! Topaz could hardly wait!

Once, her little family had ridden home in her mom's station wagon, the one that *occasionally* gave heat. Topaz had asked, "Dad, why does the church give out gifts and food?" They even gave to those who lived in the town of Tranquility but didn't attend GBBC. Topaz remembered her handsome Dad's reply.

"We do it baby, to show our Savior's love—until He returns."

Topaz had asked while eyeing falling snow, "When will that be?"

Elijah Moon's roar of laughter startled Topaz and her mom, who'd been driving. "Baby girl," Elijah replied, "that, no one knows."

Oh. Well. Topaz wanted to get Christmas goodies. She needed to play with her friends, and Doggie. She, Caley, and others had to have their snowball fight with the bigger kids. The bigs usually won, but if the littles were losing, then the Lord could return. That would be the rapture. Then Topaz wouldn't have to go back to school or do homework.

Oh, but if the other stuff she'd heard the cobweb crew whispering was true, then Topaz wanted to stay on earth a bit longer. She would sure like to meet her new brother, or her sister.

Chapter 12

WHEN Naomi's baby had to be taken at 29 weeks, Topaz cried as hard as she did. Fully-formed, he had been just weeks shy of being able to breathe on his own, outside the womb. For Naomi and Topaz, the early third-trimester fetus had been loved like he had already been born.

Elijah tried to sound soothing. He told Naomi they could try again. Really, she was too upset. People lost babies. Through parishioners, he'd been privy to many losses. They had other babies. Life rolled along. Old Preacher's death had taught Elijah that, if nothing else.

With bleary eyes, Naomi looked away. Elijah didn't understand. She had lost *numerous* babies due to fibroids, tumors with hair and teeth. They fed off her body. Elijah only knew about one baby. The boy who'd nearly made it. In her womb, myomas multiplied, thinking they were real live babies; it was disgusting! Although she'd prayed, and prayed, they were growing at an alarming rate. Naomi's gynecologist said they needed to be removed, along with a portion of her uterus. Alarmed, Naomi thought, her uterus was part of her *baby-making* apparatus!

The doctor had said she would try to save what she could of the uterus. Still, now that Naomi had gained weight, during a painful pregnancy that had yielded nothing—other than sickness and death—Naomi no longer cared. She was tired of crying, and praying. She would simply tell her doctor to do the hysterectomy, none of that partial stuff; she forgot what the GYN had called it. Naomi wanted no more heavy bleeding, pelvic discomfort, and pressure on her other organs. She didn't want the temporary relief that she might or might not get from a fibroid embolization. Nor did she want any more pills. Naomi had several, some to up her mood, or others to decrease anxiety. She had drugs for sleep and to wake. Naomi especially didn't want any more of the pills that no longer dulled the ache. For once in her adult life, she wanted to be pain-free. She didn't want to wait to see if the bloodsuckers inside her would shrink or minimize when she went through menopause. And she was tired of fighting with her weight due to the hormonal imbalance.

Naomi told herself she would have the operation. Didn't she already have a child, a beautiful, sensitive, and intelligent daughter? Taupe was nearly ten. So what? Elijah wanted a son. Who cared that she had also wanted her boy. Actually, Naomi had wanted four boys and one more girl, just like her copper-skinned, golden-eyed Topaz. But five of those babies were dead. In life, Naomi bitterly thought, dabbing the tears she would never let Elijah see, people didn't always get what they wanted. Not even people of God.

TWELVE-year-old Topaz hated to leave her mother at home alone. Naomi had been so fragile-minded and distraught. She had been for a good long while now, but it couldn't be helped. At least Naomi could take pills if she had pain. For help with Naomi's depression, Topaz thought, Mama could even pop another pill. Other than that, Topaz didn't know what else could be done.

At GBBC, Topaz had been appointed the leader of the youth choir. It was a big responsibility. That choir occasionally needed to accompany the pastor on outings. They were expected to fellowship with other churches with growing youth ministries like their own.

As she listened to popular gospel tunes, and as she learned hymns too, Topaz also had to train the combined choirs to sing for Communion. With school and her contributions to the school newspaper, she really didn't have time for much else. She practiced night and day. Then she presented songs to her same-aged young people.

Topaz nearly forgot to feel jealous when other kids called her father 'Dad.' But Elijah Moon was *her* father, not theirs. Then there were her cousins; Uncle Ezra and A'nt Tippie's boys were always around, making noise and eating everything. They called her father 'Dad.' Topaz hated it. The boys had a father—her Dad's brother! She didn't mind sharing her Dad, but she knew the other kids called him Dad because she did.

Caley, Topaz's friend, called Naomi and Elijah Mama and Daddy, just like Topaz did, but that was different. Caley Nix had no one other than her frail old grandmother. Caley's parents had been lost to drugs by the time volatile Caley was three. Willingly, Topaz shared her parents with her slender friend, but all the other church kids? And them bad-behind Willis boys up the street from Greater Bethany, why'd they need to try to steal her father? Their old man drank. Sure, Pastor Moon often went and got him, at night, from the gutter, but still, the boys had a dad.

Topaz forgot the Willis boys, and girls who were always in a rivalry with her. They had breasts. Those girls were forever slicking Vaseline on their lips and prettily pouting. They ran to her father after service to hug him. Then the baby witches would stand with their thin arms around him, silently daring her, Pastor Moon's real daughter, to say a word.

Topaz remembered that later that week, she'd would have to teach some of them a new song. Everyone thought to do so was easy. Upon hearing the youth choir, people just thought they sounded good. Who knew how much work it was for Topaz? It took a lot to make the teenagers gel. First, most did not want to listen. They felt she was bossy when she gave them notes. She asked them to repeatedly sing those notes to get them right. Secondly, the teenagers only came to choir practice to play, meet one another, and others. They wanted to joke around and jostle. They whispered, chewed gum, passed notes, and kissed out back.

Sister Myrtle, the young people's advocate, suggested having closed choir practice. That hadn't stopped the choir teens from bringing outsiders, their friends, and relatives. The outsiders sat on the back pews and giggled. The outsiders made the shy singers nervous. The outsiders made faces and opened noisy candy wrappers. It rattled the timid kids' nerves. To Topaz, serious about teaching music, it was all unsettling.

To her, the only time everyone was on the same page was for the few minutes when the choir members thought they sounded good. During those moments, Topaz, the pianist, looked at Cedric, the stocky organist. She saw Tallulah, the other organist, and Bailey, the drummer. She saw Titus too. He played bass guitar, and Amber, the heavy girl, played the sax. Those moments the band found themselves in sync with the choir. Miraculously then, the singers remembered their lines and held their harmonies.

Chapter 13

ELIJAH Moon sat in his office with his new dog, another sweet rescue, at his feet. He sure missed Doggie, who had gone to canine Heaven. Elijah thought about Naomi, who was so distant lately. He missed her too. Sure, if he wanted, she would sleep with him. If he leaned on the bathroom counter and held out a hand, if he said, "Come do me, wife," she would. But why did he have to coax her to do her duty? He disliked that. It was something about which he'd prayed, *Lord, make her willing*, but so far, Elijah had received no Heavenly help.

Naomi would also use lubricant, Elijah remembered, as though he could no longer get her wet. Then she wouldn't be all that into it, not like she had been before Topaz was born. Even before she'd become pregnant with the baby that she'd lost. At thirty-six, Naomi had wanted him more than she did now. After that pregnancy, she had changed.

Now sex-greedy Elijah had a wife who cared less about his needs, although he had a slew of women coming at him. Eager women appeared when a ministry grew. One of the older pastors had warned him.

Maybe the women who came onto him, Elijah mused, could sense he wasn't getting his needs met. Still, he wasn't sure about the ones who called his home office way over in the night. That just seemed too bold. But then again, he felt like he had been married so long, and from such a young age, until there were things he probably didn't know. At thirty-nine, he felt he'd been a holy man for an inordinate amount of time. As such, maybe he just thought women wanted him when they really didn't.

Elijah thought about it as he sat in his home office. Perhaps the late-night calls weren't invitations or booty calls at all. Maybe the women who called really did just need to speak with their pastor. Perhaps they simply needed consolation and words of wisdom. But why did each one sound so sexy? Didn't they know he was virile? He sometimes felt weak too. While listening to their sad songs about how the men in their lives weren't doing them right, he thought of how right he could do them.

Lord, please forgive me; Elijah intoned, as he put his face in his big hands because nowadays it seemed as though temptation was everywhere. Now Elijah really had to wonder, how had *Jesus* handled

Mary Magdalene? She'd followed him all over the countryside. How had The Christ dealt with that other Mary and Martha—Lazarus' sisters? Hordes of other women too had just wanted a good hammering from the carpenter's strong, miracle-working son.

Elijah Moon sighed and knew he had to stop thinking. He was a man of God, and those thoughts were wicked. He shouldn't think about his savior that way, either. However, Elijah asked himself, didn't the bible say our High Priest was tempted, the same way we are?

If that was the case, then women actually had attempted to entice Jesus, many times. That led Elijah to wonder how his savior had handled those encounters. The bible didn't specifically say. It only depicted how He'd dealt with the temptation from Satan.

But, Elijah mused, how would *he*—a modern man—sound, following the Lord's example? How sanctimonious would he appear if he told every temptress, 'Get thee behind me, daughter of Satan, for it is written…man shall not live by bread alone…' When oh, how Elijah wanted some nice soft brown 'bread!' He would use oil on those plump round buns, just before he would sink his—

No! Elijah had to stop thinking wicked thoughts, but see? This was what those women—the new members at the church—had reduced him to, rubble. They'd done so with their tight skirts. Often Elijah tried to pray as they marched toward the collection plate. Closing his eyes and knowing he appeared pious, many times he tried not to notice their jiggling bosoms. He tried not to see some female members who'd been there a while; some of those women got him going too. A few of them insinuated things as they sidled up to him after service. Others weren't so subtle. Truth be told, there was one woman in particular…

Elijah didn't know how it had begun, but now he just couldn't seem to get extricated. He was caught up in her clutches. He told himself he didn't know why he frequented her apartment. The place he thought of as her den, of iniquity, but that was untrue. At his own home, he disliked the way Naomi floated around—like an unresponsive *ghost*. Elijah couldn't even talk to her about it because his Nae was in a fog.

Elijah wanted to ask the Lord for forgiveness, but then again, he didn't. The Lord had to understand. Big Elijah was a *man*, and a lusty one. A man like him had needs. Now those needs were being met outside his marriage. Well, some of them…

Chapter 14

In the early 1980's

HE was getting on her nerves. This Topaz thought, but internally, she vowed not to let the sixteen-year-old know it. He was a buff golden shade, a light brown really, and one evening in church, unpredictable Caley announced, "SED-Rick's skin is yella. Yep, like the color painted on every numba 2 pencil I ever had!" She and Topaz cracked up while trying not to draw attention to themselves.

Nevertheless, the yellow boy had seen them; so had some disapproving adults. Cedric had known the girls were laughing at *him*. He'd frowned, which only made them bury their heads in their laps to keep from snorting any louder because they were supposed to be quiet. Seeing the chortling and wheezing girls, an usher deftly marched them from the sanctuary until they could behave.

Forgetting silliness, Topaz knew Cedric Stable thought he was better at the keyboard than she was. She also knew he thought she was a kid, but she was probably his mental equivalent. Maybe she was more astute.

Cedric's actions also let Topaz know he thought she got preferential treatment at the church because she was the PK, the preacher's kid. The pastor's Baybay. Cedric could not have been more wrong. Everyone expected more from Topaz than they did anyone else. Heck, she was now thirteen, and she couldn't even say that word aloud. It would have been a sin. Lord knew *she* wasn't supposed to commit any sins. She was held to a higher standard than everyone else. Topaz couldn't even have a boyfriend. Her father said no boys, not until sixteen. Topaz was mature for her age, though, *she* felt. Elijah Moon's word was law, at home and at church. Topaz sometimes hated it. She couldn't go anywhere or do a thing without her Dad's consent. His large presence loomed. She was a prisoner. Topaz forgot the man whom many women found one big luscious hunk. She often heard them in the ladies' room. They thought it was only them in there. It was disgusting, the way they drooled and said how good he smelled. He was the *preacher*, for crying out loud! And he was her father! Ick; Topaz only wanted to concentrate on the song she was playing. She could master the second chord progression. She needed to get the key change. It would take them into the third song of the medley. If she got the notes right afterward she'd make them her own. She'd get yella-behind Cedric off her back. This was the song he'd taught the combined choirs, but he didn't have to police everybody—the lead soloist, the singers, and the musicians. Topaz understood, though. He wanted *his* song, to be better than the others that she taught because she had a gift. It wasn't something Topaz was haughty about because perfecting that gift took work and dedication, but she *was* talented.

She had never minded competition, although it seemed too many people strove to compete with her. For some strange reason. Truth be told, Topaz was sick of stocky Cedric, who wasn't very tall. That she could smile about because she knew he wanted to be taller. He elongated his spine, even when sitting on the organ seat. It didn't matter that he was taller than she was, because, for a guy, he was short—ha!

Sure, he was older by three years. She strove to master the notes, but that yella boy was overbearing. He despised her...even though he really did smell nice. However, she couldn't think about that as he again leaned over her to place her fingers in the correct chord structure. As Cedric did, he didn't deem her worthy enough to pay attention to; he spoke to the drummer about the downbeat.

Topaz sighed. All she wanted was to go home and get it, on her own, with Puppy nearby. She was the Moon family's new dog. Home was where Topaz did her best work, on the piano that Mother See had bought when Topaz was little. People around the church said Mother See thought she was the first lady's mother and Topaz's grandma. As far as Topaz was concerned, the older woman *was*. Heck—there was that troublesome word again—but Mother See was more a grandma to her than Cozi Moon, or Naomi's mother. Topaz rarely saw her real little Gran because she lived in Carolina. As Topaz managed to play the right notes, the golden-eyed girl forgot grandmothers.

"Again," Cedric told the musicians. See? He was a scuzzball; he could always point out every mistake but never a triumph. Forgetting the stocky boy-man, Topaz listened as Cedric told them where to take it from; bars before his dastardly chord progression. She played and recalled her father's mother. Cozi was nothing like her name. She wasn't interested in Topaz, or any of Topaz's other cousins. Cozi didn't even care for drunken A'nt Tippie and Uncle Ezra's kids, and the boys often stayed with her—when Cozi couldn't badger Naomi into keeping them.

All her grandmother cared about, the thirteen-year-old believed, was trying to pretend she was the church's first lady. Oh, and clothes. Cozi always told Naomi she didn't own the proper clothing for this or that. Well, duh, Topaz thought. Mom didn't make much money as a social worker. Naomi did her job for the love of the kids she helped and protected. Topaz's good-smelling Dad *had* made money at his courthouse job, but he'd had to quit because of his mother. No, he had done so to manage all that was associated with the church. Now things were really tight. Topaz didn't get an allowance. Yet her father always gave someone outside the family a handout. Usually, the receiver had a job! Topaz played on because some things she would never understand. Ah! She did it!

"Again," Cedric called, and Topaz wanted to grind him under her boot. She knew he only wanted her to mess up. What Yella didn't know though was once she got something, it stayed. Aware that Cedric Stable had no idea; Topaz smiled, even as the stocky dictator yowled, "Again!"

HE saw her smirking while seated at the piano. She thought it was hers, alone. He guessed that was okay. At least she'd gotten the notes. She was young, but she seemed older, probably because she didn't talk much, unlike most females. The only time the kid ever really talked— well, gave directions—was when she rehearsed the children's choir, or the adolescents. In combined choir rehearsals, she barely said a word. Maybe because he and the minister of music did most of the instructing. However, when the kid did make a soft-spoken point, it was valid.

Cedric liked that she worked hard. The kid never came to rehearsal unprepared. He liked that on a fast song, even without the drums, she could keep the beat. She'd slap her little foot against the shiny wooden floor and keep things bumping. Her style, was unlike any he'd ever heard, and he had heard quite a few. Cedric's mother was a jazz singer. She'd sung in lounges, hotels, and supper clubs. Right now, she was trying to die. Sure, they said his Mom had the disease that everybody dreads. She'd been to chemo and had radiation. She didn't look the same. Mom no longer cared about the records he and she had listened to, Cole Porter, Dave Brubeck, Dinah Washington, and Miles Davis.

Cedric's Mom was tired. Last week, she'd whispered to him and his dad that she would accept no more treatment. She said she was going to leave here as she was. Cedric hated to hear her talk like that because she was his best friend. If she left, whom would he have? His jukey older brother? When Carlton wasn't working, he was chasing skirts. Cedric knew his father would be around, but the stocky older man would be at his bar. Business owner Mr. Stable didn't have time for much else, including his youngest son. Cedric forgot his sad life. He told the church musicians to play it again, from right before the changeover. He said so because he was trying to figure out what Miss Topaz—Baybay—was doing with her copper-colored skin that looked so soft.

She'd gotten the notes, but then her lightning-fast little fingers had tripped over the keys, incorporating trills he hadn't even known would fit. She had some jazz in her soul, Cedric could tell. She wasn't just church. He told the musicians to play it again; he wondered where Babybay could have heard such musical licks. Did she listen to the likes of Ella and Satchmo? Cedric walked away from the piano, where the preacher's kid sat. He had to because she smelled nice, sort of, and inviting. He'd noticed, although he hadn't been trying. Her scent was soft, like cotton candy or cake icing. It rose up from her thick, longish hair that was brown and pulled back into a neat ponytail. What he'd really noticed was her most capable little fingers. They were pretty. The kid wore no rings or bracelets. Cedric thought she would because she had to be spoiled, a rotten brat who got everything she wanted. The kid had golden cat eyes too. Scary. They seemed to see right through him.

Cedric suddenly wondered what all that shiny hair would look like if he undid the clip that held it. What if he could feel that sweet-smelling hair, just wrap it around his hand as he— Ah, there was Lela. Seconds ago, she'd slipped in the door. That meant this session was over. That tone-deaf girl was nothing, if not prompt. Man, did she have titties on her! She liked to show her double Ds. She liked them handled, and handle them he would! Cedric couldn't wait to leave and get at Lela.

Now *she* was something to think about, unlike that little girl, the PK …even though the preacher's kid was turning out to be super talented.

One day, Cedric thought as his mind went back to Pastor Moon's cute kid. Cedric might even challenge what's-her-name—Baybay—to a keyboard competition. Then, what lil cutie was made of, Cedric would definitely find out.

Chapter 15

Eᴌɪᴊᴀʜ lay in bed trying to breathe deeply, like he might have been asleep. However, what he really wanted to do was get up and go home. He didn't belong here, in this bed, with this woman. He belonged at home, in bed with Naomi, his wife. There, old Doggie would lie on the floor beside his bed. No, the family had Puppy now; Doggie had gone on. Elijah covered his eyes. He was so ashamed of himself, catting around on Nae. Yet, for some reason, he kept finding himself back at the apartment that belonged to *her*. She was okay, not anything special, not someone for whom he would leave Naomi. First, because he did not believe in leaving. Secondly, he loved Nae. This one didn't believe him, though, because he came to her bed. Elijah didn't try to explain anymore. But he came to this one's bed because he had so many worries and bills at home. The monstrosity he'd bought, where his family lived, was a money pit. It ate up every dime he and Naomi could lay their hands on.

Being with this woman was an outlet. Well, it had started that way. Now, it didn't matter where he was, all his problems assailed him. And blast, did he hate the feeling that said he'd become 'entangled.'

At the rate Elijah was going, he would have to do speaking engagements and hire himself out for weddings and funerals. He'd have to do so until the cows came home. Now see? Elijah breathed heavily. That was another thing. He, the church administrator, and the treasurer had sat for long hours attempting to juggle church funds. It was tedious, the day-to-day business. While Old Preacher lived, Elijah hadn't known what all had gone into making the church go. Now, he sometimes felt Old Preacher had gotten off easy. The man had done what he loved. He'd preached and spoke to God afterward. He had then gone quietly home to Jesus. It didn't get any easier than that. Now Elijah was stuck.

He realized his heart was crazily pounding. Again. Elijah wondered if he was developing a heart condition, like his dad. He wondered if trying to keep the church lights and water on was giving him chest pains. Was maintaining and servicing the boiler, printer, copier, piano, organ, and other instruments worrisome? Repairs for the parking lot were steep. Insurance prices, paper, cleaning supplies, Communion and teaching materials, and the cost of hymnals stayed with Elijah. Had thoughts of property taxes given Old Preacher angina and heart palpitations?

Elijah didn't know. All he knew was that radio was not doing what he needed anymore. He would have to branch out, maybe take Greater Bethany Bible Congregation on TV. The board said it was too expensive. It was too expensive not to. The church had to expand its reach. If it didn't, Elijah mused, they'd never keep up with all that came at them. Again, Elijah sighed and wished he were at home, in *his* bed. There, Naomi would not have asked what was wrong. She knew. He hated when this woman did that. This one didn't realize. She couldn't help. All that could help was money, and the Lord. Since he no longer pretended he slept, Elijah rose altogether. He pulled on his clothing.

There she went, talking again. Why couldn't she be like his wife and keep her mouth shut? Elijah made the mistake of asking her that once. She'd gone ballistic saying he hadn't wanted her to keep her mouth shut when his big dick was in it. She said he hadn't wanted her like his *wife* when he'd been getting her good pussy. He'd told her he abhorred it when she was vulgar. She'd said she despised when he was crude. Coming to *her* bed and talking about his wife. "Especially," the woman huffed, "when *I'm the one* gave you *a son!*"

She was never going to let him forget it. Elijah got his coat. He wondered. How had he let himself get into this? At forty-two, he was too old for mess. How'd it get this far? Sexy Elijah knew. It was his wife's fault. If she hadn't become spacey, if she'd opened to him, instead of closing like a clam, he'd not have sought attention elsewhere. Naomi Ruth was the one he wanted, even now. It was his greedy pecker's fault, too. Elijah tried to get out of the apartment without a scene. He had never sought this woman's attention. She'd just been there. They worked in close proximity. He'd talked to her about the mountain of debt under which the church struggled. Now, this one wanted him to leave his wife and make her the first lady. He'd said get in line, "Behind my mama," and others. The woman had said he should quit playing; she was serious.

He had known she was the first time she'd said it. Now, he had grown tired of telling her. That leaving mess was not gonna happen. Elijah would not leave *Mrs. Moon* or his kid, petite golden-eyed Topaz.

Outside, in the chill morning air, he got into his car. He'd almost given up hope of getting a new one. Elijah couldn't see that coming anytime soon. In his old car, he could only see condensation caused by his breath. In the cold, Elijah waited for his shuddering vehicle to warm.

Moments later, he opened his eyes and headed for home, all the while feeling bad. As he went, Elijah asked God for forgiveness. He also asked for help, just like the clergyman in the movies. However, in real life, Elijah Moon didn't believe his angel had shown up, evidenced by his predicament. No man who looked like Denzel had appeared. In 'The *Preacher's* Wife,' Washington had portrayed the angel. Guess God was ignoring him, Elijah mused. Probably because he was a reprobate, a repeat offender, screwing outside his marriage. What was worse was the other woman was more sexually timid than Naomi had ever been. This one never got wild or free. She didn't want to experiment. He and this one didn't lay up, sharing snacks. He didn't want to hold her or just gaze steadily at her. They never laughed together. This one was always angry.

Elijah thought of his wife. She didn't complain, although there was much to complain about. Naomi just went on, in her laid-back way. To Elijah, she was as cute as she had been way back when he'd met her. Nae had been seventeen, and he a little older. She'd been slender and shapely. No longer a girl, Naomi was a woman now. Sure, she was currently a few sizes bigger, but she was beautiful, inside and out. Naomi made Elijah laugh too; that girl wore *shoes* in the house! He couldn't get over it. She hated the cold floors –and that cracked, awful linoleum in the kitchen. Waiting for a green light, the preacher almost guffawed right then, thinking about his wife and her little weirds. He had to admit, with heels on, Nae always looked sexy, swanging what her mama gave her.

Elijah drove Tranquility's near-empty streets to get back to where she was, the one woman who had a hold on him. Elijah tried not to think about certain things, now, after the deed was done. Still, he knew. He had been away from Naomi in a devilish way. He had been with another woman. That he could not forget. Good Lord, what was he doing?

Forgetting his wife, the other woman, another kid, his own shortcomings, and Hollywood movies where anything was possible, Elijah remembered. He had taken to calling his rod, his plug, Satan. He did so because it had led him down this path. The road to degradation. Now, that path seemed to be a road off of which he could not turn… because Satan kept leading him on.

Chapter 16

CEDRIC Stable taught fourteen-year-old Topaz the bass pedals on the Hammond organ. How could he resist? She had asked him nicely. She had also claimed she'd asked because Lula was busy.

"Who?" Cedric wondered with a frown.

"Ta-LOO-lah." She'd said it like he should have known, "Loo-la."

"Oh." He nodded. She called Sister Tallulah Lula. Okay.

"Lula's busy," the kid shrugged. Topaz thought all the church musicians knew the other young woman was always rushing in from, or rushing out to, one of her jobs. Lula worked at the bookstore up on Main Street, and she worked at the hospital, Tranquility General.

If Lula wasn't rushing to or from work, she raced home to feed her obese father, whose health was rapidly failing, or she sped to class.

Cedric liked that Tallulah was in college, trying to make something of herself, despite all the obstacles in her life. It was what he would do, too. Forgetting the other organist and her busyness, Cedric told the preacher's kid he would show her a few things. Then mentally, he tried to block the sexual images that his words conjured.

IN the weeks to follow, Cedric kept his word, and the PK progressed. Good thing, too, because not long after Topaz started becoming proficient on the organ, Mrs. Oraleen Stable, Cedric's Mom, passed.

Yet, the kid managed to keep up with him. In the name of staying in touch, Topaz often called the Stable residence just to ask a question or two. She'd stand in the big kitchen at her parents' drafty old house, lift the receiver from the wall phone, and dial. On the yellowed linoleum that her mother despised, while sweet Puppy thumped her tail, Topaz would speak with the boy who once caused her to get a lump on her head.

Although he sounded a little like he had died right along with his mother, he would make an effort to give Topaz a few moments. Cedric did so because the preacher's kid was young. Maybe she didn't have a heap of friends, not outside Tallulah and that long tall skinny wild girl whose hair had never seen a process. Caley Somebody. Oh, and Topaz had that giant old faithful dog. Or had Doggie gone to heaven? All of that was why Cedric asked how the kid was coming along with her music. He didn't care, but it sounded like the right thing to ask.

Breathlessly, the kid would mention chord progressions. Topaz would cite the new song she'd mastered. Somehow Cedric would wind up feeling nearly as enthusiastic. He'd forget his pain, for a while. Sometimes the pastor's baby even said hold on, that she'd get the extension. Then in what, good-looking Sister Naomi, called the family room, in that big funny-colored house, the kid picked up the other phone. She'd say, "Yella, hang on, okay?" As if he had nothing better to do. Then he'd hear her walking to hang up the kitchen phone. He knew she'd been referring to his skin. He knew because his Gran, too, called him 'that yella boy.' Maybe coffee-colored Gran did it because his dad, her son, was dark. It was a bit comical; that *and* the preacher's kid, clomping around in the huge house. Since he'd been lying around, pitying himself after his Mom's passing, Cedric really didn't have anything better to do.

Back in the family room, with the receiver wedged between her ear and shoulder, the PK would plant herself before her apartment-sized Baldwin piano. It was a beautiful walnut-colored upright. The kid proudly said, a hundred times, that her grandma had bought it for her. Mother See, that's what the church members called the woman.

Topaz would begin to play, but not before she would proudly say that the piano was the *second* that her grandma had bought for her. For the two hundredth time. Topaz said Mother See had done so simply because she, the kid, had wanted a piano. One that she could play at home.

Then the preacher's baby would begin to play. She would thereby transport herself, and Cedric, to a world where melody alone ruled.

HE realized he had been away for nearly a year following his mother's death. He hadn't wanted to see anybody or talk to anyone, not even his neighbors or the church people who'd simply wanted to offer condolences. He hadn't wanted the old mothers to hug him, squeezing him against their pillow-y, powdery-smelling bosoms. He hadn't wanted the women in their fifties and sixties to bring casseroles and pies. Cedric had just wanted somber men to leave him alone with his sorrow.

Now it was time. Cedric had had a dream. In it, he had seen his mother. She'd looked terrific. She had been wearing a light-colored beaded evening gown, one like she'd worn when she had headlined at jazz lounges all over Manhattan. Mom looked like she had, back in the day when he'd been a kid. Her short hair was waved. It lay flat on her head. It had been glossy, and she'd been made up. Mom's nails were done, and she'd appeared healthy, with no trace of illness.

In the dream that had seemed all too real, Mom had stopped just short of hugging him, but still, Cedric had felt her love. She'd spoken to him, but not really. She'd telegraphed a message to his mind. Receiving it, he knew she was telling him she was okay. Mom was saying she was happy and no longer in pain. Cedric's mother had let him know, through some type of telepathy, that she wanted him to seek contentment, too.

Then he was awake. He had tears in his heart, but Cedric also felt a type of buoyancy. He hadn't felt that since childhood, way before his mother's illness. As he lay in bed, he tried to memorize every detail of his dream. Cedric wanted to always remember Ora Stable, Sister Oraleen, as the shining star that she had once been.

As he lay there, he realized. He had to get back into the swing of things. He had very nearly allowed life to circumvent him. Since it was January, Cedric had to get his grades back up. He wanted to graduate, on time, in the spring of the current year. He had to check in with his friends and cousins. In addition, he had to get back to church, to GBBC.

He had to again see the preacher's kid. What was her name? Toe-something, Tone-yah? No, Toe-PAZZ—that was it! Cedric wondered why he thought of her. She was a baby, a child. Well, she was younger than he was, that was for sure, and he had never really cared about her. Well, he had never really had any interest in Baybay…but she *had* called a few times. She'd said she was checking on him. Other times she'd called to ask how she would play something she'd heard in her head. She'd hummed the notes and explained exactly how she wanted to trick them out. Cedric hadn't been much interested, but he'd gotten the gist of what the kid wanted to do. So he'd told her, start in B flat. Then he'd coached her on the necessary modulations.

Why was he thinking about that lil girl anyway? She would probably not be glad to see him return to church. She'd never seemed happy for his presence at any time before. Cedric didn't even know why she bothered to call—other than the fact that the kid wanted to use him, musically. He grimaced because that wasn't fair. At least the kid had called. Who else had, besides her dad, after Cedric had been so remote?

Big Pastor Moon had even stopped by the house. A couple of times, Pastor had visited his dad's bar. Pastor Moon had prayed with Cedric's father. The preacher had called Cedric's dad 'Brother Stable' –like the man had ever set foot in a church. Well, any time other his wife's funeral. Pastor Moon sure had nerve, Cedric fondly thought, praying in a *bar*. And the funny thing was Cedric's dad had been quite moved by the preacher's actions; bar patrons had felt the same. They'd loved Ora.

One regular said, "That holy man is alright with me."

Cedric's dad had called out, to the astonishment of those in the bar, "Come on by anytime, Reverend—my place is always open to you!"

Cedric had thought that was stupid, but Pastor Moon had waved. He'd eased his immense shoulders through the door and out into the night.

Cedric wanted to forget that the preacher had given him a few dollars on several occasions. The big man, who always smelled nice, had even wrapped his huge hand around Cedric's neck. The man said, "Son, these things happen. Still, you get your head right. Accept what's taken place, and bless the fact that you had a mother, a good one. Start back on your studies and live your life. It's what *I* had to do..." Pastor Moon had swallowed emotion. "I lost my dad; I wasn't much older than you."

Cedric could still remember the shock he'd felt when the preacher divulged his desire, long ago, to fall apart. "As men, though, we don't have that luxury. We gotta be dependable and solid. Those are my old man's words. You play cards, young man, so you know; you gotta make use of the hand that you were dealt."

Pastor Moon's father had been Old Preacher. Cedric had heard about him. There was even a color portrait of the man in the church narthex. Cedric stopped recalling those things because they caused him to think about the kid, Pastor Moon's kid. *Baybay*.

Why did she often cross his mind? Cedric wondered, even as he got himself to church the following Sunday.

Chapter 17

ALTHOUGH he told himself, repeatedly, that he wasn't, Cedric still found himself eager to see the preacher's kid.

He slipped into a pew near the rear of the sanctuary just before offering time. Cedric noticed the minister of music. Sister Tallulah was on the electric keyboard, but no one was on the organ or the piano. How strange. He looked around. Where was she—Baybay? Cedric didn't *want* to look for her, but he had never known her to be absent from church, not even when she'd had a stuffy red nose. It seemed Topaz had always been there. So where was she, the kid?

Oh, there. The kid was on the pulpit, crouched behind her father who sat on one of the throne-like chairs. If it weren't for the spaces between the chairs, Cedric would not have seen her. The kid nodded, as her father, wearing his magnificent robe, seemingly instructed her. Facing the congregation, not her, the big man's lips barely moved.

Cedric's breath caught as she stood on impossibly high heels.

Lil shorty descended the stairs to the side of the pulpit. She looked like joy come to life, with her inviting copper skin and beautifully thick swinging hair. It was loose today, and Cedric couldn't take his eyes off it. But why'd she go that way? The piano was the other way.

Watching her lithe movements, he realized he had almost made himself believe that after being away for so long, he'd forgotten her. He wanted to think he'd gotten her out of his system, because really, she was too young, for him. Sure, she seemed mature, but she was a kid, and he was a man, almost. He was seventeen, soon to be eighteen. He had seen and done things that the pretty petite one probably couldn't imagine. He'd do good to remember that. Cedric told himself this as he dragged his eyes away from Kid's lengthy, heavy hair with the blunt cut ends.

However, there was something about the PK that called to Cedric. He knew it as he watched her go to the organ. So… she'd flipped the script. She'd left the piano, not for good, he hoped because she was great at it. Yet watching her slide onto the organ seat, Cedric nearly felt pride because *he* had helped her transition to that beast. She looked so little up there. But *he* had helped her learn to use the swell and vibrato, the treble and the bass. *He* had taught her how sound emitted from the huge Leslie that sat in the corner. *He* had explained that the Leslie was a specially constructed amplifier/loudspeaker that created distinct audio outcomes. *He*, Cedric, had said that using the Doppler Effect, the singular organ speaker was named after its inventor, Donald Leslie.

In another life, Cedric might have felt jealous while watching Topaz begin to play as though she were an old hand, a tiny little pro. He would have felt so because since he'd been gone, out on bereavement, she had picked up his duties. And she was doing a fabulous job.

Where would *he* fit, now? Cedric wondered because it appeared Topaz and Sister Tallulah, the minister of music, had seamlessly meshed. He had always felt like sis with the glasses was kind of deep. She was about nineteen and really into the word of the Lord. As far as he knew, Tallulah had never had a boyfriend. Quite possibly, she'd never even worn a pair of pants. After reading the whole bible, she'd said she considered those the 'apparel of a man' and definitely not for her, a young woman of the Lord. Cedric had simply thought she was strange.

Now, however, Topaz and Tallulah complemented one another. Cedric noticed it from his seat near the rear. The two sounded great. The preacher's kid was on the organ, with the young woman who was a little older on the keyboard. The accompanying musicians were tight, too, Cedric had to acknowledge. He did so as Topaz raised a small hand and closed it into a loose fist to signal the song's shutdown. Cedric noticed the fifteen-year-old had everything flowing right.

As her father walked to the podium, Cedric realized. The kid been born to carry the service. Softly, she played behind Pastor Moon as formally, he addressed the Lord's people.

Kid was amazing, and so was her dad.

God, he'd missed this! Cedric couldn't deny that often he'd longed for the ordered worship service, the reverence, the quiet, and the feeling of…*love* that was the skein throughout. Now he was here, again.

Cedric found that he liked watching Baybay. Being seated in the rear was great, nearly as good a vantage point as sitting up high on the organ seat. Pushing aside twinges of jealousy, Cedric wondered. Did other male congregants, the deacons included, notice Baybay's shapely little legs moving back 'n forth over the organ's bass pedals? And she wore those impossibly high, sexy heels. He hoped the men didn't. Cedric recalled that when the kid stood, she was such a tiny thing. She couldn't have been that strong, either. Suddenly, Cedric felt quite protective.

Appearing regal in his robe, Pastor Moon was at the podium, and the man mentioned...*him.* Huh? Church members turned. Nodding, they acknowledged Cedric's presence, like the reverend had, and Cedric felt funny. His heart skipped a beat, but he felt good, as though he belonged again. He felt like he'd come home, and all because the big man had taken notice of *him.* Cedric knew he wasn't anyone special, but he *felt* special, and it was nice. It was how his mom had made him feel.

As Pastor Moon intoned that he felt the need to change the order of the service, Cedric silently but genially shook hands with nearby well-wishers. Then he returned his attention to Pastor Moon.

With his deep voice drizzling over the congregation, like honey over silken skin, into the microphone, the big man suggested a song.

Topaz immediately began to play it. Then her father softly spoke. "Come on my jewel, sing unto the Lord."

The big man, that many said was good-looking, stood with closed eyes as the music flowed. He bowed his head as his kid closed her own eyes and lifted her melodious voice.

She leaned forward slightly, so her glossy lips neared the microphone. It was angled toward her. Cedric refused to think of her mouth nearing his dick that way. The kid's throat worked as her soft, breathy, but mature soprano trilled like that of an angel, one descended from heaven.

"God is moving, by His Spirit, moving in all the earth..."

The microphone setup was new, Cedric thought, listening.

"Signs and wonders prove His moving."

When he'd been the organist, well, one of them, there had been no mic suspended by a bent metal elbow so *he* could sing. Not that he *could* sing. Still, Cedric guessed, whatever baby wanted, Baybay got.

The kid sang on, wrenching emotion from every syllable. *"Move, oh Lord, in me."*

He had to stop being petty. This Cedric told himself as that girl's— no, that young *woman's*—voice grabbed hold of him. It would not let go.

Then she shocked Cedric by using the very chord progression that *he* had taught her, seemingly so long ago, back in combined choir practice! However, it was no longer his. It was all hers because of the way she played it. Then with mastery and dripping-water-sounding notes, Topaz segued into a different song. A song that was similar in tempo and temperament. *Genius*! It was all Cedric could think as words mellifluously rolled from Topaz's tongue. *"Even Me, Lord…"*

Man! Now she sounded like a nightingale, so – very – euphonious. The highs and lows of her voice should not have been there, not yet. But Cedric's mother would have argued, saying that Topaz wasn't too young to be capable of wrenching such emotion from a song. Mom would have said that a gift –like the gift of song– knew no age.

Jeez! Cedric thought as Baybay's voice dragged him from his musings; she was legit crushing it! Man, did her tiny fingers, and feet make that organ sing! Cedric could barely breathe as he listened. He noted that Topaz and the organ sounded like one. Her mastery of the instrument caused it to sound like she and another *person* were singing in tandem. Suddenly, Cedric wanted to play, right then! And he hadn't wanted to touch the organ, not since his mother died. Hearing Topaz also made Cedric want to *sob*, such a strange feeling for him. Oh—God. It was all he could think as people all over the church rocked, waved, or stood, while some uncontrollably wept.

That little girl —no, he had to stop calling her that. She was no such thing any longer. That *young woman* was better at playing the organ, and singing –in the spirit– than could ever be hoped for by most worship leaders.

It was because she was devoted. Cedric knew. There was no other word to describe Topaz. She had been devoted, to the piano and to her calling, ever since she'd been little. She had been drawn and had willingly followed. Now her hard work and her gift had faultlessly interconnected. What a thing of beauty it was to behold!

That, Cedric knew, was what the old folk called '*the anointing*.'

It was the Holy Spirit, using Topaz, for the glory of God.

Cedric scrambled up to join others who stood. He knew his was a huge grin, but Bay had come into her very own. Baybay did not see him, or anyone for that matter, so lost in a spiritual world of music was she.

Yet watching her and feeling something ridiculously overwhelming, Cedric knew. Musically, Topaz Moon was worlds beyond him. Period. The funny thing was: the knowledge didn't even bother Cedric. All he could feel was…pride.

Cedric Stable was proud of *his* Baybay.

Chapter 18

HE saw her after church. He forgot how she and her taller friend with the natural used to giggle and make him uncomfortable. Approaching, them, they actually seemed quite grown up. Cedric wondered, had he been away that long? He walked to the organ where Baybay and her giggle partner sat. Long, lean Caley swayed as Topaz played.

Cedric noticed people, including quite a few guys, surrounding Topaz. Most were laughing. They joshed as her slender fingers moved over the keys. Her high heel-shod feet tap-tapped the bass pedals as she created the sweetest background music. Every few minutes, teenagers would break into song. Perhaps they did, Cedric thought because Topaz's playing caused even the least likely person to feel like singing.

Service had let out twenty minutes ago but there was one thing about Greater Bethany Bible Congregation. Rarely were the members in a hurry to leave, not when it was sunny out. Rain and snow were excuses to hole up within the sanctuary or the fellowship hall. People hung. If it was warm out, they'd spill into the parking lot or onto the steps or the manicured back lawn, like a family. Sure, some complained that anybody holding a position of importance at GBBC was related to the pastor. That wasn't true. Look at *him*, Cedric mused; *he'd* been one of the organists, an important position, and he wasn't related to the Moons. He was the son of a former jazz singer and a barman. One who rarely, if ever, set foot in anybody's church.

Cedric noticed that young people, including Topaz's tall skinny erratic friend, Caley, began to disperse. As many made plans to see one another later in the week, Cedric moved forward. Looking up, Topaz's eyes registered surprise. Was she happy to see him? Maybe she was wary because, in the past, he had tormented her.

"Hey, Baybay." Dang! He hadn't meant to call her that, he said.

She chuckled. "Actually, it no longer bothers me. I think it's cute. Like me." She grinned while still playing. He could tell. Her mind was mostly on her music. Still, she said, "Good to see you, Yella."

"You too," Cedric said as the little minx abruptly stopped, collected her purse, and the tote in which she kept her sheet music. "Sometimes," she said, sounding as though she thought aloud, "I have to *make* myself get up and leave." Closing the organ, she stepped down beside him.

Cedric quickly averted his eyes. He didn't want Topaz to know that he'd checked her, ogled her bottom. Mmm...she had a little shape on her. Now when had that come about? She smelled good, as always.

Cedric recalled Sister Naomi. Topaz's mom had that hourglass thing going on, too. So it was true, the apple didn't fall far from the tree.

Looking up at Cedric, while passing empty pews, Topaz announced, "You've stretched out." She hadn't meant to blurt it. But he was no longer short, for a man. He wasn't stocky, but strapping and strong. *Ooh...*

Cedric laughed, and Topaz liked the sound as he quipped, "Yeah, I have." He made it sound like an inducement for her to find out. "I'm 'taller' in a *few* places...some of them hidden."

Fifteen-year-old Topaz felt funny, as though she and Cedric shared something, although there were others around. Two girls flitted about, and older kids laughed. An usher picked up paper. At the same time, a young mother rocked a baby as she and an older woman had a chit-chat.

Cedric felt the shift, and he was aroused. It was the strangest thing, having his rod strain inside his clothing –because of the *preacher's kid.* He closed his coat, about to take off, but Topaz began to speak.

"You coming to rehearsal this week? I mean, since you're back now."

Cedric gazed down at her. He felt himself swell, as his eyes roamed her from head to foot. "I mean," Topaz amended, caught in the gaze that caused her to experience strange sensations, "You *are* back, right?"

Looking up at Cedric caused Topaz to remember a man in an anatomy book. She'd stared at the naked man forever. Now she wondered, did Ced look that way? *What* was she thinking? What a sin!

Clinging to her second question, Cedric quietly asked his own. "You want me back?" He wondered what it would be like to kiss her.

Topaz spoke slowly, as she attempted to figure out where they were. It was unfamiliar terrain. "Ced, I want...whatever *you* want..."

Afterward, she wondered, what devil had possessed her to say *that*? Topaz nearly felt ashamed. Then again, she didn't. Still, she could barely look up at the boy—no, the almost-man—who caused her heart to race.

In silence, she and he stood for seconds that seemed like an eternity. They just stared at each other. Then Topaz worried. Was her hair okay, and her skirt? Why, did she know she would dream about kissing him? Although she'd never gotten the chance to do any real kissing thus far.

Cedric Stable grinned and broke the spell. He leaned nearer, and sure enough, Topaz noticed. He still smelled nice, like always. Cedric whispered, "Lemme tell you something, Baybaby…"

He saw her father approaching from the rear. The big man looked dapper in his winter coat while carrying his hat. Was that hat what Cedric's mom would have called a fedora? Cedric wondered. He noticed the young man who respectfully carried the preacher's briefcase. Cedric knew Pastor Moon's big leather bible was in that case, along with his hankies and other preacher paraphernalia.

Topaz's dad and his escort were why Cedric spoke quickly and only for her to hear. "Baybay, never tell a man that you want whatever he wants. He'll try to take advantage of you."

Topaz looked coyly at the boy-man, who was no longer short or stocky. She did so from beneath her lashes. She hoped she was getting it right, like big-chested Lela had. A while back, the older girl had gone out with Cedric. Forgetting Lela, Topaz asked, "But what if it's true?"

Cedric nearly choked because was the kid *coming on to him*?

Good thing her father stepped up. He pulled Topaz beneath his big arm. Protective the gesture was, even as Elijah Moon amiably said, "Young people, what's going on?" Although the man had asked it many times before, of all the youngsters in and around the church, Cedric knew. The inquiry was different this time. It contained a warning, for him. He was not to get too familiar, not with the baby.

Aware, Cedric shook the pastor's huge hand. He engaged in momentary small talk. He bid all a good afternoon. Despite wanting to jet, the returned organist made himself walk, albeit swiftly, from the sanctuary.

"Bye, Yella…" Topaz said so softly that no one heard.

Accepting her coat, she wished the person aiding her with it could be her one-time tormentor. He had been the yellow—no, the gold-skinned—little boy with whom she had once tussled. She had subsequently wound up with a lump on her head.

However, forgetting that, she wished she could have had more time with Cedric Stable. He was the young man who had long ago given her a new name.

Baybay.

Chapter 19

ON a bright sunny Saturday, Topaz walked the few blocks between her parents' home and Granny's. As she neared the rundown house where Caley's grandmother resided, Topaz thought of what she and her taller, thinner friend would do in perhaps an hour.

They would go to the park, where Topaz would meet Cedric. Then, Topaz thought, if she were lucky, she'd get a few minutes alone with him, as usual. Without others around, they would kiss. Cedric would touch Topaz in places that caused her to feel heat she had never before known. She knew her father would say she was 'fast,' but Topaz didn't care. What Cedric offered, she wanted.

"Hi, Granny." Topaz kissed the wiry older woman's brown cheek.

"Hi, honey." Granny closed her front door. "Don't you look purty?"

"Thank you, Ma'am." Topaz allowed her best friend, who wore only underthings, to pull her from the small hallway.

In her junky room, Caley asked, "Girl, whutchu wearing?"

Topaz fingered her sundress. "What's wrong with what I got on?"

"You're dressed up." Capricious Caley eyed Topaz's espadrilles, "But your sandals are cute."

Topaz felt as though she were deflating. Again, she wished she didn't always have to practice the keyboard. Lately, she'd been feeling that way, a lot. If she didn't have to continually learn songs to teach the different choirs, she too could have a real after-school job. Without church duties, she could have talked Mama into talking Daddy into it. Then Topaz would have been able to buy cute clothes, like other girls, instead of always being overdressed or looking like a nun. Therefore, she verbally defended herself. "Granny said I look pretty."

"For a *church* outing," Caley shot back. "Anyway, Granny's old. She don't know nuthin –not about fashion or what you should wear to the park." The tall, thin, brown girl turned to her closet. "You got your hair right though, up like that, because it's hot—and you have a nice neck. Them dangly earrings are working." Caley stepped over shoes that lay in the open mouth of her jam-packed small storage space. "Here, try this." Caley handed over a tube top with the tag still attached.

Topaz slowly asked, "What...to do with it?" She puzzled over the elasticized raspberry-colored piece.

Caley spoke with her head and shoulders in the closet. "Put it on, silly. Take off that dress. And your bra."

Topaz murmured, "I don't know, Cae..." but the tube top *was* cute and more risqué than anything that Topaz had ever worn or owned.

Suddenly Topaz felt a spark of excitement. She would do it! Shimmying out of her dress, carefully she laid it aside. She reminded herself, at the time to go home, she'd have to put it back on. Therefore, she couldn't allow her dress to get bunched up with all Caley's other clothes. The changeable taller girl had stuff strewn everywhere.

However, for now, Topaz vowed, she would step into something new.

Topaz looked in the mirror as something small, and denim landed on her head. She raised a hand, becoming aware of a pair of *short* shorts.

"Put them on," Caley called, fiddling with the headband that would keep her unprocessed hair off her slender, longish face.

"You know Cae," copper-skinned Topaz called out to the girl whose face and body were all angles. "You should try to become a model."

"Can't," Caley rebuffed. "Too old now. Sixteen; I'm ancient. Oh my—*Lord*!"

"What?" Pivoting in the tank top, Topaz saw her friend staring at her. In the mirror propped against the wall, the petite one peered at herself. "These shorts are too tight." Topaz pulled at them. "I think. Right?"

"No..." Caley scrambled over an upturned sneaker and a pair of inside-out jeans. "They fit *you* perfectly –better than they do me. That's why I never wore them. They cost a mint too, but you keep 'em. Dang, Taupe, look at your ba-donk-a-donk! And your bazooms. Lookit them sexy legs! Where'd you *get* all that? I'd sho like to get me some."

Topaz chuckled, even though she felt self-conscious. "I've always looked this way. You just never noticed."

"No." Caley shook her head. "No one noticed because you're always covered up. Like a little nun."

There was that word again. Nun. Topaz hated it. Well, she thought, while critically eyeing herself, no nun here. The girl in the mirror sure didn't look like anybody's Gidget today.

Topaz had a newfound worry. "My...nipples...are showing."

"They sure are. Nip. Nip. That's the point," Caley announced while using a cigarette lighter to warm the tip of a kohl eye pencil. "You can always put Band-Aids over them, if you want; make 'em less visible." Lining her eyes, Caley sounded preoccupied. "There're some in the bathroom, top drawer, but then your yella boyfriend won't get to see."

Topaz shook away the cover-up idea. She rather *wanted* Cedric to see her this way, like a real girl and not like some stuffy little saintly almost-woman. Topaz turned to take one last look at her round behind, her thighs, and shapely bare legs. Then she bent to again lace up her sandals. Wow, she mused; she had a good look going. Her body actually looked nice, now, even better than some of the girls at school. Those girls thought they were hot with their trendy clothes, but Topaz realized she, too was sexy. She would just have to find a way to get a few new clothes, cute clothes, like a real teenager. Then she would have to show the hot chicks at school that she was the same. Sizzling hot.

WHEN she and Caley sauntered down Granny's front steps to walk in the sunshine, Topaz felt nervous and excited. She'd promised to meet Cedric in Tranquility Park, near the basketball court.

As they crossed a street, tall, thin Caley described an encounter with the new girl who had just started work at the jeans store. Half-listening, Topaz couldn't remember ever feeling as real as she did right then. She also silently acknowledged that no matter what her Dad said, it was fun to be young in the eighties, which he called the last days. It was fun to be out too, with guys driving by whistling, or calling, "Yo, Shorty!"

Topaz also knew that had she been dressed like her Dad always wanted her to be, no one would have looked at her twice.

When she and Caley neared the park, it was a scene out of one of Topaz's daydreams, where she was always the outsider. Today though, beneath giant trees whose green leaves created a beautiful overhead canopy, she fit. In the white-lined parking lot, Topaz and Caley passed cars with music blaring from tweeters and woofers. Teenagers stood around talking, and some even called out to them. Others knew Topaz by name. They looked at the PK in shock, before their looks became subtly appraising. Girls looked away, while boys cast secret assessing glances.

Noticing all, Topaz felt funny but good. She and Caley passed mothers who strapped babies into strollers while fathers instructed older kids. On the grass, Topaz and Caley skirted blankets, lovers, and others.

On the walking trail, they passed concrete tables on grass and chairs where older men in shirtsleeves and straw hats played checkers or chess.

Then as she and her friend neared the basketball court, Topaz felt nervous. She saw that there were already several people in the stands, creating a blaze of color and waves of sound.

Taking calming deep breaths, Topaz took in the activity on the sidelines. Many loudly proclaimed they got next. Stepping past, she knew they would play the winners of the current basketball game.

About to sit beside a balding man holding a dripping Popsicle for a small boy, Topaz did as Caley told her. Carefully, Topaz placed her palms face-down on the bleachers. Then she sat on the backs of her hands. "This way," Caley told Topaz, with her eyes on the sinewy young men who ran up and down the court, "your thighs won't burn."

Topaz nodded her thanks. She had not been aware, and she realized. There was so much she had to learn, about being real.

Cedric saw her and grinned as he ran backward down the court.

His tank top clung to his shining, sweat-soaked skin. He looked unbelievably fit with the muscles in his shoulders, stomach, arms, and legs visible. Noticing his nylon shorts, like those that professional ballers wore, Topaz felt her heart flip. Soon, however, she calmed down enough to join those around her in enjoying the game.

Then afterward, as capricious Caley sauntered off with a different group, Cedric approached. His team had lost by two points. Not appearing disappointed, he pulled off his tank top and used it to wipe sweat from his face and torso. "Hey, Baybay." He leaned in for a kiss.

He tasted salty, like perspiration, and bubblegum. "You really have gotten taller, Ced," Topaz marveled. That was something she wanted. Height. She was tired of always looking like a child.

"And you—are *fuine*!" Cedric winked. Then he pulled Topaz up to take a good look at her, from head to toe. "Daaang, girl," He whistled, as his eyes darted between her nipples, visible beneath the raspberry tube top, and her shorts-clad curvy thighs. "You sure look tasty!"

Cedric bent to snatch a clean tee from his duffel. Pulling it over his head, he turned to clasp hands with a gangly young man. Afterward, Cedric sat beside Topaz. He leaned close. "You got time to hang out?"

She nodded because she wasn't expected at home until that evening Stating it, she announced. "I just gotta go back to Granny's."

"Ah," Cedric nodded, "Caley's grandmother's house."

Topaz didn't mention that there, her mom would pick her up. The Moons didn't want her out after dark—unless she was with the saints.

Forgetting her sheltered life and all the rules she had to adhere to, Topaz proceeded to enjoy her day of freedom. Moreover, she had to internally admit. Last year, she would never have imagined that hanging out in the park with Caley, Cedric, and others could be so much fun.

With the sound of Kool & the Gang's classic instrumental, 'Summer Madness' wafting over her, Topaz watched as Cedric gave a younger set of boys a few pointers on offense. Afterward, he again sat next to her, and she could feel heat pouring off him. She could also smell his sweat, and she thought it was strange; he wasn't funky. Actually, she could smell his deodorant, and it reminded her of her father. She recalled the way *he* smelled after he preached. The memory caused her to recall that her Dad often mentioned one of the things *he* remembered most about *his* father. He said it was Old Preacher's scent.

Although she'd been born after her grandfather's passing, she loved to hear about him. To her and others, the man was legendary. Topaz especially loved hearing that often after Old Preacher had given a sermon, his clothing, as well as his clerical robe would be nearly sweat-soaked. That was because he had conferred so much of himself on the Lord's people. Then, Elijah Moon often said, he would really smell his father's cologne. He had also smelled the sweet scent of Old Preacher's perspiration. Elijah said he'd helped Old Preacher back to his office, many times. There the older man had changed into dry clothing. Those occasions, Elijah had revealed, were the ones on which he had been most conscious of his father's scent. It was something Elijah sorely missed.

As she sat in the bleachers at the park, with afternoon sun warmly bathing her, Topaz remembered her Dad getting tears in his eyes. Big Elijah Moon's face had crinkled. Then he'd said there were some things a person never forgot about another, even long after the other was gone.

Allowing memories to fade, Topaz excused herself from Cedric and his friend. Topaz sought her sister-friend. "Cae, Ced's gonna take me for a ride," Topaz quietly revealed.

"Oh, okay." Caley nodded and asked a girl with long cornrows to wait a moment. "You know we gotta meet back at Granny's, right?"

Topaz rolled her eyes. "Mama's coming at eight-thirty."

Caley laughed. "Just before dark; one of the rules is that we need to be home before the street lights come on. Well, even if I'm not there, go on inside. Tell Granny I'll be there."

Topaz turned away, and tall Caley noticed how Cedric patiently waited. He held his duffel bag in one hand, causing the muscle in his arm to slightly bunch. The tall, angular girl shouted when Cedric took her copper-skinned friend's hand. "Have fun, y'all!"

Caley watched the petite girl with the hourglass figure that no one had known she had. Caley watched the boy that she and Topaz had often giggled about when they'd been younger. He wasn't a boy anymore, and there was no longer anything to giggle about, not concerning him. Impulsive Caley Nix wondered if the pair would go somewhere and do it. Together they looked so sexy. The muscular young man who'd shot up to about five-ten, and the petite shapely girl with the flat stomach.

The pair had a type of electricity surrounding them; Caley had heard granny mention such before, now Caley knew what it looked like. She could even imagine her petite friend and Yella making a home sex tape. *That* Caley would watch on her new VCR, her videocassette recorder, because those two just made a person want to look at them.

Caressing a cucumber, lil scraggy-haired Granny had said electricity between people was called chemistry. She said she remembered experiencing it.

Caley turned back to her other friends, and a thought struck. Cedric was gonna put his thing in Topaz. It was probably thick; he looked like it was. Caley's short shapely little sister would welcome Cedric sticking her. He would suck Topaz's protruding nipples too. Man, would Cedric teach Taupe things—stuff she had never dreamed of! He'd have her panting with pleasure. Oh, to be a fly on the wall, curious Caley mused.

Then Caley had one wish: as her small sister-friend was finally growing up—despite her seemingly sheltered life—hopefully, Taupe, or Cedric, would use protection.

Chapter 20

AFTER the park, Cedric drove Topaz to Just Desserts for ice cream. Inside the cool eatery that smelled of sugar and syrup, she slid into a booth. Cedric surprised her by sliding in on the same side. As Topaz ordered a root beer, she hoped she wouldn't see anyone she knew. She also hoped none of those people would see her, or Cedric.

Topaz was aware that the waitress was a girl from school, but Topaz didn't mind the girl seeing her. Actually, Topaz felt good because the girl had seen that she wasn't so square. At the moment, Topaz didn't feel so much like a little church girl. People in Tranquility called her that, behind her back. Now the waitress knew, Topaz mused, that she had a male friend, and he was fine. Topaz actually hoped Waitress would run tell that. Perhaps today was the beginning of Topaz, too, getting a life.

She didn't want to acknowledge that she was jealous of girls like Waitress, but Topaz was. She'd worked for the church, for *free*, for as long as she could remember. She wasn't stupid though, she knew other people got paid for the types of services she rendered. Even Cedric and Tallulah received a small stipend from GBBC! But, since *she* was the PK, everybody expected her to do everything she did for nothing.

She couldn't even buy a cheap 'n cheerful pair of sandals without having to ask her father for money. It now felt...demeaning. Topaz sensed her father liked holding the wallet. Elijah Moon had a big ego. Topaz had tried to overlook that because of love. Still, she suspected her father liked having his kid ask him for things. Maybe it aided him to feel important, just like the church made him feel prominent and noteworthy.

Well, Topaz had grown sick of feeling small and stepped on.

She sighed as she faked a smile for two little boys in a nearby booth. With their cute brown faces smeared with ice cream, they made eyes at her. Forgetting the kids, Topaz reminded herself. She didn't want to feel upset today. She only wanted to focus on the fact that for a few hours, she, too, had something desirable. Cedric. She'd had him, in secret, for the last few months, ever since the end of the winter.

As she thought it, he placed an arm around her. Topaz felt funny then and realized, again, that she had always lived in a fishbowl. It seemed she existed in clear glass where somebody was always watching, and judging. Topaz felt like she had no privacy. That had begun to grate. Although she hadn't consciously acknowledged it, the fishbowl was part of why she was crazy about Cedric. *He* had a life, one that was his own. He had hopes and dreams that not everybody knew about.

Previously, he'd divulged that in the fall, he would attend college. He would study food service management. Since she didn't precisely understand, Topaz mentioned it as they awaited their order. Trying to focus on Cedric, not soppy aspects of her life, she asked him to explain.

"Well," Cedric began, "if after my studies, I become a food service manager, I could manage a chain restaurant." Cedric expounded. He could wind up responsible for personnel. He could work somewhere that wasn't a restaurant but was still a place where food and beverages were prepared and served. Hotels fit the bill, as did stadiums and arenas.

"No place like this," Cedric amended, indicating the color-splashed eatery in which they sat. For him, it was too small a start. He wanted big. Cedric said that since his career choice meant the world was his oyster, he would leave the sleepy town of Tranquility. He happily announced that he would do so because he was anxious to see where he would wind up, in five years, then ten, and beyond.

When their ice cream came, Topaz forgot Cedric's dream. She tried to concentrate on eating. She was unable to because he kept touching her bare thigh, even the inside. She just wanted to open her legs for him, but people were glancing over. Had she and Cedric been alone, Topaz would have wanted to strip and show him her goosebumps. He'd caused them to rise everywhere on her copper-colored skin.

Kissing Topaz's shoulder, Cedric inconspicuously slid a hand up her torso. Beneath her tube top, he fondled her supple breasts. Inside her body, Topaz felt miniature explosions as Cedric said she was beautiful.

Yeah, in Caley's clothes, Topaz thought.

Then in the eatery's back lot, lined with trees, Cedric opened his car door for Topaz, but he didn't let her sit. Instead, he pulled her close. He caused her to face away. With her in his arms, he inhaled her lovely soft scent. He also bent to curve around her so he could rub that male part of him against her derriere. As he did, he whispered. "I *want* you..."

With closed eyes, Topaz didn't know what Cedric meant. Come to think of it, he'd said that more than once. Loving the feel of his arms encircling her, she wondered, wasn't she with him? Didn't they spend every moment they could together? Did he think she was going to run away? Topaz didn't yet understand what wanting meant. Still, she reveled in the intensity she felt whenever she and Cedric were alone together. Topaz felt the *other* way she often felt, too. She wanted to strip naked and liquefy before Cedric. She wanted fall into a boneless heap at his feet. She would allow him to do many new things to her.

But they were in a shady parking lot. They could only do so much.

Still, the couple did very little talking. They kissed, felt, and fondled. They laughed and joked. They hugged and rubbed. Cedric even touched her *there*. Topaz felt all melty, and Cedric felt invincible. The twosome whispered, breathed hard, and sucked face.

Then it was time to go.

Topaz wanted to stay. She felt like there was more, and she wasn't getting it. Cedric knew there was more, and he wasn't getting it. He desperately wanted it. Sex with Topaz, Cedric knew, neither of them needed. It would change them, and their relationship, forever.

Although neither wanted to part, Cedric dropped Topaz off at Granny's tumbledown house. He made her laugh when he quipped, "Don't Caley know that lawn needs mowing? That girl need to git one'a her boyfriends to do it." Cedric gave Topaz a quick kiss and told her he would see her at church, tomorrow. Tonight, he had to work at his dad's bar, "But I'd much rather be with you…"

Sunday, Topaz thought, frustrated. As she climbed Granny's crumbly steps, Topaz felt Cedric's eyes on her derriere. Sunday. Topaz nearly hated that on that day, she would have to pretend, again, as she usually did when at GBBC. Topaz would act as though Cedric meant little to her.

In Caley's room, while hooking her bra, Topaz knew. As she handled her sundress, she felt flickers of anger. On Sunday, somebody would be watching –her. Some peeping Tom or Tina might even think she was fast, the very thing her father had often told her to quit being.

Frankly, Topaz was growing tired of the fishbowl, as well as all the rules.

Chapter 21

ELIJAH was trying to leave. It was always the hardest part because she tried to make him stay, every single time. She knew he had things to do. She knew he had to get home, to his real family. Then he would have to drive up to the prison. He was the chaplain for the inmates there. He couldn't possibly let them down. They looked for him, depended on his presence. Some just needed to be seen, or heard. For other inmates, Elijah was a lifeline. He offered hope. For others, he was a father figure, so he had to leave, even though she'd started in again, as she often did.

"See?" he pointed out, "that's your problem. You're too loud."

She placed her hands on her hips. "Well, *your* problem is you're always trying to reprimand somebody." In her nightie, she thrust her abundance of bosom forward because more of him wouldn't be a bad thing. "If I'm so much of a problem," she began, tempting him, "why you keep coming here?" She touched herself, and caused Satan to jump.

Down boy. Elijah mentally instructed his wayward man piece.

"Seems to me," she said, baiting him by raising and caressing a large leg, "*Naomi* is your real problem, not me. You need to get rid of her."

Virile handsome Elijah buttoned his shirt, ignoring his body's greed. "How many times have I got to tell you? It's – not – done."

Although she was a fine woman, she looked rough when she frowned. "What do you mean? Are you saying *divorce* is not done? Or are you saying divorce is something *you* won't do? *Or* are you saying, in your roundabout way, that your marriage is not done? Why speak in parables? You ain't Jesus. In fact," the woman with the beautifully gleaming dark skin sneered, "you nothing like him, contrary to popular belief."

Elijah was so tired of the rigmarole. On the one hand, he had this one, who always wanted to hop his bones, and on the other, he had his wife. He couldn't heat her up if he tried. "Just let it be," Elijah sighed.

"No." Barefoot, the woman advanced on him, wanting to make him angry enough to just take her again. "You're not my father—" Hearing the whine of a bedroom door's hinges, she quickly turned.

Sweetly, she spoke to the little boy whose skin reminded Elijah of a Hershey's kiss. "Hey, honey. I made a cereal mix with raisins. It's in the kitchen." She turned back to Elijah Moon, who was about to make his getaway. "As I said, you're not *my* father…"

Elijah was so sick of her, yet he bedded her, repeatedly. He knew it was sick. Sin-sick. "You know," he stated, "if it wasn't for that boy…"

"*That boy*?" The woman fumed, yet she was glad her son hadn't heard. "Don't you ever call him that again," she managed not to shout. "What if he'd heard you? Then he would have felt unwanted."

Elijah said nothing, just grabbed his keys. He despised the fact that she followed him, hissing all the while.

"If it wasn't for 'that boy' Preacher, you'd be in trouble."

Elijah turned, startling her with his blazing eyes. He kept his voice low. "What's that supposed to mean? You threatening me, Eve?"

She took a step backward, but decided to hold her ground. She would *not* be like his first wife. As the second –one day— she wouldn't be a pushover. Therefore, angrily she whispered. "I'm not making threats, but… if it wasn't for me and him," the boy, "you'd sleep with some little trollop who'd out you. She would put your business in the street."

"You as good as have," Elijah snapped, not about to spend any more time fooling with her. He strode from the angry woman's apartment.

Yelling after him, she dashed into the hallway. "How'd I do that?"

While in the cold, waiting for his old Impala to warm up, Elijah's eyes narrowed. That woman knew what she'd done. In his office at the church, she'd placed framed photos of her son on his desk. In the space that many frequented. Elijah had told her she was inviting trouble, and speculation. He supposed that's what she wanted. He'd asked wasn't it enough that her son's photos were on the church administrator's desk?

She'd verbally one-two punched him. "A child's photo should be on his mother's desk…as well as on his *father's.*" She'd stood there with hands on her hips, daring him to rebuke her or remove even one photo.

Elijah hadn't said a word. Now he simply always made sure that shots of the kid, and those of his wife, Topaz, and the rest of his family faced him. He didn't want them facing whoever momentarily occupied the comfy chairs opposite his desk. Oh God, the big man thought as he drove. What a mess he'd gotten himself into.

Chapter 22

In the mid 1980's

SHE hadn't told her parents she was going skating with Caley and a few other girls. She'd just hinted, and her mother had said okay. Topaz's father had been fine-tuning a sermon, so he really hadn't paid attention. Topaz knew because he'd grunted, a little.

Now it was their first time… Topaz couldn't believe it was happening. It was why she watched Cedric, as she lay back among his pillows. She knew he'd done this before, many times. She knew he'd done it with Lela with the big chest. The skanky young woman had run around telling any other female who would listen.

Lela had put them all on alert. She'd let everyone know, the organist was taken. Now she was off somewhere, somebody said, hanging onto a motor-biking loser who supposedly sold liquor that he stole.

Topaz smiled because if only Lela could see her ex now. Cedric was on his knees, between Topaz's splayed thighs. He was so beautiful. Topaz couldn't take her eyes off him.

It always amazed her how different his body was from hers. He often said she was the one with the beautiful body. He said the female form was a dream. However, Cedric didn't know that this was Topaz's dream.

Although she tried not to seem like a novice, when he caressed her *there*, she nearly levitated off his bed. Using his fingertips as well as his rod, Topaz felt Cedric create sensation, a storm of feeling inside her.

In the past, Topaz had only felt Cedric's man piece through his and her clothing when they'd gotten heated while kissing. She loved his big soft, pretty, pink lips. She loved when he put them on her, on her neck, her shoulder, and even her boobies. Then when he kissed her, the open-mouth way—hold the phone! Cedric was the most amazing kisser, to Topaz. Before him, she'd only had sloppy seconds. She'd swatted away a few boys who'd been brave enough to try it with the preacher's daughter.

Forgetting bravehearts, and her father, who would have broken Cedric in half, had he known what she and the young man were up to, Topaz remembered. She'd felt Cedric's man part before. It had been one evening while in his living room. She and he had been seated on his dad's black leather sofa. The short, stocky older man had been away at his bar. There he spent most of his evenings. In Cedric's home and his arms, Topaz had felt so grown-up. Then she'd felt as though she'd ratcheted up another notch toward womanhood. Cedric had taken her hand. He'd wrapped it around that hard, and soft, and warm part of him. It was a part so different from anything on her body.

Now, as she lay on Cedric's bed, with the bedside lamp on, because she'd insisted, he used that part of him, and his hands, on her. Topaz felt herself become moist. Cedric had caused her to become that way on many occasions in his basement. In days past, they'd been down there listening to records. Many were the same ones he'd listened to with his mom. Topaz had felt special because Cedric shared such things with her.

Yet this time, the touching sensations were greater. Cedric was looking at her privates, too, as he touched her. He told Topaz to bend her knees. Then with him between her thighs, he lifted her buttocks.

Sure, she felt fear. For one thing, her parents thought she was out skating with Caley and other girls. If they knew she'd lied about where she was, they would be so disappointed. She'd also be grounded for life. Topaz was a bit scared, too, because Cedric had often warned her that when they did it—*if* they did it—it would hurt.

Topaz didn't care; she would handle it. That she told herself because she wanted Cedric. She wanted *this*. She wanted them to take things to the next level. If impulsive Caley and a few of the other girls at school were doing it, repeatedly, the first time couldn't be that bad, could it? Heck, if it were, Topaz reasoned, the girls would abstain. Right? Armed with that thought process, Topaz forgot inhibitions. She just made sure she watched. She held onto Cedric's strong arms as he nudged her with that all-male part of him. Ooh, that felt good, but then...

Oh...ach—his man part had to be too big! It wasn't going to fit.

Cedric laughed and broke the tension, while Topaz couldn't believe she'd said all of that, out loud! Not bothered, Cedric gave her a quick kiss. She could not know that her words caused him to swell, even more, with pride. "Okay, Bay," he told her, "here goes."

Topaz again felt a nudge, then a push. Ow. She felt herself stretching, if possible. Ow. *Ow*! "Ouch..." she whimpered. "Oh, owww-*oooch*!"

She nearly hated herself then because she didn't want Ced thinking she was a baby. But that *had* hurt –like the devil! Still, Topaz thought, she was nobody's baby. She was fifteen, a bona fide teenager, one who didn't care that her father had said no boyfriend until sixteen. Topaz forgot Mom had agreed. It was time. She, Topaz Tiara, had to do this.

She blinked because now she felt like something was wedged inside her, which it was. It was uncomfortable but amazing because it was Cedric. Topaz noticed that he rested on her, instead of balancing himself on his sexy toned arms. It was unbelievable that his weight nearly caused her to forget the fire-hot pain that radiated within.

After a bit, Topaz felt wet, and *wow*, the pain began to recede.

"What now?" she asked, even though Cedric had his face turned into her neck. She couldn't know that he attempted, with all his might, not to move. He was allowing her to become accustomed to him, and them.

"What now, Ced?" Topaz repeated and felt him breathe on her neck.

When he said nothing, just raised himself off her, but not out of her, she figured she needed to take charge. "I want you to…" Topaz stopped because she didn't know what she wanted, or what was supposed to happen now. But this could not be all there was. It just couldn't.

Without conscious thought, beneath Cedric, Topaz began to squirm.

Cedric's eyes widened, and he thought he would die from the tightness and the ecstasy. He groaned, and Topaz looked up, alarmed.

"Oh, my Lord, Yella, did I hurt you?" She'd inquired in all sincerity.

Cedric couldn't help it. He burst out laughing. "Did *you* hurt *me*? Bay, I, the experienced one, should ask you that. You're the virgin."

"Not anymore," Topaz happily announced as Cedric felt her wriggling beneath him. It was like she was trying to get something. She didn't know what, but her sexy little body spurred her on, telling her it was there and that Cedric could give it to her.

And give it to her he would.

"Move." Topaz bleated, "No, not away; move, in me!" She punched Cedric's shoulder, the little hellcat.

He laughed again, delighted that she wasn't going to be a tiny prude. "Okay," he agreed, more than ready to oblige. Cedric didn't say hang on, but he should have because Baybay was in for the ride of her life!

Moments later, she cyclically clenched around Cedric. She also trembled. As she erotically mewled, with her legs drawn up and her pretty breasts exposed, he thought she was magnificent. Watching her, his rod still within her, Cedric lost himself, as he never had before.

LATER, Topaz found that she could hardly walk. She almost felt like she and Cedric were still amid the act. It was what she got for being fast.

When he dropped her off at Caley's grandmother's house, he kissed her, long and sweet. Feeling warmed all over, Topaz also felt like an adult. She got out of the big old car that Cedric's father let him drive.

She had done 'it.' She reminded herself as she climbed Granny's crumbly steps. She, Topaz Moon, was no longer the odd woman out, like Lula. Sister Tallulah, the church minister of music. Now she, Topaz, would no longer feel ridiculed or like an outsider when the bolder kids hinted at or made sexual innuendo.

Her thigh-insides ached, so did her hips and other places. Topaz could not have been happier. She was well on her way to becoming a woman, she mused. She had Cedric Stable to thank for that. Hey, maybe she would thank him by getting busy with him again!

That was what she told Caley when in the taller girl's junky bedroom, they discussed things. Pushing clothes off the bed and onto a chair, Topaz refused to go into detail. Yet she did say that they, the girls, needed to make their Friday evening 'skating outings' a weekly thing.

With a grin, capricious Caley shook her head. "Uh-oh," the taller girl announced, "you're hooked."

Topaz pulled her knees up and wrapped her arms around them. She felt the sweet sore, the feeling that reminded her of Cedric and what they had done. "I think so," Topaz acknowledged. "And I like being hooked – on Ced."

Chapter 23

IN her cozy little home, Mother See asked Topaz to step out of her room. "Baby, come in the kitchen." She spoke over a shoulder, "I've got something for you. And I want to discuss something." In the kitchen, Mother See knew. It wasn't actually her job to say anything, but the child's mama, Naomi, was off in la-la land. The gal had been, for quite a while, ever since she'd lost that last baby. So she couldn't be counted on.

Mother See remembered calling Naomi over. The older woman had mentioned that Topaz was changing. The silver-haired woman said Topaz had become a mite more confident. Yet the girl's mama hadn't seemed to notice, or that the petite one took more pride in herself. Mother See mentioned there was only one reason a young woman would change so immediately. She'd pointed out the reason to Naomi.

The petite girl was keeping company.

Naomi didn't think so. She said Topaz didn't have time.

Mother See frowned because Naomi didn't know the first thing about time, not anymore. Naomi lost all track of it. Poor thing. She now lived in a fake world, in her head, and she preferred it that way.

Yet when Mother See pressed the issue, Naomi was curt. "It's about time my baby grew up, Mother. If she does have admirers, it's because she's such a pretty thing."

Mother See agreed. Topaz was lovely, inside and out. Still, as a young woman coming into her own, the elderly woman hated to say, but did, Topaz needed the guidance of *her mother*.

"I do guide her," Naomi rebuffed. "I'm always around."

'Yeah, bodily,' Mother See wanted to say, 'but definitely not mentally.' She'd wanted to shake her precious Naomi too, but near innocently, Naomi spoke on. "I'd hoped my baby would be a bit taller, but I guess she's going to stay little, like my mom and my aunt."

Mother See had rebuffed. "Baby girl is perfect. She just needs your guidance, Naomi. You gotta teach her to avoid the pitfalls that can come with being attractive." Topaz needed to also avoid the land mines that would explode when a girl didn't get the attention she needed at home.

However, Naomi, the space cadet, had latched onto only one portion of what Mother See was trying to say. Naomi agreed that Topaz was perfect as she was. Naomi also said, "Mother, I can't see what you're worrying about. Taupe's never given us a hint of trouble."

Naomi's daughter was becoming a woman, with eyes so like her grandfather's. Sure, other girls her age were having sex. Daily, Naomi interacted with those girls due to her social work, but not Topaz. Taupe wasn't ready for sex. Naomi didn't care that Mother See had mentioned Topaz's cute little figure, and that young and older men noticed. That kind of talk sickened Naomi. She didn't want men looking at her baby, even though she had seen them with her own eyes. Since she couldn't take a pill to calm herself, not right then, Naomi figured she would just have to get Mother See to talk about something else. A less threatening conversation, Naomi mused. That would help get her equilibrium back.

Oh no! Naomi's hands had started to shake, and her insides were churning. Jeez! Needing her pills right away, she nearly slammed a hand onto the tabletop. With the radio going, and with Mother See making up shit to worry about, Naomi's insides felt all quivery and upset. Suddenly, Naomi felt like she would lose it or have a panic attack.

Grabbing her purse, she mumbled about going to the bathroom. Naomi nearly sprinted from the kitchen. Behind the closed door, she fumbled around. Naomi plunked her purse on the sink. If she couldn't locate her pills, she would need to be rushed to the hospital. She swore it.

In the kitchen, Mother See was aware. That gal was back there self-medicating, again. Probably taking downers this time. The older woman shook her head and whispered like she spoke to the spaced-out woman who needed to wake up. "Lord knows you need to see what *I* see."

All of that stupidity, Mother See thought, was why *she* was about to chat with Topaz. The silver-haired woman would explain, as best she could, the things for which Topaz needed to be watchful. Mother See did not know how good a job she would do since she had only raised a son, Ronald. Still, she would do her best, for her granddaughter's sake.

Mother See would tell the child that, like other girls, she needed to have fun. Yet Mother See would explain male attention was nice, but if not adequately supervised, fun could lead to a world of heartache…

Mother See wondered. Should she speak with Topaz and then give her the credit card that would enable her to buy a few cute, age-appropriate clothes? Then should they have their little pow-wow?

Before Mother See could think further, the words issued forth.

Chapter 24

MOST of the time, he couldn't wait to get at her. She was so sexy, sweet, and small—but not like a child. That would have been wrong. However, Topaz was perhaps one of the most petite females Cedric had ever been with, which made him feel protective. Yet, she was fearless.

Cedric was aware that he'd been Topaz's first, but she surprised him with agreeability. She willingly tried anything he wanted. She even had other ideas, things she'd seen Lord only knew where. Maybe at frail old Granny's house because, really, was there any supervision there?

Other times, Topaz mentioned something she'd heard or read about, and she wanted to try it. The girl climbed all over Cedric, and he loved it. Topaz was ravenous. Cedric found that incredible because he loved having her bent over before him, her plump bottom undulating as he did her. He loved Topaz on top, teasing him with her tits and driving him insane. Cedric wondered, was it the hot weather magnifying their rampant attraction? He didn't know. He only knew that when he saw Topaz, especially at the park on Saturdays, he'd have to have her.

She knew too that they would go to his father's empty house. They said they were going for ice cream. Sometimes they did, before or after fantastic sex, but to the pair, their alone-time was paramount.

Topaz had thought she'd loved her music, but she realized. She now desired something just as much –or more. Cedric. Actually, her feelings gave her music new depth. She craved him. It came through in her music.

Even Cedric had noticed. He'd mentioned it once while they were unlocking his front door. He said that at church while watching Topaz play, often, all he could think of was her fingers, drifting over him, like they drifted over the keyboard. Topaz had stripped. She loved letting Cedric worship her nude body. She'd proceeded to strip him. Down on his father's living room floor, she ran her hands all over him, like he'd said. She used her tongue too. "You like that?" she asked, as nude and seated wide on Cedric, her small, nimble fingers ignited him. Maneuvering himself into her tight little sheath, Cedric told her he did, "But, I like being in here, more."

ONE day Cedric looked distant. When Topaz tried to engage him in conversation, he refused.

She tried to get him to talk to her, so they could get to the lovin'—the part that they both always wanted. However, after twenty minutes of what Topaz deemed wasted time, Cedric said he had an announcement.

Topaz felt a chill. Still, she listened as Cedric told her they needed to cool it. He said what they were doing would soon become evident to people, if it hadn't already. He mentioned people like Topaz's parents.

She said she didn't care. Topaz said she had so little fun. Then the petite one asked, "Why would you want to take even that from me?"

Cedric said he didn't, but he was older, and going away in the fall. Staring off, he said they might as well start learning to spend time apart.

Topaz felt like Cedric had dashed her with ice water. She asked was there someone else. She had seen how teenage girls, and women, looked at him. They flirted. She'd seen Cedric flirt back—not the way he did with her, but Topaz could tell; Ced liked the attention. She did, too, now that she'd started receiving it, from the opposite sex. Topaz knew she was only fifteen. Within weeks, Cedric would be eighteen, so perhaps he felt the need to trade up. But, Topaz thought, she needed him.

Cedric told Topaz her thoughts were wrong. "There's only you, Baybay. We just have to be careful. It's why I'm leaving…"

Topaz's eyes widened. "You're leaving, me?" She could barely breathe. "What did I do?" Or not do? She knew Cedric liked sex, and he liked to try different positions. She'd done most of what he'd wanted and more, hadn't she? Topaz touched her heart, crazily fluttering in fear.

"No, no," Cedric grabbed her hands. "I'd never leave *you*. I'm just gonna leave GBBC," the church. "People have started saying shit."

"Like what?"

"Well…they see the way I look at you. They know I want you."

"Oh. That." Topaz admitted that her grandmother, Mother See, had told her that when young women began 'courting,' they needed to be careful. Mother See had said things could happen, some of them unpleasant, because of all the pleasant things that courting afforded. Topaz had not altogether known what the older woman meant. Topaz had felt sad as she'd thought, now even her grandma, her only ally, was becoming a fusspot. Now Mother, too, didn't want Topaz having fun.

But like her parents, Topaz mused, Mother See was older. Sure, she'd been a beaut in her younger years. Gorgeous photos graced different rooms in her home. Mother –who had not been Mother then– had had beaus too, and quite a few. She'd had fun, yet now she and Topaz's parents were begrudging the petite one the life and love she wanted.

However, Mother See *had* made it possible for Topaz to get new clothes. For that, the young woman was grateful.

"See?" Cedric frowned, not aware of all of Topaz's musings. "Even your grandma knows. That's what I'm saying. People know, or they're gonna know. I don't want them in my business, in *our* business. I don't want your folks coming down on you either because of me."

"I can handle it," Topaz nodded, "just as long as we're together."

Cedric knew she was a bit younger than he was. She didn't fully understand yet what he was saying. Still, he couldn't resist Topaz, not when she knew just how to get him going, even when his mind was elsewhere. As he held her in his arms, Cedric realized they were fully dressed, something new for them.

He recalled that after his mother's passing, the Stable house had seemed sad. Topaz had brought the sunshine. She'd opened curtains and windows, saying, "It's dark 'n stuffy in here." Then with her shiny brown legs, bouncy breasts, shapely booty, and slightly flared hips, she'd wound up a dream come true. Topaz had rescued Cedric. She'd kept him from drowning in sorrow. While kissing her, Cedric remembered all. Within moments, their clothing was missing, and they did what they did.

Yet Cedric announced, again, after he'd had his fill of sucking and pumping, that at college time, he *would* quit Greater Bethany. The young man reminded Topaz that he would do it for them. Cedric wanted them to be together in peace.

Cedric proclaimed he would use condoms too. The very next time they did anything, and forever after. He said he wouldn't like it, Topaz might not either, but it was what they had to do.

Remembering the fishbowl, Topaz agreed. "Just as long as you, Yella, don't deprive me." Then Topaz slip-slid all over Cedric.

Chapter 25

CEDRIC loved being in college, but often when he was in class, he had to remind himself. He needed to keep his GPA up, which meant he had to pay attention. He couldn't sit there thinking about Topaz, not while the professor spoke. For the time being, Cedric had to forget the way she looked naked, like she had the last time they'd been together.

He had been seated, and she'd stood before him. She had been facing away. Slowly she'd bent, as from her neck she'd raised her heavy hair. Nude, she'd leisurely gyrated. Every move had been tantalizing, before she'd backed up and sat on his lap. She'd kept it moving. Dang, if Cedric hadn't become horny as a toad! He'd thought he would burst as he'd tackled Topaz. Aware that things were getting hotter, she'd laughed.

Lately, though, when he spoke to or saw her, things were a bit different. Things between them were a bit cooler and a lot less freaky...

TOPAZ was so sick. Although she didn't often see Cedric because he was in college on Long Island, it sure would have been nice, she thought, to lie with him. They could snuggle up in his comfy bed.

When they'd been together, not long ago, Cedric had noticed. Baybay was listless. Sure, she'd wanted to get it in, but there had been no fire. This he'd mentioned, and she hadn't argued. Topaz had known Ced was right. She knew too that something was wrong, inside her.

Topaz's breasts were bigger and so sore all the time. Her hips were slowly spreading, and her stomach was no longer flat. It looked a little puffy, or bloated. This, she one day mentioned to Caley.

In the other girl's junky bedroom, Caley's eyes widened. "Ooh..." tall and slender whispered, "You're not pregnant, are you?"

Topaz appeared shocked. "No. I just think I have some strain of the flu, that's all. I'm so tired, Cae, and I ache all over."

"How long have you felt like this?" the angular brown girl asked.

"A few weeks, maybe a month..." or longer, Topaz did not say.

Caley's eyes grew rounder. "That's too long. I'm scared for you."

"Stop making something out of nothing," Topaz quietly advised. Curling up on the bed strewn with clothes, she pulled a coat over herself. "When Mama' n Daddy go to that meeting before Thanksgiving–"

"The church thingy that they stay at for a week?" Caley interrupted.

"Yes; when they go there, I'll stay with Mother See, like I always do. I'll let her doctor me, get me well again."

Caley looked doubtful. "I don't know if grandma can cure this."

"I'm not pregnant, Cae, so stop saying it." Soft-spoken Topaz knew she'd sounded sure, but she wasn't. Actually, her sister-friend had voiced the doubts that even she'd had, lately. Perhaps she should not have been so fast. But too late now. Maybe.

"I don't know," Caley continued. "You got that long sweatshirt on…"

"It's November; it's fall. It's always cold out now."

"Not that cold. It's a little chilly, but you're acting like it's already winter. Look at that big jacket. You look like the abominable snowman."

"Shut up." Topaz laughed, "And this jacket is yours."

Angular Caley stopped laughing. "Taupe, you peed on the stick yet?"

"What stick?"

"Oh, come on." Caley rolled her eyes. "For such a smart –a book-smart— girl, Topaz T. Moon, you really are life-dumb."

"What stick, Caley?" Topaz softly asked again, ignoring the jibe.

"The pregnancy test stick. I may have one or two in the bathroom. Under the sink, I think. In the back. I put a pack there because Granny can't bend too well." Caley grinned. "This way, she won't see them."

"Don't get them, Cae." Topaz suddenly felt sicker. "I don't wanna do it. Not today."

"I'll bet your lil fast tail never told Cedric that."

When Topaz scowled, slender Caley shrugged and understood. "Okay, we'll do the stick whenever." Tall and thin transferred folded sweaters from a chair to the floor. "Tell me something, Taupe. Did you ever use anything?"

Topaz appeared the total innocent. "Anything, like what? For what?"

"Oh, *Lord!*" capricious Caley yowled and covered her face. "Everybody is going to say this is *my* fault—that I'm the fast ass, that *I* corrupted you, but you are dumber than dirt, girl! This is the nineteen-eighties; didn't you listen in class when they explained all that reproduction/sex stuff? They gave out condoms, for crying out loud!"

Topaz told the truth. "I really didn't pay attention. I didn't know I was going to have sex, not this soon, anyway."

High-strung Caley animatedly waved. "You dumb, dumb, little shit! Now you gonna wind up with a teensy yellow *baby*!"

Topaz stared at her best friend and only wanted to get to the crux of the matter. "What're you talking about—the using something part."

Caley rolled her eyes. "I guess, from your stupid little answer, that you and Cedric didn't use anything, any *protection*. You know, the stuff that people use so they won't wind up pregnant. You probably just got naked, and when he was naked too, and hard, you let him slide up in you, all bare skin, moving hands, kissing lips, and sexiness..." Caley looked like she was thinking about it and getting off on the idea.

Noticing, Topaz told her, "Get out of my business."

"Well, don't bring me your problems." The tall, slender brown girl shrugged and raised herself from the ladder-back chair. She sat on her junky bed beside Topaz. "So tell me," she said, her voice sympathetically lowered, "you two really didn't use anything, *ever*?" Wow. That must have been a dream, with no irritating latex between them. Caley was nearly jealous. But now, she no longer had to use protection either; she was headed in an altogether different direction.

Topaz shook her head. "I didn't know we were supposed to use anything. But a few weeks before Ced left, we used condoms. Ick."

"Ding dang." Changeable Caley sounded anxious. "I wish I'd known. I could've gotten you pills or some other birth control. My friend—you saw her at the game, the one with the long cornrows; she works at a clinic. Or I would have told you to tell your man to use condoms—every single time. He only had to roll them over his chubby lil yella dick. You could have watched or done it for him. That would have been so sexy."

"Yeah, we could have," Topaz admitted, "if I'd known, and his...*part* is not little."

"Ah, but chubby it is, and yella," Caley grinned, trying to imagine.

Topaz almost smiled. "You, Cae, are a nosey, sex-starved fiend."

"Be that as it may," Caley shrugged, "you could have used the sponge even. It's yucky to get out, but you'd have been protected—although no method is all the way safe."

Caley looked away and felt bad for her sister-friend. If Topaz *was* pregnant, she would never live it down, not with their parents. Mama was lovely, but she was ruled by Daddy, almost. Nowadays, Mama also seemed like a pothead, all spaced-out. Sort of like Auntie who drank, Tipsy, Uncle Ezra's wife. Caley guessed Mama was trying to keep peace in the family's peeling yellow house. Granny said women were sometimes submissive, especially when they had a giant storm of a man, like Pastor Moon. With wrinkled fingers, Granny had caressed a cucumber. She'd said sometimes a woman just wanted to keep her man happy.

But back to Taupe, who'd called Caley a fiend; Caley hadn't forgotten; however, that word better fit *Granny*. She was the sex-starved one, a true, little, old fiend, who talked junk while fondling vegetables.

Refocusing on her sister-friend, Caley Nix realized. Topaz was trapped –if she *was* pregnant, because the people at Greater Bethany Bible Congregation thought she was a little, black, holy Mary *before* the Immaculate Conception. If Topaz turned up with child, people at GBBC would want to stone her. Like them people and that woman in the bible. A few of them realized bible woman was getting a lil somethin' on the side, from a few men, then up bubbled hate. However, unlike the woman in the bible, for Topaz, there'd be no flesh-and-blood Jesus to her rescue.

"I hope you 'n your man had fun," Caley blurted. "Ay, no offense. Just look at it like this, if you *are* pregnant, then you and Cedric can do it anytime you want, now, 'cause the deed is done." Caley shrugged, "No sense depriving yourself." She sang out off-key, "Get ya freak on."

Topaz flinched. "Shush –and ain't no deed done." Topaz knew she'd sounded sure. Yet she involuntarily lurched off the bed, tossing aside the heavy jacket she'd been lying beneath. She raced to the bathroom. It had sour-smelling towels inside. The odor caused her to hurl.

Then she knew. Bent over the commode, Topaz felt like she heaved up her insides. Oh, God. Caley was right.

Topaz was pregnant.

What was she going to do?! Topaz wondered, feeling like a tiny fat mouse, one that was snapped up tight in a trap. Puking and crying, she acknowledged that she had already prayed about her situation. However, she had received no answer. Then Topaz remembered.

She hadn't consulted the Lord *before* she'd willingly gotten into this mess, so why should she expect Him to help her out of it, now?

Chapter 26

THE church administrator would never forget. She'd wanted to name her son after his father so everyone would know. However, the boy's father dissuaded her. Sometimes that man made Eve angry. Sure, he said he wasn't ashamed of their son—who was really *her* son, alone—since his father never publicly acknowledged him. Still, Eve often told her son's father she wanted him to come out and own up.

That was when Elijah gave her some bullwinkle. He said he was protecting her and 'the boy.' Eve had said many times, "Quit calling my son that." She knew what her son's father was *not* saying. The good-smelling man wasn't protecting her, or her son. He was really defending himself, and his wife, and his shrimp of a daughter—his other family.

That, the church administrator hated. She wasn't some harlot off the street. That other woman, Naomi, was no good for him. Why couldn't Pastor see? He needed to serve the bitch papers and be done with it. When Eve suggested it, her son's father said, in that long-suffering voice, the one he used when his nerves were plucked. He was doing the best he could. He was trying to protect everyone involved.

Eve yelled, "What about your *son*? He don't need his father?"

The preacher had nearly yelled back, before catching himself. Barely controlled, he'd spoken. "I'm trying to do right by all my children."

That was when she'd hit the ceiling. Eve told the preacher that one of his kids, the girl, was nearly grown.

His rebuttal had been, She's not fully grown yet." Elijah knew Eve didn't understand, but he couldn't imagine telling his family about her, or the boy. Therefore, he'd simply said, "My girl still needs her father."

Eve huffed, "You're saying she's had you all these years, and my son hasn't; but that's okay. Your daughter is more important than your son."

The preacher hadn't further engaged. He'd left.

Those types of things were why Eve had had to give her son a name close to his father's because somehow, she'd known. The preacher would lap up her honey but he wouldn't want it known. Eve wasn't going to let him off that easily. It was why she'd willfully named her son *Elisha*. Everybody knew she'd run her husband off, long before she'd gotten pregnant. Church people knew that there had only been one Immaculate Conception. Just like they knew that Eve and the preacher spent an inordinate amount of time together.

Back some years, Eve had gotten her husband, at the time, to go to a couples' session. She hadn't been interested in reconciling. Attending sessions, she'd been making a statement, to the Pastor. She'd let him know, there were problems, and she was ready to bail. She'd kept her eyes on Pastor. She hadn't acknowledged his stupid young wife. Eve had wanted Pastor Moon to know. She was available, for him, any time.

If the preacher's wife had kept her butt at home, Eve would have opened her shirt, although it had been cold out. She would have leaned forward, allowing the preacher to glimpse her cocoa-colored breasts. She knew he had nearly salivated. Sure, he'd looked like he was in check, when she'd crossed her large legs. But she knew. It had to be an act. Her tiny skirt rode high on her ample thigh. Eve had known one thing too. Although Pastor had never said it, he'd dreamed about sinking into her.

Back a while, she'd become clerical for the church. Eve mentioned her Pastor love to an older woman who warned Eve against folly. Sister Smart said no good could come of it. "Forget that mess, Sister Eve."

However, Eve Island had known what Sister Smart did not—because Eve knew men. No man could work close to her and not wind up wanting her. She'd known it was just a matter of time. Big Pastor Moon would desire her. When he couldn't stand it, he'd make his way to her, in the dark. So she'd waited. It didn't matter that his wife was shapely, or that some thought wife was attractive. Naomi was...cute, but not woman enough for Pastor Moon. Oh, but Eve was, with her super curves, smooth chocolate skin, and natural curls. To resist her, any man would have had to be blind, deaf, *and* without a lick of feeling in his body.

When she'd become the administrator, Eve wielded more power than the fake first lady! That, Eve believed. So, all in all, she had been right to ignore older Sister Smart, who hadn't been so smart, after all.

Although it had taken a bit of time, Pastor Moon had indeed found his way to Eve, and she'd welcomed him, to her bed. Then Eve had even conceived for him, when for her husband –now her ex– she had not.

However, there, Pastor Moon had gotten stuck, when he was supposed to have *married* her. Eve wished her son had been born looking just like his father, instead of like her. Then maybe Eve could have forced the preacher's hand. Perhaps, she still could…

Chapter 27

SHE told Mother See. Topaz had never held anything back from the older woman who was in all ways her grandma. Back in the day, Topaz had even told Mother how she'd felt when Naomi had grown distant, after losing the baby that might have lived had he been born weeks later.

Sure, Naomi had shed the inordinate amount of weight gained during that pregnancy. Topaz's mother had even privately had a hysterectomy sometime afterward, but she had never again been the same. To Topaz, her mother had just seemed too mellow, like someone who'd taken a handful of pills. And Naomi did take pills, for this, that, and the other.

Topaz continued to think about her mother, who had seemingly lost her fire. Naomi had turned into a woman who simply went along. As the go-along woman, she agreed with anything her husband said or did.

Topaz hated that. Sometimes, like now, Topaz just wanted her mom back. Topaz couldn't help but remember that after Naomi had lost the baby, Naomi had let Topaz do as she'd wanted. Naomi had not understood that what the golden-eyed girl had really wanted was a *mother*! However, since Naomi was all but missing in action, Elijah Moon had stepped in. He had done so on the rare occasion that he wasn't busy running church affairs. Those, Topaz felt, were immensely more important than she.

One rule that Elijah Moon had proposed was that Topaz should be in the house before the street lights came on, and Naomi had agreed. She'd done so by not disagreeing or saying anything to the contrary. *But*, Topaz recalled, it had not been dark out when she'd gotten into trouble. She and Cedric had screwed, repeatedly, in the daylight.

All of that was why Topaz couldn't tell her mother, who was often busy with her social work and attempting to rescue other people's kids. Yeah, during the few times when she seemed lucid. Other times, Naomi occupied herself with what Topaz now saw as some silly church shit.

Topaz sat in her grandma's kitchen with her eyes closed, thinking about these things while her parents were away. They were in another state, all dressed up and going to meetin' every day, with thousands of other believers. Yep, while real-life marched on without them, at home.

Realizing church meant so much to her parents, especially her father, Topaz vowed not to tell him. She couldn't because he was always right, in his own mind. Sure, he would be angry and blustery, and that, Topaz could not bear. Not now, not when she was so emotional. The big man had high hopes for her. In his mind, she was on a little pedestal. Therefore, Topaz could imagine him rebuking her, saying she had gone and ruined things. He might even say she'd ruined everything. Biggums would be embarrassed because he needed to control everything and everybody. He would think Topaz should be embarrassed too. And in the past, she'd have placated him. She might even have been ashamed, but now she was not. Now, Topaz just wanted to know what to do.

There were the church members too. Ugh. Topaz turned her head as Mother See bustled around her old-timey kitchen, the one that Topaz had always loved. She heard the woman run water into the kettle that would whistle when hot. Topaz realized that if the saints ever got wind of her situation, they'd want to stare and speculate. That darn fishbowl again. They would wonder and whisper, "Who the daddy?" They'd go to each other's houses, eat chicken, lick their fingers, and laugh while discussing her. Other fat saints would sit in a diner, late at night, eating pie a la mode, while they roasted her alive. A bold somebody might even feel as though they had the right to ask Topaz about her 'sin'—since everybody at Bethany Bible Congregation saw her as church 'property.'

To the saints, Topaz really wasn't a person. She knew she was just a fixture, attached to the organ or to the microphone that sat beside it. Some people would even want her to ask forgiveness, from them! And they were doing similar stuff and more. Fucking hypocrites!

Just thinking about everything, Topaz felt sheer anger and blurted it all out. Words tumbled from her lips with such force that she was left shaken. Afterward, she verbally acknowledged that she hadn't meant for things to come out in such a torrent, "But I've had no control—ever!"

Then, seated in Mother See's cozy kitchen, Topaz burst out crying.

Not flustered, Mother continued her tea preparations, while the child intensely wailed with her head on her arms. Placing china on the table, Mother See softly coaxed, "Up now, baby." Patting Topaz's back, she offered, "Come on. This here will settle your stomach."

Again, Topaz burst into tears because she *was* a baby! Cedric had told her so, many times, way back. Now she, the stupid baby, was *having* a baby. His baby. "What am I going to do?" Topaz cried. She had never thought this could happen—to her! She'd just been having fun. She had crawled all over Cedric, enjoying her newfound freedom. Oh, God! He was older by three years. Shouldn't *he* have known better? He should have stopped her —Nope. Topaz caught herself. She could not blame Cedric. He had not initiated anything. *She* had, repeatedly, even when he'd said they needed to cool it. Cedric had even jokingly said spooning led to forking. It sure did. And look what that led to; all one of the saints needed to do was to pin a big fat F on Topaz's chest. Why? –Because she was a fornicator, a feverishly—forking—fiend.

However, this was her parents' fault, right? If they hadn't held her so tightly, if she hadn't been so sheltered, maybe this would not have happened. Maybe if her mother had been more of a mother, instead of remaining wrapped in grief and hiding behind seemingly good deeds...

Topaz placed both her small hands around the teacup offered. Its heat felt good. She welcomed it. She only wished she could get heat into her bones because she stayed so cold these days. Maybe this week, mainly spent alone, would help get her mind right, as her father often said.

That Topaz knew she needed, because here she was, blaming everybody—but the right person. *She* was at fault. *She* had been the dumb one, like Caley said. She, Topaz Tiara Moon, was to blame for her own situation. Now, she just had to deal with what was happening. Now she had to be a woman. But, Topaz realized... she did not know how.

Mother See squeezed Topaz's shoulder. Instead of sounding reprimanding, Mother sounded soothing. "Baby girl, you ain't the first to go through this, and I dare say, you won't be the last."

Fresh tears rolled down Topaz's cheeks as she kept her small hands around her teacup.

"Stop," Mother See told her. "Stop that, now, child. You don't wanna mark that baby. They will come here cryin' all the time if you don't get hold of yo' self." The older woman spoke slowly, forcefully, willing Topaz to believe. "You – gonna – be – alright. This *will* be okay. It is not the end of the world."

But it was! Topaz told her grandma that it was the end of things as she had known them.

"Okay..." Mother See sounded pensive. "That may be, but now things'll be different. They will have to be, plain and simple as that."

Topaz felt quieted then because it really was that simple. Things were changing because they had to. In fact, things had been changing even before she'd peed on Caley's stick and nervously waited for a sign.

Topaz used a napkin to dab her puffy, red-rimmed eyes. Slowly, then she sipped her hot, honeyed tea. She felt better, even when Mother See commanded her to keep her mouth shut. "You clam up about all this. You hear me? You can talk to Caley or me, but no one else."

The older woman hadn't sounded harsh, just matter-of-fact. "Your folks are out of town right now, so you go to school from here, the same as always in November. Then when they get back, I'll call your Mama. We'll start setting things to right."

Topaz looked up, her eyes bleary. "I don't want an abortion, Mother."

"You ain't gon' have one." The older woman's eyes blazed. "Strike that word from your 'cabulary because we don't believe in murder."

Topaz felt better. As she sipped more tea, she knew that for some people, abortion was an option. She knew that it was a necessity in some cases, but for her, it was neither. For her, it would be wrong.

As she sat there in her oversized sweatshirt, Topaz began to feel warm for the first time in…forever. She spoke as gently she clinked her cup on its saucer. "Mother, I want to keep it. I've been thinking, and I want this baby. My baby." Cedric's baby.

Regal Mother See's eyebrow rose. "I don't know how well that's gon go over with Daddy Moon, since you got to live in his house and go to his church, but we'll see. Quit worrying, though, because ain't a thing that worry will fix. Just drink up. Then rest. This part, I will handle."

When Topaz rose to go to her room, she asked the silver-haired woman a question. "Mother, should I tell the father?"

"Isn't your young man in college?" Mother See knowingly asked.

Topaz stared at her grandma. So it was true, what people had said for years. Mother had the sight. Actually, she saw too much. "Yes, Ma'am." Referring to Cedric, Topaz finally admitted, "He's an undergrad."

Mother See pointedly inquired, "Can he he'p you, financially?"

Topaz wondered if the question was rhetorical because her grandma had to know, Cedric couldn't do a thing. Yet Topaz truthfully answered. "No, he can't help me, not right now."

"Then hush, like I said. You will tell that yella boy when it's time."

Topaz nearly felt relieved because her grandma really knew.

Mother See raised a wrinkled hand. "Don't ask me one question, either because only *you* will know when it's time. Your spirit will tell you. In the meantime, in 'bout a week," Mother See sounded disdainful, "I will talk to yo' Mama, pull her from this stupor that she's been in."

"Okay." In the house where she had always felt comfortable, even more so than at her parents' home, Topaz turned. She would go to the room that had been hers since she'd been a golden-eyed tot. Yet, she pivoted and dashed back across the kitchen. Throwing her arms around the woman who was only a head taller, Topaz revealed, "I've always loved you, Grandma. You always listen to me. You've always seen me, too –the real me. You've never wanted me to be something I'm not."

Mother See hugged the girl back, the one she'd held on birthing day, nearly sixteen years prior. "I've always loved you too, baby," more than life itself. "And you have always listened to me. You see me, too."

Repeatedly, the older woman smoothed the girl-woman's long heavy hair. It was getting lengthier and thicker by the day, due to hormonal changes. Wishing she could take away agony, and further wishing she could make all things right for her petite Topaz, Mother See spoke.

"Lotta folk don't listen to a person once that person gets up in age." The woman hugged the girl who rested in her arms, just like she had when Topaz had been a child. "Not you, though, sweetie-pie. You've got a great ear *and* a good heart."

Mother See repeatedly kissed Topaz. The elder held on tightly too. "I'm aware you're about to be somebody's Mama." Mother See ran her hands over the young one's heavy hair, "But lil honey, I promise you one thing… You gon always be *my* baby. You come to me with anything."

Tears streamed down Topaz's cheeks. For that, she was grateful.

Chapter 28

ELIJAH claimed Naomi's aunt was nosey. He said he didn't care if she *was* a professor living down south. The woman was still nosey.

Ignoring her husband who often went on tirades, Naomi said he was unfair. Her aunt, Petunia, had never poked her nose into anyone's business. Not when Naomi had lived with Pet, and not even when big Elijah had madly plugged Naomi under Petunia's roof. Back when the young couple had decided to get married.

Naomi forged ahead to say that as a college instructor, Petunia could homeschool Topaz, away from Tranquility.

"So you talked to *her* about this already." Elijah was fit to be tied, "Before you approached *me*, your husband—Topaz's father?"

Naomi knew Elijah was livid, but who cared? He was always having a conniption, some mood swing or other, just like a pregnant woman. It was because he still wanted to believe, as his mother did, that he could control everything and everybody.

Naomi watched the big handsome man pace the tacky linoleum in their big old kitchen. She really wished Elijah would calm down. Looking away from wooden cabinets hidden beneath decades' worth of paint, she tried again. "When I spoke to Mother See—"

"Mother See?!" Elijah literally shouted as though he were caught up in one of his sermons.

"Yes, Mother See." Naomi appeared composed, as usual, which further infuriated her husband. "Mother was convinced this is the best—"

"Mother See is convinced," Elijah echoed. Then he bellowed, "*She* knows!" He shook his head. "I should have known *she* would know. That ol' woman knows everything. She probably saw this in some vision or dream. I wish to God she'd said something or tried to stop it."

"How do you know she didn't?" Naomi retorted, sick of Elijah. At home, he always attempted to place blame and point fingers. When he was at church, he was different. He was the fearless, unflappable leader.

"Anyway," Naomi said, instinctively defending herself. "*I* didn't tell Mother. Your golden-eyed girl did."

Elijah sounded crestfallen. "Why didn't she come to *me*? Or you?"

Naomi's eyes narrowed. "With the way you howl when things don't go right around here, I guess she couldn't take that chance."

Forgetting the other part of his life, the part he hoped his wife never found out, Elijah wanted to shake Naomi. He hated that she seemed unperturbed. Yet lowering his voice, he asked, "What do you mean?"

"I mean what I said. You're so damn calm and seemingly unmoved at Greater Bethany. But *here*, if it's not your way, you race around and rage, like an ogre."

Elijah felt as though he'd been unfairly attacked. "Take it back, Nae."

"I will not." She threw up her hands and wondered, where was her purse? She needed her pills. Sure, she'd promised Mother See that she would begin backing off them. Naomi hadn't forgotten, but her meds were the only things that kept her sane in this crumbling make-believe world that Elijah had so carefully constructed around them. Now Naomi didn't know if she could stand to watch it all disintegrate because then her man, her big fine man—that so many women wanted—might fragment too. Fighting panic, Naomi felt around in the depths of her oversized purse. She shook heavy hair out of her eyes. When she couldn't locate the correct pills, she asked herself a question. Did she care whether Elijah splintered? Naomi didn't know. All she knew was *her child* needed her. Topaz needed help, and she, Naomi Moon, was going to give her child everything she had, even if she had to roll over big Mr. Moon to do it. Naomi promised, this one time pushy Elijah would not get his way.

"All I wanna know," Topaz's father bellowed, "is who the daddy?"

"Mother See and I decided that we'll send our girl to Aunt Pet."

"Later for Petunia. Naomi Ruth, you heard me. Who is baby daddy?"

Naomi would never tell Elijah that Topaz had not said; let him think she knew. Naomi realized it might give her an advantage in dealing with 'his royal highness.' As Elijah badgered her, Naomi mentally escaped by thinking about her aunt. Her mother's sister was the woman to whom she would send Topaz. Naomi knew there wasn't time to spare, not with Topaz's waistline enlarging every day, even as Elijah warned her.

"Nae, you know you can't get away with ignoring me."

"I'm not ignoring you. I was trying to have a conversation with you."

"Well, since you won't say who did this," Elijah huffed, "lemme ask you something else—even though I *will* find out who the boy is. If he's a man, God help him even more. But how on earth you gonna send *my* child away without consulting *me*? She has to play for the services!"

"The services?" Naomi's eyes widened, and she forgot her promise to Mother See. Now Naomi really needed her pills, or she would pull off her shoe. She'd fly across the ugly laminate countertop separating her and her husband. Tomorrow's morning paper would read, **Wife High-Heels Preacher to Death**. "Don't fool with me Lijah, talking 'bout some *service* that Topaz has to play for. That girl's been playing for you for years! Although you think that's all she's good for—That, and making you look big; those things aren't the issue—so forget them." Naomi said she wouldn't further discuss Topaz's boyfriend, either, "Because none of that is important right now."

"See? That's your problem." Elijah reprimanded. He peered at the woman who'd sounded eerily like the one he'd married, and not the ghost who'd long taken her place. "You don't know what's important."

"Yeah? Well, since you know everybody else's problem, Elijah Moon, why not help solve some of them?"

"I'm building something here, Naomi, and Topaz is a component in that. We are right at the door of going on TV. The ministry is growing. If things start unraveling now, how you think you're gonna keep getting them fancy clothes and hats? How we gonna pay for this money pit?"

"As I said, those things are not the point. I don't care about that stuff, Elijah. It's worn for you—you 'n your shallow-ass mama. As for this shambledy house, and GBBC, I'd quickly run off and leave both."

Naomi had almost sounded calm, although inside, she felt fire and rage, the likes of which she hadn't felt in years. Yet she tamped both down to truthfully state, "*All I care about is* protecting *my child.*"

"From what?" Elijah scoffed, "And looks to me like you a little late for that—protection." Hearing himself, the preacher felt so phony. *He* had a son! Apparently, he hadn't used enough protection, himself.

"Elijah." Naomi looked and sounded stunned. "Can you honestly stand there and ask what Taupe needs protection from? You know, a few blocks over, at Greater Bethany, your church members would love nothing more than to rip my child to bits, for what they will perceive as her *sin.*"

Not thinking, Elijah said, "Then get rid of it, the sin. Scratch it out."

Naomi's heart stuttered because she just knew she hadn't heard right. *Get rid of it. Scratch it out. The sin.* This was *a baby* they were talking about! And *she* had lost five! Suddenly she could hardly breathe.

Elijah paused, too, realizing what he'd just said, but he was not about to back down. In the stunned silence, he thought about it. Then he decided it really was the best thing for all involved. Heck, sometimes he wished he could go back and scratch out the night on which Eve, the church administrator, had conceived. Then she would not have borne the boy whose very existence sometimes felt like an albatross around Elijah's neck. So again, he proclaimed, "Topaz just has to get rid of it."

"*I rebuke the very notion,*" Naomi growled. Then she shouted, "No!" Naomi was firm in stating her daughter's wishes. "Topaz wants to keep it. And it's her body—*her* decision."

"Keep it?!" Elijah almost hit the peeling ceiling. He roared, "And her body resides in my house—so *my* decision. No baby in this house!"

"Well, then, we'll have to let the baby go to a family member—maybe to Aunt Pet—so Topaz can at least see the child from time to time. But even that solution might not fly."

"I don't care. She's spoiled, but enough!" Elijah was done. The silly females in his life thought they had a choice. They didn't. Turning from his wife, Elijah felt more disappointment with her, and his daughter, than he'd thought possible. Topaz had ruined everything, for him. Now people would talk, about him. They would think the preacher couldn't manage his household. They would say he let his only kid, a tiny thing, run roughshod over him, and just when things had begun to look up.

"Elijah?" His wife spoke to his broad back. "Elijah, turn around."

He did not, and he sounded weary because everything, it seemed, was going to hell in a handbasket. "What, Naomi?"

She made herself say, "I know you're worried about GBBC, about what the members will say, and what they'll think," because as the preacher's wife, she knew Elijah all too well. "But let Greater Bethany think my baby is still going to preparatory school. You did mention it, before, in front of the congregation." Usually, Naomi hated when her husband did that; opened up their private lives for dissection. Yet, this time she was glad he had. It would give her precious daughter an alibi.

Elijah Moon said nothing. With pursed lips, he simply stared out of the window. He didn't want Naomi to know, but he was giving the matter real thought. He had to because his daughter was much like her mama. His girls were soft-spoken. They seemed passive and agreeable, but boy did they have a stubborn streak! When the petite one set her mind on something, there was no swaying her. There never had been. Therefore, Elijah needed to figure out a way to save face. Yes, amid all that wayward girl, and her mother, had now heaped on his head.

Elijah also had to figure out how to keep *Eve* from pushing for more.

Unaware, Naomi didn't care that Elijah appeared sullen. She was fighting for her child, and for the life of her grandchild. Naomi wanted further schooling for Topaz, with as little embarrassment as possible. "Elijah," Naomi resolved, "we'll let everyone think Taupe has gone to the preparatory academy. Since Aunt Pet is an undergrad instructor, Topaz's grades don't have to fall. My aunt can guide her."

Naomi grasped at straws. "For Taupe, this—going away—will be *like* preparatory training. Yes." Naomi hated to say it, but it was true. "Nothing can better prepare Topaz for life than what she now faces."

"I wish," Elijah softly stated, "this had never happened." He meant all of it, including things of which Naomi had no knowledge. "I also wish you'd never gotten your old crones involved in my business." The preacher nearly sounded defeated. "I wish you'd abided by my rule," one of many.

What goes on in the preacher's house stays *in the preacher's house.*

Naomi bitterly laughed. When she spoke, her voice was soft, yet she meant every word. "Elijah Moon, I am not your child. And if you keep this attitude, Topaz won't be either, not for much longer."

With those words, Topaz's mother grabbed her purse. She left her husband sputtering and blustering. Without turning, she waved. Later for Lijah, Naomi thought. She would do what she had to for her child, who was now becoming a woman.

Chapter 29

THAT Sunday, while seated at the organ, Topaz wore a beautiful ensemble. Regal Mother See had taken her shopping for the sleeveless dress and matching lightweight coat. The young woman recalled trying on both. Her grandma had said, "This material won't allow you to get too hot; it looks neat, *without clinging…*" Both knew that was important.

Seated on the organ, Topaz forgot shopping, to recall being a kid. She'd loved the tiny glasses that the Mothers Board had filled with grape juice. They'd done so for Communion. Often during that high, holy part of the service, Topaz's father read from the scriptures. There, the beverage was called wine, or the fruit of the vine.

Topaz fondly remembered wondering why she couldn't have a big glass. Often as a kid, she'd thought the tiny glasses would not have been enough for one of her dolls. As she sat on the organ, listening to the announcements, she recalled that as a kid, she'd loved Communion Sundays. Then, most women wore white, like angels.

Suddenly Topaz wondered. Would *her* kid ever experience any of the things she had? As she played something innocuous, a little background music, she wondered. Would her boy, or girl, ever taste the thin Communion wafers? She'd marveled at them being nearly transparent. Would her child also be intrigued or even giggle during the foot-washing portion of the service? It sometimes followed Communion.

Topaz really did not know. At present, everything was so up in the air until she was confused. All she knew was that she could no longer remain at home. Her father didn't want her there, in her condition. In addition, her mom and Mother See thought it better for her to go away.

Down south with Aunt Pet, Topaz could still get her schooling. She could have her baby in peace, with no one poking around, peeking, and waiting to judge. *No more fishbowl.* That was why the petite one agreed.

In a way, leaving Tranquility was good, Topaz thought, for many reasons. One of them was that she no longer wanted to be in the house where she'd never really felt comfortable. She especially did not want to be there when her father deigned to put in an appearance. Heck, these days, he treated her like she had leprosy. Yep, since he'd found out.

Topaz wasn't surprised. Church people were sometimes self-righteous; still she was hurt. After all she'd done for Elijah Moon and all she had given up to make things work for him. If he hadn't acted so ugly, Topaz realized, she probably would have spent the rest of her natural life trying to please that man. Well, thank God for small blessings.

Oh, the preacher had called her into his home office, the one with the huge bay window. As a girl, she'd curled up on the cushiony window seat, just to be near him. Back then, she'd thought the world of her Dad. The other day though, with all that forgotten, Elijah Moon had been composed and formal, like she, his daughter, was one of his parishioners.

Topaz hadn't really cared because she knew all of that was just a ruse. After all, she knew her father. She had been aware too that he was seething inside, but so was she! What did *he* have to be upset about? Topaz wondered. Elijah Moon had other organists. *He* wasn't the dumb one who'd screwed up his life. He wouldn't soon have to walk around looking like a balloon. Nevertheless, he didn't see things that way. He saw them as he saw most things—through his lenses of judgment.

As he'd talked to Topaz, well really, as he'd talked *at* her, faking equanimity, he'd asked questions that she would never answer. She'd resented him then, as she never had before. Topaz had also realized; she was no longer a kid. All the things taking place in her body reminded her. As a result, she'd detested Elijah Moon. How dare he treat her that way. He'd rebuked her, too. However, Topaz kept quiet because she knew one thing. Her father couldn't often hear anyone else's words. That was because while the other person spoke, he usually didn't listen. He silently thought, of what *he* would say. To him, that was most important.

Therefore, Topaz had simply stood, formulating a plan. Since she was being banished, sent away, she simply would not return. She knew her father thought she would, afterward. He believed all would be as it had been. He believed she would again play the organ for him, and be his dutiful little monkey, but phooey on him. And if he failed? So what.

Uh-oh, she needed to pay attention. She was slated to sing again, in church for the last time, before being sent away. Sentenced, for 'her crime.' Fornication. Topaz began to play. With tears making her voice sweeter, she tried not to recall. Her father had been unable to look at her moments ago when he'd requested the sermonic solo.

Topaz did not even think about what she would sing. It was as though her fingers floated—of their own volition—over the keyboard. The words bubbled up, too, from the deep of her. *I Must Tell Jesus...*

All of my trials.

She was so glad Cedric was not there to hear or see. He would have known something was wrong. He would have had questions. He most likely would have approached her, too, because he was protective.

Topaz sang on. *I cannot bear these burdens alone.*

Cedric would have wanted to make things right for her.

Topaz didn't want him involved. Well, not any more involved.

Sure, tall thin Caley said that portion of Taupe's decision was stupid, but Topaz didn't think so. Cedric was furthering his education. That was what he needed to do. Right now, he could not help her.

Melodically Topaz sang about the one who could.

In my distress, He
Kindly will help me.

Knowing she had to allow Cedric his freedom, Topaz sang on about another. *He ever loves and cares for His own.*

She got to the soaring and triumphant chorus.

I must tell Jesus!

By that time, both she and the congregation were nearly all-out weeping. For doing so, everyone's reason was different.

I must tell Jesus!
Jesus can help me...

Topaz's heart nearly splintered as softly, brokenly, in song she reminded herself, and others, that there was only one.

Oh-oh-oh, Jesus.
Jesus, alone.
Hallelujah.

Chapter 30

AT Petunia's cute little home filled with a lovely mix of the eclectic, things garnered on many travels, Topaz relaxed. Surprisingly, her little round great-aunt did not try to incriminate her or make Topaz feel bad about any of what was happening. First, because as an instructor at the college up the road, Petunia was too busy. Secondly, the woman had never had children. She had always wanted them, she said, but she had not been so blessed. Thus, she taught the children-turned-young-adults that had been born to others. Petunia said she felt like her students, her niece Naomi, and now Topaz and the baby were her blessings.

Topaz wasn't so sure. All she knew was that she might have to leave her baby. Baby would remain with Aunt Pet *if* Topaz returned to Tranquility because her father was adamant. No bringing an infant into his house. Well, they would see, Topaz thought, hugging herself. She knew her child would have a good home because her great-aunt had always been sweet to her. Topaz's mother had even said the same, often, over the years. As a young woman, Naomi, too, had lived with Aunt Pet.

However, daily, as the baby grew inside her, Topaz just could not see leaving him or her. This she told Aunt Pet, who reminded her of a plucky little cartoon character. The short round woman didn't seem upset as she pulled a red woolen hat over her press 'n curl. She simply asked, her amiable voice high, "Then what are you going to do, my darling?"

Looking up from her homework, Topaz told the truth. She did not know, *but* she knew she wanted her child.

Wearing a wildly colorful sweater, Aunt Pet rubbed Topaz's shoulder. "You've got a strong maternal instinct." That had been all. Then Petunia had been off. Gathering her glasses and her scuffed leather school bag, she'd called out. "There's a casserole in the fridge." Slipping into her little car, she turned the ignition. Jauntily then she'd bumped away to the college, where she would instruct another group of undergrads.

AT home, Naomi was so nervous—for her daughter, until she ate, and called Topaz. She went to work. While trying to sort her way through mountains of paperwork, she ate, and wanted to call Topaz. As she went on field visits to see children who needed someone to advocate for them, Naomi stopped at fast food joints. There she ate more. At home, she cooked dinner for her man. Often he didn't make it back to the vast mustard-yellow house to eat. Eating alone, Naomi guessed Elijah wouldn't ever get around to having the old Victorian re-painted. Nevertheless, there, again she checked on her daughter.

Understandably, there were times when Topaz felt betrayed and abandoned. She refused to take the phone. Then Petunia would calmly say, "Nae, our girl is doing okay. She's just not having the best day."

When the grandfather clock in the living room gonged, signaling that it was midnight, Naomi ate again. She stood with the refrigerator door wide. She looked at the phone with its curly cord, hanging on the kitchen wall. She wanted to pick it up, but she did not. Topaz was probably sleeping, and Taupe needed rest because soon she would be unable to sleep. The baby would be too big and perhaps press on her bladder. Yet Naomi just wanted to hear Topaz's voice and know that her girl was okay. As she sat at the table in the moonlight, eating coconut macaroons, something that she did not need, Naomi thought about her life.

She had been happy, following her decision to marry Elijah. At the time, all Naomi had wanted was to become Mrs. Elijah Martin Moon. She'd wanted his good loving, and to become the mother of his children. Back then, she hadn't known what life with young Elijah would entail. Naomi had thought she knew him, but over the years he had shown her, she really had not. Back then, he had talked to Naomi. He'd told her of his dreams and his fears. All of them had included the church, and the work he felt had been foisted on him following his father's death.

At the time, Naomi had thought she could handle all that she and Elijah would face together. Now, however, therein lay the rub. They hadn't faced everything together. They didn't think the same way, either. That Elijah proved when he chose his mother and the church over Naomi. She felt like Elijah had joined Cozi Moon too often in ganging up on her. Those two rebuked Naomi for every little thing. According to them, Naomi mused. She couldn't even breathe right. They told her that her clothes were wrong. After losing her fifth and last baby, the pair said Naomi had become an inept mother to Topaz. No one cared that the baby had been Naomi's *sixth*, the fifth lost. Cozi Moon had harped on Naomi's weight too, until she'd slimmed down, for herself. Naomi's mother-in-law had also told her, every chance, that she wasn't going about her first lady duties right. Cozi said Naomi didn't need to work outside the home; Cozi had not, while Old Preacher lived. Cozi claimed if Naomi was at home more, and 'not out, trying to be *the man*,' by making a living, she'd learn to keep the pastor's house right and be a proper preacher's wife.

The pastor's Mother complained that Naomi didn't greet the bishops and superintendents and their wives during Holy Convocations and other conventions as she should have. A point of contention was that Naomi had not made Topaz go to Sunday school. Nor young people's rap sessions. Those two things the other Moons had insisted on.

Both mother and son claimed Naomi was not as active in the church, or the community, as she could have been. Yet she was doing her best. The parishioners and others loved her, but to the Moons, that meant nothing. And the litany of the things she was no good at became endless.

However, some of those things Naomi had not done, with good reason. Like not making Topaz go to Sunday school. Naomi, forty-one hadn't insisted because her child was *always* in church. Topaz was there every time the doors opened, or the little thing opened them. Even when there was no service, Topaz was at the church, by herself, practicing the organ. She was learning the pedals, the bass, the swell, and vibrato.

Naomi hadn't liked that. She hadn't felt it was safe, but her husband had blustered that she worried too much. He'd said that most times while Topaz was at GBBC, the saints were in and out. But Naomi had seen some of those 'saints' eyeing her baby. Those men looked at Topaz like she was a tasty little pork chop. Unsettled, Naomi had gone to God in prayer many times regarding her daughter's safety. She had also enrolled her girl in self-defense classes, all while popping pills. It seemed those were the only things that calmed Naomi's feelings of distress.

Naomi tried not to think about her petite young woman at the church, learning songs to teach others. Yet Topaz had been diligent in learning music for every holiday—for Ash Wednesday, Good Friday, and Easter. That child had a repertoire of songs for Mother's Day, Thanksgiving, Christmas—and everything in between. She had pieces for a host of other occasions too, Communion, funerals, for the altar call, for sermonic solos, for the different choirs, for testimony service, for offerings, the ushers' march, and for anniversaries—those of the church, the choirs, and that of the pastor. That girl had music on hand for celebrations, weddings, christenings, birthdays, and for the benediction. She played to slow things dow, and speed them up. Topaz kept everything moving. No one knew better than Naomi how hard her child worked. Well, Mother See did, but that was why Naomi hadn't put another thing on Topaz's plate. Elijah and Cozi hadn't liked it, but Naomi had not cared.

Now, Naomi realized, she and her girl had 'this' to contend with. The baby situation. Naomi ate another macaroon. She had an idea of who'd fathered the baby. Really, she *knew*, but in her mind, calling the Stable boy out, like Elijah wanted, wouldn't change a thing. Topaz would still be pregnant, and then everyone would know. They'd wonder if it had been a one-time thing or if the sex was ongoing. It wasn't their business.

At forty-five, Elijah wanted someone's head. Naomi didn't think his was the way. She would speak with Cedric Stable. They'd come to an agreement. Of that, Naomi was sure. She liked the young man that Ora's boy had become. Naomi talked to her confidant, Mother See, then she was pretty sure they'd done right, sending Topaz to Petunia. It would give Lil Mama and her baby a chance. Naomi usually felt she'd done okay, until the quiet times. In crept doubt, and Naomi wound up eating.

In food, Naomi sought comfort, perhaps because, that, her gorgeous but self-absorbed husband did not provide. Naomi ate too because, for years she'd been undermined, not so much by Elijah, but by his mother.

Sure, Naomi was ballooning up again; she looked at herself critically. She saw her skirts stretching across her chubby thighs. They even hiked up in the back, over her chunky behind. Sure, the members at GBBC were talking about her weight, but she no longer cared. She was fine. Naomi had even heard what her mother-in-law had said.

The last time Cozi saw her son's wife so big, she'd been pregnant...

Naomi nearly chuckled, because *that* was funny, seeing that her husband rarely spent time at home or in her presence. Sure, he appeared when it was time for her to fix him, or something. However, those were the only times, outside the church, when Naomi saw the man, nowadays. And she had been good to him, and good *for* him. She'd done so much for him, but she had become his slave instead of his partner.

Maybe he had another woman. Naomi didn't know, and she didn't care. She hadn't slept with Elijah Moon in so long until she no longer had the need. Not since she'd lost all those baby Moons, and not much since the hysterectomy. After all of Elijah's badgering and taking his mother's side in things, Naomi just didn't want any of him. Maybe if he'd been nicer, she'd feel differently, but who knew? All Naomi knew was that her husband needed to stick somebody, so hopefully, he'd chosen wisely. Hopefully, *his* sins wouldn't dash back to bite him—or her.

All of that Naomi would have loved to throw in her mother-in-law's ape face. She wanted the mean-spirited woman to know. No babies were being made in the Moon household. However, as she had since they'd married, over seventeen years prior, Naomi held her peace. Still, the truth stared at Naomi. Ever since she'd told her husband what they would do concerning Topaz, Naomi felt...a change.

The diffident wife had experienced a little buzz. It was strange, but somewhere deep inside Naomi, a spark had leapt to life. It gave her a feeling of being...empowered. Naomi knew she would have to do a whole lot more to get some momentum going, but for now, her little buzz was enough.

Mrs. Moon knew there was something else she had to do. She didn't exactly know what that something was, but as she put the remaining macaroons away, she said a little prayer.

Then knowing the Lord would set her on the right path, she climbed the creaky stairs. Headed to her big empty bedroom with its adjacent bathroom, Naomi would brush her teeth. The big old house would settle around her as she got into bed. Alone. In the dark, Naomi would not wish for Elijah Moon either, not like she used to, years back.

Instead, she would let herself dream...of another man, a bureaucrat with whom she worked. *He* thought she was intelligent and sensual. So did others. And indeed Naomi was. She always had been. Bureaucrat loved her glorious brown hair. He touched it every chance he got.

Reaching into her bedside drawer, she pulled out her bliss wand. The saints would call it devilish. Still, she remembered. Bureaucrat called her super-sized sexy. He often told her she smelled amazing. Well, she did.

While removing her nightie, Naomi pondered *that* sizable man. Guess she just liked a certain male type. Lying down, in her humid place, she used her wand. It was the place where she just might invite Bureaucrat...

After giving herself a few thrills, Naomi then thought about what she hadn't in nearly twenty years... What *she* wanted out of life. Now.

Chapter 31

Eᴌɪᴊᴀʜ walked down the back steps of Bethany while burly Deacon Wilnod locked up. Headed toward his car, Topaz's father saw a young man enter the parking lot from the far end.

The sneaker-shod fellow moved quickly, with a hood pulled up over his head. His face was mostly hidden.

Elijah's heart began to pound as he turned to face the man full on. If this was his time, then Elijah was ready to go. He did not fear death. With all his troubles, he would almost welcome it. His insurance would pay Naomi and take care of college for Topaz.

"Pastor Moon..."

Elijah squinted. Although there were lights in the parking lot, it wasn't full dark, so they hadn't yet blinked on. Aware that evil lurked in the hearts of men, Elijah realized he couldn't see well, a hazard of getting older, so he called out, as he often did. "Hey there. Who's that?"

"Pastor," the lean man stepped into a burgeoning pool of light. It was thrown by one of the lot's awakening lanterns. The lean man pushed his hood back. "Sir, I wanted to catch you before you got away."

Elijah extended a beefy hand. "Lance… Right?"

"Yes, sir," the man crisply stated, glad to be acknowledged.

"You've been on leave. Correct?" Elijah asked because vaguely, it returned to him. The young man had been in Afghanistan, or Iraq, with the US Armed Forces.

"You've got a great memory, Pastor," Lance admiringly stated, "and that's with having tons of people to remember."

"Hang on a sec," Elijah said and unlocked his car door. Bending, he started the vehicle that coughed to life, after a few tries.

Descending the church's back steps, burly Deacon Wilnod saw his Pastor facing a hooded young man. Reaching behind and into his waistband, Deacon Wilnod loudly rasped, "Everything ok, Reverend?"

Elijah waved. "Yes, Deac. This is little Lance—McGilroy, right?"

Corporal Lance McGilroy nodded, although he was now a husband and father. He guessed the preacher remembered him from way back.

"Well…alright," Deacon Wilnod—ever the warrior—stated. He wasn't about to leave. Snow was flurrying, but he kept hold of cold steel.

Unaware, Elijah asked the young man, "What can I do for you?"

"Well, I was wondering…if you could spot me a ten, Pastor…" Lance looked sick having to request it. "I mean, I got back here with a leg injury, among other things, and I can't seem to get much help. I've been looking for work too, but tonight it's really bad. My little girls need milk for the morning, eggs too. You know, for when they go to school. My wife works, but her pay only goes so far. It keeps heat and the lights on, but see Pastor, I don't want to send my girls out hungry."

Lance looked as though he fought not to become emotional.

Elijah looked into the face of the young man who had proudly worn his uniform and served his country. Elijah's heart went out. He also knew it took a big man to ask another man for help. It was why he pushed his greatcoat back and reached into his worn pants pocket, for his wallet.

Elijah never had much, but he was always willing to share what he had. "Lance, I've got a twenty and a ten," Elijah truthfully stated. "How about I keep the ten? I need gas, you know. I'll float you the twenty." The preacher held it out. "You get that back to me, son, when you can."

Amid the effusive thanks and the pumping of his hand, Elijah realized. He'd had to put it that way. A man had his pride. He also wanted to take care of his family. Thus, Elijah would never have damaged young Lance by acting like Lance had asked for a handout. The young man needed help, like Elijah did. "Do me one thing," Elijah said, forgetting that he had asked God for help as recently as earlier in the day.

"Anything I can, Pastor, anything."

"Let me see you and those girls of yours in church, real soon." Elijah stamped his feet. In his old shoes that needed new soles, his feet were getting cold. Forget about new shoes, Elijah recalled; there just wasn't the money. Dismissing his own needs, Elijah advised the corporal, "Come to the house afterward and eat, son. I know Sister Naomi would love to feed you and the wife." Elijah turned slightly to slide into his now warm car. "Come to my office one weekday. You know, we've got government-sponsored programs. With federal backing, we've helped get quite a few servicemen up on their feet again."

"I didn't know that," Lance admitted, holding the car door wide for his Pastor. "I sure will, Sir." He closed the door and yelled through the window. "God bless you, Pastor Moon! I mean it. Bless you!"

As burly Deacon Wilnod was about to turn away, he felt the lightest tap on his shoulder. There was no one near, no one human. Still, before the ex-cop knew it, he rasped, "Brother Lance, think you want a ride?"

In flurrying snow, the corporal surprised himself by accepting.

Elijah pulled the old Impala out of the parking lot. He was careful not to skid on gathering precipitation. Although his throat burned, and he felt like he was coming down with something, he'd make one more stop.

Joining a trickle of traffic, Lord, did Elijah want to go home! Yet, he could not. He knew Old Mother Meadows would be looking for him. Sure, it was now after visiting hours, but she'd be heartbroken if her Pastor didn't show. Therefore, Elijah turned at the light, heading for the gas station. He'd get just enough to get him to her and then home. He might even have enough in the a.m. to get back to Greater Bethany; start all over again. Pulling into the station, again Elijah asked his savior for help *and* strength because, without those, he could not make this journey.

AT Tranquility General, the gray-haired night nurse, and Elijah's daughter's friend, Tallulah, both waved him in. "Evening, Pastor Moon."

He nodded. "Nurse Sheila. Sister Lula." Elijah also thought as he walked the white-tiled hallway; good thing the staff knew him, or he'd have had to wait until tomorrow. Nevertheless, the preacher was known because he was at the hospital nearly every week. There was always another somebody to see about. "Knock, knock," Elijah softly called and eased his immense shoulders through a hospital room doorway.

Mother Meadows' rheumy eyes lit up. "Pastor, you came!" she cried, her frail hands fluttering before her.

Lil Don, her son, stood to shake hands. "Thanks for coming, Rev." The man said he would let his mom and the reverend talk.

"Mother Meadows," Elijah nodded, taking a seat, "I said I'd be here."

"I know, Pastor, but you sho a busy man, and I'm jest an old woman trying to go home to be with her Lord."

"A fine thing that is," Elijah nodded. He took the frail brown hands in his own. Forgetting his aching throat and head, softly he announced, "Mother Meadows, I want to pray for you."

"I want that too, Pastor." The elderly woman nodded, "First, I gots to tell you shomething. I wanna gi' you something too. Lil Don and I were jest speaking of it."

Elijah sat back, locking his fingers over his midsection. It had spread considerably in the last few years. Naomi's good cooking was to blame.

"Well," Mother Meadows began, looking to see if indeed her hospital room door was closed. "I've got a confession to make, Pastor. Lil Don don't know this, and shince he and I have come all this way, for nearly forty years, I'd now prefer it if he never knew."

Elijah nodded, carrying the saints' secrets had become part of his job.

"Well...I'm just gon shay it." Mother Meadows looked straight at Elijah. "I'm not Lil Don's mama. *She* died after giving birth. She was my friend, you shee, and she made me promise to take care of her baby and her man. Well, as things went, I did. Two years later, Big Don asked me to marry him. He passed on, a while back; you know. I'm leaving Lil Don, his Dad's property. Pastor, you must understand. I shlowly grew to love Donnelly but I loved his boy right away. I love Lil Don with all my heart, and I'd never hurt him. I always meant to tell him, you shee, but shomehow during these thirty-nine years, it was neva the right time."

The little woman sat back with nervously fluttering hands.

Elijah Moon appeared unperturbed. "I understand, Mother. I know too that you need me to pray, for you, for the unburdening of your soul, so I will. Would you like that?"

"Yesh," Mother Meadows vigorously nodded. "Wait now. I want you to have this. Then you can pray for thish old woman." She pulled a piece of folded parchment from her bedside table. With frail hands, Mother Meadows pressed the paper flat. "Lookit that."

Elijah leaned and squinted. He ignored his aching throat and throbbing head. "Looks like a deed, to me."

Toothless, Mother Meadows smiled, covering her mouth. "Oh. "Shince I lost sho much weight, dentures don't fit in my head anymore."

Elijah patted her hand. "You're still the fairest of them all." He remembered her from years back. When he had been a boy, she had been a beautiful young woman, and as sweet as she was now.

"Thish here is the deed to a property I've held onto." Shakily the old woman handed it over. "I give it to you, Pastor. Donnelly Jr. agreesh."

When Elijah began to protest, Mother Meadows said. "Shon, don't waste my little time being modest. Greater Bethany needs funds, and this here will provide a good deal of what you need. A developer wants to buy this land. Let him make an offer, then take it from there. This ish why I couldn't go before now." She chuckled, unafraid of dying. "I had to get you here, for you, *and* for me. Now I need you to come on back tomorra. My son, the attorney, and the notary will be here to make the transfer legal."

Elijah didn't know what to say. Therefore, he simply bent. As he had when he'd been a boy, he kissed Mother Meadows' hands. Then Elijah simply rested his head on those hands. Tears flowed from beneath his closed eyelids. *Oh my God, my wonderful God*, Elijah thought. *Isn't this just like you? I believed this visit was for her, but instead, you orchestrated it* for ME, *your humble but unworthy servant.*

"You shtop that now," Mother Meadows fussed, gently patting her Pastor's huge handsome head. "Ever'body needs shomebody to do shomething for them now 'n again." She kept patting, as without her teeth she softly spoke. "Don't fret now baby. Jest get back here tomorra at ten, and make this official—whether I'm here or I've passed on."

With a hankie drawn from a pocket, Elijah dabbed his eyes. He pulled himself together too, just enough so that he could pray. Then outside Mother Meadows' room, he bid her son adieu. Walking quickly, Elijah nodded at Nurse Sheila and Sister Tallulah. Lula had been Greater Bethany's Minister of Music until a year ago. She'd resigned to focus on college and work, Elijah recalled, hastening onto the hospital elevator.

Inside, alone, Elijah became emotional. His shoulders heaved, and the big man leaned an arm against the metal wall. Overcome, with gratitude, he rested his aching head on his raised arm. He let the storm take him. He shook with the force of his tears because the Lord was incredible. Just when Elijah had thought he could go no further, his savior heard his prayer and had sent His servant some help.

CAREFULLY, he climbed the snow-crammed steps of the big old Victorian. As he unlocked the door and heard the squeaky hinges, he felt unbelievably happy. Elijah was *home*. Tonight there was heat too, such little that it was; guess Naomi had been able to pay their too high oil bill.

In the dark, when he finally got into his blue pajamas, he looked over at her. She was bundled in their big bed. Heaven knew Elijah loved that woman. In all the years they'd been together, Naomi had never really made a fuss about anything—Well, nothing other than Topaz, their daughter. Elijah thought of Naomi as peace personified.

In the moonlight, with his head and throat feeling furiously afire, he fumbled around in the medicine cabinet. Glancing out the window, Elijah realized. Lunar light, reflected off the new blanket of snow outside. That was why the unlit bathroom seemed so bright.

In bed, Naomi heard. *Pills* in a bottle. She knew that sound. "Lijah?"

"Hey," Elijah said when she padded in on tiny vintage tiles. "Hey. "

"You sick?" Naomi glanced up, belting her robe. Illness, she knew, was the only reason her husband would ever take anything.

"Head hurts." He removed the aspirin bottle cap, "Throat hurts too."

She tapped his arm, her non-verbal signal for step aside. Elijah did. When Naomi used an elegant finger to point, he sat on the commode lid.

Ahhh, that felt so nice, Elijah thought when his wife placed her cool hands on his face. She felt his glands and touched his forehead. "You've got a fever, alright." She rinsed and slipped a thermometer in his mouth. Gently she pinched his lips closed. "Let's see what we're up to." Getting a glass of water, she set it down. She shook aspirin into his hand. Moments later, Naomi removed the thermometer and squinted.

Elijah chuckled. "You never used to do that before."

She glanced down at him. "What?"

"Squinch up your eyes. *I* do it now, too. Guess we're getting old."

"You're up to 101," she said, offering him a homeopathic cold/flu remedy. "And like it or not, we're gonna be grandparents. We *are* old."

Oh. Elijah swallowed. Nae sounded like she'd gotten used to the idea.

She pulled at the robe that revealed cleavage. "Gargle with this. In a bit, we'll see if we need the doctor." Naomi turned—and felt Elijah's arms slip around her from behind. She spoke, patting his hands at her waist. "Lemme go, hon. I –um, gotta make you something hot to drink."

"Nae, wait." Elijah did not release her. "I just wanna hold you for a minute." Still seated, he rested his head on her ample behind. "I like you like this, baby, all plush and thick." So badly did he want her. He didn't care what anybody said, not even Cozi Moon. "I ever tell you that?"

"No..." Tears assailed, and Naomi told herself to breathe because Elijah had shocked her. He did so again by asking, "Remember when we were good together?" He pressed his face into her terry robe at the cleft of her buttocks. He made growly noises as though he would eat her up.

Despite herself, Naomi giggled and remembered the sexy Elijah of their youth. "Seems like you trying to get frisky with me, Preacher."

Elijah chuckled as he snuck a hand into her robe. He caressed soft skin. "Baby, I *wish*."

Naomi patted the large hands roaming her tummy and her nudity beyond. With her eyes darting from side to side, she wondered. Was that little flutter *desire*? Did she suddenly *want* this man, after all they had been through? And despite all in which they were yet embroiled?

No, that could not be; Naomi shook her head because…Elijah was sick. And she and he had not slept together in ages. Sure, they rested and rose from the same bed, but…nothing. Until now.

Naomi had once loved getting into it with Elijah, but now? No. She hadn't a clue who he'd been with, perhaps even earlier this evening. However, with him being slightly ill, he hadn't showered and didn't smell unfamiliar. Then again, knowing him, he *had* likely been out, as usual, seeing about somebody. That, the preacher did most often.

Relaxing, Naomi realized it was nice to allow Elijah to hold her. It was nice that he wanted to. It was something they hadn't done in forever.

Elijah spoke from behind. Then he stood. Towering over Naomi, he gathered her into his massive arms, despite her protests. "You know I love you. Right, Nae?" He nuzzled her nape, as wrapped in his embrace, she felt *him* pressed to her backside. He opened her robe front, liking that no clothes were beneath. Curved around her, his fingers slid within her.

Naomi gasped, admitting, "You love me, Lijah, in your way."

He snorted, sort of a chuckle and not. "You love me too, woman."

She squeezed the hand that opened her secret gate. "I do," she divulged, feeling his male organ enlarge behind her. "In my way, I do."

"Then that's good enough for us." Elijah needed to know, "Isn't it?"

Naomi didn't answer. Shallowly, she breathed and rode a wave of ecstasy provided by Elijah. Then she patted her husband's arms. "Let me go now. I've got things to do, for you. Oh, and there's gas money on the dresser. Lunch money's in the highboy, second drawer if you need it."

Elijah squeezed his wife tighter, again making her mewl because Lord knew he needed what she offered. "Thank you, babe." Reluctantly releasing her, he asked, "Is what we have not good enough for us, Nae?"

Untangling herself, Naomi left the lunar-lit bathroom. "I don't know Lijah." Overcome with desire, she told the truth. "I'm really not sure."

AFTER drinking hot tea and steaming beef consommé, Elijah lay in bed beside Naomi. He felt nonsensically happy. His throat and head no longer hurt, and Naomi slept, nude, in the moonlight. What a gift! Propped up, Elijah's eyes and hand traced her plush curves—the way they never did when she was awake. Cupping her heavy breast as snow fell outside, Elijah wished three things. One, that lovely Naomi had never had female troubles. Leaning to suck a tit, he wanted to bury his rod within her. Elijah also felt her problems had led to many losses; his and her children, intimacy, and *her*. He had essentially lost his wife to female woes. Wanting his mouth and his lapping tongue between her v, the second thing Elijah wished was that he had been smart enough to not get caught up. Now he knew. For years, Eve had plotted. Back when she and her husband had counseling, she'd set him up. Elijah wished he had been faithful, to God, and to Naomi. He felt like such a sinner. Sure, he'd walked circumspectly three hundred and sixty-four days out of the year. However, on the three hundredth and sixty-fifth, he'd succumbed.

Down through the years, he'd counseled drug addicts, prostitutes, drunkards, and others. Sometimes they remained clean for as long as he had. But some took tumbles. Yet without anyone judging them, they often got back up on the wagon. That, Elijah felt, he could not do. He felt as though his sins were worse than those of others. He knew people would feel the same way because *he* was the preacher. In their minds, he was not supposed to sin. In people's minds, *he* was more. He was just a man though, saved by grace, like any other man.

On an elbow, Elijah stared into Naomi's lovely face. Unable to resist, he leaned over and kissed her. Elijah recalled his third and futile wish. How he would have loved it if the Topaz thing had never occurred. It caused him to lay awake at night, simply because he wanted *more* for his precious daughter. She felt like he'd rebuked her, but he hadn't, not really. Elijah just didn't want Taupe to struggle as an unwed mother. *That* was why he'd said no baby. He was trying to give her a chance. He also thought if she had no baby, then she wouldn't yet be a woman. She'd still be *his* baby. Then *he* would be given another chance to be a better father. Elijah knew he hadn't really been there while his golden-eyed girl was growing up. He had the type of job—a calling really—that kept a man busy, and away from those he loved most.

If he'd hugged his kid more and had spent more time with her than he had with all the kids who mostly saw him as the preacher, maybe things would be different. That got Elijah thinking. He pressed his rod against the curvaceous body he craved. Wrapping Naomi with an arm, he realized. Now, he had the same worries for the boy whose name was like his. Elisha. Now he worried about the kid he called Eli.

Unlike his conniving mother, Eve, the small boy had a sweet spirit.

Elijah tried to spend as much time with the kid as possible. However, the father often felt conflicted because he had to do so away from prying eyes, away from the fishbowl in which he and his family lived. Elijah had to sneak to see his kid. That meant most of the time, he had to see the boy at his mother's home. That was just what Eve wanted. She wanted to pretend they were a happy little family. She wanted Elijah to service her too. Often he refused because, really, he wanted Naomi. Eve became loud and shrewish. She sometimes frightened him. Elijah didn't know what she was capable of or what she would try next to get her way.

As his hand meandered over his sleeping wife, Elijah remembered Eve saying she wanted him to recognize her son, "As your own."

He'd said, "You know I can't do that, not before the people."

Eve had become enraged, yet she'd managed not to yell, a pastime of hers. "Why not? You're human. People need to know it." She'd said, "They need to stop thinking you're a little god. You have a life, too."

Elijah shook his head. "People will know I made a mistake."

Eve had become furious. She'd yowled that Elijah thought of her and her son as mistakes. "We're blemishes on your otherwise 'perfect' record, huh? Well, too bad. You can't have your cake 'n eat it too!"

Asleep, Naomi moaned, and Elijah realized he had always hated that 'cake' saying. Fingering the woman who widened her thighs for her dream bureaucrat, Elijah abhorred thinking it. Still, Eve honestly had him by the balls. True, Elijah wanted a son, but he hadn't wanted his son this way, outside his marriage. He'd wanted all of his children with Naomi. Any number of times, he had even thought she'd been pregnant, but guess he'd been wrong. Guess amid everything between them, he'd pickled things, just as Abraham had, in the bible. Abraham was a man who'd slept with the woman that worked for his wife. Becoming pregnant, the worker woman bore Abraham a son. There Abraham and

Elijah's stories differed. Abraham had been able to acknowledge his boy, publicly. Elijah might never be able to do that. First, because it would devastate Naomi. He knew how much she'd wanted a son, *his* son. He would never forget; she had been ecstatic while carrying his seed…but everything had gone so wrong. Then she'd let the doctor take her insides. Yet more had been taken, Elijah believed. He kept fingering her, and sleeping, Naomi moaned, wondering why her dream man now resembled Elijah. He mused on how more than Naomi's female parts were gone. Part of her, her essence, was too. She didn't seem to mourn that loss, just the baby. Elijah regretted losing *Naomi*, as she had been, smart, a bit tart, sexy, and so laid back.

Getting dream-state Naomi good and wet, Elijah further contemplated the other reason he wasn't like the bible's Abraham, the man who'd had a son outside his marriage. For Elijah's situation, the church was not ready. Sure, these types of things happened to other people, but they weren't supposed to happen *to the preacher.* Elijah wondered if it would tear up the work. And he had labored so hard and long to get 'here.'

He breathed harder. Desperate to sensually glide into Naomi, Elijah knew he'd be called an adulterer, which he was. Lying in bed, he scrubbed a hand over his stubbly face. Again he wondered, how had he become so entangled? At Forty-five, he should have known better. For years, he had walked circumspectly. He had tried to be righteous. Now all he'd worked for, and all that he had taught others, could be unraveled with a word. All that dang Eve had to say was: her son was his.

She practically already had. All she had to do was seem forlorn too, and she could amass sympathy. Elijah could be ruined. Then again, all people had to find out was that *Topaz* was having a baby, and they would look at Elijah funny. He was supposed to manage his household. Elijah sighed because it was all too much. He had bills up the kazoo. The church, and the money pit in which he lived, drained him. He wasn't frivolous, nor did he live above his means. He had simply inherited debt.

Elijah massaged the colossal hard-on he wished sexy Naomi would ride. At the same time he used his other hand to make her moan. Within her body, he could forget his troubles, for a while. But Nah. If he stayed in bed, he'd wind up *in* Naomi. They might fight –or not; Elijah didn't know. So he rose, before he did something he'd regret. Well, something more to add to his list of regrets. In the bathroom, choking the chicken, the big man asked himself, was he really cut out for this holy business?

Chapter 32

TOPAZ was in labor. While walking her round and round their little home, Petunia spoke. "My friend Jessica says this will get the baby into position and lessen the pain."

Continuing to waddle, Topaz held her throbbing back. Every so often, she stopped to catch her breath and ride out the next contraction. Yet, they weren't coming close enough to get in the car and pop up the road to the hospital. The time was nearing though, both women knew it.

Topaz was terrified and somehow excited. She was ready-ish. This was what she'd wanted for the last month. She had grown tired of the beach ball that replaced her flat stomach. It was uncomfortable. During the past four days, she'd fervently prayed for it to be time. Now it was.

She only wished Cedric could be with her. Topaz wished she'd told him. He would have taken off to be with her. Yet what if he hadn't? She'd have felt worse than she did now. Therefore, she guessed, she had done right. At least she hoped so. Topaz knew that when Cedric found out, he would be pissed—to say the least. He'd want to know why she'd kept it a secret. She hoped he would understand. Then again, how could he, when some of this had been forced on her? Heck, even she didn't understand some of what she was experiencing.

Topaz cried out. She stopped thinking and walking. Bending, she clutched her midsection. "Oh, Aunt Pet, let's go!" Topaz eyed the immediate warm splash on her feet. It soaked her pants. "What the...?"

"Going's a good idea," the little woman sang out. She grabbed a woolen hat, in June. "Bag's in the car, so come, honey!"

Despite the pains, coming faster now, Topaz nearly laughed. Her aunt was darling. If Topaz had to leave her baby with anyone, it would be plucky little Petunia. Soon, Topaz thought, she would meet Baby.

NAOMI was seriously fretting. She couldn't be with her daughter. Elijah had made her miss her flight! He hadn't picked her up on time! He had been up at the hospital. She thought he'd seen Mother Meadows. Now, at the airline counter, Elijah silently seethed because the girl in the blue jacket with the airline logo said there was a change fee.

Elijah wondered why Blue Jacket looked at *him. He* wasn't going anywhere, and Lord knew he didn't have money. The fee would have to come from Naomi. She worked. She was the one determined to go down south for the birth of a baby that no one wanted. Well, his daughter wanted the baby that some parishioner would undoubtedly call a bastard.

Elijah watched as Naomi dug into her purse. He didn't allow his eyes to widen as she pulled out a gold credit card. Where had she gotten that? And when? Why had she kept it secret? He was her husband.

He shook away the notion that he, too, had a few secrets. It wasn't like he, the preacher, could tell Naomi everything, even though she was his wife. He had to adhere to the preacher/parishioner code of confidentiality. For a thing he'd just made up, it sounded good. Elijah forgot things he kept from Naomi. Most of it would do her no good to know. It would cause problems. They needed no more of those. He watched her take the receipt. She wasn't upset, but Nae had to know. Nobody would be wasting time or money had Topaz not been fast.

Unaware of her husband's surly thoughts, but feeling their negative energy, all the same, Naomi only wanted to get on the plane. She wanted away from Tranquility and the man who acted like she was impinging on his time and keeping him from more important things. Not looking at Elijah, Naomi waved him toward his old Impala. She said he needn't spend extra money—always his worry—on parking.

Readily agreeing, as she had known he would, Elijah pecked Naomi on the cheek. She watched him hasten away, his massive shoulders wide. She turned too, heading for her gate. Had she not had her daughter on her mind, she might have been bothered by Elijah's seeming indifference. Yet Naomi forgot him and the most erotic dream she'd had, involving him. She sighed, wondering if she would ever get used to being married and alone. Naomi wondered, too, did she really *want* Elijah sexually again. Or was it just last night and that dream? It had seemed too real. When she'd awakened, Elijah had been in the bathroom. She had been sopping wet.

Taking a seat, Naomi thought of another loved one. Topaz. Wonder if she would be glad for the presence of her mother.

Lord knew, Naomi opined, her *husband* had seemed all too eager to depart from her presence.

Chapter 33

TWENTY minutes later, Elijah parked at a parishioner's house. The appointment was why he'd had to hurriedly leave his wife. Then inside the house, he had the hardest time reconciling. The atrophied girl in the bed was his *daughter's* age. Instead of sixteen, the child looked like a ravaged old woman. At death's door, the teen whispered that she had grown weary of fighting a degenerative disease.

Elijah's heart stuttered when a thought crossed his mind. Topaz would soon give birth. Yet as little as was said about it, young women, the world over, still died in childbirth every day. Seated in the straight-backed chair beside young Linda's bed, Elijah knew the girl's end neared. Still, Linda made light-hearted banter. It was what her pastor would not forget, her quick wit. Thank God that hadn't deserted her.

Elijah looked up and into the pained eyes of Linda's mother. He saw the grief-stricken face of her father. Then Elijah's gaze fell on her brothers. *How* the family needed the comfort of the Holy Spirit. Taking the waif's hand, now mostly bone, the preacher said he would pray.

"Pastor," Linda managed, in a weak voice, "I really am ready to go. Would you pray—please, that God would take me soon? Tonight, even. Oh, and pray for my family. They don't need this grief anymore."

Feeling utter compassion for young Linda and for the loved ones who suffered with her, Elijah nodded. Softly petitioning Heaven with Linda's request, Elijah asked for endurance and peace, until the heavenly Father saw fit to make little Linda a beautiful being of light.

Pastor Moon asked that the angels of the Lord would comfort the family members who would remain. Upon concluding the prayer, Elijah stood. However, not before he bent to place his lips on the girl's forehead. She should have been preparing to go to college, instead of planning to die. Some life things the preacher would never understand.

There were tears in his eyes because Linda could have been *his* child! Aware of that truth, Elijah felt a wave of longing. He ached for Topaz, his super-talented, intelligent, sometimes sassy, golden-eyed girl. On the day she'd been born, she had grabbed hold of his heart and had never let go. Now she was having her own baby.

Dashing away tears, Elijah hugged Linda's family. Her father, a short bull of a man, broke down and sobbed. In the small room, Elijah embraced him. "Thanks for coming, Rev," the bull man's oldest son nodded as his father tried to pull himself together.

At that moment, like a freight train, realization slammed into Elijah. *He* had lost sight of what was important! *Family* was important, more so than their mistakes or what others might say in judgment.

Releasing Linda's brother, a mini bull, the preacher had another thought. God knew that he, Elijah Moon, had made more than his share of mistakes. Still, *he* had time to get some things right. Maybe.

Leaving the grieving Bull family, Elijah recalled the situation in which he currently found himself. The Eve Situation. It was not unlike the one in which his daughter found herself.

Seated in his long-nosed, old, burgundy Impala, outside Linda's home, Elijah shed tears. He really was becoming a big ole crybaby, he thought. Yet his tears fell for the young woman who would be gone, possibly within hours. Elijah shed tears for his own daughter, too. That young woman believed he didn't care a thing about her or her wants.

Suddenly, Elijah could see, through the water in his eyes, that petite Topaz Tiara Moon had needed him as much as little Linda needed her family. Now with a pricked heart, Elijah saw that that he hadn't been there, again, for his golden-eyed girl. He realized it was because he had deemed her ensnared.

Oh, Lord. Topaz's missteps may have been her own, but they weren't all that different from his. *That* bothered Elijah the most.

Could he say fraud? Because, as he put his car in gear, that was what he felt like, a giant fraud, a phony. "Father God," Elijah prayed aloud, "how am I to get any of this right? When it seems, I keep making mistake after mistake."

Then Elijah heard the still, small voice.

It's not by power, nor by might, but it's by my spirit...

"Then help me," Elijah moaned as he drove. "*Please*, Holy Spirit."

Chapter 34

AFTER Naomi had seen her daughter *and* her grandson, she couldn't wait to call Elijah. He was still the first person with whom she wanted to share everything. Figure that out. Thus, when she got back to her aunt's charming little house, Naomi dialed. She said, "The baby's a boy. His name is Ar-MOND, spelled A-R-M-A-N-D, and—"

Elijah wanted to know one thing. "When are you two coming back?"

"Well…" Naomi had to tell him the rest. "You know the ladies, and I decided that Taupe would stay here a few months—"

"A few months!" Elijah interrupted. "No. That is unacceptable."

"We discussed this," Naomi rebuffed, feeling her joy dissipate.

"*We* did not. You may have chewed it over with all the old biddies in your life, but *you and I* didn't discuss that. I'd never have agreed."

"Be that as it may, Lijah, I told you. Now I'm telling you, again, that after having a baby, a woman has to get back on track."

"We're talking about Topaz here."

"Yes, we are." Naomi sighed, "And you have to get used to the fact that she is no longer your little girl. She is a woman, now. If you saw her, you'd know. Something in her is different."

"Later for that," Elijah huffed. "Just tell me. When'll y'all be back?"

"*I* won't be back for a while. Remember, you told me to take off. I put in for it on my job, so I'll remain here. Pet and I are going visiting."

"And while you're cavorting," he snarled, "what about my daughter?"

"Um." Naomi knew she sounded stupid. "Your daughter is in love with her son. Taupe said," Naomi quickly stated, "she's not returning."

Elijah could have spit fire. "What?!" He needed that girl to run the music department! He nearly said so before he caught himself. That wouldn't go over well, so Elijah managed not to growl. "What the devil do you mean, my girl is not returning? This is her home."

"I said that to her, and Lijah, she said it is not. She said it never has been. She said Mother See's house is more her home." Naomi shook her head. "There's no way we're going to wrestle that baby away from her, and I don't want to. He's hers. I'm going to help her raise him."

"She's spoiled. Since you're the mama, make her turn him loose."

"As *the mama*," Naomi cut in, softly but firmly, "I will not make another mother cut loose—as you call it. My daughter has rights, too."

"And *you* know what *I* said, Naomi. No babies in *this* house."

"Elijah, I have gone this far along with you, but I'll go no further." Naomi began to sound exasperated. Involuntarily, she reached for her purse, seeking her pills. "Topaz said she's not coming back, so what you gonna do, big man? Fly down here and make her?"

Something within Elijah turned over then. Naomi sounded indomitable and like she taunted him. Like the old Naomi.

Elijah realized his daughter was just like her. If they'd both fallen for this baby, how could he control them? Elijah did not know, and he began to have heart palpitations. They came on all too swiftly nowadays. Therefore, he abruptly told his wife he'd speak to her later. All of this had become too much.

"What does that mean; we'll speak later?"

Elijah clutched his chest, really needing Naomi with him through the frightening, angry hammering. But she was away. "Means," he choked out, "got – to – go." Silently he prayed, *Lord, help.*

"Elijah!" Naomi called because he hadn't sounded right. "You okay?" No answer. She stared at the phone. He was gone. Immediately, the preacher's wife prayed, because, from Petunia's house in the south, Naomi could fix nothing back in Tranquility.

"Lord, keep my stubborn man. Please."

Naomi also got a glass of water. After downing a pill, she hoped her family would come to an agreement, sooner than later. It needed to be beneficial for all, yet in the realm of possibility, Naomi could not see it.

IN his home office, Elijah fell onto his big leather chair. Naomi had found it for him at one of her 'junk' stores. Elijah was aware that he needed to see his doctor. The knocking in his chest was worsening by the week. He had too much on him. Elijah tried not to stress about things, but that wasn't his way. He prayed, but at each turn, the walls seemed to close in. Many things seemingly squeezed and suffocated him.

Elijah, too, had pills. He'd gotten them a while ago from the family physician. He'd never taken them, though, because Elijah didn't want to become dependent, like Nae. Now *his* heart meds had probably expired.

Suddenly, in the big empty house, Elijah felt like a prisoner. It was a cage of his own making. Elijah thought about spending time with the boy whose name was similar to his. It was Elijah's attempt at relaxing. He liked the plush headrest on this nice chair. Thinking about something safe allowed him to calm down. As he slowly massaged his chest, Elijah recalled how he had always wanted a son. Now, the more time he spent with little Eli, the more pronounced that desire became.

In a way, Elijah really wished he could acknowledge the boy. Then he would be free to be a Dad to Elisha, perhaps an even a better one to Eli than he had been to Topaz. –Now, *there* was a problem if Elijah had ever had one; Topaz Tiara Moon; Elijah needed that girl. And she wasn't coming back, to him, or to Greater Bethany. The preacher had to think. He was doing something wrong, but what?

Uh-oh. His heart began to jackhammer again.

Massaging his chest with one hand, Elijah used the other to cover his eyes. He prayed the longstanding prayer that he had often prayed for Naomi –with little or no results. Stubborn Elijah prayed it anyway. *Lord, make her willing.* He prayed it for little Miss Inflexible too.

Then he prayed differently, this time selfless. He asked for a *solution*.

F̲AR from her, Cedric thought about Topaz. He'd heard that she was away. Well, good, she was someplace learning, preparing for life ahead, like he was. But why could he not get her off his mind? Maybe he should call her. She had been staying in his head, even while he slept. Cedric had dreamed Baybay was sad. Maybe she was just missing him. He sure missed her. Perhaps he could cheer Bay up when he called. He'd tell her all the sexy things he'd been thinking about her.

But nah, Cedric second-thought, wherever cute Bay was, she needed to concentrate, right? Never mind that he couldn't because he kept imagining her, in all her naked, copper-skinned glory.

That night, Cedric promised himself he might call. Even if he didn't, he would definitely dream of Bay, of sliding into her tight little sheath. In his dream, there would be no condom, either. He and Babybay would screw the way they had in the past, just raw-doggin' it. *Ahhh…*

Nope. Cedric caught his horny self. He reminded himself. Slip-sliding bareback was how babies got made. And neither he nor Topaz needed that. Not now. Right?

Chapter 35

AFTER her baby's birth, Topaz could see so many things. Now she wanted different things out of life. One of those things was: no more foolishness.

When her big blustery father received the message that she would not return, he'd called, telling her mother, "Lemme speak to my daughter."

While changing the infant boy that she'd named Armand Cedric Stable, Topaz refused. She was busy. She recalled why she had given her son his father's name. She wanted Cedric acknowledged. Chances were, too, her own father would never see her son's birth certificate.

Refusing to relinquish the line, Elijah told Naomi to ask Topaz to reconsider returning to New York. Holding the phone, Naomi said, "Taupe, he's not yelling." Naomi smirked, "Your Dad asked nicely."

While lifting her son to rub his tiny back, Topaz said she would think about speaking later, which her mother promptly relayed.

That afternoon, while the baby slept, Topaz began a list. She wrote that if she didn't stay with Aunt Pet and enroll in school, she would need Greater Bethany to pay her. She now had her son to think about. She was also unwilling to accept pennies, fair wage, or no.

Topaz needed a title, not because she was power-hungry, but so she could get more done. No more people looking at her like, 'Who are you?' She wrote that she would no longer answer the monikers 'the preacher's kid,' 'the PK,' or 'Pastor's daughter.' She was Topaz T. Moon, *a person*, an individual, separate from the pastor in many ways.

Topaz was a mother now. She needed an assistant, one to whom she could designate duties. She'd need copies of songs, etcetera. She would also never go back to living like she had, as the GBBC slave girl.

In the wee hours, a little before her son's feeding, she called her father. As she dialed, she knew she would wake him, like his other parishioners did—if he was at home. She would do so because before she'd left, he had tried to treat her like a parishioner. Now she'd be one.

When he answered, sounding sleepy, she said, "Hello, Pastor Moon."

"Topaz…" It was so good to hear her voice! Big Elijah thought it but didn't think to say it. "Ev-everything okay, baby girl?" He felt awkward with his kid now. "How—how are you?"

"A few days ago, I gave birth to a baby. A boy," she stated, startling Elijah by admitting what he'd chosen to hide from. "That's how I am."

"I heard. Um... I hear he looks just like you did at that age."

"I guess." As soft-spoken as ever, Topaz now possessed a steely determination. Elijah Moon heard it as his daughter declared she could only return if stipulations were met. She'd faxed them.

In bed, Elijah sat up to listen. He nearly felt proud. Nae had been right. His baby was no longer a baby. Elijah was a bit annoyed, too, because Topaz didn't have to make a big deal. They were family.

However, that was why she did it. She didn't want to be taken advantage of, like in the past. She heard her son, her priority. Over his whimpers, she told her father, "I'll call you in two days. I'll see what you and the board come up with." *I love you, Daddy.* That, she'd wanted to say, but he'd have taken it as weakness. "Good night." She disconnected.

"THIS is the deal," Elijah told Topaz. Used to doing things his way, he'd had the hardest time waiting for her to get back to him. "Greater Bethany will pay." He named a figure for so many hours of work.

"Unacceptable." Her voice remained level. "Refer to my fax. The scope of work is outlined, so is my figure. It's fair. Yours is not." Topaz said when services were televised, renegotiation would be in order.

Elijah wanted to howl, but his daughter's no-nonsense attitude said she'd not brook his shenanigans. Therefore, he pouted. "Understood."

The sixteen-year-old took Elijah through her list, point by point. They agreed or disagreed. "Return to your trustees," she advised, knowing how it worked. "Get back to me. Not at 2 a.m. That's my son's time."

Oh, that was how she wanted to play it? "Well," Elijah huffed, "I'll have Sister Eve," the church administrator, "get back to you."

"No. You will not," Topaz softly stated. "No minions. I deal with you." She recalled an essay and a paper. Their deadlines loomed. "Touch base Friday." The young mother dismissed her father, "Godspeed."

On his end of the line, big Elijah laughed. His daughter was becoming a true, hard-nosed businessperson. And he liked it! Dealing with little Miss Reserved was worrisome. Still, it was turning into a chess match. It was *the* most *fun* he'd had in... Elijah could not remember when.

DAYS later, the Moons came to an agreement. Before parting, Elijah cleared his throat. "Uh, my jewel, lemme speak with your Mama..."

"She's not here. I'll ask her to return your call."

NAOMI wanted to scream, to rant and rave. She wanted to run, but she was out of shape. She didn't do cardio. No Jane Fonda either, so she'd probably have a heart attack. Therefore, she sought her purse and her pills. Anxious, with shaking hands, she emptied some onto her palm.

What had Elijah done, and why did he allow such foolishness?

Because it involved Cozi Moon, Naomi thought, downing Lexapro Oral. Naomi had told Mother See that she'd scale back, but she needed her pills, now more than ever. These were for all the mental/mood fluctuations brought on by outside circumstances—no, by Elijah Moon.

Naomi placed a hand at her mouth. She wondered how to tell Topaz. Not about the pills, but about what Elijah had said. Their young woman was not going to like it. Topaz might even call off the deal that she and Elijah had so tenuously struck. She *had* been up at the college, checking it out, so who knew what Topaz would do? Things between father and daughter were strained, but Naomi had to tell Taupe. In Petunia's cute guestroom, Naomi slid beneath the cover. Pulling it over her head, she needed to hide out for a bit. Then she would get up. She'd do what she had since marrying Hurricane Elijah. Naomi would brave the storm.

"WHAT do you mean?" Topaz stood in the small solarium. Upset, she stared out into the gathering dark. More foolishness. She didn't notice fireflies. Topaz thought about the woman who had never been a real grandmother to anyone. "So, she actually said that..."

Naomi nodded. According to Elijah, his mother had church members believing their first lady was in 'the family way.'

Naomi remembered when Cozi had started that rumor. It had been about the time that Naomi had begun to gain her current weight, back when Topaz announced *she* was pregnant.

Topaz had only told three people—her mom, Mother See, and tall, slender Caley. Since Topaz had been quickly hustled away, Cozi had not known a thing. She had only seen the results of Naomi's worry.

At the time, Naomi had dismissed Cozi's jawboning as harmless, although it never had been. Now, seeing how damaging Cozi's words were, was infuriating.

"So GBBC believes you're with *your* family." Topaz was livid. "Supposedly, they're caring for *you* while you have *my father's baby.*" Saying it sickened Topaz. She gazed off into the thicket and the dark. "Who would believe that?"

"Some people," Naomi spoke like it was rational, but she too felt ill. "They'll believe because they want to." Her life had begun to feel like a foul play, and the plot kept thickening. Naomi wanted no more drama.

She had never been a liar, of that she had reminded her husband. She even asked him to recall her hysterectomy.

"You and I," he pointed out, "are not the ones telling lies."

"Semantics," Naomi rebuffed. "*We're* not lying, but we stretched the truth when we sent Topaz away. Now we're expected to go along with this other stuff?" Naomi's body convulsed. Cozi Moon's prevaricated pregnancy/fat mess was too much.

"I can't call it back." On the phone, Naomi couldn't see Elijah shrug, but she imagined him doing so. "Just go along, Nae, for Topaz's sake."

For *his* sake, Naomi thought, recalling that conversation. She forced out, "Topaz, you're a woman now, so I can speak plainly. I'on't like this shit, or the way your father said, 'This can work to our advantage.'"

Topaz frowned. Rocking sweet infant Armand, Petunia averted her eyes. "He meant," Topaz blurted, "Grandmother's lies can work to *his* advantage." The young mother turned away. "I can't believe him, or her. Then again, I can. It's always about them. That's how this goes."

Naomi nodded because she understood her husband far better than anyone. Therefore, she acknowledged, "You're right. Elijah can ask us to go along because it suits *him*. I'm tired of going along. If we do this, your father gets what *he* wants. He gets *you* back. You'll run the GBBC music department, and he'll go on TV. He'll get me back, too. It will look like his wife has returned, and she wasn't a pig, after all. In his mind, his mother simply validated me, the chubster. But, he stated, amidst, you'll get to bring your baby back. Your father didn't fail to mention that. He knows it's the only way you'll return; if you can bring Army."

Topaz looked at her beautiful baby, resting in Petunia's arms. "But it'll all be a lie! I'm no actor—and what about when Armand starts talking? Do I teach him to lie too?" Topaz plopped into a rattan chair.

"I named that baby Armand," she softly revealed, churning with indignation, "because it means strong. I gave him his father's last name because it also means strong—war leader—and stable. When I gave my baby those names, I didn't know he would need strength or stability so soon." Topaz could no longer control herself. She yelled. "*I* have lived lies! I don't want that for my child."

Topaz squeezed her hands together. She wanted to pull something apart. She looked over at her tiny son in her great aunt's arms. "*I* am his mother," Topaz stated. "I don't want to pretend otherwise." Nor did she want to go back to the fishbowl, she suddenly realized. Topaz looked up at her mother. "*I* am Armand's mom."

It broke Naomi's heart when her daughter's lower lip trembled, just like it had when she'd been a golden-eyed girl.

"I just may stay here." The young woman sounded resigned. "Aunt Pet and I discussed it. With my accelerated classes, I'll finish high school early. I can apply for both enrollment and work at the college. It'll be hard. I'll even have to apply for the college's daycare program. Yeah, and let somebody I don't know keep my baby.

"But back at GBBC," Topaz stated, "I have a sure position, one where I'll do what I love. I'll be paid what I choose. In Tranquility, Mother See will keep Armand, and I can graduate with honors. I can go to the college of my choosing.

"So maybe you can see, this is my dilemma." Using her hands, Topaz mimed a scale. "Here, I'd have to scratch out an existence. In Tranquility, I'd have seemingly everything, *except* I'd have to live *a lie* to keep what's rightfully mine."

Topaz quickly covered her tear-filled eyes.

Naomi was ashamed of her husband for even placing them in this predicament. "Taupe," she sighed, "we're just real people, with a real situation. It's why *I* want to go back and tell the truth."

Chapter 36

BEFORE she'd given birth to Armand, Topaz had vowed not to return to Tranquility, or to GBBC. Yet it was September, and there she was, on the organ, with her eyes wide open.

Topaz nodded at regal Mother See, holding her three-month-old. The baby got many looks, wearing a tiny, blue serge suit that displayed his chubby legs.

There had been dozens of comments, too, the first Sunday back at Greater Bethany. Most people had oohed-'n-ahhhed and remarked that Pastor Moon and Sister Naomi's small 'son' looked like a beautiful doll; he looked just like 'his sister.' It had nearly made Topaz sick. Ever watchful, she'd itched to snatch her son from her mother. Not because Naomi wasn't good with him, but Topaz had ached to shield Armand from prying eyes, even as she fielded questions about her preparatory training. Topaz did so while willing Mother See to cover the baby in Naomi's arms. Topaz did not know how to keep up the pretense, so she resorted to saying nothing. She just allowed people to think she was lost in her music. It seemed Mother read Topaz's mind and covered the baby.

This day, on the organ seat, Topaz realized. She had always seen a multitude of things. But she hadn't really paid attention. She wondered why. As her father preached, Topaz dragged her eyes away from Armand's curly head. She didn't want to appear as Cedric had once said; longing. But *how* Topaz longed to hold the baby who was now trying to keep his little head up. She longed to be back with Aunt Pet, in the safe cocoon of her cozy little home. There, Topaz could have cradled her baby to her breast. She'd have derived comfort from his warm little body pressed to hers. Since she couldn't, Topaz looked around.

Some female parishioners were obvious, Topaz now realized, when before, she'd not noticed. Those women's attraction to religion was *sexual* because of Topaz's father.

Taking a good look, Topaz acknowledged that The Right Reverend Elijah Moon was massive and robustly built. He appeared patently virile, a man who naturally exuded sensuality. With his smooth brown skin and good looks, it flowed from him in many ways; in the silken slide of his husky voice, and the fluid way he moved his large hands, adorned by both a wedding band and his seminary class ring. He captured attention.

Watching certain women, Topaz knew they thought of her father's hands, moving over them. Topaz knew because she'd often thought of Cedric's hands the same way. He had even admitted to thinking the same, in reverse. Cedric said he did so while watching her fingers. When they traipsed across the classic Hammond's waterfall keys and its pre-set panel. Cedric had ogled her shapely legs and feet, too, as they'd moved over the bass pedals. He said he had even imagined Topaz on him, the same way women in Greater Bethany's congregation undoubtedly imagined Pastor Moon on them.

Topaz forgot Cedric, whom she had not seen or spoken to in months. She guessed he had moved on. Her life was so full, though, that she couldn't dwell on it. As a new mom, she had the added pressure of being accepted to the internationally recognized Manhattan School of Music.

Making melody, the new Minister of Music forced her thoughts back to her father. As a preacher, he was so much more. Why had she not seen it before? Big sexy Moon was an actor, an orator, and a performer, all rolled into one. He involuntarily projected masculinity, and luridly so.

Topaz also noticed classic frenzy, when he got to the high point in a message. Then came the shouts, the struts, the pleas, and the hoarse invocation. And on the organ, *she* was Moon's accomplice. With her skill and talent, she heightened the mood in what she began to see as a dance. To Topaz, the dance was spasmodic and unpredictable, but it was also carefully choreographed. Her innumerable hours of practice, and all her father's hours of studying, writing, and rewriting proved that.

Like any love affair, Topaz realized, the whole dance exhibited exaggerated calm, in the beginning. That was when her father offered his text. He mentioned scripture and gave the title of his sermon. Then the affair built to a frenzied crescendo. It was a lot like sex.

Topaz watched, as doing 'the dance,' and staying true to the love affair credo, her father darted here and there, making use of the pulpit, his stage. She glanced at her fingers. They coaxed melody from the keys as he slapped the leather of his giant bible. She knew some women immediately envisioned him slapping their nude behinds.

Topaz played on, her part in the dance, as inwardly she wondered. Why did the saints often act as though they held disdain for one of the most basic human activities? Why did they often pretend that *sex* wasn't as much a part of life as eating or sleeping? If they could see what she saw, they would know. Sex and the dance that they and the preacher did each week were nearly the same.

Both the lover and his love, the preacher and the congregation—in the black church—heaved, perspired, labored, and ultimately trembled with ecstasy.

As many left the pews to head to the altar, Topaz knew some did just to be near their love, the big beautiful brown preacher.

Sure, her father had expounded on hellfire 'n brimstone. He'd claimed those things were the rewards of the flesh. For allowing lust to rule and getting caught up, a person would receive their 'reward.' Knowing what she now knew, Topaz played on and was aware of one thing. Big Pastor Moon was preaching, first and foremost, to *himself*.

He spoke of pincers and spirit beings, the djinn, and demons. He mentioned those who assumed human or animal form, while poking fire-hot pitchforks into the ripe flesh of sinful humans. Pastor Moon had to have had himself in mind. Was he being punished and tormented for lascivious behavior? Topaz did not want to know.

When her father said sex had been created for procreation and those united in holy matrimony, he could have been speaking to her. However, Topaz knew. Elijah Moon was most likely again talking to himself.

He claimed the bluesy music that made a person want to move was often that of the devil. He said if one listened for long, Satan would get his due; Satan would possess that person's body and mind through the music. When her father said that person would writhe and wriggle, before doing lewd and lustful things, Topaz had no doubt. Her father was reminding *himself* to walk circumspectly.

Topaz thought it fitting when her father asked her to end the service with the little song made famous by African-American hymnist Andraé Crouch.

Complying, Topaz opened her mouth and sweetly sang.
Always remember Jesus... Jesus.
Keep HIM on your mind.

Chapter 37

The late 1980's

ONE midweek morning, the Moon household was alive with the routine. There was running water, brewing coffee, and breakfast for Elijah, who sometimes fed the baby. This day Grandad got baby dressed. In the big old kitchen with the ugly linoleum—with which Naomi had learned to live—she reminded Elijah of things. He passed his grandson over. Kissing baby and Naomi, Elijah strode through the front door.

In her workday heels, slacks, and a nice blouse, Naomi grasped her travel mug. Reaching for her purse, she looked over at Lil Mama.

Bent, Topaz pulled a hat onto nine-month-old Armand's head. Hefting him from his high chair, repeatedly she kissed his pudgy face.

"Time to go, man," she said, settling him on her hip.

The women headed toward the back door, just as the house phone rang. About to pass it on the kitchen wall, Topaz said, "I'll get it."

Car keys in hand, Naomi took her grandson. "Ooh," she murmured, "Me-Maw's boy is getting big!" Exiting, Naomi kept cooing.

Topaz picked up the phone. "Hello?"

"Baybay."

Her heart stuttered, then did crazy little summersaults. "Ced..."

"Hey girl, I know you're busy, doing all kinds of morning stuff, but I wanted to catch you. I didn't believe I would, though. But I just wanted to say hey, you know?"

Topaz found her voice. "Hey you, Yella. It's been a long time."

"It has, but that don't stop me from thinking 'bout you."

He did? Topaz admitted, "I do the same." She didn't say it, but he really needed to know something, and it weighed on her.

"I know you gotta go, Bay, but I just wanted to hear your voice." Before she could reply, Cedric announced, "I hear you got a brother."

Topaz felt as though Cedric had dashed her with ice water. He'd gotten wind of that perpetration. Now, how was she to tell him? He'd think her contradiction was a lie. Feeling crestfallen, Topaz glanced at the clock. Cedric probably believed they'd simply grown apart. People often did while starting new lives, but he needed to know. That had not been the case. "Ced, we need to talk, but not now."

"Sure, Bay," he said, "Call you soon?" Unaware that anything was wrong, he revealed, "I'm in 'n out of town, but I'd love to see you."

She would love to see him too. Then tell him things, mainly the truth. Yet, none of that could Topaz say. So she remained silent, staring at the ugly floor. Sure, seeing Ced would be great, but doing so would make her ache, all over again, for him. It had taken her nearly a year to *almost* get him out of her system. Now, that fast, it seemed as though her world had brightened and dimmed, once more, because of him.

"Baybay, you there?"

"I am." Topaz's voice was softer than usual. "Call me any time, Ced."

His eyes narrowed because Bay didn't sound right. "I will." Despite how subdued she'd sounded, he felt it was a good day, simply because he had spoken to her. Before he rang off, Cedric just had to tell her.

"I'll never not love you, you know."

"I feel the same." Although she felt deflated –defeated really– she softly said, "Kisses." She hung up before either could say more.

Behind her, Topaz closed the old Victorian's back door. Descending the stairs, she didn't see the morning sun rising. Nor did she smell earth fresh with the promise of spring. The young mother didn't feel wild winds or notice them blowing her thick lengthy hair. She only felt empty as she opened the rear of her mother's idling car. She stowed her baby's gear, purse, and books. Quickly she checked the baby seat, always a precaution. In front, as a passenger, she slumped.

Driving, Naomi glanced over. "Who was on the phone?" When Topaz didn't reply, Naomi called her. "Lil Mama. You okay?"

With eyes on the sun-splashed windshield, Topaz nodded. "That was an old friend." They pulled up before a house more familiar than their own. Unbuckling herself, Topaz thought, that had been her *lover*.

Opening her front door, silver-haired Mother See took Armand. Then her eyes narrowed. "You're not okay…are you, Lil Mama?"

It was the second time she had been asked that. When she looked up at her grandma, Topaz's golden eyes, Old Preacher's eyes, shone with tears. "My heart is splintering, Mother. All – over – again."

The silver-haired woman surmised. "You…spoke to this baby's daddy." She took her great-grandson's necessities.

Topaz watched Armand try to pry open the older woman's mouth. He let out the sweetest giggle when she let him. "Mother," Topaz knew she needed to depart. "This boy's father...thinks he," despite tears, Topaz kissed her baby, "is my *brother*." It was so very upsetting.

The woman swore. "Curse them cackling hens down at that church! They always talking!"

From the car, Naomi watched the petite woman. With her hair brown-gold in the morning sun, Topaz was lovely, inside and out. Her fitted car coat, her jeans, and her heeled boots were all stylish. Yet, she appeared devastated. When she slid onto the passenger seat, Naomi guessed. "That was Cedric, Army's father, on the phone. Right?"

Speaking softly Topaz felt mean. "No, Elijah Moon is Armand's father. That's what we're letting people believe, and you're his mother."

"This mess has gone too far," Naomi said as she left Tranquility city limits. She headed for the 59th Street Bridge. Upon crossing it, in Midtown, she would let Topaz out. Nearby, Topaz would catch the train to MSM, the music college. While driving, Naomi felt anxious. She longed to stop, get her purse and take a pill—or better yet, she wanted to take her daughter in her arms. However, she kept driving.

"Taupe, I never wanted to go along with this. I just wanted you to be able to have your baby, in peace. That's why I suggested going to Aunt Pet. If you recall, I insisted on being called Me-Maw. I know I'm Armand's grandmother. I don't care what anybody thinks. I don't have a problem with the truth. You, my daughter, are that baby's mother. You're a good one, too, and I'm proud of you."

"I know, Mama," Topaz's voice was soft, although she wanted to yell—at her father. She hated her stupid self, too, for going along. Then again, her father was the absolute best with her boy. That, Topaz had to admit. He laughed, and snoozed with Armand, the Giant and Baby Bear. Elijah fed Armand, and when time permitted, great big Grandad looked out for the little one. One night, in blue PJs, big Elijah had even walked the floor with the teething baby, rocking him and soothingly singing.

Shaking her head, Topaz tearfully asked a question. "How can I tell my son's father any of this?" The mess that both she, being fast, *and* Cozi Moon, gossiping, had gotten them into; the mess none of them had corrected.

Naomi admitted she did not know. Yet she offered five words. "My darling Taupe, just try."

Chapter 38

AS she sat on the organ, Topaz wondered why she kept returning to Greater Bethany Bible Congregation. Was it because she had once loved it and the ordered worship service? Like her father, she'd loved the people too, before she'd started seeing them as she saw herself. Flawed.

She wondered why she no longer felt the same joy that she'd once felt. Why had the fire and the fervor gone out? Why was she no longer glad to enter the house of the Lord? Was she becoming a shell woman? Was she no longer who she had once been—like her mother?

Those things Topaz pondered as she sat waiting for the deacon to finish his diatribe. Perhaps she should play something to help him along. Then maybe she'd get home at a decent hour, get some homework done.

That was something else she had to rectify, her living situation. Topaz remembered that although the walls of the old Victorian weren't thin, she often heard her parents. Lately, they sniped at one another. Something was brewing. Topaz could feel it, and she wanted no part of it.

She nearly shook her head because the misconception was: women kept drama going. Yet, most of the drama in her life had stemmed from one source. Her father. It seemed the man thrived in chaos, perhaps because then he could swoop in, like Zorro, and do his silly rescue bit.

Topaz was so tired of the shenanigans. She just wanted peace.

She looked over at her son. Growing as fast as a weed, the boy belonged to the pastor and his wife. At least that was what some people thought. When she hadn't been much older than Armand, Topaz had also been dragged to revival meetings like this one. However, before that, she and her best friend had been tapped to pass out flyers. The papers announced the Old Time Religious services.

"Yeah, like these people will come," tall thin Caley had grumbled, referring to neighborhood occupants. "Please."

Burly Deacon Wilnod was still up, about to pray. In singsong, he rasped, "Oh Lord, here we are today, knee bent and body bowed…"

Topaz played softly as he sing-sang on about being saved from death and the like. She remembered. Naomi had aided her to lose the fear of such things. Back then, Naomi had been more herself. She'd comforted her daughter while sitting bedside. Topaz remembered snuggling in her mother's arms and how her nightmares had ceased.

Back then, Topaz could not have been happier. Glancing over at Naomi, who was no longer Naomi, the woman's daughter wondered, what happened? What changed her mother? Was it the trials of living with her father? Were his idiosyncrasies what had broken Naomi?

As the revivalist rose and began speaking in unknown tongues, Topaz suddenly made a vow. She would *not* become a shell of herself. She just had to find her way back to herself. The person she used to be. The one who had enjoyed things, especially music. Topaz suddenly vowed she wouldn't allow anything or anyone to make her become like her mother.

Topaz's father wouldn't do so, and neither would the loss of Cedric.

Topaz would remain her true self, if only for one reason. Her son needed her, like she had needed her mother.

AT the old Victorian, Topaz heard the sniping. Yet, she reread the score. She tried to concentrate. She had an upcoming live performance. Nevertheless, studying her student piece was becoming impossible because in her parent's bedroom Naomi was apoplectic.

On this evening, Naomi did not sound at all like her docile self—of late. There was a bunch of banging around in that upstairs bedroom too. Big Elijah Moon also tried to speak in hushed tones.

Hearing it all, muffled though it was, Topaz knew. Something was seriously wrong. That was why she made the call.

"Sure, baby, you know the piano here is yours." The elderly woman advised, "You come on over. Then you work on it all you want."

Replacing the receiver, Topaz packed toiletries, clothing, toys, and cereal. She called a cab. She gathered her school paraphernalia and her heavy, sleeping, twenty-two-month-old. When the horn tooted out front, she didn't say a word.

Struggling beneath her burdens, Topaz left the peeling yellow house.

Chapter 39

BACK at the Moon residence, heavy Naomi bent and clutched her midsection. "You stabbed me!" She said it because she'd heard the talk. It was being whispered all over town. She hadn't wanted to believe it. Now she knew it was true. *Eve's boy was Elijah's.*

"I could take you having an affair," Naomi spat, "more easily than I can swallow *this*!" She couldn't even look at the man she'd married so long ago. "And why her?" Beyond upset, Naomi snorted, "Guess you finally got your son. You wore out my behind trying to get him, now you've got two—and ain't nare one of them mine!"

"I do not have two sons," Elijah feebly shot back.

Naomi narrowed her eyes. "Oh, you don't? Did you forget? You 'n your Mama have put it about that Armand is ours! Now you wanna give Topaz her boy back? Elijah!" Naomi tossed a bottle of cologne at his head. "How could you do this, to me? And let me find out this way?"

And after all she had been through, with and for him, "I deserve better—at least a smidgen of courtesy." Naomi's eyes were red-rimmed, and her nose was red, as the smell of Elijah's cologne rose from shards of glass. "You must really hate me, to let me find out like this."

Elijah would just bet his mother, malcontent Cozina Moon, had derived great pleasure from telling Naomi. Cozi had said *all* her grandsons would spend the night at her house. Then Cozi had gone on to name little Elisha, along with Ezra and Tippie's boys.

"Cozi named that kid, Eli, before she said the names of all your brother's kids, like I don't know them. I've kept them all their lives!" Naomi hurled another bottle and didn't wait to see if Elijah ducked. "When your Dad passed, you really should have married your Mama! Lord knows you 'n she are closer than you and I have ever been."

Elijah tried to calm his wife. He did so by slowly approaching her. Softly, he called her name. "Naomi. Nae…"

"You know what," she said, fighting pain while seeking her purse. "I want you outta my house." Naomi's fingers trembled as she fought to remove the Vicodin cap. She needed Lexapro too, but she couldn't see through vision-blurring tears. She had been crying for the last hour. Now she knew if she didn't take something soon, she would wind up in jail tonight. Why? –Because she was so angry she could kill.

Naomi screamed. "Get the devil out my house, man!"

"Your house," Elijah repeated. "When has this not been our home?"

"It changed when I found out you stuck that woman." Feeling like fighting, Naomi asked, "Did you do her at the church? You pig."

Backing away from Naomi, who seemed crazed, Elijah glanced in the mirror. He looked crazed or worn, himself. Forgetting that, Elijah watched his wife and realized what he had not before.

The first lady was a drug addict.

The fact that she stood before him with a hand full of pharmaceuticals made it glaringly obvious.

Naomi recognized Elijah's look; she had seen it on both Mother See and Topaz's faces. They, too, had realized Naomi was a functioning addict. Well, Naomi thought, Elijah didn't get to judge her. Not when he was partially to blame for her predicament, trying to have all those babies –for him. "You know what, Mister Holy? Fuck you. That's right, fuck – you – you fornicator. Whoremonger. You adulterer."

Ouch. That hurt, Elijah realized. He also recognized that he had never wanted to hurt Naomi. He felt sick about the whole sordid deal, but she wouldn't let him say so. And she would never believe him. Poor Nae… She was the gentlest, most accommodating woman he knew. Well, it wasn't apparent at the moment, but she was. His Naomi. Elijah especially hadn't wanted her to learn of his betrayal, and not this way. It was why he reached for the pills filling her hand. He reached for her, too.

"Nae," he called, thinking he could smooth things over a bit. "It's done, now. I can't call it back, but I truly would if I could."

"Oh, shut up. And don't touch me!" Naomi hissed like a cornered cat. "I should have known you'd say that. That's your line for everything." Deepening her voice, Naomi mimicked Elijah. 'It's done, now. Can't walk it back.' Oh, and to answer your question from before," Naomi blathered on, well past angry. "This became my house when I went to work; when we transferred it into my name. You quit work—at your Mama's behest—so you could become the church gigolo! That's when this stupid, overly-ornate, ugly, shambledy house became mine."

That stung, a lot. "Naomi, I'm no gigolo, not by a long shot."

"Oh, no? Well, since you've gotten used to another title—Preacher, I guess you believe that. But to finish what I was saying, this became my house when I made the payments, so my daughter could have a place to lay her head. So, as I said before, get the fuck – out – of my house."

Elijah appeared stunned. Who was the raging woman before him? She didn't even love the place like he did. Raising a large hand, palm face-up, he quietly asked, "Where am I supposed to go, Nae?"

Turning toward the bathroom, Naomi shrugged. "I don't know." Her voice floated back, "I don't even care. Go to your whore—that boy's mother. Or to your Mama. Go to hell; you just can't stay here."

TOPAZ called her mother because she was so excited. She wanted to let Naomi know. She'd worked with a professional jazz pianist, at MSM where she had rigorous conservatory training. There, the petite one also received a plethora of opportunities to perform and network. Offered by the Manhattan School of Music, the program for young jazz musicians was one of the finest in New York City and elsewhere.

Topaz wanted to tell her mother that she would become a union person. She had joined AFM, too, the American Federation of Musicians. That wasn't the only union she would join, but they, Topaz wanted Naomi to know, would make sure Topaz was paid scale. It was the going rate for musicians of her caliber, whether she did studio, performance, or road work. Whoop-woot! Tiny T. Moon was on her way!

One day, she would even make a handsome living for herself and her son! Never again would she put up with the pittance that she once had, simply because she'd been young, uninformed, and working for family.

Yet when Topaz called Naomi, Topaz's joy dimmed. She struggled to breathe as she asked her mother *why*? Why had Elijah Moon done such a callous thing? However, Topaz really wasn't surprised because the vagaries of her own life had taught her. Anything could happen.

Upon finding out about the boy Elijah had fathered with the church administrator, Topaz decided. As she and Mother See watched little Armand—the joy of their lives—toss himself into Ronald's arms, Topaz said, "Mother, I've got to move out of that house."

With her eyes on her fifty-something son, Mother See nodded, "I've known this was coming."

Topaz thought her grandma was speaking of the mess with her parents. Then Mother See spoke. "I know you're a young mom with a life. I know you probably haven't considered it, but I would sho love it if you came here. I know you won't stay long, but I want you and that baby here, for as long as you choose."

In the waning sun, Topaz squinted at the elderly woman. "What about Uncle Ronald?" Didn't Mother's son want to come out of the basement? "If Armand and I weren't here, Uncle could sleep in my room."

"No, he could not." Mother See was firm. "That has been yo' room all your days. It will *be* your room, from now until. Ron uses the basement entrance. He has his own life. Anyway, he and Annette are trying to reconcile. I suspect he'll soon return to their home, *but* until he and his wife make amends, at least our boy will have another male influence. You *are* going to let me continue keeping him, aren't you?"

"Of course," Topaz nodded. She smiled because Armand was having such fun. She just wished he were tossing himself into his father's arms.

"Army will be with you, Mother, until pre-school. Topaz mentioned her pay from Bethany and the new work coming her way due to her training and networking. A portion would be Mother See's payment.

The silver-haired woman said, "Lil Mama, I just want you to concentrate on getting your degree. Forget paying me. We'll manage."

"We will," Topaz nodded, internally calculating just when she could make her first payment. She felt ridiculously happy, until she remembered her mother's unhappiness.

Aware but reserving judgment, Mother See spoke about something different. "Annette is dropping Ron's boys off this weekend. I know they," twelve and six, "won't mind sharing their dad with a little one. That is if you don't mind him hanging with them."

Topaz didn't have to ponder it. As her son flung himself at his Uncle Ronald, she did the same to her grandma.

The elderly woman placed her arms around the girl-woman she had loved ever since the golden-eyed one was born, nearly twenty years prior. Mother See tried not to sound choked up. She failed, but she did manage to offer the meaningful words, "Welcome home, baby."

Chapter 40

ONE summer day, while quickly walking in colorful, bustling Manhattan, Topaz's mind was on a question. She would ask her theory instructor. Thinking only of rapidly getting to Claremont Avenue, she didn't see the woman who hurriedly approached.

When the taller woman was nearly upon her, Topaz blinked. The person in the long skirt looked incredibly familiar, but who was she?

"Topaz?" The woman called as they were about to pass each other. The woman gestured as if to say, 'It's me, remember?'

Then it hit the golden-eyed one. Bethany's keyboardist, "Loo-la!"

Amid swirling color and the going and coming of Manhattan foot and vehicular traffic, the two women screamed. Reaching for one another, they jumped up and down. They also attempted to hug at the same time.

"Okay," Topaz visibly breathed as Sister Tallulah held both her hands. "We have got to calm down." Yet they both laughed and screamed and hugged some more. They asked questions all the while.

"Where have you been?" "How have you been?" "How's your dad?" "How's your dad, Pastor Moon?" "What're you doing now?" "Where are you on your way to?" "Why have I not seen you?" "It's been so long!"

"As little as is said about it," Topaz stated, deciding to tell her old friend the truth, "I had a baby. A boy. He's three years old now."

Tallulah looked momentarily confused. "So you and Sister Naomi have children the same age?"

Topaz chuckled. "That'd be something, but no. The baby is mine."

Topaz knew that her sister-friend, tall, slender Caley would say, 'Taupe, you're skating on thin ice,' simply because Topaz had told. Caley would point out that GBBC members loved to talk. She would say the proof was the fact that Tallulah had even heard about the baby. The keyboardist had been gone from the church for at least four years. Slender Caley would say it didn't matter how long Lula had been gone. She was, in essence, still a church member. Therefore, she too might talk, and that talk might get back to Greater Bethany, or worse, back to Daddy Moon.

Nevertheless, Topaz felt a little glow inside because she was becoming powerful. Ever since Armand's birth, she'd felt like she was morphing into a type of Wonder Woman, one who made her own rules.

Trying to recall what she had heard, Sister Tallulah said, "I moved away from Tranquility. Still, somebody said there was a baby boy. He's supposed to look like you, but I thought he was your mom's..."

Topaz sighed. "That's a long story, but I'm telling you, Lula. The boy is mine." Topaz knew her father wouldn't want it to get out, but it was time. She would no longer live lies, since she no longer lived in that big old Victorian house of lies. Moreover, if her father dared question her, Topaz would toss his standard line back at him. 'It's done, now.' She would also say, as he often had, 'I can't call it back. Not now.' Hee-hee.

"Wanna get a quick cup of coffee?" Sister Tallulah inquired.

Glancing at her watch, Topaz realized she had at least forty-five minutes. "Sure, let's go down this block." She grabbed Tallulah's hand. Dodging taxis, bike messengers, and pedestrians, they quickly crossed the frenetically paced street. Then when seated at a countertop, with coffee and pastries before them, the girl-talk wound around to Cedric.

"I haven't seen him in a good while," Topaz admitted.

"Well, *I* have..." Tallulah, who was now an evangelist, grinned.

Topaz shrugged off a frisson of dismay and told herself Cedric was grown. As such, he could see anyone he desired, even holy Lula.

The woman in the long skirt pawed around in her leather hobo bag. "Taupe, a few weeks ago, I was at the airport, picking up my fiancé," She wiggled her ring finger. "A man hugged me. Devon, whom I'll marry, was displeased." Tallulah grinned, "because Cedric is fine."

Topaz said, "I remember," even though she hadn't seen him in what felt like a lifetime. Oh, it really was that long; it was *Armand's* lifetime.

"Well, trust me," Tallulah nodded, "the man is hot." She pressed a small rectangle onto Topaz's palm. "You need this card."

"It's yours?" Topaz fingered it.

"Nope, turn it over. It's Cedric's. I've been carrying it around for weeks. I meant to get over to GBBC one Sunday. I hoped you'd be there. I never made it, with me planning to move to DC and my wedding and all coming up, but here you are! This is providence."

Again, the two hugged. Afterward, Topaz fingered the card, at which she had yet to look. Despite Tallulah's protests, Topaz covered their bill. She listened too as Tallulah announced, "Cedric made me promise to find you. He asked you to call him. He said he's not in town much, but he wants to reconnect with you." Tallulah laughed. "He called you Baybay. Remember that? I think he's based in Vegas, doing big things, but…" Tallulah wiggled her eyebrows. "Girl, he's got it bad for you!"

The ladies parted. Topaz jetted to MSM, clutching her cross-body purse like she often clutched her son. Cedric's son. She held her satchel against her, the way she longed to hold Cedric, one more time.

AS Tallulah got farther away from her old friend, she could not get Topaz, or the Moon family, off her mind.

Growing up in sleepy little Tranquility and going to Greater Bethany Bible Congregation, Tallulah had often felt a little envious of Topaz. The girl –whom some of the kids had called cat-eyed– had two parents. That was something young Tallulah had desperately wanted. However, when Lulu, her mother's name for her, had been a toddler, her mother had left. Everyone had thought the couple had been happy. Lulu's father—God rest his recently departed soul—had been heavy and sick. He'd done the best he could, but Tallulah had wanted what she'd thought Topaz had.

Back then, the older girl had only seen beautiful and poised Sister Naomi with the gorgeous hair. She'd been a very present mom. Then. Tallulah had loved big Pastor Moon too. He'd smelled so nice, always, with his giant engaging persona and booming voice. He made everyone feel special. He had always seemed so proud of his 'jewel,' his 'baby girl,' both of which he had often called Topaz.

At one point, Tallulah had even wanted to *be* the pretty, petite, and seemingly highly-favored daughter who lived in the big house.

Yet on this day, Topaz had intimated that all had not been perfect in the inner sanctum.

For Tallulah, looking in from the outside, everything had appeared to be peaches and cream. However, the golden one had had a secret love child! That was something. To Tallulah, it was also a reminder.

Things behind closed doors in sleepy little towns were usually *not* what they seemed.

Chapter 41

MEETING Caley for lunch in a small Mom & Pop Italian eatery, Topaz revealed that she had seen Cedric. Topaz didn't say that she had done so several times.

Wide-eyed, the taller, slender woman had one question. "You and ol' yella do it?"

Laughing, Topaz said, "You know what, Cae? You're the exact same as when we were kids."

"I know." Caley feigned misery. "I'm a fiend, but hey, I'm immensely more attractive now. I've grown into these angles and legs."

"You have, Cae. You're certainly a head-turner." Shaking her own head, Topaz could never say that for old time's sake, Cedric had picked her up in his dad's car, a smaller, newer version. Cedric made sure she knew he had his own sporty little something out in Vegas.

Cedric took Topaz to an upscale Moroccan restaurant. He spoke about his job as a food service manager. In addition to making sure hotel patrons got the correct order delivered to them in a timely fashion, he dealt with complaints. He attempted to fairly resolve each issue, while he monitored all that occurred in the kitchen. Cedric said he had to maintain sanitation standards according to code, and he did administrative work.

Hearing that he also handled credit transactions and cash and that he managed end-of-the-night surveys and lock-up for one of the major hotels on the strip, Topaz was impressed. "You're really doing it, Ced."

He'd gazed into her eyes as softly he said, "You are too, Bay."

They had both been unable to do much more than pick at their food, although it was delicious and well presented. Yet their minds were elsewhere. The Gap Band's *Yearning for Your Love* began to play in the new Stable vehicle. Glancing over, Cedric saw that to the music, the petite beauty gently bobbed her head. Without thinking, he reached for her hand, and she squeezed his.

She mouthed the words, *My heart is yearning…*

He sang the part; *Let me inside your love.*

"Come home with me," he whispered, and she agreed.

In the Italian eatery, Topaz didn't tell Caley that Cedric's home had not changed one bit. She didn't say that she'd felt like being with him there was what she'd had to do.

Topaz didn't say that slowly they'd removed one another's clothing. Nor did she speak of Cedric bending to lave her breasts. As he took her nipples into his mouth, she'd felt so different from any time before. Topaz felt she'd been armed and ready, no longer a naïve young girl. When she and Cedric could no longer wait to be joined, Topaz did as Caley had once instructed her. Topaz produced a condom.

Cedric watched her sheath him, and while seeing those nimble fingers foray over him, the same way they still skillfully tripped over keyboards, he'd moaned. Then he laughed because Baybay took charge.

Doing so, Topaz felt glorious because now she was strong; all she had been through had made her so. She only wondered if, after the loving, she would be strong enough to say what needed to be said.

Caley, who had grown into her bohemian look, forked into eggplant parmigiana and asked if Topaz had taken Armand with her.

Topaz scooped up first-rate broccoli Fettuccini. "I did." Topaz recalled the trio hanging out, a couple of times. Then as a couple, she and Cedric had gone to dinner. Afterward, they'd had alone time, again.

Direct as ever, Caley queried, "Does your old flame like Armand?"

Topaz looked down at the red and white checkered tablecloth. "Well, I'll just say this, when he dropped me back at Mother See's, he carried Armand up the steps and into the house."

"My godson must have been asleep."

"Yep. Then back outside, Cedric said, 'That kid is cute.' He thinks Armand is so funny. Ced even joked that maybe he and I could have one just like him…"

"What?!" Caley appeared flabbergasted. "And you didn't *tell* him?" She didn't care that with her outburst, she'd startled a small family nearby. Leaning forward, Caley yipped, "Cedric still doesn't know. That was your cue, girl! That was the perfect segue into telling him that Armand is yours—and his! You blew it. You know that, right?"

Soft-spoken, Topaz admitted she knew. Then she sounded defensive. "I couldn't just blurt it out, Cae. Why would he believe me?"

"Why not? You want him to know! He would want to know. He needs to know! What are you waiting for—a skywriting sale?"

Topaz did not raise her eyes. "I'm not…waiting. I just don't know why I kept my mouth shut. It didn't feel right. It was too soon."

"Almost three—no, four—years of this madness, and it's 'too soon.'" Caley rolled her eyes. She could feel herself becoming upset. "Okay, Taupe. 'You kept your mouth shut.' No, you didn't. You sucked that man's dick. Your mouth was open then, but you said nothing. You claim 'it didn't feel right,' but I'll bet you and him getting it in felt right. Him freakin' you, and y'all rolling around was perfect, but you kept quiet."

Topaz averted her eyes. "I didn't say we did any of that."

The taller woman who currently excelled in a gemology course waved. "You didn't have to, Taupe. I can look at you and tell. I know you, how you feel about him. I know he's probably sexier than ever now. You couldn't resist climbing all over him, and I don't blame you. I just think *he has a right to know*!" Caley's eyes shimmered with tears. "Hell, the man has lost so much time. That's time and memories, with his kid, that he'll never get back. Do you understand that?"

Caley huffed, "As a kid whose parents weren't there, I ask you to think about your son." Fun-loving Caley appeared choked up. "Ponder how your boy will feel when he learns you didn't bring him and his dad together sooner." She collected her things. "Do you think he'll like that? Will either of them even forgive you? Will they want to?" Quickly, Caley stood. "Ask yourself those questions, Taupe."

Topaz turned her head, not wanting to see the other woman's pain. Angrily, Caley stomped away. Hoping she'd return, Topaz had to admit her unpredictable friend was right.

Topaz's actions were unfair to both Cedric and their son. However, none of that changed the fact that hers was still the most significant dilemma. How would she even broach the subject with Cedric, now, after all this time? And after she and Cedric had slept together again. A couple of times.

Chapter 42

IT was as though she couldn't get over it. Sure, she had been betrayed, but didn't that happen to people every day? Didn't they let it go, at some point? Naomi knew they did, but the lies and the lust. It had led to all of this. That was what had her stumped. That and the fact that Elijah kept coming back, to her, to her house. He kept letting himself in. He followed her around, saying things she didn't care to hear.

He was sorry. He hadn't wanted her to find out this way...blah, blah.

He stood before her even now, attempting to make things right, but he could not. Naomi nearly laughed because it was ironic. It seemed like she saw more of Elijah now than she had in all of the last five years. Yet every time she saw him, she saw his betrayal and nothing else.

Naomi even 'saw' her son, often. The one who would have carried his father's name, and his and her DNA. In her musings, her boy looked just like her copper-skinned girl. That tall boy, her boy, was the male version of the tawny-eyed girl who, to this day, still looked so much like her father. But, Naomi recalled, nothing about her son was to be. Of that, she reminded herself as she kept cleaning out the refrigerator.

Elijah had stolen her dream. Since the doctor had cut away her insides, Naomi had held onto one dream. Sure, she had been aware that it wouldn't come true, but the notion had been comforting. Now, even that had been stripped away. All she had was a pack of lies.

How had Elijah stuck himself into *Eve*—repeatedly?

Naomi was so angry she could spit. Before she knew it, she'd dropped her sponge, hauled off, and slapped the fool out of the man!

Elijah knew he deserved that; it was why he had again been trying to make amends. Instinctively, he grabbed both of Naomi's forearms. "I'll give you that one, Nae." He shook her; "but I ain't gon *keep* letting you hit me." It was sick, but for some reason, at that moment, wet and skeezy entered his mind. Elijah wanted to rip Naomi's clothes off and make her love him again. He had once loved her fire. He guessed he always would. Elijah held onto Naomi, but despite his strength, she struggled like a little wildcat. He knew she was hurt, and angry. He knew she would never believe he was too. How many times could he say it? He hadn't wanted this. He had gotten caught up. Elijah repeated it, wishing he could make Naomi see; *she* was his world. "Nae, I never wanted this…" Elijah said he never meant to get involved with Eve Island. Looking back, he said, he almost felt like he'd been played, lulled, and lured into everything. Moreover, Elijah said, he hadn't been trying to have a baby.

Naomi yowled, "But that's what happens when you screw people!"

Since things didn't appear to be getting any better, Elijah figured he didn't have much else to lose. Therefore, he told his wife the truth. "I wanted my son to come from you, out of your body, Naomi." She appeared stunned as he spoke on. "You hear that, Nae? I wanted *our* son!" Elijah bitterly divulged that now he had a boy he couldn't acknowledge, not before the church or the world, and the truth was…he was growing to love that child.

Naomi didn't care to hear that. Elijah wasn't talking about her son, the one who didn't exist on this earthly plane, so Elijah could clamp it.

"But," the man continued, "The bad thing is: this boy's existence has driven a bigger wedge between you and me than there was before."

When Naomi just stared, Elijah said, "Girl, don't play stupid. You know we had very little before all this. Now, that innocent child—yes, I said innocent—because he had nothing to do with his birth; that child has become the equivalent of a sword. For you, for his mother, and for my mother to wield at will, and everybody keeps hurting everybody else."

Naomi waved and tried to turn away. "Oh shut up, Elijah."

"No. You stop this." He spun her. "You threaten to throw me out of my own home. The boy's mother threatens to expose me at the church. My mother threatens to reveal little Eli's parentage when she wants to control me, and Nae," Elijah sounded worn, "I am so tired. I detest all of it." He threw up his hands, releasing his wife. "Now I know how Abraham in the bible felt when his wife's hand-maiden had his baby."

"That Eve bitch is *not* my hand-maiden!" Naomi slammed the refrigerator door, "And do not preach –to me."

Elijah spoke on. "I know my case is different from Abraham's, in a way. His wife pushed him to make a baby with the help." She'd mistakenly believed that was the way she and her husband could get the son that God had promised. "But Nae, you would never have done that."

Getting out a frying pan, Naomi announced, "I'm not listening."

Regardless, Elijah reminded his wife, "Back in the day, Naomi, you became a hellion anytime you thought some woman got too close to me. I miss *that* woman. I miss *you*. I really do, and I'm sorry."

Naomi heard her husband pleading for her to pay attention. "Your fire, your slow burn was one of the things I loved about you, Naomi." Elijah bitterly tossed out, "Then came the ghost—"

"Don't you blame me!" Naomi rushed over. "You Romeo in a robe!"

Elijah grabbed her raised hand. Holding it, he pried the fry pan from her fingers. "I'm not blaming you, Nae, but after our loss, you know you floated through here, and through all other areas of our life, like a ghost."

Elijah didn't want to hurt her, but he had to say it. "It wasn't just your loss, Naomi. It was *my son*, too, that we never brought home. You went back to work afterward." Her addiction to pharmaceuticals escalated. He softly said, "You barely spoke to me unless it pertained to Topaz. If it had to do with the church, you said to speak with my administrator. You left me alone, with grief, and our daughter. You let me carry the church alone, when that was part of why we wed. Our deal was to do things together. You, my rock, disappeared. Your body was here, but you? No."

"So you're rebuking *me* when *you* got someone *else* pregnant?" Disgusted, Naomi shook her head. "I know you and your appetite, Elijah. You probably fucked the daylights out that woman." Noticing her arm, held high by her husband, Naomi spat. "Let go of me."

"Screwing's not why I wound up with her," Elijah stated. "I was stupid and carnal, but you didn't talk to me half the time, or you ignored me. You were in a shell. That's how we wound up here. And for the record, she's nothing like you, sexually, or in any way."

"Shut... it up," Naomi advised. "I don't want to hear this."

Elijah grabbed her. Beneath her breast and at her waist, his big hands clasped struggling Naomi. "Oh, but you will hear me, wife. *You* were sexually adventurous, inventive even, once upon a time. She's not. *You* were my best friend. She's not friend material, and because I fooled with her, I've lost the girl I once knew; *you*. I hate that. Half the time, I hate myself." With tears in his eyes, Elijah shrugged. "That's it, in a nutshell." He released her, prepared to stalk from the old Victorian.

Naomi stopped him with words. "That's not it, Elijah. That's not even half of it." Broken-hearted, she softly spoke. "You knew there was that baby, the one I nearly carried to term. He wasn't the only one."

Elijah pivoted, as laboriously he breathed, "What – do – you – mean, Nae—*he wasn't the only one?*" His eyes blazed. "There were others?"

Naomi did not look at her husband. "He was the *fifth* baby. Lost. We'd have six kids by now, but my doctor told me that *I* had to stop getting pregnant. She said I had to know when enough was enough – when my body couldn't take any more. She said the next time, I could be the one lost. That was when I decided. That was when I let them take my insides because I knew if they didn't, I'd keep trying. I'd keep letting you hump me until we got our son. Even though I was ill and had bloodsuckers feeding on my insides, I didn't want to worry you. But I was headed for the burial ground, Elijah. And now you blame *me* for us not having the life we planned." Naomi raised tear-filled eyes. "After I nearly killed myself—for us, in so many ways."

Bitterly, she wept. "Just go, Elijah," Naomi hiccupped. "Please?"

He watched her turn away, shutting him out as effectively as ever. Elijah was hardly able to breathe, yet snatches of memory danced before him; Naomi deathly ill, on several occasions, there had been bleeding and torn hospital bills; the devastating termination of a pregnancy at 7 months; 29 weeks, resulting in the loss of his fully formed son. The baby's lungs had not yet been ready to breathe independently, said the doctors. If baby boy could have held on just three more weeks... That Elijah fully recalled. He remembered his wife, inconsolable and sobbing. Now he knew, not just for that loss, but for many. Then came her addiction, leading to the final retreat.

Unable to process everything he suddenly knew to be true, Elijah wanted to take Naomi in his arms. With tears clogging his throat, he crooned, "Oh my poor baby, *you*... I *wish* I had known the extent of things. You didn't talk to me, Nae." Elijah really wasn't an ogre. "I wanted to know things. Maybe life would've been different had you let me in." He could have even been there for her, like she'd been for him.

Crying broken-heartedly, Naomi heard Elijah approach. She flinched.

Elijah noticed. His wife wanted nothing to do with him. He couldn't take her in his arms to console her. He felt nearly as hurt as she. Maybe this *was* the end... Elijah turned. Without a word, he left the house, and the woman. She—not the bricks and mortar—had been his home.

Chapter 43

NAOMI knew it was time. She had to move forward. She had to put what was done behind her. She would start by getting off those pills. For years, she had been taking prescription drugs. She knew it was why people often believed she was mellow, but if they only knew. She was an addict. She didn't know when she'd started thinking meds were the only way. But they helped her cope with the demands of being the first lady and with life. Looking back, she saw; all she had ever wanted were two things: to be Elijah Moon's love and to have his babies. Naomi had never wanted all this, all that being a preacher's wife entailed. She'd never dreamed she'd be judged, every single day, on every little thing she did, or wore, even though Mother See had warned her. Still, Naomi had never dreamed there would be competition for her husband's attention, even *after* they married. Although, again, Mother See had warned her. Mother had said the malcontents would always be around. Mistakenly, Naomi had believed that after her nuptials, the stupid stuff would end. In a way, it had only intensified. Women were attracted to what they perceived as power. Thus, in droves, they were attracted to King Elijah Moon. Therefore, it became their mission to dethrone her.

One of those women was her mother-in-law, Cozi Moon. Naomi had never met a more conniving woman. The pastor's short stylish mother truly felt as though Naomi had stolen her spot. To Naomi, Cozi did not seem rational. Did Cozi ever think? Her position had been *lost* when she'd lost her husband. If Cozi wanted to be angry with somebody, Naomi mused, Cozi should have been angry with her husband, for dying.

Naomi knew sometimes she felt anger, directed at Old Preacher. If he hadn't died, Elijah would have kept his job at the courthouse. Ambitious man, Elijah would have been promoted. He might have even started his own business. Then they would have had money. They'd not have been in the cold old house that her husband had had to put her name on to save it. They could have had a new one, or they could have had theirs refurbished. No house being so drafty in winter and hot in the summer. Had things indeed been correct, Naomi mused, she would have been woman enough to bear more children. She would have had four sons. Six kids had been her dream. Elijah had also wanted them, and she would have had another daughter, Jade, who'd have been beautiful like Topaz.

And Topaz...she was another story. She had grown distant. Now she was always off somewhere with the baby or with slim vivacious Caley. Naomi forgot her kids to focus on her addiction. Elijah was right about the pharmaceuticals. She was dependent. It started after Topaz's birth. Naomi had found out that fibroids were multiplying. They'd impeded her carrying several pregnancies to term. Then after she'd lost what Elijah thought was their second baby—when it had really been her sixth—she'd had a D&C, a dilation and curettage. That led to cramping that doubled her over in screaming pain. After her then-prescription had run out, Naomi coerced a friend in the medical field to get her another. Oblivious. When Naomi took them, she didn't ache or remember. Then she'd had the hysterectomy. Again, she'd desperately needed meds. She'd needed something more potent, though, and she'd grown to like the way the pills made her feel. When she took them, there was no constant reminder that she'd lost Elijah's son and any chance of giving him another. In lucid moments, Naomi had felt ungainly, and not womanly. Losing her fire, she'd closed herself off, as Elijah had said.

Now Naomi wanted to be authentic. She wanted to walk in truth, be real, and live in the moment. Naomi wanted to be present for all of life's little moments. Therefore, she sighed and vowed to call Elijah. Mrs. Moon wished to have what might prove to be another hurtful conversation. Still, she and Elijah had to get everything out in the open. Start in truth, again. If they could. From there, they would see.

Sure, it would take time, and help, to get off the meds and fully get past the betrayal. This Naomi knew because everywhere she went, the hurt loomed. Still, she was willing to try. She would do so by going to see someone. Sure, some black folk believed seeing a shrink was taboo. Instead, they consulted the preacher, but *that* Naomi could not do, so...

She would seek professional help. Right away.

HOW, she wondered would she change her future if she couldn't stop pondering the past. Thinking about it wouldn't change or erase it. How many nights would she wake—she asked herself—splenetic and angry, due to visions of her big man with that wild-haired woman?

Sitting up on the side of her empty bed, Naomi wondered. Where was her husband? She could not know that a parishioner had used his one phone call to telephone the preacher. She was unaware that quietly, so he wouldn't wake her, Elijah had done what he had for decades. He'd gotten up, got dressed, and had gone to see about that one who needed him.

Naomi sighed and reminded herself. For the majority of her marriage, she had been alone. Headed into the bathroom, she wondered if she should make it official. When she realized she'd run water into a glass and held a handful of pills, she knew. Death and divorce weren't options, neither were antidepressants. Naomi had to talk to Elijah. In the past, she'd shut him out. Early in their marriage, she'd done so by thinking she didn't want to 'bother' him. She had been so conscious of not being a complainer, like Cozi Moon, until Naomi had kept Elijah in the dark. There were so many things that he should have known. He would have wanted to know. Sure, he was big and blustery—her Hurricane Elijah— but that was his way. And now, *her* way had to change. She had to open up, in more ways than one.

Naomi remembered something. Back when she and Elijah had been young, he'd mentioned wanting them bound, irrevocably, to one another. Guess that prayer of his had been answered. It was evidenced by the fact that she'd never left him. Naomi couldn't. Her heart belonged to Elijah.

In her big ugly kitchen, Naomi sat in the dark. She thought about visiting evangelists. For them, she'd cooked and made beds. For her husband, she'd fielded calls. She'd taken care of the church and neighborhood children, along with her daughter, Caley, and her five nephews. Yet, images of that woman bent over as Elijah pumped her from behind, pushed in. Naomi felt queasy and wanted to puke, like she had while carrying Elijah's babies. The babies who were not present. Knowing the other woman delivered Elijah's baby made Naomi see red! Wondering if he'd been at appointments and at the birth caused Naomi to want Eve dead. Naomi wanted Elijah naked. With a wire brush dipped in bleach, she'd scrub him free of evil. And that woman was evil. Way back, Eve had plotted. Naomi remembered; she'd been carrying Topaz then. The woman had come for a marriage-wrecking session. And sex-greedy Elijah had fallen into her trap.

Naomi wanted to dismiss vile thoughts. But had Elijah put his mouth on that cunt? Suddenly Naomi wanted the pills she'd flushed. She longed for the way they would make her feel. Numb, and like she did not care.

Chapter 44

ELIJAH loved Naomi, yet he felt she had pushed him into Eve's arms. In a way. Naomi had left him vulnerable after they'd lost his son. She had been so depressed until she'd lost interest in him and them. Oh, she'd let him pounce on her, but gone had been the joy, the connubial greed, and the way she had once been so hungry for him. Gone had been the kisses, the playfulness, and her dirty talk. Her nasty mouth he'd loved, for a couple of reasons. Gone had been erotic soaks in the tub that was too small for him—let alone the two of them. Gone had been togetherness and quickies in his office, or their car. Now he knew why.

He hated to think about it, but now he knew something else. Eve was a shark. She'd sensed blood in the water. That was why she had gotten after him. After Naomi had lost his son, Nae had no longer been vibrant. Elijah had tried to wait her out, believing she would one day go back to being Nae, but she had not. And Lord knew he had needed to be touched. He had needed *her* touch, but she'd withheld affection.

She had cried and asked him to pray that feeling would return to her. She hadn't even been able to put her mouth on his, forget her putting it on his penis. Then when she had, there was no suction, and by all that was green, that was the one thing that Eve could do well. The witch knew it. Eve knew that was partially why he kept returning, but she wanted more. Elijah had repeatedly told her there was no more. Nevertheless, his returning had fueled Eve's hope.

Each time he'd left her, he'd felt sinful and defiled. The memory of her crawling all over him—just because he'd needed the contact—had haunted him. Unlike when he'd jostled with Mrs. Moon, the woman who had become a figment of his imagination. Sexy Naomi had no longer existed, not outside of Elijah's mind, or the photos in his bureau. He loved the Polaroid where she wore a see-thru baby-doll nightie. Stretched tight over her bulbous breasts, it separated to display her rounded stomach. Her nude legs were spread. A hand parted the gates of her garden, just for him. They'd taken the photo just before Topaz was born.

Elijah knew some people didn't think of him, or his wife, that way. That was why their thing had been exceptional. It had been a secret, messy, inventive, and exciting. And it had been theirs, alone.

Over the years, Elijah had kissed Naomi's photo countless times. He and she had been happy. Sure, they'd been busy and feeling put upon because Old Preacher had recently died, *but* they'd had each other.

Now, what did they have? A silent house, a sham marriage, and a kid outside their union. Oh, and a woman hell-bent on destroying them.

Elijah realized, if she could, Eve would destroy his reputation just to get what she wanted. She would gladly hurt all of those he pastored or had become a father figure to, all the people who believed in him. She would not hesitate to spew out that he, the preacher, had not lived a blameless life. The type of life about which he preached.

However, what Eve didn't understand was that type of life did not happen overnight. That was why it was called a '*life* of holiness.' One had to work up to it. It took years, and much prayer, fasting, and many times failure. That kind of life had to be guided by the Holy Spirit.

That, Elijah now saw, more clearly than ever. He saw that Eve did not respect the office of the preacher—his calling. She cared nothing about ministry. Eve only sought a certain position.

Suddenly Naomi's rebuke floated back to him. *You Romeo in a robe!*

Elijah scrubbed large hands over his aching head because he genuinely did not want to be seen that way, and especially not by his wife. From his youth, Elijah had disliked priest and preacher predators, those who preyed on parishioners. Now, was he one of them?

How had things gone so wrong? How had he gotten off the straight 'n narrow and onto this slippery slope?

Once again, Elijah asked for forgiveness. Then he prayed, *Lord, please don't take your spirit from me.* Unashamed to do so, he let his soul cry out, *Wash me over again, Lord! Would you please.*

Then as he sat in silence, Elijah Moon wondered. Was there any way he would ever feel restored, or right, again?

Chapter 45

Aт Greater Bethany Bible Congregation, Elijah Moon spoke to his daughter. "Come on, my jewel. Sing a song unto the Lord."

Topaz sat beside the organ because burly Deacon Wilnod's grandson sat there. Amil, a teen, was in training. Topaz forgot that now she didn't want her father calling her that, not when he had stolen her baby, in a way, and not when all along, he'd had a baby, with another woman.

Yet Topaz rose. She forgot the organ, with its swell and sound effects. Allowing young Amil to remain, she whispered that he should follow her lead. On stilettos, she crossed the church, appearing to all, the dutiful, beautiful daughter. Longing for the simplicity of the notes that the piano would refract back, Topaz sat. Wasn't she training Amil Wilnod to accompany others? This would be one of his most significant tests.

Seating herself on the piano that she had once loved, Topaz didn't even think about what she would sing. Forgetting all the eyes that were on her, Topaz forgot jealous rivalries. She dismissed young women who despised her for no reason other than she was the pastor's daughter. She didn't think about the young men who came just to ogle her, or about the little kids who adored the very ground on which she walked.

On the piano bench, Topaz sat. She closed her eyes. Slightly, she raised her fist to let Amil know, not now. Stretching elegant fingers, she did not need to see where she would place them. She had learned long ago, she only needed to feel. After all the practicing and attempts to get the notes just right, there was a point when the song simply came to her.

This, she knew, would be one of those times.

Melodically, Topaz began, a virtuoso, exercising fingers up and down the board. As she had known, when her fingers connected with the keys, sweet music flowed. She and the stringed instrument became one.

With eyes closed, blocking out all but what she felt, Topaz slid into an overture. She savored the clear high notes. She caused them to sound like dripping water. Then slowly, she allowed the music to trickle downward. It became somber as she transitioned into the key of B.

Topaz began to sing softly, and someone verbally shivered, calling out, "Ooh Jesus!" She had chosen a hymn because those she loved. Sure, in the youth choirs that she taught, the other young people, and even her best friend Caley, thought of hymns as 'old people songs.' Topaz did not.

To her, hymns were the songs that said what the soul could not say when words escaped one. Hymns spoke when a person could only feel, or when that person found themselves deep in trouble.

It was why she sang the hymn, *"Tis so sweet...to trust in Jesus..."*

In her heart, she knew *He* would not let her down. Her savior would never leave her to fend for herself, like her mother, Naomi had, so long ago; Naomi, who should have heard her heart's cry. Topaz's savior was not like her father either, the man of God, who sometimes did not hear from God. Topaz's savior would not hurt her, repeatedly. Lately, her father had not allowed his family to live in truth. However, Topaz's Savior ever admonished her to walk in truth, in the light.

Approaching the chorus, Topaz seemingly banged out thunderous notes. Simultaneously, she slapped the sole of her shoe on the wooden floor. It was as though, without words, she demanded that those congregated listen. Candidly, she sang, *"Jesus, Jesus, how I trust Him; how I've proved Him o'er* [over] *and o'er..."*

When she got to the part *"...Precious Jesus; oh, for grace to trust Him more,"* most of those over forty nearly wept.

Topaz sang on, and signaled for Amil on the organ to join her. *Jesus, I'm so glad I learned to trust Him, Precious Jesus, Savior, Friend.*

When she crooned the sweet somber refrain, her heart both broke and soared, each time. *"Oh, for grace to trust Him more..."*

Rocking and hugging herself, Naomi dabbed her eyes. In the corner, Mother See simply nodded. Although he appeared stoic, inside, Elijah Moon had totally melted. He'd have preferred not to, yet he felt the anguish and the tears in his daughter's every intonation. Bending to stare at his steepled hands, inwardly Elijah inquired, what could he do? What could any of them do, now, to make so many wrongs right?

Jesus, Jesus...

Aware that he appeared to most of his parishioners to be in worshipful contemplation, Elijah Moon reminded himself. He and his family were in this thing up to their ears. All any of them could do at this point was ask for God's forgiveness. Then maybe they could go on.

Precious Jesus.

Continuing to sing, Topaz euphoniously gripped the congregation. She barely allowed them to breathe. Singing with such sweet intensity, she saw none of what took place. She was unaware of what her father told himself, again, as tears rolled, unchecked, down his cheeks. He had simply tried to protect his family, the one at home, and his church family.

It was really all he had ever done.

Topaz was so wrapped up in the music. So lost in song was she, until she only felt the height of what those listening and watching felt.

Suspended between earth and heaven, she experienced being lovingly enveloped in her savior's arms.

Now, somewhere in the back of her mind, she knew what Old Preacher meant before she'd been born. Often, her golden-eyed grandfather had thanked God for using him, a willing vessel.

As she sang on, Topaz knew. *That* was what she, too, had always been. A willing vessel. And she would ever be so, because it was what she had chosen, long ago.

Oh, for grace to trust Him more.

Moreover, as the Greater Bethany congregation witnessed such rapturous beauty in song, they became the young songstress' willing captives. Until she chose to release them...and herself.

Slowly, she drifted back to earth.

Then the healing of the Holy Spirit flowed.

Chapter 46

Eliajh asked Ezra, "Wanna take a ride? I gotta get uptown."

Inches shorter, stocky Ezra shrugged, "Why not?" He and his older brother spent so little time together until a ride would do them good.

Getting in the car, Ezra asked, "So where to?"

Big Elijah turned the car around, "Sylvia's."

"Good." Stocky Ezra nodded. He loved the soul food restaurant located in Harlem. On Lenox Avenue, the famed eatery pulsed with color and vitality. There, locals and celebrities alike broke bread together.

As Elijah left Tranquility, merging with traffic on the Expressway, Ezra remembered that his brother knew the proprietor. The culinary queen was a brilliant and talented woman. Ezra thought about his and Elijah's last time at the eatery. Reverend Al Sharpton had been at the table next to theirs. Not far from him, Magic Johnson and another baller had sat, enjoying, as quietly they'd conversed.

When he and Elijah sat with succulent dishes before them, Ezra again noticed. Sylvia had created a homey atmosphere, and his brother Elijah seemed to relax within the eatery walls. The elder told a tale of intrigue and suspense. When Elijah enumerated a few situations, those in which he was currently embroiled, Ezra felt shocked.

As Ezra ate and listened, Elijah admitted to having stepped out on Naomi. With nary an interruption, Elijah said it wasn't like he'd often slept with Eve—a church member—although that was just what she wanted. Elijah said he'd had needs, they hadn't been met at home. He divulged that Naomi hadn't cared what he did. For a while, she'd turned a blind eye to her husband's extracurricular activities with other women. Elijah said then came Eve. Although she was a handsome woman and could have her pick of men, she had never turned him away. Elijah said he'd seen some deacons and others, checking her out. They kept their distance, though, because there was a running joke. People thought he hadn't heard, but very little didn't reach Elijah's ears.

Eve was left alone because she was 'set aside for the master's use.' Elijah thought that was ugly, but the consensus was: Eve was generally viewed as the 'king's concubine.' Where that thought process had originated, Elijah did not know. Then again, he did.

Eve had been known to contribute to circulating gossip. She did so in the attempt to force his hand because she wanted her son acknowledged.

Ezra said nothing, but his eyes widened because he hadn't guessed there would be a child, too —a son, even though his mom had hinted.

Big Elijah Moon continued, saying his son's mother wanted everyone to know about him, and that she'd had relations with the preacher. "She even invites church members to her home," Elijah divulged, "where she has her son's *birth certificate* framed. It's hung on the wall!"

Ezra tried not to appear shocked, but he had to ask, "Who does that?"

"Only someone a bit unstable or deranged," Elijah admitted. He even said that on numerous occasions, he'd asked Eve, "Why don't you take that down?" He'd reminded her, "Other people don't have their birth certificates on their wall." He said she'd had given him a long stare, before retorting. "Other people know they're wanted. They don't need reassurance, like my son does. His birth certificate is displayed to let him know that *somebody* wanted him."

Elijah said he'd growled, "The kid can hardly read yet!"

Stocky Ezra tossed his head back and laughed.

Elijah also said he wished he had never gotten involved. After all the pumping and grunting, which were supposed to relieve stress, he still felt anxious and hassled. "And I never gave her my best." Following the act, Elijah said, he didn't ever feel good or mellow. He only wanted to get his clothes and get home, where he could lie beside Naomi—whom he couldn't touch. Elijah divulged that his guilt and her indifference wouldn't allow for anything more. "So we lay there, like strangers."

Ezra ate and said nothing until it became clear that Elijah was spent.

"Rev, you need to talk to Nae. Tell her what's really going on."

"I did," Elijah divulged. "I had to; Mom spilled the beans—on purpose. You know how she is; always keeping something going."

Ezra shook his head. "Our mother, forever the little devil."

"Now Naomi hates me," Elijah groaned. "I think. Then again, she made me go to the doctor. She ordered me to bring her a note, of my 'clean-ness.' She mentioned some dream. She said, '*I just might* wanna ride you, biggie.' She said I owe her a good screw, said I owe her a few."

Ezra sputtered with laughter. "That girl! Remember back in the day? She was a teen when y'all met. Then she was twenty 'n you were twenty-three. She always did have a mouth on her—if someone got her started."

Elijah grinned. That was his Nae. "I guess she loves me," he shrugged, "but it's mixed with hate. I don't know which is worse; I used to think her ambivalence was bad, but with her loathing me, I'm torn."

Stocky Ezra laughed. He couldn't help it. "I can't say I have ever experienced loathing," not with Tippie, his imbibing wife. "Indifference, yes; for years, because Topeka is always tipsy. But," the younger brother said, leaning forward, "forget me, back to you. You do know that in this situation, bruh, you're living on borrowed time. I mean, since you've told Naomi, now you've got to tell your church members."

Elijah Moon's eyes widened, and he wanted to bellow, but he caught himself. "I can't do that!" he hissed, hoping eatery patrons didn't hear.

"You can't, or you won't?" his brother inquired. "Listen, Rev, I'm telling you; you say nothing, and it's just a matter of time before all of this comes out, anyway. So *I* say...you've told your wife, now get in the pulpit 'n tell your people. Take the wind out of Hester Prynne's sails."

Elijah guffawed, something he hadn't done in forever. "You did not just reference that book, *The Scarlet Letter*." It was about adultery. Sobering up, Elijah shook his head and stared at his pie. "I can't."

"You can, and you had better," the younger brother advised. Looking a lot like Elijah, stocky Ezra said, "You're human. Remind the people of that. Let them know that like anybody, you too became weak. Say it was a random thing. Show 'em how strong you are now, though, by being able to admit you were wrong. Rise above, bruh. Request forgiveness."

"They do wrong stuff, too," big Elijah pouted. "Remember, *I* know."

Ezra chortled. He did so until tears eased from his eyes. "I luh you man—wit' yo funny self!" Wiping his eyes, stocky Ezra called out, "Reverend Elijah Martin Moon, you and I both know, people do shit. Still, my brother, *you* are the preacher. People think you should never do wrong. So tell them that occasionally, you do." Ezra leaned forward. "I'ma tell you something. Your flock will feel betrayed once they know you've fallen, *but* if they hear it from *you*—first, they'll better be able to digest it. They love you, man, like they loved Dad. Who was ever able to resist Old Preacher? The people at Greater Bethany feel the same way about you. Just ask them, Elijah, to forgive you."

"Why would they do that, or trust me again? Even Nae's having a hard time with it."

"Sure she is. Wives are different." Ezra waved. "I ain't Dr. Ruth, but maybe to them, we're Superman. They put so much faith in us. But back to your church members. They trust you, man. So tell them that you understand that in going astray, you betrayed their trust."

Calmly, Ezra raised his coffee. Then he forked up his second slice of pie, like he hadn't a care in the world.

Watching him, Elijah knew his brother had many woes. With a half-drunk wife, and five feral teenagers, all boys, there was no way Ezra did not have problems. Yet, the younger man's advice was irrefutable.

Ezra then sounded sage and grounded when he said, "Big brother, I'm looking up to you. Don't let this come out any other way. Please."

On the ride home and all that evening, Elijah thought about his younger brother's words, even as he fine-tuned his sermon. At one point, Elijah also found himself chuckling because Ezra really was a wise man. Ezra was one whom Elijah had not given enough credit. For that, he asked forgiveness. It seemed he was doing a lot of that lately.

Elijah turned his mind to asking forgiveness from the members of Greater Bethany Bible Congregation. With his heart beating double-time, Elijah wondered. Could he really go through with it?

He also wondered if he had a choice.

The way he saw it, he did not. Not if he wanted to one day walk freely down the street...with *his son*, Elisha. The precious boy whom he called Eli.

Chapter 47

ON a rainy summer Thursday, Topaz could not believe she had a little time to herself. At Mother See's house, she couldn't believe that she was actually writing her resignation letter. She felt elated and a bit sad.

In the correspondence, she explained. Burly Deacon Wilnod's grandson, Amil, would take over a portion of her duties...

AT the big old Victorian, Naomi was about to have a conversation with the man she'd married so long ago. This mess with him and Eve had helped her realize. She had wanted a house full of children. Well, she had actually gotten that. More children had stayed, eaten, and slept in her home than she could count. When those children grew up, they brought their children to her. Often those grownups, the parents, told their children of all the fun they'd had at their pastor and first lady's home. Some even said the huge old Victorian had been their safe haven.

Therefore, Naomi recognized. She had *not* really been robbed of her children, as she had previously believed. Although the hordes of children hadn't come from her body, yet they loved her and their pastor, *and* she got to send them home, when she'd had enough. Indeed, it was a great way to parent. This Naomi thought as her smile began to widen.

She found herself chuckling because she'd made a vow. Naomi would put Cozi Moon in her place whenever necessary. No longer would she, Elijah's wife, allow his bitter little mother to rule her. Those days were over! Naomi was nobody's doormat. Just as Mother See had said, so many years ago, Cozi had her time. Everyone wished it had been longer, but God had not seen fit. Back when stylish Cozi had been Greater Bethany's first lady, she had done things her way.

Now, Naomi would do things her way.

Dusting her hands, Naomi felt satisfied as she recalled the prior Sunday. She'd cornered Elijah's mother outside his office. Dumbfounded, Cozi had stared. Naomi informed the overdressed old bag that she, Naomi *Moon* would run her home and affairs *her* way until God called her away. Stepping into Elijah's office then, Naomi was clear. Until that time, she would do her best *without* ridicule. "Cozina Anetta

Moon, I hope you understand. I'll take no more of your mess." Closing Elijah's door in Cozi's face, Naomi effectively shut the woman out.

Now all Naomi needed was for Elijah to put *Eve* in her place because, for the Moons, divorce was not an option. Naomi felt her little spark. Actually, inside, it was now a flame. Feeling most empowered, she entered her husband's domain. The room with the bay window. His home office smelled so good, just like him. Seating herself behind his massive desk, Naomi took the place of power. Then she called in King Elijah. She gestured for him to sit. Over there. When she spoke, Naomi didn't care that her man stared as though he had never before seen her.

When she got to the part where she said, "Elijah since there'll be *no more* catting around, this is what *you* are going to do..." The man couldn't help but grin. He didn't care that Naomi's instructions sounded a lot like the advice from his brother. All Elijah could think was *wow*. Nae sounded like her old self again. The woman he'd thought was lost was reemerging. Thank God!

Puzzled, Naomi stopped speaking. "Elijah Moon, what—may I ask—are you grinning at?" She mumbled, "Like a big ol' Cheshire cat."

Elijah shook his head wanting to say, 'Nae, you're back!' He did not though. He didn't want to jinx things or unnerve her. He shrugged. He continued to stare, with his heart and another part swelling, with love and pride. In that silk blouse, she looked delectable, very bubble-licious...

Ignoring the silly and salacious way her husband outright ogled her, super-sized sexy Naomi decided to end her speech. Rising from the big chair, she pulled at the short skirt that clung to her curves. "From now on, Elijah, you will seek *for others* what you'd seek *for yourself*. As servants of the Lord, and as servants of His people, it's what we'll *both* do." She turned to teeter away. Elijah couldn't stop himself.

He rushed that girl, wearing shoes in the house! Placing his arms around her from behind, he held her tightly, inhaling her intoxicating scent. Squeezing her bountiful goodness, the big brown man pawed her heavy hair aside. Repeatedly, he kissed her nape. "I love you, girl."

Instead of trying to untangle herself, as he had expected her to, Naomi simply placed her arms atop Elijah's. Loving the feel of him wrapped around, fondling, and grinding against her, she held his wrists. Then she did something she hadn't, in she didn't know how long. Naomi laughed.

Hearing what was truly joy, Elijah found himself chuckling too. When Naomi continued, feeling anger and thoughts of retribution disperse, tears trickled down her cheeks. And in her husband's arms, she turned.

Seeing her tears, Elijah took Naomi's face in his beautiful hands. Looking deep into her eyes, he asked again, "Forgive me, babe, please?"

Touching his wedding band, the one he always wore, Naomi nodded.

"I love you, Nae. I vow to be a better man, and a better husband."

"I know, Lijah," Naomi said as she held to the man who grasped her tightly. He ran his hands over her back. It was soothing. When his big hands eased down to cup her bottom, that became arousing. When he squeezed and lifted her off the floor, her breath emitted in spurts. Yet with her lips against Elijah's, Naomi whispered. "I love you, hon. I honestly do. I'm sorry too; I wasn't the best spouse."

"Yes," Elijah told her, "you always were, even when you were just doing the best you could."

Naomi really was bound to the man, irrevocably, as he'd wished, way back in the day. Of that, she reminded Elijah.

Holding her, he admitted that never could he have left her, either. "You Nae, are my *whole world*. You've always been. I hope you know."

There were tears in Naomi's eyes when she allowed Elijah Moon to fully kiss her. She kissed him back. Naomi also began to unbutton her silk blouse. Looking up, craftily, she asked, "You want some?"

What a gift! Towering over Naomi, Elijah saw an exquisite lace bra and all that filled it. Then he simply said, "My cup runneth over."

Boldly unzipping the man's pants, Naomi made him an offer. "How about some wet 'n skeezy, big preach? Would you like that?"

Elijah sensually growled. "I'm so glad you asked." Shoving things off his desk, he quickly lifted Naomi, high heels and all. On his desk, he shoved up her skirt and tore the triangle of lace beneath. Around his girth he arranged her great legs. With pants still on, hurriedly Elijah slid into Naomi. For a moment, he simply rested on her, savoring the feel.

He was home.

Then she lightly punched him. "Get to work, man! You owe me."

His laughter thundered out. "So I do." He took her buns in his huge hands. "As you wish, my lady," he said, and impaled her.

Amid the pulsating act, Elijah and Naomi were still half-clothed. Neither cared. Fervently kissing, laughing, and enjoying, while struggling to disrobe, they held on for dear life.

All tangled up, the couple found their way back…to each other.

Chapter 48

TOPAZ lay on her bed. With moonlight streaming over her, she couldn't sleep for thinking. She knew she needed to tell him— everything. She'd start with the baby, then her father's no-baby rule. She'd spill everything. Would he hate her? Would he feel she had been part of the cover-up, the conspiracy? That's how she often thought of it. Topaz wanted to even tell Cedric she loved him. She always had, ever since she'd been a single-digit kid. The one who'd just wanted to play the piano. Back then, he'd been a royal pain in her neck.

Many times, over the years, he'd intimated that he loved her. Had he loved her even way back, or had it begun when they were teenagers? He had been older, so perhaps he had been surer of his feelings.

Unlike her, he had lived. Not stuck in the church, early on, he had known about life. She had been sheltered, then shattered, when real life came crashing in on her. It came in the form of a pregnancy she had not known could happen. Nowadays, she wondered, how she could have been so stupid—no, so naïve.

Now she knew about the rhythm method, a natural means of birth control. It was based on fertility awareness and her cycle. Never again would she be so passé and unassuming about her body. Of her body, she was the landlady. Now she knew things, and one of them was that she had to have a conversation with Cedric. Topaz would speak with the man whom she thought of as one of her closest friends. It didn't matter that she didn't see or talk to him like she spoke to Caley, almost daily. It didn't matter that their lives had taken different directions. Cedric remained in her heart. Topaz hoped she was in his.

In the moonlight, following a magnanimous sigh, she rolled over. Used to be, she recalled, when she really needed him, he would call. It had been as though they were connected by some invisible bond. The only time that bond had been shaken was during that period, when she'd been skirted away and hidden, to have her baby. His baby.

Topaz slid a slender brown arm over her eyes. She needed to sleep and stop thinking. When she finally found herself drifting off, she heard her phone. She put out a hand. Into it, she whispered, "Hello?"

"Baybay."

"Cedric!" Tears stung her eyes because there he was, the only one who had ever called her that. "Hey, Ced."

"I got one question for you." His dense, rich, masculine voice was soft and soothing. "Are you as lonely for me…as I am for you?"

She could not contain the emotion she felt. "I am," she hiccupped. The truth was she was always lonely for him. She always longed for him and wanted to be with him. She wanted to hear his voice, touch his skin, kiss his face, his lips, and smell the scent that was only his.

"Then meet me outside Bay, in fifteen minutes."

"You're back in Tranquility?" she managed as she sat up. The top sheet fell away as she asked, "Where are you?"

"Doesn't matter. You wanna see me or not?"

"You know I do." She always wanted to see him, even when she'd thought she hadn't, during that scary time.

"Bay, what's up?"

She knew he asked because she was quiet. Swinging her shapely legs over the side of the bed, she said, "I'm getting ready."

"Good," he told her. "Since tomorrow's Saturday, I'm gonna keep you, maybe until late evening. I'll drop you off then, but only because I know you got church on Sunday."

She could hardly breathe. She felt much like she had back when she'd been an infatuated teenager. "Oh, pick me up from my grandma's. I'll bring a change of clothes."

"If I had my way, you wouldn't need clothes."

Topaz chuckled. "Well, Yella, you might not have your way."

"Girl, if I believed that, I would tell you to stay your sexy-self home."

She chuckled. "See you in a bit."

When Cedric pulled up, she was standing in the shadows. Topaz had apprised Mother See of her plans. She had then quietly exited the back door, hoping not to wake Armand. She'd walked on the side of the house where there was very little moonlight.

As Cedric stopped, she stepped from obscurity. To him, she looked like a small beautiful apparition. Drawing in a breath, he couldn't believe how shapely and lovely she was, after all this time. He couldn't believe she hadn't gotten dressed either. Walking toward him, he noticed she wore a short pale gown. It was cotton, paper-thin, with bra-like cups and spaghetti straps. She was pulling on a denim jacket. Her thick, glorious hair hung to her shoulders, and she wore dangling earrings and sexy sandals. Man! College sure agreed with her.

Getting into his sports car, she pitched her quilted bag into the back.

"Hey," Cedric said, as with a barely audible thud, she closed her door. He smelled the soft scent that ever floated about her. And his rod rose.

"Hey, you," she said. Her arm was yet high from depositing her bag. Her hand perched on his headrest. Comfortable, she leaned in for a kiss.

Turning to face her, his plush, pretty, pink lips parted, meeting hers. It was such sweet sensation. He kissed her succulently, a couple of times. With a hand, he held her face. His tongue swirled with hers. He realized. They were sitting outside her grandma's house, where that woman, or perhaps someone in a neighboring house, could see them. He sucked on her lips anyway while telling himself to get a move on.

Putting his vehicle in gear, Cedric advised, "Seatbelt, please." Then he zoomed off, wanting Topaz only to himself.

As they rode Tranquility's darkened, near-empty streets, with her heart excitedly racing, Topaz asked where Cedric had been. She said, "I ask because while kissing you, I tasted liquor." She knew somewhere he'd drank, perhaps even at his dad's bar.

"Does it matter?" Cedric asked. "Just know that wherever I was, I was trying to forget you."

Had she not known him as well as she did, she might have felt offended. However, she didn't and inquired, "Then why'd you call?"

"Why did *you* call *me*?" He kept his eyes on the road.

He was so popular and busy when he was in town until she would not have known the first place to look for him, much less to call, and on a Friday night, too. It was why she admitted, "I didn't touch the phone."

"You didn't have to; you've never had to. I'm connected to you."

She looked away from him. Sexy in a tee and worn jeans, he smelled like man and drive-a-sista-insane. Suddenly she only wanted to climb all over him. Forgetting that, she looked down at her hands in her lap. With the passing of every street lamp, her skin took on a golden hue; then, she could barely see it for moments again in the dark. Passing her parents' large old Victorian, she noticed. Her father's old Impala was gone, as it often was. Forgetting that, Topaz told Cedric, "I had only been thinking about you a little bit."

"I know." Cedric stated, "Thus, you called—you summoned—me." He seemed to change topics. "You know I'm gonna wind up on you, right?" He could see it as he stopped at a light on the near-empty boulevard. They would both be slick with perspiration and maybe massage oil. Cedric's voice became husky with need, "I can't wait to get into you." He'd feel her band around him. She would moan, make all her womanly little noises, and drive him crazy. He stepped on the gas.

Having similar thoughts, Topaz sure hoped to wind up all over Cedric. She desperately needed to feel him, his hard body on and beneath hers. She wanted his strong arms surrounding her. And his kisses! Boy, did she need those. Whenever he put those big, soft, pillowy lips on her, anywhere, she nearly liquefied; she would do whatever he asked. Heck, she had not met another man who had such power over her.

Looking up, she noticed. They were at his house. She didn't wait for him to come around to get her. She simply opened her door. Topaz turned, causing her seat to spring forward so she could grab her tote.

Cedric stiffened, seeing her bent in the moonlight. Her tiny panties were but a wisp of fabric beneath her transparent gown. Noticing that her undies barely covered her bountiful bottom, he stepped behind her. Cedric pressed his pelvis to her buttocks. Grasping her hips, he rocked. He slid up, then down, feeling her, as his breathing became labored.

With her head and shoulders still in the coupe, Topaz didn't move. Yet she felt, as Cedric gently used a foot to spread her legs. When his hardness, bulging inside his jeans, met her cavern from the rear, ohhh, just that limited amount of contact nearly undid her. Topaz backed up on Cedric, wishing he were within her.

All too soon, his large hands eased her from his vehicle. "Watch your head, Sweet," he said, taking her bag. Hell, if he hadn't gotten her up from there, he would not have been able to contain himself. He thought it while kissing and caressing her as they leaned against his coupe. With fingertips at the small of her back, beneath her trendy denim jacket, in the moonlight, Cedric turned. Then he guided Topaz up the front steps.

She stood with the storm door open as he reached around and before her. He was so close she could feel him, his thighs, his rock-hard chest and abs, and his heat. Giving her and himself a reprieve, he flicked his wrist and unlocked the oak door. Removing his key, Topaz walked into the dark. Behind her, Cedric locked the door. Before she knew anything, he jerked her to face him. With one hand, he took his keys, dropped them on a nearby table. With his other, warm at the small of her back, he pressed her close. "Why'd you come outside nearly naked?" His lips scintillatingly moved over the column of her graceful neck.

"I've got clothes on," she argued, wanting to lose them.

"No one considers a lil pair of panties, a see-through gown, and sandals, clothing."

"I've got on a jacket."

"Not anymore," he told her, disposing of it. Then as she stood there, in the moonlight, he slid his hands down her shapely little arms. Dipping his head, he kissed the rise and fall of her breasts. The swell of them was visible, just above her sexy gown. Cedric allowed his hands to slide down her sides. With hands on her back, he drew Topaz closer.

Unable to stop himself, Cedric took his lips on an exploratory hike. Over Topaz's shoulders and her neck, he slid into the valley between her breasts. Open-mouthed, Cedric kissed and sucked. He did so through the thin fabric, a semi barrier between his mouth and her. He left the material clinging as he ordered, "Take this off." He helped her peel her nightgown away. "Leave those," he said of her teensy panties. Removing his tee, Cedric started music.

Eyeing his moonstruck muscular back, Topaz heard The Rude Boys croon, *I Need You Girl*.

When Cedric turned back, Topaz could barely breathe, watching as languidly he drew his belt. Cedric stepped from his jeans and was... formidable. Topaz just wanted to touch him as the R&B quartet sang about sunshine on the worst of rainy days.

"Commere," Cedric coaxed, pulling Topaz close. Seating himself on the leather sofa, he placed hands on her hips, level with his eyes. Slowly he eased her panties down so she could step from them. Leaning forward, Cedric kissed her navel and inhaled. As he did, his hands spread to encompass the lovely round mounds of her bottom.

"I've never forgotten your scent," he said, holding her. He very nearly added that he had searched for it everywhere and with every woman with whom he'd tussled. Cedric didn't want to explain, though, that with them, he'd used condoms, something he hated. He'd have had to tell Topaz again. Although he wasn't sure she altogether believed, she was the only woman with whom he went bare. She was the one. With her, it was the best he'd ever had... perhaps because she held his heart.

Sure, other women were more experienced. This Cedric acknowledged with hands cupping Topaz. Sure he enjoyed their play and teasing, but he had found out something. It was what he hadn't cared to know. Sex was just that, if not with the one he loved. However, with that one, it was an all-inclusive trip to the stars!

As she stood unmoving before him, with her hands softly cradling his head, Cedric suddenly felt different from the way he had a moment prior. Somehow, he felt protective and tender. Therefore, he said, "Sit, Bay." Turning Topaz away and easing her onto his lap, he didn't try to maneuver into her. He simply rested his head on her pretty back. Wrapping his arms and legs around her, he slowly caressed her.

"Sweet," Cedric began, "you do know that no matter what happens, I'll always belong to you. Right?" Cedric asked because… He did not know.

Dropping her head, Topaz sniffled. She wondered if Ced would feel the same way after she revealed a few things.

She remained silent.

Cedric felt what? Hot…tears? Onto his forearms that were wrapped about her, the tears plopped. "What's the matter?" he asked, alarmed. In the dark, over softly playing music, Cedric inquired, "Bay, why you crying?"

Not sure she could, but knowing it was time, Topaz spilled all.

Chapter 49

THAT Saturday, she woke with sunlight pouring over her. Topaz blinked. Cedric stood at the window as fresh summer air caused the curtains to rise and fall around him. Then Topaz remembered. Last night. She'd sat on Cedric's lap. He'd held her as everything tumbled out of her. She'd included that she loved him and probably always had.

Well, she thought, he hadn't tossed her out because she was still in his home. Therefore, croakily she called, "Ced."

Appearing determined, he slowly turned from the window. Facing her he said, "Lemme ask you something."

She struggled up in the comfortable bed that smelled decadently of him. "Okay."

"Does my son know he's mine?" Cedric had barely slept, thinking of nothing else since he'd heard. He also realized that had Topaz wanted, he could not have gotten freaky with her. Not last night after hearing all. Good thing she'd been exhausted from crying and maybe from having kept such a secret for so long. Most likely, she hadn't wanted to get busy either. Cedric didn't know. All he knew was that ever since, his mind had stayed in overdrive. Realizing she hadn't answered him, again he asked, "Bay, does Armand know I'm his father?"

"No." She told the truth. "Not really, but you have to understand. At five, he's essentially still a baby." She didn't want Cedric to feel dejected, as *she* had on so many occasions. Soothingly she added, "You're special. That I've made sure he knows, but it's our secret."

Solemnly, Cedric nodded. "Now I know the real reason you made him keep your and my 'friendship'—even my seeing him—quiet."

Cedric slammed a fist into his palm, "That lying bastard!"

Topaz knew he meant her father.

"I could kick Pastor Moon's ass."

"What would that solve?" Topaz inquired, dreading the very notion. Pushing hair from her face, she revealed, "This right here, your reaction, is why I didn't say anything—and you can't, either."

"Yeah, because who would believe me anyway?" Cedric sounded bitter. "Who would take my word over the preacher's?"

"It's not just that," Topaz stated, very nearly wishing she had never left home last night. "If this came out, it would hurt a lot of people. The congregation believes in him. They'd be devastated, and—"

"I don't care!" Cedric was heated. "What about me—and *you*?" He dropped to his knees before her. "What about *Army*? Dammit. I missed so much with him, and with you. What if I had wanted to know and be there? I hate that he was born without me! I wasn't the man to hold him or give him a bottle. *I* should've given him one of his first baths!"

Cedric was torn up inside. "Damn it, Taupe, what about that boy— *our* boy? Is he supposed to live this lie just because your father decided? Am I supposed to live it, too, because it was the preacher's decision? Who made him God? Does he think I don't want my kid—that I can't take care of him? Granted, when all this happened, I could'na been much help, *but* I could have *been there*! Your father don't rule me! He doesn't own me. I'm a man, and shit has got to change." With wild eyes, Cedric felt insanely angry. "I swear." He spun. "I should go choke him out!"

Scrambling up, Topaz reached for Cedric. "No!"

Squeezing the hand that pulled on his arm, Cedric knew Topaz was distressed. He was too, and he had to ask, "What gives Pastor Moon the right to fu—*fiddle* with people's lives this way?"

Topaz could not answer, partially because all those questions she had already asked a thousand times and because she had no answers.

Cedric's voice became soft as in the morning sunlight, he pulled Topaz to him. "I want to see him—Armand—today. I want my boy to know." On his knees before Baybay, Cedric kissed her, her mouth, eyelids, and cheeks. He thought as he had all night, how hurt she'd had to be…living in that house, under that criminality. Then unable to acknowledge the boy she loved with her all; the little chubby-faced kid who was hers, and *his*. Not the preacher's! Cedric wanted to go get his boy right now. But racing around would scare the kid because shorty didn't know him like that, not yet.

Down on his knees, with Topaz facing him, Cedric pulled her onto his lap. He wanted her on the rod that sought her heat, despite his jeans. With parted knees on the floor, he held her tightly. To calm himself, he inhaled her; he felt her, the little body that had given his son life.

Now he knew why Topaz had always seemed like such a loner amid people. Now he knew why she connected with certain songs and could sing the devil out of even the most wounded soul. *She* was wounded, and *he* had further placed her in that spot by not knowing.

He had caused her pain. Just like her effin' father. Dammit! Cedric thought, he should have left Baybay alone, when she'd been young and naïve. Had he not had to get inside her, she'd be different. Had he not wanted to feel her sexy little body clamped around his, had he not wanted her elegant fingers drifting over him, the way they floated over the keyboard, things would be different. They'd be much less painful.

Cedric would never forget what she'd told him, what she had been through. The worst part was that he had been unaware. That Cedric hated, and he'd missed so much! He wanted to kill somebody. Sure, another man would not have believed. Nevertheless, Cedric knew Bay. He had known her nearly all her life. She didn't make up stuff. She wasn't given to lies. Cedric knew something else. Out of all the time that he'd believed he was just banging Bay, he had never used protection. Well, maybe twice or thrice, but looking back, he could see. He'd poured so much love into her until there was no way she would not have become pregnant. At the time, however, he hadn't seen it. What had he been thinking? Cedric wondered. *He* had been the adult! Well, nearly.

Cedric's princess. That brought him back to what she'd said. Her father had been furious. Elijah Moon had wanted to have the baby's father charged with statutory rape. Elijah had wanted the scoundrel—whoever he was—in jail! Topaz said that was when she'd dug in her heels.

Recalling her words, Cedric nearly smiled because when little Bay chose, she could be challenging. "Sweet," he heard himself call, because nothing had changed since her revelation. He still wanted her, with the same intensity that he always had. It was crazy. The only thing was: now, he knew better how to control himself. And he had a kid!

"Baby," Cedric crooned. "Baby," he repeated because she really was his baby. And when she had been but a sheltered baby herself, she had had a baby—*his* baby. And he hadn't been there for her, or their kid.

Cedric kissed Topaz. With hands beneath her buttocks, he lifted her. He wanted to right everything, for her. Removing his jeans, he re-settled her more firmly on his package. Desiring only to be inside her, Cedric wanted to correct things for himself too, and for their kid.

Dammit, why hadn't he known? The preacher's wife had never appeared pregnant, not to him, but then she'd come back with a baby. Stories had circulated. That had been the perpetration, *the lie*! The timing fit perfectly, though. Topaz had returned too, shapelier, and sad, and near-sullen. Why hadn't he recognized? Often when he'd attended services on the low, on weekends stolen from college, Cedric had seen how she'd looked at the baby, with such longing. He guessed he'd miscued because people said the baby was her *brother*. Yet she'd gazed at the baby—Armand—the same way that he, Cedric Stable, had often gazed at her.

Why hadn't he recognized that she sometimes brought the kid around when her parents were out of town, and he was in town? There had been a time or two when she and he had made love. She'd shushed him, saying she didn't want the kid, sleeping in the next room, to hear, just like real parents. Heck, they were young, but they *were* real parents!

Damn. There was so much he needed to know and do. Now he would have to play catch up. That hurt. It made Cedric feel he'd been robbed.

Why hadn't he seen the tenderness that she'd lavished on the kid? The way Topaz often kissed Armand's pudgy face, as though she could just eat him all up. Why hadn't Cedric realized? He, too, had more affection for Armand than had been explicable. Cedric had even thought that were he to ever have a kid, he would want one just like the boy who looked like Topaz. *His* boy.

Bumping into the remarkable little woman who rested in his arms, Cedric wanted her to feel *him*, his heart. It was hers. He wanted her to know. Unable to stop kissing her, he said she needed to know just how he felt about her. He no longer cared that her father wanted more for her than a barman's son. The truth was he, Cedric Stable, was doing well for himself. At twenty-four, he was quickly working his way up to becoming highly sought after in his field.

And he loved Topaz Moon. However, "But no," was what Cedric said. Looking at his chest pressed to her lush soft breasts, the ones that had probably nourished his son—he didn't know—he made himself speak. "This right here, my getting into you, is what got you in trouble."

With widening eyes, he couldn't believe her. Why was she crying and scrambling up? Off his lap, Topaz sobbed as though her heart would break. She spoke in a desultory fashion, seemingly digressing, so much until he could hardly follow. She plopped onto his bed—the bed that had gotten them in this situation. "Should'na...told..." she blubbered. "Knew. Wouldn't want me..."

"No! No, Bay," Cedric dismissed that. "I do want you. I just don't wanna complicate shit." He raised her tear-streaked face. "Baybay, I don't want things to be harder, for you."

"I could stand this," Topaz hiccupped, "all of it, because of you...because I had you, always, in a way, in my heart. Now..."

Oh, man! She undid him, he thought as he kissed her. With gentle hands, he brushed back her tousled hair. And Cedric's heart broke.

There were so many things he wanted to tell her, or did he? Watching her toss herself dejectedly amid his mussed cover, he felt a storm brewing inside. Cedric realized he was unaware of how to handle his spiraling emotions. He wanted to inflict pain on her father, but he wanted to comfort her, too. Cedric could no longer string words together as on his knees he kissed Topaz's arm. With his own tears assailing, he kissed her shoulder as she curled up on his bed. Though her coppery-smooth back was to him, he kissed it, lifting thin pale fabric.

Wondering what to do, Cedric ran his hands over Topaz. Never again would he be that dude, the seemingly carefree man that he had been, just a day ago. Now that he knew about his son, he had to do something.

He wanted to pull the skimpy gown from her, the one she'd replaced last night after she dropped her bomb. Cedric made himself do no such thing. However, he did tell Topaz, as she lay staring glumly away, that he wanted to remove it. As he did, she raised her arms, her way of helping. He saw his discarded jeans. Then hovering over her, with his rod straining for her, he laid her back amid sun-warmed rumpled sheets. All along her body, he slid, several times, the friction inciting and delighting them both. Cedric whispered, "I won't cum inside you, Bay..." like that would help.

With his scent surrounding her, Topaz looked up and into the now-chiseled face that she had always known. The face of the man that she would always love. She was attuned to her body's rhythm. Thus, like a flower, for Cedric, Topaz opened as she advised, "Yes. Yes, you will."

Tenderly they moved, together. All hard planes and muscles, Cedric eased in and out of Topaz. He did so while kissing her swollen, red-rimmed eyes. His mouth covered hers as he gave her his breath, his life.

Joined, she breathed life back into him, and Topaz realized. This time was nothing like the time that had produced their son. This time, she and Cedric knew what they were doing and why. They loved. For them, there would be no more hiding. This time, coupling, for two consenting adults, was Heaven on earth.

Chapter 50

SUNDAY morning, Elijah was nervous as he sat on the pulpit. Today was the day. He remembered as the time neared for him to give the sermon. In a minute, he told himself, he would do as promised. He would not back out. He would apprise his congregation of his wrongdoing...

ELIJAH began as he often did, exhorting the Lord's people to worship. Then he asked them to turn with him to Genesis. There, he showed them Adam and Eve. He showed how the pair wound up sinning. Elijah pointed out the couple's fear of being naked or uncovered.

"Brothers and sisters, often *we* too fear being naked, uncovered, or even found out—after we have sinned." Elijah admitted, "This fear harks back to the garden of Eden. This fear is predicated upon sin. Fear began when sin entered the garden through disobedience. In *our* lives too, fear enters through disobedience—when we've sinned."

Elijah instructed those gathered to turn with him to II Samuel, chapters 11 and 12. He did so with trembling fingers and a frantically beating heart. There, he summarized the story of King David, and Bathsheba. Elijah elucidated how the King had seen a woman so beautiful that he'd just had to have her. "King David didn't stop there," Elijah stated. "He found out the woman was married, to a soldier in his army." Yet that did not slow the king; he had the woman brought to him so he could lay with her. Then later, the woman sent word. She was with child. The King had the woman's husband, the soldier, placed in the forefront of battle. There the man was to surely be killed. "After the woman mourned her husband's passing, the King felt free to have her."

Elijah explained to the members of Greater Bethany why the King's actions had been wrong on so many levels. Elijah said a prophet appeared before the King. The prophet said God revealed certain things...

"Confronted with his sins," Elijah stated, "the King repented. Unlike many of us today, King David truly sought God's forgiveness."

Standing before his congregation, feeling naked and so like the shamed King, Elijah bowed his head. Softly he spoke. "I am here today to do the same thing." Elijah said *his* sins had come up before the Lord. "Thus, I want to repent, publicly." With raised hands and uplifted eyes, again Elijah asked God to forgive him. Then as tears of remorse streamed from his eyes, Elijah asked his congregation to forgive him.

On the organ, for perhaps the last time, since she had tenured her resignation, Topaz did not know what to play. Feeling confused, she recognized. That was the only time she had ever been at a loss in any service. She almost wished she was anywhere but in GBBC. Topaz felt hot, like she was under a microscope. She felt it more so than usual because people glanced at her, and her mother, to gauge their reactions.

Therefore, Topaz relaxed her features. She watched her father, who was so obviously broken up. Tripping over the organ keys, her fingers did not touch them. No music came forth. In the stillness, where not even a baby cried, Topaz scanned her memory.

At last, she came up with one song. *I Am Thine O Lord.* It was sometimes called, *Draw Me Nearer.*

She played it with the volume on low, as many in the Greater Bethany Bible Congregation began to stand, all over the sanctuary. Yet her father spoke on. He stated that, like Adam and Eve, he too had realized he was naked because he too had sinned. Elijah said he wanted to be right, though. He lamented that with his whole heart, he wanted to follow God.

Topaz reached the chorus, *Draw me nearer, nearer blessed Lord*, and her father was crying—something she had never before seen. Her mother was too but lovely Naomi appeared encouraging, and as did others.

Speaking haltingly, as he stood before the congregation, the Pastor looked regal in his robe. Tearing his eyes away from his wife, big Elijah Moon was grateful. Nearly invisible had been Naomi's nod. Seeing the little copper-skinned boy seated beside her, Elijah chose not to mention Armand. Remembering all the parishioners he'd counseled and countless others who'd confessed, Elijah recalled. None of *their* confidences had he ever betrayed. Thus, he would afford his daughter the same courtesy. What had become her secret was now hers alone, to tell, if she so chose.

But *his* secret? It was one he was tired of carrying. The weight of it sickened him. It caused him to feel fraudulent, and like a failure—which he was not! This he explained to the people. He explained that wrongdoing and sin did that to a person. It drove a wedge between them and God. It forced them away from those they loved.

"However," Elijah resolved, "today, I remove that wedge. I choose to go back to the place, with my God, where I felt free and unencumbered."

Topaz began to play *Take Me Back* by hymnist Andraé Crouch as Elijah spoke of having a son. The child had been born *outside* his and Sister Naomi's union. Elijah let the people attempt to digest that.

Feeling a bit more sure, Topaz softly played on.

Yes, Elijah had shocked many with his revelation. Some even murmured, looking wide-eyed from one to another. However, Elijah continued to speak as he descended the pulpit steps. At the front of the church, he stood before the altar. There, he called for little Elisha.

"Come, Eli, stand before the Lord's people."

Rising, Eve did not know how to feel. With her heart beating locomotive fast, she too watched as her beautiful child obeyed.

Slowly but without fear, the small boy made his way down the center aisle toward his father. As he did, Topaz played the verse.

Lord, I feel that I'm so far from you, but still, I hear you calling me...

Elijah Moon laid a big hand on the boy's curly head. "I acknowledge this child," Elijah said. "*My* child. He was created, like all of us, in sin and shaped in iniquity. Yet, *he is no mistake. He is truly loved.* My actions before his birth are questionable, and they are why I beg forgiveness." Hugging the boy to his side, Elijah beseeched the people not to lay the sins of the father at the feet of the child. As the child clung to Elijah's robe, Pastor Moon's big bejeweled hand stroked his curly head. Elijah asked Bethany to love little Eli as they had loved him.

"Many of you have loved me from the time I was younger than my boy is now. I pray you will continue to love us both."

Playing *Renew my strength, restore my joy*, Topaz could only see swirls of movement and color. Tears swam in her eyes, yet she was vaguely aware. People moved toward the altar, where prayer took place. There, one by one, the old mothers of the church began to hug their Pastor, who never let go of his son, the small boy who sat on his arm.

Lost in a world of music, Topaz played, *And dry my weeping eyes.* Still, she noticed other people. Appearing stricken, a few quickly slipped from the church. Perhaps her father's revelation had been too much for them, or maybe he'd hit too close to home. It could have been that those people would have preferred it if the preacher had never sinned, or if he'd continued to live a lie. Topaz did not know. All she knew was that she was *proud* of her father. Aware that his revelation would be harrowing, yet he'd offered it. He had not tried to sugarcoat things either or place blame elsewhere; Pastor Moon had simply laid all on the line.

Topaz segued into and began to sing, *Is Your All on the Altar*. Sure, she knew there would be repercussions. There would inevitably be those who would say Elijah Moon needed to be removed from the office he held so dear. They would say he didn't deserve to lead. Others would not agree. Topaz would be rooting for her dad because he had done right, at last. Realizing it, Topaz felt a swell of love for him. In recent times, it had seemingly dwindled. Now love flowed back into her heart.

After the benediction: *Now let the power of the Holy Spirit rest rule and abide; now, henceforth and forevermore...*

The people of the Lord sang 'Ahhh-men.'

With a holy kiss, they went forth to greet their neighbors.

Packing up her sheet music and other paraphernalia, Topaz heard those nearby. They said things she'd not hoped to hear. The service was so anointed; it had been lovely and so moving. As she stood beside the organ, she watched a line of people, all waiting to embrace their Pastor. Men quickly shook his hand before ambling away, and it stunned Topaz to realize. The capacity of the Lord's people *to forgive*...was enormous.

WHEN Naomi left Bethany that Sunday afternoon, she couldn't recall ever having been hugged so much. Not in such a short time. She couldn't remember how many times someone had said to her in passing, "We'll get through this, Sister," or "God bless you."

As she drove, she wanted to cry. For so long, she'd wanted to hold Elijah's sin against him. She'd wanted him to pay, not realizing that he *had* paid, in feeling guilty and soiled, and in other ways. Naomi also became cognizant that she hadn't ever thought about *herself*; she wanted forgiveness when she was wrong—and she *had* done wrong. She wasn't blameless in her and Elijah's woes, not by any means.

As she drove, another Sunday crossed Naomi's mind. On that day, when she'd gotten home, the house had been cold. The oil bill had not been paid. Naomi had been angry, especially when she remembered that Elijah had made sure the church had heat. Thinking back, Naomi saw. Those things had not been important. She recalled too that at home, she had simply turned on the oven. Then she, Elijah, and their baby had gotten through the cold. When Naomi looked over their lives, she saw that she and Elijah had come through many things. Many storms they had weathered together. Mr. and Mrs. Moon would continue to do so because they took their vows seriously. For better or worse. At this point in their lives both wanted to be true, to each other, and to their God.

In the big old Victorian, Naomi bustled around her kitchen with high heels on. She tied an apron over her lovely lavender summer dress. She'd hung its matching sheer coat aside. Naomi heard a car door slam. On the driveway, she heard another and another. She looked out the window and nearly laughed. A bunch of kids had come home with Elijah, and so had an older mother from Bethany. Teenagers poured from a different car.

Placing a hand to her mouth, Naomi fondly realized. Youngsters and others had been in and out of her home for more than twenty years. Naomi thought about her man as he unlocked the front door because that was who Elijah Moon was. He was *hers*; it didn't matter what had transpired. He and she had come through many things. Those things had only made them stronger, together. They and Greater Bethany still stood.

Naomi knew Elijah had to be worn out after the morning's ordeal. When he came in, she looked up and took the beautiful giant in her arms. With children skirting them and making themselves at home, as they often did, Elijah kissed Naomi. Then he said he'd go up and nap.

She gave the kids a few tasks, like setting the table. Naomi gave the responsible teenagers the job of watching the currently heating large dinner that she always prepared—just in case parishioners needed a meal. Then Naomi told all her children, and sweet Mother Jones, that she'd be right back. "Oh, and y'all pour that soda in the punch."

Naomi ascended creaky stairs. Elijah was abed. In the hot room, she started the fan. Naomi pulled the sheet up over Elijah. Pivoting, she hung the clothes that he'd quickly discarded. She knew the day, and the night leading up to it must have taken a lot out of Elijah. Meticulous man that he was, never would he have laid his shirt and suit down, otherwise. As she turned from the closet, she heard Elijah's muffled voice.

"I love you, Nae."

About to leave the room, she softly admitted, "I know, Lijah."

He heard her downward tread. With closed eyes, he smiled, aware that his wife loved him too. Over the years, she had proved it in a multitude of ways. Earlier in the day, she had again been his rock. Although she might not want to, Elijah *wished*. With Naomi, he wanted to share his unique way of saying 'I love you.' However, since her hysterectomy, she'd often had little interest in sex. Then other times, here lately, things were spicy. Yet, *he* always had a voracious appetite for her.

That led Elijah to remember the female attention that he often received. He recalled that for a while there, it had kept him riled up. His being riled was how he'd found himself involved with Eve.

Every day after that, he'd wished he had kept his horse in the stable. Then he'd not have had that woman breathing down his neck at every turn. Elijah shook his head. His stint with infidelity had taught him; he had too much to lose, and catting around was not worth it.

Wearing nothing beneath the cool sheet, he turned over. On his back, he wondered if he heard movement. Had Naomi returned?

Indeed, she had, and she spoke. "I forgot something Lijah."

His eyes remained closed as he inquired, "What's that, Mrs. Moon?"

"I forgot to tell you...that *I want you*." She sounded like she was grinning when she added, "And had you not brought all these people home, I'd have shown you." So what, she'd rounded out? So had he. He was big and beautiful. She was voluptuous. Sexy, but in a more confident and adult way, Naomi knew it. Soon her man would know it again too.

"Know what Lijah? I might yet have my little blue nightie around here, somewhere."

He roared with laughter. It was the one she'd worn in the super suggestive photo taken just before Topaz was born. What a gift.

"Oh, you find that funny, do you?" Naomi sounded like she really pondered it. "I wonder if I'd even be able to get into it again..."

Supremely pleased, Elijah guffawed. "I'd love to see that." Opening his eyes, he reached for Naomi. "But, woman, I like my presents already unwrapped. That way, I can get to the good stuff faster."

With a chuckle, she leaned down and gave him a racy kiss. "Then one unwrapped goody coming up." She poked her head under the sheet. There she open-mouth kissed his lower head, surprising him. Back out, she said, "I promise, you'll get a *suck*. This evening. Think you ready?"

He couldn't help but pull her down onto him and their bed to show her. He was more than ready. Through the sheet, she felt his mighty proven sword. "Good Lord!" Naomi eked.

Suddenly, desiring big gorgeous Elijah, his wife straddled him. Wanting to discard her panties, she rode the bronco. Quickly rising though, Naomi said, "This has got to stop." Still, she turned back. Unable to help herself, she used a hand to mold the sheet to Elijah. Through slatted eyes, he watched her gaze at his length and fondle his heaviness. Then Naomi flung back the sheet. She ardently slid on nude Elijah while kissing him, for a blessed few moments. "Okay. I gotta get downstairs."

Both people felt they hadn't nearly had enough.

"Let me go, hon." Breathless, she said it because the man who smelled tempting pulled her back onto him. Fervently kissing her and molding her curves with his warm hands, he indeed started something.

Feeling like a young-married, erotic thoughts flitted through Naomi's head. Their effects coursed through her body. Still, Naomi untangled herself. "Stop now, man." With a quick two-step, she managed to evade Elijah's seeking fingertips. "No more tempting me. Pull that sheet up, Lijah. But later, I will be having *some of you*! —Because you owe me."

He loved owing her. Actually, he had a lot of lost time to make up for. They could start with him licking her, or getting some from the back.

Before the mirror, Naomi smoothed her lovely lavender dress and her apron. She touched at the gray in her heavy satin hair. Then knowing her man watched, on high heels and great legs, she sashayed from the room. Grinning, she made sure to shake what her mama gave her.

Lying beneath the tented sheet, Elijah Moon laughed loudly. That girl. Wearing shoes in the house. Always. Then Elijah groaned because *how* he *wanted* forty-something Naomi, right then! He desired her with the same intensity he had when he'd been a younger man. But as he knew, no one ate her good cooking and left. They lingered and ate some more. Getting up, he found a shirt and slacks. In minutes, he would eat and linger too, with the great big family God had seen fit to give them.

"Gotta feed my children!" Naomi called from the stairwell. All of her Greater Bethany Bible Congregation babies.

However, the husband and his wife both knew. Although Elijah's skeezy stuff had to wait, he would get it, and so much more!

Chapter 51

AT her little apartment, Eve was stunned and angry. She tore sheets off her bed. They were the ones that held a hint of that man's scent. She should have changed them months ago, when Elijah had stopped coming around, but she'd wanted to feel close to him. Now, she felt like he had made a fool of himself. He had done so before Bethany, earlier in the day. He had made *her* look supremely stupid and skanky too.

Angrily Eve wondered. Why had Elijah done that? Why had he publicly humiliated *her*, by choosing Naomi over her? In the past, he'd said that he believed she, Eve, was unstable. Months back, he'd said he only slept with her to appease her. Now Eve knew. He'd done it to keep her quiet—until he could out her! Now he had other people thinking she was the church tart! Now she looked like Delilah, who'd betrayed Sampson.

And the saints! Most skirted around her like she had the plague. After service, old mothers had shaken their heads at her, like she should have been ashamed. A few had hugged Eve. One said, "I'm praying for you, daughter." Eve had approached others who'd stood talking, as they often did after service. Quieting, they refused to look at her, so she knew. They had been discussing her, the preacher, what he'd revealed, *and* her son.

Eve felt overwhelming anger. Why was no one treating *the preacher* like a pariah? Sure, people were shocked. Sure, they'd discuss it for months to come, but Elijah Moon was being hailed, by some, for coming clean, for confessing his sins! Now he would be legendary too, like his father. Eve had even heard burly Deacon Wilnod rasp that he felt more like his pastor was a true man of God. Really?

The stupid fat deacon had rasped, "You admitted you'd fallen, Rev." Wilnod said it took a big man to tell his sins to others. "Yass, when that man knows them others will judge and maybe even try to derail him."

What made Eve most angry, though, was *Naomi*. Now *she* was cast in angelic light! *She* would forever be praised for being long-suffering and prayerful, while Eve had become the outcast. All in the space of a few minutes. Eve had hurried, with bowed head, to her car. In the parking lot, she'd felt people watching her. Suddenly Eve wondered. Why hadn't she believed Elijah when he'd said he really wanted to be able to acknowledge his son? She should not have provoked him, not by telling him to prove it. Eve had believed he'd been just talking. That had given her a false sense of power. She'd felt like she held all the cards. She'd had something on the preacher. It was what he had been unwilling to own up to; that she had held over his head. Now, she had very little power left.

Eve remembered how she sped out of GBBC's parking lot, nearly hitting another car. She'd recalled Elijah's words at the same time.

"You know I can't very well get up and do what you want, Eve." He had said it time and again. "I can't tell people about this that's happened between us."

She recalled taunting him. "You always worry about the way stuff looks, but one day—"

He had cut her off, slowly enunciating, "You don't worry enough, Eve. That's your problem. It's why you could never be a preacher's wife, or the first lady."

The man might as well have punched her, the way that had hurt!

She'd screamed. "I'm good enough to screw, at night, but not good enough to be seen with in the light!" Eve had long known she wasn't the type of woman to whom someone like Elijah Moon would commit, but she had ignored the notion. She had been determined to level up in life. Elijah Moon had been her way to do it. What had he called it? Oh, yes, he'd said women wanted to climb up in the world, on *his* back. Eve knew she was just that type of woman, but unlike the others, she was smart. *She'd* had the preacher's baby. *That* could not be ignored.

Eve had also ignored Sister Smart. Down through the years, the church secretary had often shook her head. The older woman always mumbled, "This can't end well, Eve. Not for *you...*"

Eve had ignored the fuddy-duddy because what did Sister Smart know?

Elijah had gotten his coat and placed a large hand on her son's head. His son's head. She'd wanted to shove Elijah as he bent to softly speak to little Eli. Their son had appeared sad. He'd wanted his father to stay. When the man had drawn up to his full height, Elijah Moon met the mother's angry eyes. "I've said it from the beginning, Eve. This had nowhere to go. I never lied to you. I always told you. I'm committed."

Yeah, Eve knew, but through the years, she'd taunted Elijah. She did so once more. "You're so 'committed' to a woman that you step out on. You're 'committed' to the members of a church that would crucify you, if they knew about the real you!"

Elijah had said nothing. He'd simply headed for her apartment door. "I'm figuring, and I guess you should know Eve; you and I end here."

Her eyes had widened. "What? —us? Ending? No way."

The man had never been anything other than truthful when speaking to Eve. "I feel this thing has run its course. This is over."

What the fuck? Eve had been so angry she'd felt volcanic! She felt like the man saw her as nothing more than a roll of bathroom tissue, to be used and discarded.

In the outer hallway, Elijah had nodded. "I'll take care of my boy."

"Oh, because you're so *committed* to that chick who once tried to give *me* marital advice; I haven't forgotten. Eli, go in your room." Angry, Eve had pointed, and the child obeyed. "Well, Pastor Moon, give your little *wife* some advice from me! Tell *Mrs. Moon* that she should suck her own husband's big black dick—or he'll seek someone who will."

Elijah had sadly shaken his head as Eve hollered after him. "You'll be back! Then I'll make you beg." She'd screeched, "I'll make you pay, preacher! I won't let you 'n that other kid of yours rob *my son* of his inheritance!"

Now, Eve angrily thought as she laundered her sheets – the ones that the preacher had lain with her on. The man had gotten up in church and he had shamed her. Big time.

Well, *she* had something to say about that.

Chapter 52

CEDRIC knew he should have been readying himself for his flight back to Vegas, but he had to make the stop.

He drove to the preacher's house. There, he banged on the door like a crazed man. He rang the doorbell, but that produced no one. As he stood waiting for someone to open up, he recalled Topaz. She'd begged him not to go to her parent's home. She'd said, "Let me go back to school," and back to Mother See's house. Topaz said she had only a year and a half left when she should have had a full two. She said she'd worked so hard, had heaped a ton of credits on herself. She reminded him of her double major and that she worked like a yoked ox.

She told Cedric of her plans, of how she would move out of her grandma's house. "It's getting time that I had my own place," she admitted. "I need it for Armand and me."

For *his* son, Cedric thought. Solution-oriented, he'd asked, "Where you go gonna go?" He'd pointed out, "You quit GBBC, and although you've got a few sessions lined up, you've got no real money. You got a job waiting," he asked, "one I don't know about?"

She'd felt pummeled by all the statements and questions.

He felt like he had been making her see. She needed him. "Let me help you. You'll have student loans to pay back, and if you're doing another few years to get your graduate degree, you're gonna need some serious help. You can't live without money."

She'd been angry. Topaz had asked if Cedric was trying to belittle her. She huffed that she'd accomplished a lot as a *single* mom. Every week, she paid into a college fund for her son. Everything he ate or wore, she bought, with her own earnings. "Just because I live with Mother See doesn't mean I live for free. I can do this—I *been* doing it!" she'd spat.

Cedric recalled pulling her into his arms, his fighting mad little kewpie doll. "I know Baybay. I just want to help. I can, you know."

It was why he was there, at her parent's house, to let *them* know. Things would be different. As he banged on the front door, again, he remembered. Topaz had sighed and leaned against him, refusing to look at him. "How?" she'd asked. "How are you going to help me?"

Standing in his kitchen, he'd suggested, "Stay here."

She'd been shocked. "In your dad's house?"

"Is he ever here?" Cedric asked. "No," he'd answered his own question. "Dad's with his squeeze," Dolly, the top-heavy barmaid. "She loves having him with her. He's hardly been here since my mom died.

"Both his name and mine are on this house," Cedric had divulged. "My mom saw to that. Now my dad can't bear to be here; one night, he told me."

Before closing, Mr. Stable had stood behind the bar, polishing glasses. "You understand, right, son? It just isn't the same without Ora."

"I do," Cedric had said because after his mother's passing, if *he'd* had anywhere else to go, he would have. Never before had he told Topaz that, or that often when he was in the house that he still thought of as his mother's, he had soothing one-sided conversations with her.

Cedric had lifted Topaz's chin. "Look at me. I want you to have a safe haven. Bring my son here and spread out. Give him my old room. Move in the master with me. I'll get new locks. I'll get your piano delivered—even though there's an electric keyboard downstairs," where they used to listen to records and do naughty things.

Topaz didn't breathe, hope, or believe. "But you'll be in Vegas."

"You'll be here, still needing a place to live. There, I basically live rent-free." In a hotel. "Here, I pay the bills. Been doing it while the place sat empty. Heck, do this for me. Please? A day here, maybe two there, I'll be around. Armand and I will get to know each other. I need this, Bay. I'll send for him in the summer, and on holidays. Please... *Mom*."

It was so good to be called that, finally, by Armand's father. Topaz thought it as Cedric continued to speak. "If you're good, too, Bay, I just might send for you. Oh, and he's going on my insurance."

She'd wanted to smile, but there was a tug of war going on inside. "I want my own place, Ced. This is a wonderful offer. I'm grateful, but you've got your life, and I need to stand on my own two feet."

"Then get out of college, with your graduate degree. Then I'll get out of your hair, but until then, I gotta take care of my son. Period."

Those same things he intended to tell Sister Naomi, Cedric thought; as on high heels, she stood with her front door open. Of all things, she was smiling. "I've been waiting on you, Cedric."

Entering the peeling yellow house, the young man vowed to tell the woman's husband too, big Pastor Moon.

Chapter 53

THE following Saturday, Topaz dropped her son off. Naomi had asked to keep her grandson. As Topaz stood on the steps of the old Victorian, her mom mentioned Cedric. "He was mighty angry at first, but he and I got it together. It seems he's determined to be in his son's life."

With a wistful smile, the petite one placed a box on Cedric's kitchen table. Remembering, she was grateful to her mother for the reprieve. Now she and Mother See would not have busy little Armand underfoot as they completed tasks. Although Cedric was gone, Topaz needed to settle in his home—her and her son's temporary new abode. She smiled again because Cedric's father, Armand's Papa Stable, had sent a truck and two employees over to help.

Mother See hadn't particularly liked the idea of Topaz shacking. Mother didn't like Topaz living with a man, "But since you and he already *know* each other, in the biblical sense," she grinned, "I guess I could look the other way."

Topaz laughed. "Grandma, Ced is in Vegas most of the time."

"Well, I just won't think about all the times he'll fly back." Mother See chuckled. Hugging Topaz, she knew Lil Mama was bright and that she would do what she believed was best, for herself and their boy.

THAT Sunday, after church, quite a few little boys hung around Naomi. She addressed the Missions Club; the kids were running around, excited, because they were going to the Pastor's house for dinner. Eve's small son Elisha appeared downtrodden as she stood holding his hand. The woman with the shock of curly hair knew. She should have been gone following the benediction. No one really wanted her around, she felt. Yet, she couldn't take her eyes off the woman she despised. Eve knew Elijah Moon's foolishness, getting up before the congregation, spilling the tea, and making her look like a villain, was *Naomi's* doing. That chubby chick thought she had won, but Eve would see about that.

Little Elisha watched Sister Naomi too. He watched other boys darting around. They waited to go to her house. Eli knew he would never be allowed to go. His mother often said mean stuff about Sister Naomi, even though he couldn't see why. Sister Naomi was pretty, she smelled nice, and she felt soft when she hugged him and other kids. But none of that mattered, the little dark-skinned boy thought. He'd have to go home, by himself, again, while the others went to Pastor Moon—*his* dad's house. They'd play with Armand. Army was little. He was Eli's brother or his nephew. Eli didn't know which. He just knew he would cry in a minute. His lower lip trembled. It was all so unfair! He wanted to go!

Noticing the child who barely clung to composure, Naomi's heart went out. Eli wanted to romp with the other boys, at her house, at his dad's house. Naomi knew Eve despised her simply because she, Naomi, was the wife. Eve also despised her because Eve thought they were playing some game. It was one that Eve felt she needed to win. It was sick, Naomi thought, and stupid, and oh so childish.

Naomi flashed back to when Eve and her husband, now long gone, had come for a marriage session. A lot of good that had done them, Naomi wryly thought, because Eve had had plans, way back then. As she turned to gather the surrounding children, Naomi forgot recriminations. She realized something. It wasn't little Eli's fault that his mother and the Pastor had slept together. The cute little boy had done nothing wrong. The kid whose skin reminded Naomi of smooth chocolate had simply been born. A result of the actions of two errant adults. That, Naomi understood. It was why she could look into Eve's narrowed eyes.

It seemed the woman was always attempting to stare her down. Naomi only cared that little Eli wanted to visit his father's home, with the other boys. "You know," Naomi stated, despite feeling hatred emitting from Eve, "your son is welcome, too."

Eve wanted to shout, '*My* son? You bitch! My son is *the Pastor's* son!' Yet she did not, even as her boy joyfully shot forward. Eve watched, feeling sickened as her son's little arms wound around Naomi's shapely thighs. Eve wanted to pull him back, even as in his exuberance at being invited, he nearly knocked Naomi down. That would have served her right, Eve unkindly mused. Breathing deeply, Eve vowed not to make a scene. Elijah Moon wouldn't like that, and for little Eli's sake, she would not provoke his father. Eve had to remember. Daddy Moon could still come back to her, if she was good.

Leaning forward, Eve tapped her son on the shoulder. She wanted to bring her heavy fist up and suddenly catch Naomi beneath the chin. Hell, Eve couldn't even rub her own son's back! Naomi was bent over doing that, as little Eli's arms stayed around Naomi. Eve felt like bawling as others watched. She knew they thought Naomi was a saint. Eve hated that her son betrayed her. He knew Naomi was their enemy! Eve had told him; Naomi kept them and his dad apart.

Naomi straightened, looking into Eve's stony face. Aware that Eve, wanted to say no, Naomi prayed Eve wouldn't hurt Eli like that.

As though she'd read Naomi's mind, curly-haired Eve summoned a nonchalant mien. Sure, she felt many things, two of which were rage and jealousy. Still, she couldn't disappoint Eli, not with all the onlookers. They pretended to greet one another, but they were paying attention. They wanted to see what she, the church outcast, would do. Eve also knew there was so little that Eli, her sweet-natured child, requested. Therefore, she pulled him to her. Embracing the little chocolate boy who meant everything to her, Eve fought irrational jealousy. Eve ignored the preacher's wife, whose nosy ass stood watching—like what Eve said to her own son was any of Naomi's business. Eve made her boy face her.

In hushed tones, Eve admonished Elisha to be good, just before quivering with excitement, he ran to Armand. Eve resented that kid. If it wasn't for *him*, she thought, *her son* would be the heir, not the smaller copper-skinned boy. He looked just like that other bitch, his sister, Ms. Snooty, who trained the deacon's grandson to play the organ. Amil was the new lead organist. And Topaz. She was just like her Mama, standoffish. Ms. Vertically Challenged probably thought she was better than everybody, just because she and Naomi were related to Elijah Moon.

Unaware of most of Eve's thoughts, Naomi turned to shepherd the surrounding children out to her car. Standing in the sunshine, she offered Eve a curt nod, silently thanking her for doing the right thing.

Watching her son go with *that woman*, Eve wanted to fight! And when had Naomi gotten a new car? Eve's mouth twisted. That vehicle, and everything else, should have been Eve's—as the new first lady. Filled with rage, Eve just had to snarl. "I ain't do it for you."

Naomi shrugged, aware of those nearby. "Doesn't matter."

Tremendously angry, Eve let it be known, "I did it for *my son*."

The unsaid words hung in the air. *The Pastor's son.*

Naomi dismissed Eve. Whatever. Without a glance, the preacher's wife drove away, with the pastor's son in her car.

Chapter 54

1995

IT was mid-summer. Elijah Moon was taking his first real vacation since Old Preacher had died. This was the big one!

He recalled how Naomi had laughed. She'd said that at nearly fifty-four, he was as excited as the children. It was true. He and his boys, Eli, his son, and Armand, his grandson, were headed to Disney. The boys might have been a bit old for it, but Elijah figured better late than never.

Seated on the plane, he looked over at his son, Eli. It felt good to say that; *his son*. It was nice to have folk know. The handsome kid, technically a teenager, but not quite, sat in the window seat. He nodded off but woke every few moments. He didn't want to miss a thing.

Elijah Moon glanced down at Armand, Topaz's boy. In the middle seat, with copper-hued skin like his mother's, the nine-year-old no longer looked just like her. Or was he ten? Elijah didn't remember. He just knew the wide-awake kid was starting to look more like Cedric Stable.

Elijah had not been shocked to find out that his onetime organist had been 'the culprit.' Yet he no longer bore the younger man any ill will. How could he? Cedric was a great father. He'd taken to it like a duck to water. Elijah smiled, looking down. His grandson swung his feet and could barely pay attention to the in-flight movie. The intelligent, funny kid had brought such joy to the Moon family.

WAKING, thirteen-year-old Eli looked over at his dad. The tall, lanky boy with the sweet spirit grinned. He was thrilled. He didn't often get to spend time with his father, not when no one else was around. Still, this week would be different. Having others around was okay too, Eli thought. He knew Elijah Moon was important. The big man, acquainted with everyone from restaurateurs and celebrities to politicians, was always busy. Eli recalled the outreach programs that registered people to vote and to become active in the community. He thought of the food drives for the less fortunate, and the classes that enabled young people to become job-ready. His father spearheaded those things and more. Therefore, whenever Eli and his dad got to spend time together, without others around, it was great, like now.

For Eli, Armand didn't count as an 'other.' The petite boy was fam. Actually, the kid was Elisha's *nephew*. It had been confusing for a while, but Eli now knew. Short-Stuff, Topaz, was his older sister. Tall, lanky Eli liked being an uncle to her kid. Kiddo worshipped him. Eli loved Mama Nae too, his step-mom. She was the mother of his half-sister, but Mama Nae treated him like he and Topaz were wholes. Despite all the mean things his mom said about her, Mama Nae made Eli feel like he was her real son. Topaz did the same, but Short-Stuff was bossy, sometimes. Eli was already taller than she, but his Dad said he would grow more still. Eli's tiny sister, who always wore high heels, had taken him to Vegas a few times. Eli's nephew went too. Boy, had those trips had been fun, but *this* trip with his dad would be awesome!

YOUNGER, Armand couldn't stop excitedly swinging his feet. He would hang out all day at the park with Grandad and his uncle, Eli. The older boy was so much fun. Eli knew cool stuff too.

Armand frowned. Some people at Grandad's church thought he and Eli were brothers. That was stupid. He and Eli had different mothers, and fathers; Grandad was Eli's father. But, copper-skinned Armand thought, *his* dad was the best! Topaz's boy recalled his middle and last names. They were his dad's. Yep, and Armand Cedric Stable's dad lived in a Las Vegas hotel, on The Strip! Eli said it was cool. Dad's penthouse had marble floors and almost no walls because of all the windows.

Whenever Armand stayed with his dad, all they had to do was pick up the phone and say what they wanted. Burgers 'n fries, or the clams—yick—that his Dad liked would be brought right up. Dad never cooked, like at home with Mom and Marva, the housekeeper. They and Armand all lived in New Canaan, Connecticut. In Vegas with his dad, veggies were optional, so was making his bed. Housekeeping took care of that.

Armand's mom was twenty-five or twenty-six. She was an international composer. Classically educated, she played piano for people like Natalie Cole, Rod Stewart, Tony Bennett, and Michael Bublé. Bigwigs called her from all over the world. His dad said. Dad claimed she was tiny but dynamite! Armand was going to be taller than his mom; he knew it. He was already her height, and he wasn't even ten.

Armand forgot his mom to think about his dad's silver sports car. It was low to the ground and loud! Cedric said the louder, the better. Mom said it was too loud for her, but Dad said she was a girl, a pretty one. Dad was always calling her pretty. He usually called her Baybay because, he said, she was his baby, from way back—yick. Mom sometimes called Dad Yella. She said it was because of his skin.

Armand's parents didn't see much of each other because Mom lived in New Canaan, while Dad was in Vegas. His mom traveled too, for work, just like his dad, who oversaw the food service aspects of a chain of high-end international hotels. Still, whenever Armand's parents got together, they were gross, like they were on a honeymoon. His parents kissed a lot. It was noisy, and they touched each other. Dad always pulled Mom onto his lap, and Armand couldn't look. Dad slid his hands beneath Mom's shirt. The parents didn't really want to go out either; they just wanted to stay in, naked, in their big bed, like they were exhausted.

Armand's uncle Eli said *his* mom, Eve, never kissed anybody anymore. She never stayed in bed either with a man. Armand didn't really like Ms. Eve, not like he liked his own mom, Topaz. She was tiny—she called herself petite—and she smiled and tickled him. Mom was teaching him to play the piano and to read music. She said Grandad had taught her. Mom was fun, sometimes, but Eli's mom was not. Ms. Eve was scary, and she had a mad face, all the time.

Eli had once told Armand that his mom was angry with his father. Armand wondered why anybody would be mad at Grandad, the pastor of Bethany church. Grandad was great. Armand's mom must have thought so, too, because why else had Topaz bought Grandad a car? Grandad walked around that shiny new car with the plush interior, touching it like Dad touched Mom, so lovingly. Then Grandad shook his head while saying, "A *brand new* touring sedan. Will you look at God…"

Still walking, looking, and touching, he said he'd asked God for a pretty car, fresh off the showroom floor. "Baby girl, that was so long ago." Grandad had hugged tiny Mom then. He'd lifted her off the ground in front of the family's yellow house. Grandad sounded chokey too, when he said, "I just couldn't figure out how God would deliver it." Tiny Mom laughed, and so had her mom, Me-Maw. Naomi. They'd all stood staring at the car instead of getting in and going somewhere. Weird.

Oh. Armand remembered Eli's angry mother. Eli said Ms. Eve was upset because his father hadn't married her. But Granddad, Eli's father, was *already* married—to Me-Maw. Strange. Armand shook his head.

Armand's mom said Me-Maw's real name was Naomi. Me-maw was Armand's grandmother. He had a great-grandmother too. She was good to him. People at Granddad's church called her Mother See. She was kind of old, with silver hair, and she had a cane, but people said she looked good, just like Nancy Wilson, the singer—whoever that was.

Armand's dad said, "Army, you've got another grandmother too." Gram Ora Stable lived in Heaven. Armand had a second grandfather, Papa Stable. He lived with Dolly. She had a big chest, funny colored hair, and she worked at the bar. Dad said Dolly's hair was bleached. Armand thought bleach was for clothes. Oh well. He loved Dolly, and Me-Maw.

Armand remembered his Aunt Caley, his mother's sister-friend from way back. It was funny to think that his Mom had once been a kid. Anyway, tall Aunt Caley, who was also his godmother, made jewelry. She used precious gemstones and metal. Mom screamed when she saw Aunt Caley's stuff in the places she called boutiques, the exclusive ones, like at Dad's hotels. Aunt Cae's stuff was in Mom's magazines, too.

Armand closed his eyes and stopped thinking. All the family stuff was giving him a headache. He really just wanted the plane to stop, so they could run into Disney!

SEATED next to Armand, robust Elijah Moon inconspicuously watched him and Eli. The lanky older boy reminded Elijah of Eve... A good while back, she'd resigned from her position as the church administrator. She'd claimed the self-righteous folk at GBBC made it hard for her to get anything done. Eve had also maintained that they had even poisoned outsiders, members of other congregations, against her. She said she couldn't fellowship with anyone anywhere in the sleepy town of Tranquility anymore. Eve said she was moving away.

Elijah had not been unhappy to see her go. But before she'd gotten the notion to do so, he'd figured she would. It was why he prayed for guidance. He'd wanted to know to whom her vacated position should go. Then gray-haired Sister Smart had applied, since for years, she had been the secretary, Eve's backup.

Both Elijah and his wife, Naomi, thought Sister Smart was a great choice. Thirty-six years married to Deacon Smart, Sister Smart was sage and not full of folly. She was direct and discreet, not a gossip. She was all that a church administrator should be. She was what Eve was not.

Unbeknownst to Pastor Moon and his wife, Sister Smart had even advised Eve, long before Eve had begun traveling Troublesome Road. Sister Smart had told Eve to leave the man of the Lord alone. *"Touch not mine anointed.* That's what the word says." Reminding Eve, Sister Smart had often tried to offer the wisdom of a mother.

Thinking about Sister Smart caused Elijah to recall the incident that had occurred soon after the gray-haired woman began facilitating church business and affairs...

IT had not been four p.m., but because it was winter, it had nearly been dark out. Elijah noticed, peering into the church parking lot. There, the lights yawned on. At home, he knew Naomi prepared chili. Hankering for a big bowl of it and a slab of hot buttered cornbread, he suggested that he, Sister Smart, and the church treasurer call it a day. The treasurer, a trusted male of the church, said he would lock up. Elijah got his hat, donned his coat, and headed for the door. Chili and cheese were on his mind. Saying he wanted to check a few locks, the treasurer veered down a different darkened hallway.

About to exit the church annex, Elijah reached for the knob, but the door opened. It was pushed inward from the outside.

Someone largely built stepped into the dimly lit interior. Squinting, Elijah made out a baseball cap, pulled low, and some type of puffy windbreaker jacket. That was when he heard an ominous click.

Knowing it was the safety of a gun, Elijah silently prayed, even as the person with the weapon gestured. Elijah took it that he should retreat, go back the way he'd come. He found himself in the still-lighted church administrator's office. Where Sister Smart was, and where the treasurer had gotten to, Elijah did not know. He only hoped they wouldn't show up, startle the intruder, and wind up hurt, or worse.

When he tried to speak, to talk the person down—the one who seemed all too familiar, gruffly, the person told him to shut up. That voice, Elijah knew it. It had been disguised, but he just had to think...

Sister Smart entered the office, wiping freshly washed hands. Therefore, she stood—wearing her quiet, no-nonsense lace-up shoes— *behind* the intruder. With his eyes, Elijah bid her to remain still, even as the intruder pulled the baseball cap from his head.

When he saw the shock of curly hair, Elijah frowned. "*Eve?*" With a *gun* trained on *him*? Lord knew he was sick of her. "Eve," he called, exasperated, "You pulling weapons on people now? What's this about?"

"You know." She brandished black metal. "You stand there, acting all holy." Angered, she tried to cry, "But you know why I'm doing this. You need to die! Don't play stupid with me."

Elijah sounded calm, although inside, he fervently prayed. He thought he might have to rush his son's mother. He would have to overpower her, even though in the attempt, he might get shot.

"Eve, what do you mean by that— 'I know why you're doing this?'"

She waved her gun. "Don't play with me!" An angry boiling cauldron, she yelled, "You were supposed to marry *me*!" With her free hand, she slapped her chest, "*Me*! I was supposed to move in with you." She hit again, "We could have been happy." Then she snarled, "But you had to go and listen to *her*." Naomi. "You had to be her puppet. Now *I'm* the outcast. Everybody hates me. She's in my house. The new car was supposed to be mine. Y'all even stole my job."

Elijah shook his head while remaining still, but he had to rebuff because Eve was wrong. "No, Eve. You *quit* your job. You said," Elijah clarified as slowly he took a step forward, "no one wanted you around anymore. You said people treated you like a pariah, or like you didn't exist. You said people reprimanded you like you were a child."

"Because of *you*!" Eve screamed as angry tears welled up. She forgot those who'd tried to befriend her in her hour of need. "You fucked me, then you betrayed me! I sucked your dick! Then you got up there that Sunday and cast me in the worst light! You made me look like a floozy, like some loose change. The worst part is: you used *my son* to do it!"

"I did not. I asked the Lord's people to love our son. I said nothing about you, Eve. I only spoke of *me* and of *my* wrongdoing."

"With *me*!" Again, Eve slapped her chest. "I was your whore. People know! Eli is proof of what we did, and now you've walked away. Now only a few old ladies, who pity me, will have anything to do with me."

Elijah was so close that he could snatch the gun. However, Sister Smart beat him to it, and hearing a loud crack, Elijah involuntarily ducked. When he looked up, the grandmother of thirteen shoved Eve into a straight-back chair. "You should be 'shamed of yo'self, Eve Island!"

Carelessly, Sister Smart dropped the weapon into a drawer, which she promptly locked. She scolded Eve, "You put a hole in the church wall!"

Sister Smart waved Elijah aside, speaking over him. "Now I'ma tell you what we're gonna do here, *Ms. Evil*." Elijah, and the treasurer, who had returned with two officers, all silently waited to hear.

"You, Eve," Sister Smart pointed "are gonna first apologize to our Pastor. How *dare* you act so ugly! And cussing, in the house of the Lord, using all that vulgar language. Girl, when I told you, near 'bout fourteen years ago, not to pursue this man, *did you listen*? I told ya things would never work out. Did I not?" Sister Smart yelled, "Answer!"

Seated, Eve sullenly nodded. Feeling angry, stupid, and sad, Eve wished she'd just poisoned the man. Then she wouldn't be sitting in the administrator's office, her old office, feeling like a truant teenager.

"Well," Sister Smart sighed. "You apologize to our Pastor here. Then these good officers," she gestured at them as they walked further into the room, "will arrest you." Eve sputtered, but Sister Smart continued. "Yes, we gotta get your info on file, in case you come back, do this again. They'll pick you right up. So this evening, Ms. Eve Island, you get arrested. Because of yo' foolishness, I'ma give a statement; the treasurer, too. Maybe you'll cool off and think about your lil boy. He don't need his mama behind bars. If you see the light 'n get it together, we close this case. If you don't, you go away on a host of charges." Sister Smart appeared to be thinking. "I b'lieve you made terroristic threats, while attempting to murder our Pastor here." The woman looked around. "I know you defaced church property. Putting a hole in that wall there, and you're trespassing; you no longer work for this church.

"Officers," Sister Smart gestured them forward, "she is all yours."

Seated on the plane, Elijah recalled telling Sister Smart she was something. Watching Eve and her weapon disappear, Sister Smart waved. "Honeybunch, Deac Smart and I raised five wild boys; got *nine* grandsons, too. After all that testosterone, I could *never* be afraid of one lil ol' angry *girl*."

Elijah recalled Sister Smart's suggestion. "While Eve is on ice, Pastor, as that boy's daddy, *you* need to apply for custody. It really would be nice if y'all could have joint..." She pursed her lips, "But just to be on the safe side, Precious, get on down to family court. Start there."

Looking over his grandson's head, Elijah thanked God for Sister Smart, his guardian angel. Lovingly, Elijah Moon gazed at his lanky teen. The boy stared from the airplane window. Suddenly Elijah felt such love for the boy who was growing up in his household.

Unstable, Eve kept manufacturing drama. Elijah remembered. Thus, he had been granted custody. A thorn in his side, Eve had really gotten the ball rolling before Eli was ten. Elijah knew she'd done so as a last-ditch effort to create tension between him and Naomi. Ms. Vindictive believed his marriage would finally crack under the strain. Calling day and night, Eve had blown little things out of proportion. Eve said she could no longer handle Eli. Eve wanted physical help with him. She couldn't teach Eli to be a man she said. She swore he didn't respect her. She claimed he'd gotten to where he would not listen, to her.

Elijah knew the boy needed a man's hand, *his* hand, to guide him.

Eve told Elijah she'd had enough. She'd yelled. "I can't do this anymore! This awful boy needs to be with his father!" Eve had yowled, "You come get your son, and keep him in *your* house!"

Although the woman had said so for her own selfish reasons, she had been right. Elisha had needed to live with his father. Feeling bad, as well as glad, about how things had turned out, Elijah thought back to that troublesome time. He realized what handsome Eve had not.

Unbeknownst to her, Eve had granted Elijah and his wife the very thing for which they had long prayed. *A son.*

Elijah forgot trials, tribulations, and blessings in disguise, as a capable male voice emitted through the plane's loudspeaker.

"This is your captain speaking…"

Elijah laughed as copper-skinned Armand poked his young uncle.

"Eli," the more petite boy excitedly whispered. "E, we're almost there!"

Big Elijah Moon grinned because he felt like the kids. They were going to the most wonderful place—just him and his boys!

Chapter 55

2010

ELIJAH Moon spoke to his daughter. "Take an old man for a ride."

As he sat beside Topaz in her swanky coupe, he recalled holding Naomi tight, and really kissing her. He did it before he left the mustard-yellow Victorian. Looking at her, he thought her voluptuous. Where her hair had gone gray, it was now highlighted. To Elijah, Naomi was more lovely than she had ever been, and he told her so. He also said, "My darling girl, you are the sun, where I'm the Moon."

Naomi chuckled before Elijah bowed and said she was his queen. "Woman, I love you her more now than I did, way back when."

Taking Elijah in her arms, Naomi fussed about him appearing tired. "You need to let some things go, Lijah; let Eli do more of what he's been trained to do. You and I can go on a cruise. Wouldn't you like that?"

Elijah agreed. He was weary and ready for a change. He told his wife that he'd prayed about unleashing Eli. Elijah Moon believed it was time.

Feeling somber, he rode with his daughter. Elijah, whose close-cut hair was now more light than dark, looked out the window. On the Merritt Parkway, he noticed the beauty of fall foliage. He knew Topaz was headed for New Canaan. In Connecticut, she had a lovely home. His big old Victorian was now fully paid for, thanks to her. Seated aside, Elijah softly spoke. To his daughter, now forty, he divulged that he hadn't done everything right, not in this lifetime. "But," Elijah said, "I tell you one thing, my jewel…"

Topaz no longer minded her father using the term of endearment.

"Your old man did what he knew to do. I always tried to make it so you'd never wind up stuck, like I was, in a life that wasn't of your own choosing. Sometimes I felt that was what happened to me. Other times I felt this was the life I was supposed to lead."

In his beautiful orator's voice, Elijah revealed that he had only wanted his precious daughter to have all she now had, and more. "That was why I did what I did with Army—Armand. Before he got here, Taupe, I really didn't know he would become such a blessing, to all of us." Elijah admitted, "Back then, I was mixed up. I truly wanted a son, not that *you* lacked in any way, but it was my and your mother's dream, even though we had our problems. Then you turned up pregnant. We didn't want stigmas attached to you because of that." Elijah sighed as he stared, unseeing, out of the window. "So we went along with lies."

Driving, Topaz could smell his cologne. It was one of the things she remembered most about her father when she was away from him. She thought of him often as she traveled. A busy career woman, a skilled pianist, and composer, she was internationally pursued. She was also the mother of a *college graduate*, a man that music industry insiders well knew. Many turned to him when they needed to climb the charts.

Sometimes, she couldn't believe she had a *daughter* too. That had been a surprise. Topaz checked her rearview mirror and realized how her father had once felt, being tied and bound to Old Preacher, then to Greater Bethany Bible Congregation. It was similar to the way she'd felt. She'd wanted her *own* life, her way, but now she recognized. People often didn't get to choose. They simply had to do what Cedric sometimes said. They had to make the best of the hand they'd been dealt. He'd even nodded after saying it. "Those are old dude—your dad's—words."

Unaware of his daughter's memories, Elijah Moon continued to speak as he rode aside. He told Topaz he had always tried to protect her. "Yes, your old man might have been overbearing. I know I held on too tightly, but there was a time when I couldn't bear to think you'd be ridiculed by the saints. Your mama helped me see. Your life is your own. Your path will always be yours alone to trod. Nae kept at me because there were things concerning you that I had a hard time acknowledging."

Topaz smiled and switched lanes. She wondered why her father, sixty-eight, told her such things, now, and seemingly on a whim.

"You do know," Elijah said with a smirk, "I was hard on you because a PK isn't allowed to fail. No 'falling from grace,' or making mistakes."

"Now, how would *you* know that?" Topaz teasingly asked.

"I may be getting up there, but I remember how it was," Elijah chuckled. "Believe it or not, it was hard for me, too. You think *I* was bad, as your dad? Well, you should have grown up Old Preacher's kid, or you should have been your grandmother's child. Cozi Moon was something."

Topaz mumbled, "That ol' battle ax sure was." Her father's mother had passed a few years prior. She'd fallen, broken a hip, *and* a piece of her precious furniture. *That* she had been most upset about. Months later,

Cozi died. The undertaker had been unable to remove her frown. Topaz chuckled, "Remember Mama before the funeral?" Naomi had stared into the coffin whispering, "As frowny-face lived, so she died."

Elijah forgot his meddlesome mother to ask, "You think *you* had it bad? Taupe, I'm your old man, and I lived. Imagine what *I* went through. My old man died, doing what he was best at; what he loved. He instantly became legend. I couldn't see how I, a youngster, could step into his shoes, shoes that were way too big for me."

Elijah sighed and sounded weary. "Topaz, my jewel, sometimes I still feel I'll never fill that man's shoes. Now I'm just tired. Your Mama has always said all I ever had to do was be me, but the truth is: I made so many mistakes. A lot of them regarding you." Elijah pressed his lips together. "I made a mess with your Mama, for a while there. The Lord knows I messed up with Eli and Eve, too. However, I really don't regret any of it." Elijah Moon folded his large hands. "I don't regret marrying your Mama, or having gotten shoved into the ministry, or any of my time at Bethany. I have never regretted being your Dad, and I am overjoyed that Armand was born. It's hard to believe he's twenty-something. I tell you, it sure is nice being Grandad to such a high falutin fella.

"I don't regret my Eli's birth, either. Naomi and I have loved having him live with us, from the time he was ten, all up until he went to college. She adores him; you'd never guess she didn't give birth to him. He gave me a grandson too. *That* was a scare! You and him and these babies in your teens! Guess you two really are lusty—like your old man. Still, when Mercer Ellington Moon came along, I was better prepared to handle another grandson. Now my boy is in his twenties, and his boy is nine. My Eli's got his own place. He brought the sunshine, that boy did, and Lord, is he smart! Like you, he did well in college."

Elijah sat for moments in deep contemplation.

Still driving, Topaz supplied, "My brother is a New York Theological Seminary alum."

Seated aside, Elijah Moon nodded. "We all know he will one day take over the work." Elijah closed his eyes while thinking aloud. "*My boy* will expand things in ways that I never could have.

"Actually, right now," Topaz's dad said in reverent tones, "*I pray every blessing upon him. I confer every blessing upon you too, my beautiful girl. I pray that the angel of the Lord goes before both of you, in all that you ever do. May everything that your hands touch prosper. I bless my grandsons too, Armand and Mercer, and I'll not forget our little surprise. Baby Lace. I ask the Lord to bless and keep Cedric. That man is a fine father, and I pray he will remain your perfect mate—AND that y'all marry. I call forth blessings for Caley, the daughter of our hearts."*

Lace, Topaz thought. Now that little gold bundle had surprised them all. As her eyes scanned the road, Topaz's heart rate sped because had her father had just bestowed *the* blessing upon her? And her brother. Her dad hadn't forgotten her grown son, his cousin, or her small daughter.

Elijah Moon done so in the manner of the bible patriarchs! Recalling how her dad had rebuked her in the past, at present, Topaz was honored to receive his approbation. She told him and quickly squeezed his huge hand.

Elijah Moon nodded as he rode alongside. Speaking of his son, Elijah announced, "I think that even if Eli hadn't been groomed for ministry, he would still love it. Eli loves it in a way that amazes even me. He said that in seminary, he loved the African Spirituality in America elective. Baby girl, he doesn't feel put upon, as I sometimes did. It's why I believe my young man was born to take the reins." Stroking his chin, Elijah said of his son, "That boy—well, my young *man*—will probably turn out to be much better than his old man. That, I pray for."

As she drove, Topaz suddenly felt melancholy. She wondered why her father told her all that he did. She almost felt as though she were a priest, listening to confession. She felt as though in some way, her father was unburdening himself, right there in her presence. Therefore, she simply listened, and kept her eyes on the ever-winding parkway.

"Baby Girl," Elijah went on, "I am worn, tired of many things—like the daily grind. I'on't like all these slick new politicians, either. Coming 'round wanting to use my podium, but only when election time nears.

"However," Elijah stated, "I *do not regret a minute of serving the Lord, or His people.*

"When I stopped feeling sorry for myself, back when I got over being angry about Old Preacher leaving me, the work, although tough, became my joy." Elijah visibly puffed up. Appearing proud, he asked, "How many men can say what I can; that they pastor the very church that they *grew up* in? *That* has been my honor. You hear that, my jewel? I am a true son of the church, and now, so is my boy.

"I'll tell you something else, Taupe. I've heard many a confession on the saints' deathbed. Some things were innocuous, while others were truly heinous. But," Elijah intoned, as though he were on the pulpit. His voice even became louder, "The one thing I *will* do, is take the saints' secrets to my grave.

"Like my father before me, never have I breathed one word of some things to anyone. I've not even told your mother. Now that woman? She should never have put up with me. Yet she did. God bless my sweet Naomi Ruth. She is a true saint."

With that, Elijah Moon said no more. The preacher and the woman who had once been his kid rode along in silence until they reached Connecticut. They neared Topaz's impressive home, seated on five acres. Pulling onto the circular, light brick drive, she parked beside a large alabaster fountain.

Every time he visited, Elijah pulled himself from the car while gazing up at the immense but fine-looking Colonial. It was white with black shutters and a multitude of windows. How his God had blessed! With eyes on trees towering in the rear, Elijah raised both large hands. With his massive shoulders wide, he again pronounced, "Daughter, may this house be blessed, and a blessing to all who enter it. May even those who simply trod upon these grounds be blessed."

He allowed his firstborn to take his arm. Tiny thing, she escorted him up the front steps, as he murmured, "In Jesus' name. Amen."

In the grand foyer, on polished wood, he again looked around. He saw custom millwork and unadorned transom windows. These rode up the wide, white, and wood staircase. As he again walked through the tranquil home on shiny planks, Elijah saw decorative wood beam ceilings, and cozy furniture. All he could think, again, was that God had truly blessed. Indeed God had smiled upon Elijah's girl, and the man that she had been with, for so long. By now, Elijah mused, she and Cedric were as good as legally married. At least, in the eyes of the law.

THAT night after dinner, Elijah Moon rose from the gleaming mahogany table. He retrieved the bible that he never left home without. He had been reading before the meal. He patted his shirt pocket. Assured of his glasses, Elijah said he wouldn't go back into the den. There, with the Indo-Persian rug and appealing furniture, he had nearly fallen asleep. He said he would go up to the guest suite, "The one I've been assigned."

Topaz sat in the breakfast room with her six-year-old. With Lace Leilani in her arms, Topaz chuckled. Humming, Marva, the longtime housekeeper, tidied the kitchen. "Dad, don't act like I ever forced you into that wing. You always have your pick. But those are the rooms you've always chosen, even when Army was a single digit kid."

"I know, baby girl." Elijah nodded at his daughter, seated and rocking her sleeping mini-me. He nodded at the chuffy other woman, the one who was now family. As he ascended the stairs, he called down, "Nite, Marva. Topaz, my darling, I believe I'll take my rest now."

She watched the big man whose hair was nearly white, until she could no longer see his feet on the kitchen stairs. "I love you, Dad…"

His voice floated from the landing. "I know, baby girl. I love *you*."

Later, when she passed his room, after having tucked her daughter in, Topaz noticed golden light. It streamed from the suite door that was ajar. Approaching it, Topaz told herself she would just make sure her father wanted nothing more before the house was settled for the night.

"Dad…" she called, her hand on the doorknob. Her eyes were on the pale gold pooled on the plush hallway carpet. "Daddy?"

Slowly, Topaz opened the door and entered the room that smelled faintly of his cologne. In the pretty room, her father was propped up in bed. Half glasses were perched on his nose. He referred to them as cheap lil magnifiers from the dime store. Behind them, his eyes were closed.

My, my, Topaz mused. She could see why women flocked to her father's church. Even in his late sixties, Elijah Moon was a handsome man. Topaz smiled because his ever-present giant bible was open, resting words-down on his chest. Softly she walked, careful not to wake him. Her intent was to simply remove his glasses and lay his bible aside. She'd do it to make him more comfortable. Then she'd turn off the light.

Bending to gently take his specs, Topaz realized. For as far back as she could remember, her dad had worn blue pajamas, just like those he wore tonight. He kept a pair here. Light blue, navy blue, royal blue, it didn't matter the shade. Her dad's PJs were always blue, and she smiled.

Then in the soft glow of the bedside lamp, Topaz really looked at her father. Most of his hair, especially the crown and his temples, were now white. The bristles in his trim mustache were the same. She noticed his face, and the slight grooves etched there. His skin was no longer taut, as it had once been. Elijah Moon also had minuscule laugh lines outside his eyes. The skin on his neck was looser than in the past, what she could see through his formal PJ shirt collar. Yet somehow, to his daughter, Elijah looked the same as he always had, robust and impressive.

Oh, God… Topaz realized, after she'd smoothed the sheet and pricey velvet coverlet, turned back. Both lay across his lap…

Her father – was – not – breathing.

Topaz's heart stuttered, and she touched his shoulder. Then with a finger, she poked him. Nothing. Unable to gasp for air, ever so slightly, she shook her Dad. When his lion head lolled to the side, she recalled his words, the ones he had spoken just before going up to bed.

Topaz, my darling, I believe I'll take my rest now.

With tears assailing her, the golden-eyed one knew. The angels had come to bear her beloved father's spirit home. She knew she could try to revive him, but what for? He had lived, as well as he knew how. He had said, repeatedly, that he was tired. Therefore, Topaz let Elijah Moon continue to rest. Indeed, she would see him again, on the other side.

Topaz knelt. Beside her father's bed, she did as she had seen him do, so many times in church. He'd done so at the bedsides of the saints. Topaz took his still warm hands in her own, and in her heart, she prayed. With tears streaming, Topaz prayed for her father's transition… into the light. She prayed that he would be welcomed into Heaven, ushered in to rest in the bosom of the Lord. For he had been a most faithful servant, a stalwart soldier. A truer servant of the Lord's people there had never been. With tears racing down her cheeks, Topaz knew her dad had had his faults. Still, he had served, as best he could, and he had done it well.

It was why she squeezed his big hands. Nearly unable to breathe, due to the sobs that bubbled up and out, she kissed those hands. Those beautiful, oh so capable hands. They were the large unselfish hands that had reached into an aging leather wallet, time and time again for the saints. He'd done so too for those that her grandma called the ain'ts. Topaz kissed the hands that had tinkered with many a church boiler. Those bejeweled hands had signed countless marriage certificates. She kissed the hands that had signed for young men to be released into his custody. She kissed the hands that had kept many a boy on the straight 'n narrow. Then that boy-turned-man had become a productive member of society. Some were now fathers, deacons, architects, trash collectors, firefighters, teachers, coaches, husbands, and naval officers.

Topaz kissed the wedding banded hand that had held and christened hundreds of babies. She kissed the hands that had soothed and comforted the fevered, the aged, the dying, and those who remained. Repeatedly, she kissed the hands of the man who had taught her to pray. He had also been the first to teach her to play. He'd taught her to sing. He'd started her on the very instrument that brought her, and countless others, joy.

With her face crumpling, sorrow painfully wrenched its way up. From her solar plexus, it emitted. Through her mouth, sobs burst aloud.

Topaz had really believed that they—she and her precious father— would have more time. But that was the trick. *Always thinking there was more time.* Now there was no more, for them. No longer would her father's hands hold a bat at the church picnic when the summer rolled around, greening up and beautifying everything. No longer would he lovingly grab her mother's hands or Naomi's waist. The blessed hands upon which she sobbed would never again administer communion, or wash the feet of present-day disciples.

Inching up to rest her head on her Daddy's broad warm chest, she, who had once been the preacher's kid, sorely wept...

Then dabbing tears, Topaz rose. Noticing the time, she attempted to compose herself. She reached in her trouser pocket for her phone. She nodded too at saddened Marva, who'd heard the keening.

Wanting only to help, chuffy Marva ushered frightened baby Lace from Grandad's room. Remaining, Topaz called the authorities.

The woman with Old Preacher's eyes called her mother. Slumped in her office, Topaz said the hurtful words. *"Mama, Daddy is...gone."*

Naomi wept, accepting it. She said she'd seen it coming. About a month ago, Naomi said she'd asked God to help her. Naomi had needed to face that at just shy of seventy, Elijah Moon would leave her.

"Taupe, your dad appeared worn. His step had gotten slower. To get up in the mornings, it took everything he had." But what had alerted Naomi like nothing else, she revealed; what had started prayers for grace to be able to accede to God's will was: when Elijah began to speak of Old Preacher. Elijah had spoken of his father as though the man, now legendary, was again present. Naomi had known then that her husband drifted, ever closer to the other side.

When she could at last disconnect from her mother, Topaz called *him*, her stabilizer. When she said his name, Cedric heard the brokenness. He instantly knew; they had lost someone, but whom? Unable to speak, Topaz whimpered. She held the phone, wishing for the man to whom she had been faithful for untold years. Needing his strength, Topaz realized. Like her father was for her mother, Cedric was her heart. For her, it was indisputable as she said, "Yella, we lost Daddy."

Afterward, she called her oldest and dearest friend. Topaz braced herself because Elijah Moon had been the only father that high-strung Caley had ever known. Thus, in tandem, the women lamented their loss.

Then Topaz called not only her own son, Armand Cedric Stable, but she reached out to her father's son. She rang her big brother. Topaz, informed the younger, strapping, handsome, Elisha Moon that their father had left them. "He went peacefully, Eli."

When disconnected, despite anguish, Topaz smiled. Her brother had had tears clogging his voice, yet he'd taken charge. Eli said he and Topaz would get with Mama Nae. He'd said the three of them would do the needful. He said he would make the announcement. He would tell the Greater Bethany congregation that their esteemed pastor had gone on.

Topaz loved that brother of hers. The one who was now a man.

Again, she looked into the room where her dad had seemingly slept. His body had been removed, but she had hovered. She'd made sure the authorities took care with him. Now lifting his pillow and holding it close, she remembered.

When on the phone, twenty-six-year-old Eli had been calm, supportive, and soothing. My God, Topaz thought, her brother was only two years older than their father had been when he'd lost Old Preacher.

With tears streaming, Topaz pressed her face into the pillow. She desperately needed to recapture her father's scent, for all time.

When she lifted her head, she recalled riding with her Dad, earlier. Elijah had said he would soon unleash Eli. Topaz knew her father had been right about his son. Eli was ready. Tall, good-natured, seemingly reticent Eli *was* the man.

Son was *the only one* who could step—easily—into Elijah Moon's formidable shoes.

EPILOGUE

TOPAZ Tiara Moon sat in her room and remembered her mother's presentation. *"Eli, my precious, this bible once belonged to Old Preacher, your grandfather. Then it passed from him, Reverend Ezekiel Moon, to his son, your father, Reverend Elijah Moon. I often wondered if it would one day pass to my son . . . and now I know it will."*

With tears assailing her, Naomi forged on. "Today, according to your father's wishes, I give his beloved bible to you, our darling son.

"Elisha Immanuel Moon, may you be as blessed by this gift as your father was by it, and his father before him. I sincerely pray that one day you'll pass it on to your son—or your daughter." Reaching up, Naomi had hugged the new Pastor Moon. She did so, moments before Eli officiated at the Homegoing Service of The Right Reverend Elijah Moon.

As she sat in her luxe bedroom suite, Topaz recalled. From far and wide, people had come to the sleepy little town of Tranquility. They'd wanted to pay their last respects to the man whose life had touched so many. Topaz remembered that night... and *Corporal Lance McGilroy,* the U.S. Serviceman who had once needed milk money for his girls. *He appeared with his wife and one of his grown daughters. They and others passed, touching her father.*

Elijah Moon lay in state, appearing dignified and powdery, while sister Tallulah softly played the keyboard. Devon, Lula's husband, and their daughter had accompanied her from D.C.

Thirty-something Amil, Deacon Wilnod's grandson, had been on duty. Topaz remembered teaching him to play the organ. *Greater Bethany's organist, also a new father, had told Topaz, "I'm glad my grandpa didn't live to see this day."* The adult Amil somberly said Deacon Wilnod, with the raspy voice, had nearly worshipped Pastor Moon. *"Your dad pulled my grandpa from the gutter when grandpa became a drunk. Gramps had been a cop. Your dad gave Gramps purpose, and he was sober for the rest of his life."* Amil nodded. *"Since he went on ahead, now Gramps and Pastor can reunite."*

Although his mother had passed years prior, Lil Don, Mother Meadows' adult son, was present. So was the family of sickly little Linda, who'd become an angel of light. Topaz's aunts, her dad's sisters, and his brother had been present. Uncle Ezra had escorted Aunt Tippie. She could no longer be referred to as 'Tipsy.' Their sons—once the greedy unruly children who were always at the yellow house—were all present. Such upstanding men Topaz's cousins had become.

Topaz was so proud of her brother. Reverend Elisha Moon had done a tremendous job. *Using their father's giant leather bible, Eli delivered a most eloquent eulogy.*

Eli's mother had been proud too. Her son was now the bona fide heir. Following the services, handsome Eve headed back to her abode, several states away.

For the momentous occasion, someone had assembled the old church band. It included Cedric, the organist, Bailey, the drummer, and Titus, who'd played bass guitar. The saxophonist, Amber appeared. She was no longer a heavy girl. The band had been missing a member, but no one expected Topaz to play what had once been her beloved piano.

Cedric's father, Armand's Papa Stable, and top-heavy Dolly with the bleached hair had appeared. For the night, they'd abandoned their bar.

Now retired, the church administrator, Sister Smart, had been present. It was she who had once advised Eve against folly with the pastor. Bent before the preacher's kid, who sat on a front pew, the elderly woman shared a story. As those too numerous to count passed, behind Sister Smart, the woman said Pastor Moon stood with her when she'd suddenly lost a son. "During that time, Pastor was my rock."

Tranquility residents, business owners, visiting dignitaries, and parishioners alike, glimpsed the body for the last time. As they did, Sister Smart dodged those reaching to hug or consolingly pat the PK's hand.

"Had your daddy not been with us then," Sister Smart opined, "I tell you true, Deacon Smart might not have made it."

Discreetly, ushers had to remove Topaz's sister-friend Caley from the sanctuary. The fine jewelry maker had been inconsolable. Because Caley fell apart, her wife thought it best to leave, but not before blowing the family a kiss.

Not seeing her bedroom, but the Tranquil Gardens Cemetery, Topaz recalled the loveliest day. It had been then that her father had been laid to rest. *Beneath weeping willows, Cedric and the family had turned from the gold-tone casket. However, Topaz remained, staring into the clear blue sky. As the fam trod toward the limo, the gentlest autumn breeze lifted the ends of Topaz's hair—just like her father had, way back when!*

Pivoting to where his body would be interred, Topaz gazed over the idyllic scene. Silent, with little Lace on his arm, Cedric knew Topaz was memorizing the placid lake near where her father's headstone would be erected. Dabbing tears, the tiny mother finally slid into the limo. She sat beside her brother, Eli, and his son, whom the family called El. Behind Topaz, Cedric scooted their daughter in before him.

Across from them, stately Naomi sat, dabbing tears. Ninety-something Mother See sat beside Armand, Topaz's grown son. As all rode in silence, the golden-eyed one recalled many moments that included her father. She remembered the sound of his voice, offering memories of Old Preacher. She remembered his love for her and her brother. He'd loved their offspring too; Eli's El, and her Armand and baby Lace. Topaz knew her father had loved Cedric, but most of all, Elijah Moon had loved her mother. Naomi had been Elijah's heart and soul. He'd always said it.

Quickly pressing her face to Cedric's chest, Topaz wept. She recalled her father's scent, and the fact that after he'd preached, his clothing and his robe had been nearly sweat-soaked. Like Old Preacher, Elijah had conferred so much of himself on the Lord's people. Remembering only caused Topaz to weep harder.

Then comforting Lace, as she and the six-year-old nestled in Cedric's arms, Topaz thought she smelled her father's cologne. She raised her head because warm and rich it was—as though the man was present. Then Topaz knew. On her journey, Elijah Moon would still watch over her, just as he had in life. Hurricane Elijah, her mother had called him.

In her luxe bedroom, Topaz recalled that prudent ninety-something Mother See had offered sage advice. *"You know Lil Mama, it isn't always how a person dies that matters, but how well that person lived."* Regal Mother See nodded. *"Big Pastor Moon might not have done everything right, but Lord knows, in his heart, that man wanted to be right. And no one can rebuke a man for trying—and yo' Daddy's trying sho trying made a great impact on many."*

Grateful for the reminder, Topaz found that she could remember happy times. *Her father teaching her to play the piano, him lifting the ends of her hair and acting like he hadn't, him batting a softball at the church picnic. The two of them, the big man and his golden-eyed girl, cracking open the nuts that had been nestled in her Christmas stocking.*

Forgetting the limo, as she sat in her bedroom, Topaz remembered other things and occasions. There had been of Kool & the Gang's classic instrumental, '*Summertime.*' That song had wafted over her and her forever-friend, tall, capricious Caley. They'd hung out in the park, ablaze with sunshine and color. As younglings, they'd watched Cedric play b-ball, after he'd grown taller. Topaz remembered that beneath the vibrant sun, he'd sat next to her. And fondly, she remembered their first time.

She couldn't forget being pregnant, or the birth of her son, and plucky little Aunt Petunia, now gone. Topaz remembered the day Cedric told Armand, "I'm your Dad." She remembered her son's high school graduation. Topaz had been ill then, but she'd kept quiet, not wanting her pregnancy to overshadow Armand's day. Topaz recalled being thirty-four when Cedric's Lace Leilani was born. Caley called her his yella baby because of her skin. Lace had been a surprise, although with their carrying on, her parents should have expected her years before.

At thirty-seven, Cedric had been excited. He'd said 'this time,' he'd get to do things right, from the start. Cedric relished his dad duties.

Topaz remembered their big fine son. Later in his college cap and gown, Armand grinned winsomely. His dad had snapped photos. Nearly four years old then, little Lace, with two large hair puffs, one on each side of her head, had ridden on her big brother's shoulders.

Suddenly, while seated in her bedroom, one memory stuck out from all the rest. Months prior, Topaz had watched her Dad eat cake with Lace. On her sixth birthday, the little one had licked icing off her Grandad's big bejeweled hands. Jostling her on his knee, Elijah Moon had roared with laughter. He'd growled into Lace's neck too, making the child happily squeal. Standing nearby, lovely Naomi whispered.

"You know Taupe, your father's life has been immense. I'm only glad we get to recognize it, *now*, while he's still with us." Naomi had sighed. "He and I didn't know to do that with Old Preacher; perhaps because we were so young. We never thought he wouldn't be with us." Naomi had quickly turned away. "Don't make that same mistake, Lil Mama."

Topaz shook melancholy from her mind to remember the fishbowl. She'd resigned from her Minister of Music duties. She'd left Greater Bethany Bible Congregation. At the time, she'd thought she was done with peering eyes. However, her music career ballooned shortly after. Then it was apparent, she'd traded her old fishbowl for a larger one, with millions of eyes. Like her brother Eli, who had been groomed for ministry, Topaz was also groomed for public life. Hers was in music.

In the bedroom of her beautiful New Canaan home, Topaz smiled and dabbed at straggling tears as she realized. Early in life one was prepared for what they would later take on. For that, she was grateful, like she was grateful, every day, for her father. Early on, his demanding and conscientious ways had unnerved her. Yet, they'd prepared her for the luxurious but equally as hectic and demanding life that she now led.

Recalling Pastor Elijah Martin Moon, Topaz acknowledged that she had truly loved the man. The man who had lived large, in the truest sense of the words. She also, now, found no fault in him.

STEPPING into the bedroom of his spacious second home, Cedric knew. His baby's red nose and teary eyes said she was thinking of her Dad. Cedric had been the same when he'd lost his jazz-singing mother. Topaz's loss had been seven months ago.

Continuing to dab her face, Cedric saw her look up. Wearing jeans and nothing more, he had a thought. Therefore, he asked, "How about when we're both back in Vegas, we do this thang, my cat-eyed girl?"

Wearing heeled slippers and a satin robe, the petite one smiled. Topaz knew Cedric spoke of tying the knot. She chuckled. "You're kidding—right?" They had been chiefly together for over twenty years. They had several homes and two kids, one grown and one under ten. "What makes you wanna switch it up now, Ced? Something wrong?"

"Ain't a thing wrong. It's just time—and your old man would agree."

"Ooh, that's dirty, using my Dad to get what you want." Topaz narrowed her eyes. Slowly she asked, "Is this what *you* want?"

"It is." Cedric's eyes dropped to the cleavage between the lapels of her slinky robe. "It's what you want, too." Reaching inside, he cupped a breast. Leaning to kiss it, he heard Topaz moan.

Cedric winked. "Gotta coerce you any way I can." Kneeling before Topaz, the man then appeared earnest. "Bay, I've been waiting. I thought you'd mention it, but for years you haven't said a word." He took her beautiful hands in his. "Not even when we found out Lace was coming." Cedric kissed Topaz's musical fingers, one at a time. "I'm tired of waiting on you." He looked up. "I know you weren't ready before. I know you had to make it and all. You even brushed me off saying you wouldn't give any man license to order you around. Now, no more excuses, Bay. Let's get legal; do your old man proud." Cedric stood. "He'd say better late than never."

Topaz felt her heart stutter. "You're serious..."

The gold-skinned man nodded. "I know a cute lil chapel."

"Mama would never forgive me if we left her out. My grandma," Mother See, "wouldn't either. Oh, and neither would Eli," her brother. He now pastored Greater Bethany Bible Congregation. Eli would need to officiate. "Caley—*and* your son," Armand, "would want to be there too."

Cedric rolled his eyes. "This thing is ballooning." Still, he raised Topaz's unadorned hands to his lips. Kissing both, he realized. His baby's pretty ring finger should no longer be bare.

"Since it's got to get bigger," he sighed, walking into and returning from the closet. "I'll ask again." Cedric slipped an incomparable ring on Topaz's finger. "Marry me—soon?"

"Oh my God, is this..." She held out her bejeweled hand, turning it from side to side. "Is this *topaz*? The stone, I mean."

Cedric nodded.

His woman laughed, unable to take her eyes from the fiery golden stone. It threw off prismatic color. "Well, yes, I'll marry you." Topaz draped herself over Cedric. "We should invite your brother." Carlton. "And Papa Stable," Cedric's dad, "and Dolly— Oh, and Sister Tallulah."

Cedric held Topaz as he muttered, "Can't forget holy Lula."

Topaz grinned. "Without her, and your card, we'd still be apart."

"Don't you believe that lie," Cedric cryptically advised. "But whatever," the man acquiesced. "Just marry me already, Bay. Aren't you—the woman—supposed to be the eager one?"

The little mother dismissed that with a wave. She became lost in thoughts of the gazillion things she'd need to do. Suddenly, she gushed, "Lace! She'll be our flower girl! And Army can do the music."

Cedric watched Topaz, knowing her mind was going into overdrive. Soon she'd be making lists. "Just let's do this, Bay. And we ain't got to discuss it to death, either. Pick a date and time and I'll be there."

Topaz laughed. "You know what, Ced? We'll do this, without the extra as you say, because..." She said what she had, nearly three decades prior. "I want," she looked slyly up at him, "whatever *you* want."

Grabbing her up, Cedric said into her neck, "You know I gotta take advantage of you now. Right?"

"Oh, I'm counting on it."

Raising her eyes to the ceiling, Topaz internally whispered. *Dad, like you wanted, Ced and I are finally going to marry…*

Topaz only wished one thing. That big Daddy Moon could physically be there to see it.

If you've enjoyed **REBUKE**, then meet the family again in…

SON

~ A Tranquility Tale ~
of love, lust, hard decisions, and coming of age.

Rebuke - *April Alisa Marquette*

Acknowledgements:

Hymns
I Must Tell Jesus - Elisha A. Hoffman, 1893 *v. 4 arr.* Public Domain

Tis So Sweet - Text: Louisa M. R. Stead, c. 1850-1917.
Music: William J. Kirkpatrick, 1838-1921.

Always Remember - Andrae Crouch, © Crouch Music (ASCAP)

Take me back - Andrae Crouch, 1975, Light Records

I am Thine O Lord - Text: Fanny J. Crosby, c. 1820-1915.
Music: William H. Doane, 1832-1915.

R&B
Yearning for Your Love - Gap Band 1980, Mercury; Oliver Scott, Ronnie Wilson

Are you Lonely for Me - Rude Boys 1990, Atlantic; Tony Nicholas, Joe Little & Mike Ferguson

I Need You - Rude Boys 1990, Atlantic; Larry Marcus

www.ingramcontent.com/pod-product-compliance
Lightning Source LLC
Chambersburg PA
CBHW032046240626

47154CB00003B/1097